More Th

Dawn Barker is a psychiatrist and author. She grew up in Scotland, then in 2001 she moved to Australia, completed her psychiatric training and began writing. Her first novel, *Fractured*, was selected for the 2010 Hachette/Queensland Writers Centre manuscript development programme, was one of Australia's bestselling debut fiction titles for 2013, and was shortlisted for the 2014 WA Premier's Book Awards. Her second novel is *Let Her Go*. Dawn lives in Perth with her husband and three young children.

Also by Dawn Barker

Let Her Go
More Than Us

more than us

DAWN BARKER

CANELO

First published in the the United Kingdom in 2018 by Canelo

This edition published in the United Kingdom in 2020 by Canelo

Canelo Digital Publishing Limited
31 Helen Road
Oxford OX2 0DF
United Kingdom

A CIP catalogue record for this book is available from the British Library.

Print ISBN 978 1 80032 024 6
Ebook ISBN 978 1 78863 051 1

Look for more great books at www.canelo.co

Printed and bound in Great Britain by Clays Ltd, Elcograf S.p.A.

Prologue

Emily

It hadn't taken long to feel like an old hand at hospital visits. After only a few days, I knew the best place to park, and how to find the correct lifts that would take me straight to Cameron's floor. The day he'd been rushed in here with sirens screaming, I'd staggered along the corridors with bloodshot eyes; now I strode along the corridors, into the lift, and up to the fourth floor with ease. I'd learned to avert my eyes once the lift doors closed, smile humbly and look at the floor. The new fathers were easy to spot, flustered, grinning, with their toddlers in hand, holding a shiny balloon or new teddy bear from the gift shop. Others were like me on that first day: shattered, clutching a child's backpack and a soft and worn old toy. Then there were the pros, the parents who had adapted to their new status as Parents of Sick Children. They carried folders of information, smiled at the familiar nurses and doctors who slid in and out of the lift, and knew they had to be there early in the morning to catch the Consultant's ward round.

I watched the red numbers on the lift display change from G to 1 to 2 to 3. There was a ping as the lift slowed. Oncology. I nodded slightly to the woman who took a deep breath and stepped out, blinking back my own tears. This is what I'd been trying to explain to Paul: it could be so much worse. I couldn't imagine the horror of the parents walking onto Floor 3. They clung to each other for survival; they didn't let their child's illness pull them apart.

Sometimes I envied that bond – not their children's illness, God no – but the way that they supported each other. Paul thought it was my fault that Cameron was here. It's not. And if we're going to start looking for someone to blame, I could remind Paul that he needs to look at himself. Cameron has been ill for years, and him being here has nothing to do with what I've done. Nothing. But, if he was on this floor, they'd have a test to tell us what was wrong with him, and I wouldn't feel so alone. We don't know what our son *has*, or indeed if he *has* anything at all. There's no blood test for what Cameron has, no X-ray or CT scan. And if the thing that is wrong with Cameron has a name, it doesn't have a ribbon or a wristband or a fun run for it.

I breathed in deeply then blew out slowly. I had to stop letting my thoughts get away from me and be mindful of now. Now, Cameron needs me. He'll be coming home today, then Paul and I will sort everything out, and he will get better.

The lift ascended again. It pinged at Floor 4 then it stopped. My stomach twisted a little as the doors hissed open. A woman pushing the breakfast trolley waited while I turned myself side-ways and squeezed out into the corridor onto the Kookaburra ward. Neurology.

I walked straight along the corridor towards Cameron's room, where I assumed the discharge meeting would be. He had a single room. I had smiled wryly when I'd first told Paul. One of the benefits of having a mental illness. *No one wants to share with you.* He hadn't smiled back.

There was no one at the nurses' station on my left: nothing unusual. I glanced at my watch; I was right on time. I'd hoped to be here earlier, but Tilly had taken ages to get ready for school and wouldn't finish her breakfast, and then the slipway queue at school had been busy, and then I'd slowed in the sludge of the school traffic. I snapped an imaginary elastic band on my wrist; I was here now. I wasn't late, I wouldn't look like the bad parent after Paul had spent the whole night here. Before this, our unspoken tally chalked up during heated arguments was about normal things: who cleaned up after dinner or took the bins out each week. I hated that it had become a tacit competition to prove who cared about Cameron the most.

When my friend Anna went through a divorce, I saw how she and her ex used their children as the currency in their bargaining. I had sworn I'd never do that if I was ever in her situation, although I had been smug back then in the knowledge that Paul and I were solid. But recently, I had heard myself making comments about Paul to the children. Just a little here, a little there. '*Your dad is busy at work today... I don't know why he isn't here, maybe you could ask him the next time you see him...?*' And, oh, how my face burned as I said the words. I knew it was wrong, but after everything that'd happened, I needed them on my side. Anyway, he would be doing the same, I was sure.

I walked past the shared ward and turned right off the corridor into Cameron's room. When he had first arrived a couple of days ago, he spent hours in the emergency department, separated from sick strangers by only a flimsy curtain. For Cameron, that was torture. Not only was he terrified about what was wrong with him, but underneath, the symptoms that have stalked him since he was a child were still there. He wouldn't eat the food, and he couldn't sleep for the light and the noise and the smells. I had taken the bottle of hand sanitiser from him before his skin became cracked and red from endlessly rubbing them with the gel.

I rubbed my own hands with the sanitiser mounted on the wall outside of his room, hoping the alcohol rub would dry up the sweat on my palms. Taking a deep breath, and fixing my smile on my face, I pushed open the door.

I stopped. His bed was empty. Had they gone for the meeting already?

But the bed wasn't just empty: it was stripped back to the mattress. The bedside table was bare, with no signs of his iPad or magazines or water bottle or bag of jelly snakes. My heart

3

beat faster. Had he been taken to another ward? For a moment, I wondered if I was in the wrong ward, that I'd walked out of the lift on the incorrect floor, overconfident that I knew where I was going, and instead had emerged into a carbon copy ward a floor higher or lower. But no: the small whiteboard above the bed still read 'Cameron Napier', but otherwise, the room was empty.

I entered the room, letting the door swing closed behind me, then walked into the ensuite bathroom, hoping I'd find him in there packing up his toiletries, but it was empty except for a damp towel crumpled at the bottom of a laundry bin.

I hurried back out into the corridor. The muffled quiet of the room gave way to the sound of distant coughs and chatter, cries and chirps of machinery. I paused and listened hard, but couldn't hear Cameron's voice, or any sounds of him that I'd been hearing every day for almost fifteen years, not his footsteps, his breathing, his presence. He wasn't here.

I sensed someone stop behind me. I turned around to see one of the young nurses, Jasmine, her frown matching the one that I knew was on my face.

'Emily,' she said. 'I thought…' She stopped, her eyes darting towards the door of Cameron's room.

I followed her gaze, but the door remained closed. I looked back at her pale face, tilted my head to the side, and waited for her to speak.

'I thought you…' Her voice trailed off and as it did, my heart beat faster.

'Where's Cameron?' I said, trying to keep my voice steady.
'Paul said…'

'Have you moved him already? Where's the meeting? I'm here for the meeting.'

Her eyes widened, then she looked at the floor as dread crept through my bones.

'Jasmine, what's going on?'

'Come with me,' she said, turning around and heading back towards the nursing station.

4

I followed quickly. 'Where is he? Is he okay?' My voice wasn't steady any more. I had the sudden fear that they had stripped his bed and packed up his possessions because he'd died in the night. That in all the confusion and fuss, someone had forgotten to phone me. Paul had been whisked away to wherever they take people who pass away in hospital and the nurses had been upset but now they were changing the sheets and wiping down the latex mattress to make room for the next patient who was waiting in the emergency department to come into the ward, and the whole process would start again. My legs were hurrying automatically now; surely, she was taking me to a quiet room where she'd break the news. What would I tell Tilly? How would I explain what had happened and that I had been the one who started it all?

But I knew that didn't make sense. As much as Paul and I were at each other, he wouldn't forget to call me if our son had died. And Cameron had been perfectly well – physically – yesterday. They must have moved him to another ward, or a waiting room before he was discharged, that was all.

Jasmine paused at the nurses' desk and murmured to another nurse whose name I didn't know. This woman raised her eyebrows and opened her mouth in a way that could only be interpreted as alarm, then saw me looking at her and closed her mouth again. She nodded then bowed her head and Jasmine turned back to me. 'We're just paging Dr Chan to come and have a chat. He'll be here as soon as possible.'

'I'm just here for the meeting. Wasn't it at nine-thirty?'

Jasmine bit her lip then spoke. 'The meeting was cancelled.'

'Cancelled? But no one told me. Why?'

Jasmine stepped towards me, gently, her hand raised towards my shoulder. 'I'm sorry, Emily, we need to wait for Dr Chan, he'll be here in a few minutes and explain everything.'

I stepped back, my hands starting to tremble. 'Jasmine. Where's Cameron? Is he okay? Has something—'

'Oh, Emily, Cameron's fine, I promise. I thought you… Paul said you knew.'

5

'Knew what?' My chin began to quiver as I understood what had happened, who had cancelled the meeting, and why. I reached for the back of a chair. Paul. 'When—'

Jasmine was almost whispering. 'First thing this morning. About two hours ago.'

I had always thought, despite everything, that Paul loved Cameron and wanted the best for him. But now, for the first time, I no longer knew who Paul was, and I no longer knew what he was capable of. He had gone, and he had taken Cameron with him.

I turned around and I ran.

One

Five Years Earlier

Emily

I tilted the air conditioner vent away from my face as I drove up towards the house. I was only just starting to cool down after having to park miles away from Tilly's ballet and walk her in, then trudge all the way back to the car, where Cameron had waited with the engine running, playing some game on my phone. By the time I'd got back to the car, the heat had turned my mood like sour milk, and then Cameron had niggled at me all the way home because he wanted me to stop at the bakery for a particular bun for afternoon tea, and I had refused because Cameron *knew* that sugar made his behaviour worse. It was still forty degrees in March; the heat of Australian summer days like this made me long for the chill of the Scottish winters that I'd grown up in.

I indicated to turn into our driveway, noticing the yellowing patch of brittle grass in the corner of our verge. I'd been asking Paul to fix the sprinklers for weeks but with the soccer season still in full swing, he hadn't had time. I made a mental note to call the gardener and get him to do it when he was here to mow the lawn next week. I slowed down as I turned onto the concrete driveway, waiting for the electric gates to creak open, then frowned as I realised Paul's car was already there. I looked over at Cameron, sat in the passenger seat next to me.

'What's your dad doing home at this time?'

7

He didn't look up from the screen of my phone, but shrugged. 'I don't know.'

I raised my eyebrows, sighed then drove forwards, parking next to Paul's car. I had barely stopped when Cameron opened the door and was out.

'Cameron. Take your bag! I'm not—'

The passenger door slammed shut. I shook my head, then got out and wrestled my own bag out of the back of the car as well as Cameron's schoolbag and sports kit, then slammed the rear door closed. The sun seared my shoulders as I hurried across the few metres between the shade of the carport and the front porch, where Cameron was knocking on the door.

'Excuse me, Cameron!' I found my keys, pushed past him then unlocked the door.

I stepped into the cool of the hallway, Cameron following me, then dropped the bags and quickly closed the door behind me. I kicked off my sandals. 'Paul? Paul!' I shouted.

'In here.' I could barely hear him.

I sighed. 'Where?' I yelled.

'In the bedroom.' He had spoken louder, but his voice was flat.

Cameron trudged towards the back of the house. 'Cammie, unpack your bag and get yourself a snack, I'll be there in a minute.'

I turned right and pushed open our bedroom door, which was ajar. Paul was lying on the bed, on top of the blankets, his head propped up on the pillows. His kit bag was on the floor next to him. I took a breath in; his eyes were red and when he looked up, his lip started to quiver. Paul never cried. I closed the bedroom door behind me then stood still, my heart pounding.

I spoke softly. 'What happened?'

'It's over.'

I bit my lip, then moved closer and sat on the edge of the bed. I waited.

'They said it's too risky to play again. I'm out.'

'But the physio—'

'I'm out, Emily. No more physio. No more pills – all the painkillers and anti-inflammatories and injections that they've given me have done nothing except get me onto the pitch to do more damage to my knee. The doctor said it's completely stuffed, as worn out as someone of seventy, and there's no way to fix it. I'm only thirty-four.' He shook his head, looking away from me then croaked, 'It's over.'

I felt my own eyes prickle and blinked frantically. I couldn't cry; that wasn't fair to Paul. 'Oh, sweetheart. I'm so sorry.'

He sniffed loudly. 'I'll get paid for the rest of the season, then that's it. What's that, a month? I'll lose the sponsorships, the car...'

The school fees? The house? I wanted to ask, but couldn't. I swallowed hard and forced myself to speak brightly. 'Don't worry about all that. It doesn't matter. We'll be okay. We've got savings.'

'What else am I going to do? Football is all I know. I'm not good at anything else.'

I grabbed his hand. 'That's rubbish, Paul. You can do anything. You're amazing. You're smart, you work so hard, everyone loves and respects you. We always knew it could never go on forever.'

He didn't move his gaze away from his knees. 'I know I'm getting on now, but I thought I'd get a couple more years.'

So did I.

Paul still hadn't looked at me and I knew he was fighting back tears. I knew his reaction was not so much about losing his job, but losing his pride. The shame of a grand final loss, rather than the celebration of reaching it.

But it wasn't really a surprise. Twelve years playing in Australia, and years before that in Scotland: that was a long time for a soccer player. I knew he'd been nervous about the meeting with the doctor by the way he'd shrugged it off as if it was nothing. But we both knew it wasn't a routine check-up. We both knew that he couldn't carry on like this. Some

9

mornings, he could barely get out of bed from the stiffness in his knee. After a hot shower, some painkillers and a heat pack, it loosened up and his limp became barely perceptible. Somehow, he had made it through the games with a shot of steroids and even more painkillers but even then, we both knew that the next day, it would be worse, and the day after that.

I put my hand on his leg, just above the knee that I had strapped for him so many times, and saw him glance at it. I moved my hand away again, not too quickly, and leaned forwards and put it on his shoulder instead. 'It'll just take some time to get used to the idea. What about asking Jock? Agents must deal with this all the time, he'll have some great ideas for work, I'm sure.'

His back muscles stiffened beneath my arm. 'Is that what you're worried about? The money?'

'No!' I said, feeling my cheeks burn. 'No. Not at all.'

He nodded and sighed. 'Sorry. I'll get a media gig, commentating maybe.'

'Oh sweetheart, of course you will. You'd be great on the TV.'

'Or coaching, training, something like that.'

I nodded, the soft mattress undulating from the movement in my body. 'Definitely. See, there are lots of things you can do. Think of everything you've learned, all the connections you've made. It's just a different stage of life, that's all. No one has the same job their whole life.'

He rubbed his nose and sat up a bit, glancing at me. 'It'll be good, won't it, to spend more time with the kids?'

'Definitely. No more trips away, early morning training sessions...' It *would* be great to have him around more: it was the thing that we had fought about most. I squeezed him and felt his strong arms grip me tight. I took a big breath and stood up. 'Come on. Let's go tell Cameron. It's just the next stage of our life. We'll pick up Tilly from ballet then go out for dinner.'

He nodded, and I saw how hard he tried to smile.

The next morning, we both lay in bed before the alarm went off. I knew Paul was awake; I knew *he* knew I was awake too, but we both lay still, feigning sleep, listening to the sounds of the day beginning. A dog barked in the distance, a car door slammed, and an engine started. A train's horn sounded from the tracks, three kilometres away. Usually Paul was up by now, out walking off the stiffness by 6am, or off to training while the kids were still eating breakfast. I'd wanted so many times for him to skip his morning routine and be with us, but now that he was here, my heart ached for him.

Eventually, the alarm on my phone began to chime. I reached onto the bedside table to switch it off. Paul stretched out, yawning loudly.

'Did you sleep okay?' I asked.

'Yeah, pretty well,' he said. We both knew he hadn't.

I wriggled over to his side of the bed. He automatically raised his left arm up so I could lay my head on his bare chest, then he curled his arm around me and rubbed my back. My mouth was dry and my head pounded; I hadn't slept either. The worries about him and our future had niggled at me every time I closed my eyes. I had reminded myself that everything seemed depressing in the middle of the night, and worries always dissipate with daylight. And now, as I listened to the magpies cooing and kookaburras cackling outside, I let the fear evaporate off me like the morning dew in the sun. It would be okay; it always was. We were good like that, Paul and I. We always coped; we always found solutions.

I heard feet thumping along the floorboards as Tilly ran into our room.

'What can I do while I wait for you to get up?'

'Good morning to you too! Come here.' I laughed, lifted my head off Paul's chest, then held up the sheet for her; the duvet lay rumpled at the end of the bed after the cloying hot night.

She climbed up and snuggled into me. I ran my hand over her hair, nestled my head into it and inhaled. She was getting so tall now, and I loved every inch of her. She was eight now, already seeming to grow away from me as she grew up, but at the start and the end of the day, she forgot to act like the teenager she so desperately wanted to be.

'Do you promise to always give me cuddles? Even when you're older?' I murmured into her ear.

'I don't know!' she smiled and I gently flicked my finger on her freckled nose.

'What about Dad?' I said, nudging Paul.

'Where's my cuddles?' he said in a fake deep voice and Tilly laughed, clambered over me and squeezed into the gap between us. I sighed as the last remnants of my nocturnal anxiety floated away. We would be fine.

–

'Cameron!' I shouted. 'Come on, time to get out of the shower!' I turned to Paul, who was sipping his coffee and flicking through the paper as he sat at the breakfast bar. 'Go and knock on the door, would you?'

Paul slowly stood up, not moving his gaze from the newspaper.

'Now, Paul, please. Help me. We've got to be out the door in twenty minutes.'

Every morning I swore it would be different. I'd ignore the pit of dread in my stomach. I wouldn't yell and let myself get into a frenzy. I'd smile, be calm. I'd have packed everything the night before. And maybe Cameron, for once, would get ready without any fuss.

I thought this morning in particular might be different given that there were *two* adults to get them ready for school today.

'Paul. Please! They'll be late.'

'There's plenty of time!' He looked at me, frowning and shaking his head.

I raised my eyebrows and spoke tightly. 'No. There isn't. Cameron takes forever to get dressed. If we don't get to school on time, we don't get a car spot outside, and if Cameron's not at school early enough to go to the library first to settle himself down, it will all fall to pieces. If he thinks he's late, he'll escalate until he's in a frenzy. I do this every day.'

'Yes, I know you—'

I held my hand up. 'Not now, Paul, that's not what I meant. Please just help me, and get him out of the shower. Maybe he'll be better with you.' *You always say I overreact and make him more stressed*, I wanted to say. *Let's see if you can do it any better.*

He took a big sip of coffee, shook his head, then stomped off. I looked up and exhaled slowly, like I'd learned in yoga. This was day one of Paul's new life and I was already thinking that it was easier without him.

I should have gotten up at 5.30am as usual. It really did take me two and a half hours every morning. Paul never believed me. But he never saw what I did: showered first, before the children woke, because otherwise, exactly like now, I'd still be rushing around in my pyjamas with my glasses on and my hair unwashed and I'd have to put my gym gear on and pretend I'd been for a run when I did school drop off to explain why I looked so bedraggled. After showering, I'd do the usual things: emptying the dishwasher, filling the water bottles, making sandwiches and slicing fruit and trying to put something healthy in the lunchbox in case a teacher looked in it and thought I was a bad mother for giving them a honey sandwich *and* a hot cross bun on the same day. The rest of the time was taken up by Cameron.

Paul came back through. 'He's coming.'

'Did you hear the water go off, he always says—'

'Yes!' he glared at me.

I felt my eyes fill with tears. Since when did we talk to each other like this? When did the respectful, warm conversation stop, and bickering and resentment creep in? I blinked hard and swallowed down my retort. There was no time for this now. Paul had just lost his job; he was allowed to be snappy.

I opened the top drawer and took out the correct spoons. I walked over to the dining table and put Cameron's cutlery down in exactly the right way, parallel to the grain of the wood and placemat. Oh, how I longed to swipe it and spin it around sometimes. But I never did.

–

I often try to remember a time before my life tiptoed around Cameron. I know that memories can be deceiving, pages of a history book written with the bias of hindsight. I also know that memories are etched more deeply into us with the acid of strong emotions, and for Cameron, the more powerful emotions have been negative.

My own first memories aren't really my own: they are my mother's, laid down in my mind from her desperate repetitions as we looked through old photo albums, trying to keep her Alzheimer's at bay as it crept in to steal her memories away. She was far too young to have dementia. I remember her smile as she recalled that my first word was 'more', and that was why I was a chubby child in those photos, and how I wailed and clung to her leg on my first day of nursery just after the smiling photo of me on the doorstep was taken.

Then the memories become my own: the fumbles of my first kiss; the devastation of my first breakup; the joy of being accepted into the physiotherapy course at Glasgow University; the pride of marrying Paul when we were both so young and in love.

I do have special, wonderful, first memories of Cameron too, those that make me smile as they bubble up: the first time I told Paul I was pregnant; the first time I gave birth and cried with exhilaration and relief to see a healthy little boy; the first tiny nappy I changed with the midwife hovering over me telling me it was on backwards.

Tilly's first sweet smile and gurgling laugh.

My face burns to admit that I don't remember Cameron's first smile. I'm sure he did smile at me, look into my eyes and let out a laugh, once, many times. He must have. It seems so long since he's been happy that I've just forgotten what it ever sounded like.

—

When Cameron was born, Paul and I were like any other parents, I imagine. We were convinced that Cameron would be the most handsome baby – of course. He would be bright, like me, and athletic, like Paul. His hair would be red – not bright orange, but a handsome, dark auburn – which was exotic in Australia rather than ordinary back home in Scotland. He *was* a handsome boy. He's still beautiful, at ten.

But as his fine strawberry-blonde baby hair fell out and his thicker hair grew, just brown, we still searched for highlights of red in the sun. It was ridiculous to spend so much time looking for uniqueness in him, when now I would give anything for him to be ordinary.

Cameron was a fractious baby, always on the go. Paul said he was destined to be a striker. We wondered whether he'd play for Scotland or Australia. When Tilly was born eighteen months later, and was so sweet and calm, I knew that it proved that my parenting wasn't to blame for Cameron's behaviour. She slept better than he did at night; she allowed me to soothe her while he raged for hours; she ate what I put in front of her. Cameron's milk always had to be in the same blue sippy cup. His bowl had to be the one with Peter Rabbit on it, and the spoon yellow. He wore the same pair of shorts and dinosaur T-shirt for, I swear, a year. Paul told me to just throw it out, but when he tried to dress Cameron in something different, he too would give up after the screams and tears started. Gradually we just gave in.

As he became a toddler, Paul and I looked at each other with strained amusement when he threw his dinner across the room. Paul always thought I was overreacting. 'He's just a boy,' he would say. 'I was just like him when I was a kid. You should hear some of Mum's stories about the things Alasdair and I used to do as kids.'

My own mother was, by then, in a nursing home in Scotland and Dad was working in Canada where, eventually, he'd marry again and settle. I had no one else in Australia; Paul was my only family, and he was busy. I joined a local mothers' group and craved our weekly catch up, when we'd all trudge in, exhausted from another relentless night, comparing stories to reassure each other that none of us were failing: this was just the way babies were. But as our children grew, I started to dread the mothers' group meetings. Everyone else's boys were, well, normal. They cuddled into their mothers' chests while Cameron ran the other way from me. I began to feel nervous every time I went out with Cameron, always ready to leap to my feet and sprint across the room to grab him. It was as if the magnet that was meant to pull us together had flipped over in one of us, and instead, we repelled each other.

As a little boy, Cameron wasn't *just* angry; these weren't the normal temper tantrums that Tilly grew to have, where some distraction and bribery could make her calm down and look at the beautiful butterfly or the pretty bird. Cameron was never just angry; he was completely consumed with his distress. Sometimes I wondered if he was really my child: I saw none of myself in this feisty little boy. Cameron's real strength wasn't in his little arms that pummelled into me when I tried to put him in his room; it was in his ability to know exactly how to push me. When he was calm, I tiptoed around him, taking the time to sit on my bed with the door closed for ten minutes, my cheeks burning with the awareness that I felt better when I wasn't with him.

When he went to school he had to have the same sandwiches (white bread, butter, two slices of ham, and the crusts cut off and cut into three equal fingers), a strawberry yoghurt (only one brand, no bits in it), six rice crackers and a green apple, peeled, cut into even slices and sealed in a sandwich bag. At birthday parties, he wouldn't eat cupcakes because he hated the texture of icing on his lips and the idea of getting messy was too much for him. I smiled when the other mothers told me how lucky I was that he didn't like junk food. But I *wanted* him to like junk food; I didn't want him to be different.

Paul told me he'd grow out of it eventually. But he didn't; he became more restrictive. But it wasn't just food. It was everything: the route we took to school, the bedtime routine, the way I made his bed. And before I knew it, Paul had given up complaining. Sometimes I saw him open his mouth as Cameron's face contorted with anxiety, but he learned to close it again. We all learned to live Cameron's way. As long as his world was the way he needed it to be, he was happy. And what other job does a mother have but to make her children happy?

–

Now, Cameron was ten years old, but I still tiptoed around him and arranged his cutlery on the table just the way he liked it.

I finished setting the table for breakfast. Maybe Paul would be able to handle Cameron better than I could, now that he was going to be home more to help. He'd lost his job, his entire career, only yesterday. We all had to adjust and I had to let Paul try things his way too. It wasn't fair of me to push Paul out; he needed us around him.

'Hey, Paul. I'm going to have a quick shower now, okay?'

Paul nodded, not looking up from the paper, which he had resumed reading.

I made my voice calm and sweetly pitched. 'I'm sorry to say it again, but if Cameron's not out in five minutes, can you give him a gentle reminder to get dressed?'

I saw Paul's chest rise, then fall. He looked up this time, and nodded again.

I started to walk out then stopped and turned around again. 'I forgot. I've got a meeting with Cameron's school this afternoon, before pick-up, just to talk about how he's settling into Year 5. Can you make it, or do you have…?' I paused. 'It's not that important, it's just routine. But I'd love you to come.'

He glanced up at me. 'I'm going to the physio this morning, but then I can come.'

'That's great.' I smiled.

He nodded and smiled back, then his eyes glistened and he quickly looked back to the paper again while I pretended not to notice.

Two

Paul

I watched Emily's back as she retreated towards the bathroom. I took a deep breath, cleared my throat and sat up straighter on the kitchen stool. It was no good letting the kids see me like this. I glanced at the clock on the front of the oven; she was exaggerating, there was half an hour before they had to leave. I drained my coffee, then stood up and went to put another pod in the machine. I felt hungover, even though I'd only had a couple of beers last night with dinner, just to try to keep the panic down. The alcohol hadn't helped me feel more relaxed; it only made me feel hot and thirsty and anxious in the middle of the night. In the end, I had gotten up and taken an extra painkiller, the strong ones left over from my last arthroscopy, even though the pain wasn't any worse than usual. At least they helped me sleep, even if they had done nothing at all to help my knee. Although now that I wasn't playing, what did it matter if I'd had a bad night's sleep or a headache?

I had known when I left Scotland for Australia that I couldn't compete in the UK leagues any more, even though I was barely in my twenties. There were lads of sixteen, seventeen, coming through and they were far fitter and hungrier than me. They were the ones the managers, and fans, wanted. Emily and I were both smart enough to know that it was a great deal to be offered a contract in Sydney. Not only would the team pay us to move to Australia and set us up with a house and car, but I would have more chances to play: the competition wasn't as fierce as in Scotland, or Europe, but it was gathering momentum and everyone was getting behind football – or soccer as they called it in Australia. I was a *good* player – it's not easy to get to the premier league in the UK – but I was never going to be a superstar. But here, people had loved me, loved the team, and I played well. But as the years went on, I started missing games, then missing parts of seasons because I just couldn't do it. Really, I had known for a long time that I had passed my peak, no matter how much I tried to tether myself to the top.

When they told me yesterday that my knee had finally failed me, I let go. I knew my time was up. Still, I had wanted it to be my decision to go, not the medics'.

I sighed, rubbed at the back of my neck and tried to quell the stress rising up towards my throat. What would I do? How would I support my family now? If I had chosen a career other than sport, now, in my thirties, I'd be soaring.

'Dad,' Tilly said.

I looked up suddenly, my heart racing. 'Sorry, sweetie, I was daydreaming. You okay?'

'Where's Mum?'

'She's just having her shower. Can I get your brekkie? What do you usually have?'

She shrugged. 'Nutella toast?'

I frowned, and looked at her face as she stared straight back at me for a moment, then her lips began to twitch.

I smiled too. 'Does your mum really let you have Nutella on toast before school? I thought that was just a treat on the weekends...'

'Sometimes...' She broke into a grin and started giggling as I cocked my head to the side and grinned back. I stepped towards her and ruffled her long brown hair, then pulled her into a hug, the stress receding again. What did work matter, as long as I had moments like this?

'Okay,' I said. 'Go and sit at the table, but don't tell Mum.'

'Yay!' she squealed and jumped up and down.

I laughed. 'Go and give your brother a shout, will you? Does he like Nutella?'

'Nah, he just has cereal, but he'll do it himself. He's very...'

'*Particular,*' we both said in a fancy voice, laughed, and then Tilly skipped out of the room to fetch Cameron.

—

That afternoon, I waited for Emily outside the school gates in the shade of a fig tree. The sun was scorching, the humidity choking. My knee throbbed from the physio and my face ached from forcing myself to smile all day as I reassured everyone in the team that I was okay, that I had expected it, that I was excited about life after playing. And I *was*. A cloud of anxiety about my future had been suffocating me for months, as I lay awake with my knee achingly stiff in the dead of night. Now that I knew it was over, some of that had lifted. Throughout the day, I'd had moments when a lightness bubbled up in me, a sense of possibility that I'd never really had until now. My life from when I was a teenager had revolved around the structure of soccer and a strict schedule of training and games and events. It was always about the team. I had loved that, but now, for the first time, I could think about what *I* wanted.

I saw Emily's car swing into the school car park and a few moments later, she hurried over to me. She wore a loose dress, black with a white floral pattern, and silver flat sandals. Her strawberry blonde hair was tied up in a messy bun with her sunglasses on her head. Her normally pale shoulders were pink from the sun.

'Sorry,' she said. 'I thought I'd quickly run into the library to return some books and the time got away from me. How did the physio go today?'

'Fine,' I said, smiling. 'It feels a bit better.'

She smiled up at me then stretched on her tiptoes and kissed my cheek. I put my arm around her slim shoulders and squeezed her. 'Okay, let's do this.'

She laughed. 'You sound like you're getting ready to go into war. It's just a routine meeting.'

I raised my eyebrows at her. 'That's what they always say. Then we get in and they say the same things – he's not listening, he's not sitting still, he's failing…'

Emily shook her head, no longer laughing. 'Paul! That's not fair. He was much better towards the end of last year.'

'We'll see.' I straightened my back and tried to look confident as we walked along the smooth concrete path towards the main building. As a kid, I had never set foot in a private school; it had never been an option for people like me. I had always planned for my own kids to go to the local school too. After all, when Cameron was old enough to start school, we were living in the well-to-do Eastern Suburbs of Sydney, not the rough housing estates of Aberdeen: the local school would be more than adequate. But when he started kindergarten, Cameron was constantly in trouble. After a terrible year, Emily had persuaded me to send him here, Oakfield Grammar, a private boys' school that had promised us the world. They said that they knew how to teach boys, that while Cameron had a different learning style, they could help him thrive. We paid the fees and forked out for the uniform, but nothing has really changed in the years he's been here. When Tilly started school, we sent her straight to the girls' school, but her parent-teacher interviews were always great, and we always left smiling, with our egos plumped up, like the way Emily pounded the sofa cushions before guests arrived. It made Cameron's all the more heartbreaking.

Inside, the receptionist smiled warmly at Emily and greeted her by name. We sat on a sofa opposite the reception, whispering small talk to each other, until his teacher arrived and shook our hands. We followed her past some classrooms to a small office.

After some brief pleasantries, she started. 'I'll get straight to the point. I'm a bit worried about Cameron. He hasn't settled in to Year 5 as well as I'd have hoped.'

I closed my eyes for a second, deflating, then opened them and saw her peering at me, looking for my reaction. She hadn't even started by stirring in some praise to sweeten things. Why had I even bothered to hope that this meeting would be different?

'He's not playing very well with the other boys, not joining in in class. I thought it was maybe just nerves at starting a new year, and we do have some new boys this year, but the other boys seem to have settled in. How has he been at home?'

I glanced at Emily who caught my eye, then sat up straight and leaned forward. She took a deep breath. 'He's been okay, well, just the same. You would have heard from the other teachers, and the school counsellor, that we've had some problems, that Cameron's had some problems I mean, for a long time, haven't we, Paul?'

I nodded, then put my hand on her leg. She put her hand on top of mine. I felt tears well up; I kept my eyes down, horrified at my reaction.

Emily was still talking. 'He was like this last year, but he's not good with new things and we thought—'

I cleared my throat, able to look up now. 'Do you think it could be that he's just a bit nervous? He's just started a new year, new teacher...'

'But he's always like this, Paul,' Emily said quietly. She looked up at the teacher.

'I also need to tell you that there was an incident yesterday,' the teacher said, hesitantly.

'What kind of incident?' Emily said, her voice high and wavering.

'Mrs Vanetti was on playground duty and she heard a commotion, on the grass beside the tennis courts. She went over and there was a ruckus.'

'A ruckus?' I said, frowning.

She carried on, still looking at Emily. 'She saw Cameron on top of another boy, hitting him, and the other boys were in a panic.'

23

'But...why? What happened?' Emily said.

I felt sick. 'You told us that no one is playing with him, they've probably been giving him a hard time.'

'Paul, that doesn't excuse him punching someone.'

'She didn't say he was punching him, Emily,' I said, then turned to the teacher. 'That's not what you said, is it?'

'Regardless, he was very distressed, and was using physical violence—'

'You don't know what happened. Maybe the other kids hit him first...'

'You're right,' she said, smiling sweetly. 'That's a possibility. But the other child denies hitting Cameron first. They agreed that they'd had a verbal disagreement over who was sitting on the bench first, and the other child says Cameron became aggressive. When I asked Cameron, he agreed.'

I could see Emily wiping a tear away and trying to calm herself down. She tried to speak light-heartedly. 'I never thought I'd be called into school to discuss my son being a bully.'

'Emily. No one's saying he's a bully,' I said. 'That's not what you're saying, is it?'

Emily pressed her lips together then looked at the teacher, who was shaking her head. 'What will we do? What do you suggest?'

The two of them started to talk about the same old things: psychologists and buddies and team sports and family counselling but I could barely hear them for the noise of the blood pumping through my head as the fibres of my muscles all over my body swelled and tensed, but somehow, I managed to grip the arms of my chair and stay calm and nod at the appropriate places until we heard the school bell ring and we too were dismissed.

There wasn't time for Emily and I to discuss anything as the boys poured out of the classrooms. We met Cameron outside, both smiled brightly and talked too loudly, then I drove him home while Emily went to collect Tilly and take her to her dancing class. I said nothing to him of the meeting, and he said nothing to me of the fight.

That evening, after we'd had dinner as a family and put the children to bed, Emily went outside in the warm twilight to hang the washing. I opened a beer, then sat down at the kitchen table, opened my computer, and scrolled through my emails. After a few minutes, Emily came back in, filled the kettle and switched it on. She slammed mugs down, then dropped teaspoons into them with a clang. I closed my eyes and sighed. She walked over to me, then put her hand on my laptop and closed it.

I sighed. 'What is it?'

'I spoke to him,' she said. 'When I went to kiss him good-night. It's true, what the teacher said. He started it.'

'He's only ten years old, he just lost his temper.'

'Don't excuse it. Would you think it was okay if Tilly punched someone over and over? You need to teach him that it's not acceptable to be violent. And you need to tone down your behaviour, your reactions.'

I screwed my face up as I looked at her. 'Me? Why's this my fault?'

'He asked me if you were going to be angry with him. He looked frightened. Paul, you forget that you're big, and when you snap at them, even if you don't mean to, your voice is loud and you scare them.'

I tried to keep my voice quiet, though I wanted to raise it. 'Emily, I don't know where this is coming from. What does this have to do with what Cameron did? Anyway, we don't know what the other kid said. Maybe it was self-defence. We can't hover beside him to fight for him; he needs to learn to stand up for himself.'

'Stop defending his behaviour, Paul!'

'He's just a kid! I'm sick of all these people deciding that he is a problem. I was the kid labelled as the troublemaker before I found football; there's only so many times that people can tell you you're bad before you just give up and do what they expect.'

She shook her head, exasperated. 'I'm not *expecting* him to be bad. He *is* being bad, Paul. Don't blame me. As if I wouldn't give anything to see him happy.' Her voice broke.

I let out a long breath then nodded. It wasn't worth a fight right now. 'Okay. Sorry. You're right. I'll talk to him tomorrow. Sometimes I just feel so sorry for him. It's like... everyone's always on at him. He never gets a break. At least he was honest.' I tried to smile.

'That's even strange, don't you think? Kids usually lie to get out of trouble, but he didn't seem to care, or to understand. It's like he doesn't understand the social... usefulness... of it. I've been reading about empathy and social skills and I think—'

'Emily, are you really saying that our son has something wrong with him because he's telling the truth? He's doing what we've always told him to do – be honest, own up to the consequences of his actions.'

Her eyes were wet. 'Can't you for once just admit that we're having some problems with him? No other parents are being called up to see the teacher. Maybe it's not him, you're right, maybe it's us. Me, if that's what you're implying by rolling your eyes, Paul. Regardless, I'm not coping with this and I don't know how more clearly I can put it. I need help!' She wiped away a tear, waiting for me to respond. I didn't know what else to say. The last two days had been a nightmare and I had run out of space in my head to think clearly. I looked away then opened up my laptop again. Emily stormed out of the room, and I heard the bedroom door slam.

–

Emily had always struggled with Cameron. From the moment he was born, I knew something wasn't right between them, and it became even clearer later, when Tilly came along. She and Tilly bonded so tightly from the moment she was born, and they're still the same. They go shopping together, go out for tea and cakes in the cafés, watch movies and musicals. It warms my heart: that's what mothers and daughters should do. But she was never like that with Cameron.

I'd always imagined a close relationship with Cameron too. I pictured us going to matches together, and spending weekends cheering for him and his mates on the field, just like my dad used to do with me. Dad was always proudest of me when I was on the pitch; he knew that football was the thing that would lift me into a world wider than the home town that he'd never left. I don't remember talking about anything else with Dad but the how the Dons – the Aberdeen football team – were faring, or my own game. We were closest when we were singing the team songs with thousands of soaring voices in the stands at Pittodrie pitch. But Cameron wasn't like me: I had to edit that image of our relationship pretty quickly; I'm not sure Emily has ever adjusted.

Maybe it wasn't Cameron. Maybe Emily would have struggled regardless of which baby came first. We hadn't planned for her to fall pregnant so young. We had only been in Australia a couple of years, we had not long married, and were living a brilliant life full of parties and travel. When she became a mother, it was hard for her to adapt to not being able to do everything that she wanted to, as she tried to cling onto the threads of our life before kids. When she was pregnant, we'd sworn that our children would come with us wherever we went, do what we did, learn to love travel and eating out. But once Cameron was born, and then Tilly, we realised that was impossible. Those threads of our previous life snapped and instead she became knotted up with a toddler and a baby. I know it was Emily who was tied most tightly to them; it was my role to support her and the children, and I took it seriously.

When the kids were little, I was playing all the time. Emily would tell me I worked too much and that she wished she could come with me when I travelled or went out to a function. I honestly would have rather stayed home than go out and make small talk with strangers, but I had to go. I know it seems glamorous, but every awards dinner is the same: the same people, the same meals, same wine. It was just work. She didn't believe me. And, as I started to take longer to recover from injuries, I used to float around the function room with that familiar cloud of anxiety building up around me, aware that when the wind changed, I'd be forgotten like all the others who had been dropped back into real life before me. Retirement was inevitable. I had to work harder at networking than I ever did at football; that was my future.

I tried to spend as much time as I could with Cameron. When I was home, he and I kicked the ball to each other over and over in the back yard, scoring goals between the jacaranda tree and the trampoline. When he was five, I signed him up for kids' soccer. I couldn't wait for Sunday mornings down at the oval.

But I missed the first day. I was away playing in Adelaide.

Emily was stressed about taking him before they even got there, which would have stressed him out too. Sure enough, about half an hour after the session started, while I was at the airport, waiting for a flight home, she called me. I picked up straight away.

Emily didn't even say hello. 'It was a disaster.'

I groaned. 'What? Why?'

'You didn't tell me I had to actually take part! You should have seen me – I had Tilly with me in one arm, while I'm trying to kick the ball to him, and he was crying because I couldn't kick it straight, and Tilly was crying because she was being jostled around and all the kids were yelling. You could have warned me!'

'I didn't know! I've never been before either!'

'I thought the coaches taught them. He didn't want to do it, as soon as they did some game where they had to line up and kick at the goals, he lost it.' I could hear the anger in her voice.

'Lost it? How?'

'You know, the way he always loses it? He started to cry, then got worse when I tried to calm him down, so I had to pick him up in one arm and drag him away while he punched me.'

'It was his first time, Emily, I'm sure he wasn't the only one who was a bit worried. Weren't any of his friends there?'

'All the other *dads* were there, Paul. You should have seen me, in my sandals with two kids having meltdowns. I didn't even know how to kick the bloody ball. Eventually some other dad took pity on me and tried to look after Cameron as well as his own kid.'

I stayed silent. 'I'll be there next week.'

'This was meant to be *your* thing with him. I felt like an idiot.'

'I'm sure Cammie felt worse.'

Silence. Then, 'I can't do this on my own.'

'It's my job,' I said, keeping my voice even.

And that was how it was, little jabs at me for not being there, for not doing what dads were meant to do. Jesus, when I was growing up my mum and dad both had to work, and when Mum wasn't working, she was looking after us. My kids wanted – want – for nothing. They have their mother full time. They never had to go to childcare. They go to a great school where they learn languages and music and they get taught PE by an ex-Olympian. They go to parties in cinemas and trampoline centres and science centres, they go out for smoothies and sushi and yum cha, they download movies instantly at home. One day in their life is like the best day ever for me when I was growing up.

What I really wanted to say to Emily when she complained about me being away was, *I'll just stop working then, will I? Give up my career to make sure that both his mother and his father see every little thing that he does and praise him whether he won or lost? Then not only would we have to move to a new house, and a state school, but he'd have to quit the bloody soccer because that all costs money.*

But I didn't say that.

'I'm sorry,' I said. 'I wish I had been there to help you.'

And now that my playing career was over, I would be here to help her. But still fears lingered: had I left it too late to try and slot back into my family? What if I'd listened to Emily back then, said no sometimes to work, put my family first like she wanted me to? Would Cameron be different? Perhaps if we'd had less, life would have been simpler for all of us.

Three

Emily

Weeks passed, then months. It wasn't all bad. They set Paul up with a psychologist to help him adjust to life after soccer. They linked him up with a mentor, another player who had left the sport and became a PE teacher at a private school. Paul's agent, Jock, arranged for him to be interviewed on some radio shows, although that was unpaid, and found him some jobs here and there: opening a fun run in the city, writing a couple of pieces for a magazine and a paper on the retirement of athletes. Paul turned up and said all the right things, he did everything that was expected of him but I could sense he was slipping away from us as it became clear that by leaving school at sixteen and going straight into football, he wasn't really qualified to do anything else. We had savings, things weren't desperate yet, but we had been living as if his income would stay the same forever.

He hadn't wanted me to go back to work at first.

'I want to,' I'd said, after I poured us both a glass of Pinot and we sat down to dinner. The kids were in their rooms watching something or other on their iPads. We often ate separately from them; it was too stressful to watch Cameron fussing about everything, so we just took the path of least resistance. My stomach fluttered as I spoke quickly. 'You know I've missed it. While you were playing, it was too hard for me to work and look after the kids.' I saw him flinch. I leaned towards him. 'Paul, it's not something that we have to avoid talking about any more. It has happened, let's deal with it and move forward.'

'But when I get something permanent, what will we do with the kids?'

That exact thought had been playing on my mind too. 'We'll manage, everyone else does. They're not so little any more. There's after school care, and they do so many clubs and co-curricular activities anyway that we'd work it out between us. And in the holidays, well... we'll sort something out. Look, I'll start part-time, try to work school hours and we can see what happens.'

He nodded. We were still fine financially, but after six months without any steady income, I could see the countdown in our bank account balance wouldn't last another year at this rate. I didn't want to see what happened when it hit zero.

I sipped my wine, cracked black pepper onto my steak then slid the grinder to him. 'I know you'll get something, I'm not worried about that. I just... well, I'd quite like to do something other than this.' I waved my hands around the room. 'I've loved being at home, but I feel like it's my time now, you know?'

Paul pressed his lips together and nodded, but didn't look me in the eye. 'I guess it gives us a backup.'

I reached over and put my hand on his for a moment, then pulled the salad bowl towards me. 'It's not about a backup. I have absolutely no doubt that you will find something brilliant soon. I'm not worried about money, Paul. You know I've wanted to go back to work for ages.'

He nodded. 'I know. It'll be good for you. You'll enjoy it.'

'I will. Now that the kids are at school all day, I do feel like I drift around, taking all day to empty the dishwasher. I used to enjoy it, but now, I'm a bit envious of the working mums rushing to drop off their kids in their work clothes and complaining about daytime events at school. Part of me would quite like to have something else to talk about, like they do.'

'Okay. You're right. You used to love work.'

I chewed some salad, swallowed, then began cutting a piece of my steak, avoiding his eye contact. 'The reason I thought of it – I was speaking to Lucy the other day at assembly, you know, Connor's mum? She's a physio at the practice just off the highway near school. Anyway, she was saying how busy they were and that I could essentially rent a room from them and they'll book people in with me. I thought I could just start with maybe two mornings a week.'

'That's a good idea,' he said quickly. 'Then when I get work, you might not need to increase it.'

'Exactly. They start early there for clients who come in before they go to work so you'd have to get the kids to school sometimes, just on those two days.' I deliberately kept my voice light.

'That's fine,' he said, without hesitation. I could hear the strain in his voice.

'Great. I'll call her tomorrow.' I reached for my glass again and sipped my wine. I glanced at Paul; he did the same. I noticed his hand trembling on his glass. 'Are you okay?'

He nodded, then noticed that I was frowning at his hand. 'Yes. It's just these stupid painkillers. They're trying to get me off them, but the bloody club doctors gave me so many over the years, for nothing, that now I'm getting the shakes trying to reduce them. What a crock.'

Maybe that explained some of his irritability over the last few weeks. I knew he hadn't been sleeping; I often woke up in the night to see him lying on his side, doing something on his phone. 'You're doing so well, Paul... Do you want some mustard?'

He nodded, then picked up the remote and switched to the news that we always watched while we ate dinner.

I reached for my drink again, noticing my hands were tense. I was relieved the conversation was over; I hadn't been sure how he'd take it. I'd already spoken to Lucy of course, and the registration board because it had been years since I'd worked, and I'd printed off the forms to enrol the kids in before and after school care, just in case, and worked out how to get the

33

Childcare rebate from the government. I'd found out how the kids could get the school bus home if they needed to. But I was also deflated that Paul hadn't protested or told me that I was being ridiculous. His resignation to me going back to work confirmed that he too was worried that he might not find a new job, or, that he'd lost his fight.

–

Life took on a different rhythm. I worked, and the money trickled in, enough to let us tread water. I grew to love the time away from dealing with the children, and increasingly, Paul. I hurried out of the house in the morning with a sense of importance as I left him with the squabbling kids and the dirty dishes. Clients at work thanked me for helping them, and I felt useful, not only for helping people feel better from their sore necks and backs and hips, but also useful to my family. I began to understand how difficult it must have been for Paul before, with his focus and identity pulled between us and his sport. And as much as it hurt me to admit it, Cameron did seem more settled: maybe I really had been making too much of his symptoms, or maybe now I just had other things to think about.

Perhaps Paul had been right.

Four

Emily

'Remind me of everyone's names,' I said as I kicked off my black heels and rummaged in the bottom of my wardrobe for some strappy sandals. 'I'm never going to remember them all.'

'I don't know them all yet,' Paul said, tucking his shirt in. 'It's mainly Damian I've been working with. I'm not even sure exactly who he's invited. It's all been so quick really.'

'So, what's Damian's wife's name at least?'

'Shelly? Cheryl? Something like that.'

I smiled. 'You're hopeless.'

Paul shrugged, then grinned. 'I can't be expected to know everything. I am opening a restaurant after all, hanging with the movers and shakers of Sydney.' He raised his eyebrows at me.

I smiled back at him. 'Alright. You stay quiet, I'll introduce myself and get all their names, then I'll remember.'

He laughed. 'Yes, that's your job at these things.'

It was so good to hear him laugh again, and even though I could see he was anxious about the dinner, we were both so much more relaxed than we'd been for a long time. It had been hard for the past eighteen months, since I'd gone back to work, but eventually, finally, all those connections from Paul's endless corporate functions had paid off. About a month ago, he'd been asked to go to lunch with Damian, a businessman that he'd met after one of his speaking engagements. Apparently Damian had approached him out of the blue, said he'd followed his career as a soccer player, and knew that Paul was the right man for this job. Paul had no experience running a business, never mind an Italian restaurant, but as he'd said, we'd eaten out in enough of them to know what a good meal entailed.

I'd hardly seen Paul for the past three weeks as he got up early, dressed smartly and rushed off to meetings. But I hadn't minded; it was so good to see that spark animating him again after so many months watching him fade. And I felt a spark in me too, excitement that the pressure on us would ease with this job and a steady income. I had cut back on the luxuries: the cleaner, the lawnmower man, the pool cleaner, but I'd been living with an unease that other, more important, things might have to go too. Maybe the kids' school fees. Maybe the house. Before getting this job, Paul had at times come home late at night from the speaking gigs beaming, waving cash around and laughing; at other times, he came home with his shoulders hunched and his voice flat, complaining that I'd left the lights or the air conditioning on. I craved stability. And now, we had it again.

The doorbell rang. 'That'll be Georgia.' I still hadn't found the sandals; I hurried out of the bedroom in my bare feet and down the hall to answer the door. Georgia was our neighbour's daughter. She knew the kids well, and she was studying medicine at University, which always made me feel happier about leaving the kids with her. Tilly loved her, and Cameron, well, he was fine with her. Cameron was fine with most people as long as you didn't make him do something he didn't want to.

'Come through, how are you? Kids!' I called, 'Georgia's here.'

Tilly came running out, a big smile on her face, her hair tied up in a high ponytail. Georgia bent down and gave her a hug; Tilly beamed. Still not too big for a hug, even though she was ten now. I smiled.

'God knows where Cameron is.' I rolled my eyes. 'I've downloaded a new movie for him and he's allowed to watch that on his iPad in his room. He shouldn't give you any trouble.'

'He never does.'

'Georgia, I've got the coolest thing to show you in Minecraft,' Tilly said, pulling Georgia away by the hand. Georgia looked over her shoulder at me and shrugged, grinning.

I went back into the bedroom. Paul was tying his shoelaces. He stood up and smoothed down his trousers. 'Does this look okay?'

'Perfect! Are you nervous?'

'Nah.'

I tilted my head and raised my eyebrows.

'A little bit.'

'You've already got the job, babe. This is the fun bit, meeting everyone. Just be yourself, and they'll all love you. Are you worried I'll show you up?'

He smiled at me and tapped his index finger on his lips. 'Hmmm...'

'Hey!' I threw a discarded sock at him.

Paul ducked, then stepped towards me and hugged me. 'No. Of course not. You're the best thing about me.'

'Aww...' I mumbled. 'That's a nice thing to say. But it's not true.' I wriggled backwards. 'Careful, you might get my make-up on your shirt! Okay, we should get going. Where are my shoes?'

I looked in the wardrobe again, found the tan sandals I'd been searching for and put them on. It was hard to know what to wear. We were going to a fancy restaurant, but I'd never met these people before and I didn't know what was appropriate. I had decided on a jade silk dress, knee length, tied at the waist. It had spaghetti straps but a high neck. Covering all bases. I'd blow dried my hair as best I could, though it was a poor effort compared to when the hairdressers used to do my hair for functions. Back then, when Paul was playing, everything was paid for: flights and hotels, designer clothes, hair and make-up, meals, endless drinks. But we were no longer being flown around the country by sponsors.

I thought back to our first big event after we'd moved to Australia, before Cameron was born: a weekend in Melbourne for Australia's biggest horse race, the Melbourne Cup. Then, as our driver had pulled up to Flemington racecourse, excitement had bubbled through me like champagne. Later, once the races started, the ground shook with the thunder of the horses pounding around the track. I had put my weight on the balls of my feet to stop my heels sinking into the soft grass outside the marquee, checking my race ticket for the number of my horse. The animals were blurred as they galloped around, brightly dressed jockeys bouncing up and down. It was impossible not to be carried along by the thrill that charged the air, the nervous energy as the punters waved their betting slips, gripped their drinks and jumped up and down on the spot. As the horses turned the final corner and neared the finishing line in front of us, I saw the orange and white bib of the horse I'd picked, and the blue of Paul's bet bobbing up and down between the others. As we watched, Paul's inched ahead while my horse fell back. I shrugged and leaned forwards, willing Paul's horse to speed up, to pull ahead some more and before I knew it, Paul had grabbed me and lifted me up off the ground as he whooped in my ear, laughing. I laughed too and then kissed him. It was a perfect day. We couldn't lose.

We had many more days at the races. The excitement of that day had left an indelible mark. We would go together to Royal Randwick, Sydney's racecourse, and then, once I had the children to look after, Paul would go without me. We lost so many more times than we won, but it wasn't hard to convince ourselves that the fun we had was worth the money we shredded up.

But back then, we loved taking risks. After all, we had left our families and moved half a world away from our life in

Scotland. Back then, what was the worst that could happen? We had become too used to always winning, until Paul couldn't play football anymore. Now, the stakes were higher. If this job didn't go well, everything was at risk.

I shook away the thoughts, and reminded myself that everything was fine now. I looked in the full-length mirror on the back of our bedroom door. It would do; I looked happy, at least. I *was* happy: I was excited about our future for the first time in a long time, and so relieved that Paul was excited too.

The dinner was at a restaurant in the casino complex, overlooking the lights of Sydney harbour. Back in Scotland, the casinos were small, often hidden behind heavy black doors down alleyways, where we'd stagger in brandishing our membership cards for a drink after the nightclubs had closed. Here in Sydney, the casino was part of a big, brash, collection of expensive restaurants run by celebrity chefs, designer shops, and bars, surrounding a bright lobby with a shiny car tied up with a ribbon in the foyer. When you stepped from the foyer onto the casino floor, you were besieged by rows and rows of slot machines and roulette wheels and poker tables and blackjack tables and halls of mirrors and bright lights and jingle-jangling noises.

The taxi stopped at the main entrance and a doorman from the casino opened the car door. As I stepped out, I looked behind me back into the car. I took a deep breath. My eyes prickled with tears as and saw Paul take his wallet out of his pocket and pull out his credit card to pay the $70 taxi fare that I'd watched creep up with unease.

Paul closed the taxi door, put his wallet in his back pocket, then pulled back his shoulders. I could see how nervous he was. I pulled my own shoulders back too, then took his hand and squeezed it. So what if we'd worn these clothes before and were a little older? We were wiser. We were more cautious now; we had beautiful children to think of and we were as strong as ever: no, stronger. This was the turning point for us. We were together; everything was right where it should be again.

We walked from the glare of the casino foyer through a door and into a dark corridor lined by glowing candles, my heels clicking on the dark oak floors. I held Paul's hand as we approached the maître d' at a pedestal at the front of the restaurant. My stomach churned; why did I always feel intimidated in places like this? I didn't need to prove myself any more.

'Good evening, sir, madam,' the maître d' said.

'Hi,' I said.

'We're with—'

'The Talbot party?'

Paul nodded. 'Yes, Damian Talbot.'

'Come this way.' He picked up two menus and glided towards the back of the restaurant, towards a table next to the open kitchen where at least ten chefs with white aprons were bustling around, heads down, steam billowing and pans sizzling around them. I felt a flurry of excitement.

The table seated eight; we were the last to arrive. I recognised Damian, who stood up immediately on our approach, as did the others at the table. Three couples. Two were around our age, I guessed, and Damian and his wife were maybe in their early fifties.

'Paul!' he said warmly, shaking his hand. 'Great to see you.' He turned to me. 'And Emily, it's been too long. You look beautiful.'

Despite myself, I felt my cheeks turning red as I couldn't help but smile. 'Hi, Damian. Great to see you again.' I went to shake his hand but he leaned in and kissed my cheek. Of course.

'Have you met my wife?'

'No, no I haven't.'

I looked across the table and held out my hand to a woman with long reddish-brown hair worn down in loose curls, who was smiling warmly at me. She shook my hand.

'Hi. I'm Emily,' I said. 'Paul's wife.'

'Shona,' she said. 'It's lovely to meet you at last.'

Shona. Not Cheryl or Shelly. I felt a smile play on my lips; I glanced over at Paul, but he was now shaking hands with the others and I could tell he was concentrating on remembering names.

We finished introductions. Damian and Shona, Lucas and Amina, and Tim and Sam. I recited them in my head. They had left a space for us, opposite each other. Tim and Sam were at one end of the table, then Paul and I, then Damian and Shona, and at the other end, Lucas and Amina. Boy girl boy girl. Very well planned, I thought. I sat down, placed my bag at my feet, then exhaled slowly as I tried to look relaxed.

'Have you been here before?' Sam asked, looking from me to Paul.

Paul nodded, 'I have.'

'Not me,' I said. 'Paul used to come here with work but since having kids I don't get out much!' I tried to joke but I saw Paul stiffen. 'So, I'm very pleased to try it, I've heard great things. How about you? Have you been here before?'

We chatted for a few minutes as I periodically glanced around the table looking for a drink. Paul was talking to Damian but I knew he'd be more comfortable when the small talk was over. As if by magic, a waiter appeared and a hush went over the table as he introduced himself and explained that he was the sommelier. As he spoke, another waiter offered us still or sparkling water and filled our glasses. I picked mine up and sipped at the bubbles, only then noticing how dry my mouth had been. I picked up the cocktail menu on the table, glad to have a break from talking, and scanned the list. Would a cocktail look too indulgent? I looked over at Paul, but he was listening to the waiter.

He was coming around the table now taking drinks orders. No one else was looking at the cocktail menu; I closed it with some disappointment. I ordered a glass of the house Prosecco and went back to chatting.

A few minutes later, the waiter returned with a tray: one bottle of beer with a tall frosted glass, and one glass of Prosecco. He put the drinks in front of Paul and myself, then walked off.

I caught Paul's eyes and he briefly raised his eyebrows and gave a little shrug. Had I done something wrong? Jeez, we'd got a taxi all the way here so I was going to have a drink. I could have driven and saved $140. I quickly took a sip, keeping my eyes down.

We all kept talking and, after a few sips, I forgot about it and the tension that had been tightening my shoulders lessened. I looked over; Paul was laughing at something Sam had said. There was a time I might have been jealous of him laughing with another woman, in those endless early days when I had to stay home with the kids. But the time I spent with the kids when they were little was worth a thousand dinners out, and Paul and I had been through too much for there to be anything but complete trust between us now.

Entrées arrived. I had West Australian scallops, with chilli, lemon and chorizo. They were delicious. I had ordered a Scotch fillet for main, medium rare. It didn't appear that anyone had ordered a bottle of wine for the table, so I ordered a glass of cab sav. I sipped it through the meal, uneasy, but determined not to be intimidated. The steak was delicious. Paul had a steak too, but no one else did, which was odd for a restaurant that specialised in them. But it was fun. The food was great and the company was good. We spoke about restaurants, what we all thought worked well, what we didn't like, and how we could achieve something even better. I couldn't stop smiling at the thought of Paul – and me – being involved in this; we were back. After we had finished, I declined the waiter's suggestion of dessert as, once again, no one else seemed to be ordering anything.

As we stood to leave, Shona leaned in to kiss me goodbye. 'It's been so lovely meeting you,' she said. 'Damian really likes Paul, I think they're going to do great things together. We should catch up.'

'I'd love to,' I said, although I'd barely spoken to her during dinner and thought it would be awkward. I reached into my bag, found my purse and took out one of my business cards. 'Here, my mobile's on this.'

She looked at it. 'A physiotherapist? How wonderful.'

'That's how Paul and I met. I was working with a practice who looked after the players.'

'And you're working now?'

'Yes,' I nodded.

'Hopefully you won't have to soon, if I can believe what Damian says about Paul.'

I stopped myself from frowning. I didn't want them to think that Paul had needed to be supported by me. 'I love my work. No matter what happens, I'll keep working.'

She laughed and touched my shoulder. 'Of course!'

We all walked out of the restaurant together and said goodbye again in the foyer. The others were heading to the car park; we were heading to the taxi rank.

Paul and I held hands as we walked slowly towards the glass doors out to the road where a line of taxis waited. We were almost there when we both hesitated and turned to each other. Paul said it first. 'A drink?'

'Oh my God, yes.' We both laughed and turned back inside.

The rest of our night reminded me of when we were younger. We were affectionate and playful with each other, laughed, drank, cheered when someone at our roulette table's number came in. A band was playing in the sports bar and eventually, we drifted in there. I found a table, sat on the couch next to it and tapped my foot to the music while Paul went to the bar for another drink. They were playing eighties music. *Sweet Dreams Are Made of This*. I laughed as it came on, thinking of Annie Lennox, of home in Aberdeen, and nostalgia came over me. It had taken a long time to realise that Scotland was part of me, but it no longer *was* me. I was proud of it but here was my home now, and Paul and the children were what was most important.

Paul came back with a gin and tonic for me. He put it down on the table. He sat down and sipped his drink as I settled back in the chair. He was biting at the inside of his cheek.

'Are you okay?' I asked.

'Yes. Why are you asking me that?'

I held my hand up. 'No need to bite my head off. I was just asking.'

'I'm fine.'

I raised my eyebrows and swirled the ice around my drink.

But he wasn't fine. He sat on the edge of his chair, pretending to listen to me while his eyes darted around the room. Then he stood up, grabbed his drink, and walked off. 'I'll be right back,' he shouted above the music as he disappeared into the crowd.

'Where are you—'

He had gone. My pulse quickened. He must be going to the bar again. I sipped my drink, checked my phone in case there were any messages from the babysitter, then watched others dancing as I waited for Paul.

Five minutes passed, then ten, twenty. My drink was finished. Had I just drunk it too quickly? No, there had been at least a few songs played since he left. *Living on a Prayer, I Wanna Dance with Somebody, Come On Eileen*. Maybe he'd gone to the toilet. But why would he have taken his drink? Anyway, the queue for the toilets couldn't be that long, not for the men's. He'd probably met someone he knew, or who recognised him. I checked the time, waited for another couple of songs then called him. No answer. I'd lose the table if I went to get him but now I needed to use the bathroom, and I needed another drink, otherwise I'd start to feel tired and have to go home. I gathered up my bag and stood up.

I went to the ladies', then checked the bars and walked around the tables. He wasn't there. Where was he?

Something pulled me towards the casino floor, my eyes blinking hard in the bright lights. I couldn't see him on any of the tables there either, although it was a pretty big area and he could have been anywhere. I walked past the roulette tables, the blackjack tables, the poker tables, and towards the rows of slot machines.

Bandits, we used to call them in the UK.

There was a sad delineation between the frenzied action of the main casino floor, with groups of people milling around tables, drinking and laughing, and the isolation of each solitary body perched on a high stool adjacent to each machine. I hesitated as my eyes scanned the bent backs of the figures pressing the buttons over and over and over. At that moment, for that fleeting second before it really registered that it was him, Paul looked just as stooped and defeated as the others, as they robotically fed coins into the machine with one hand and pressed the buttons on the machine with the other. Paul's blue checked shirt stretched across his broad back, dark crescents under his arms. The patterned carpet of the room was sticky underfoot, and even though smoking had been banned years ago, the stench of stale cigarettes still clung to the paint. The noises that had been faint background chatter from the main floor were, in here, overwhelming: beeps and buzzes and clicking and jangling and ringing and canned laughter and electronic applause.

I walked over to Paul and from behind him, rested my head on his shoulder. 'You winning?'

It was as if he hadn't heard me. He pushed the flashing button again; the four reels spun and stopped seconds after each other, from left to right, thunk, thunk, thunk, thunk. He shook his head, then curled his hand into a fist and hit the button again, hard. 'No. I've put forty dollars into this, and nothing back.'

'Oh well,' I said in a voice that even to me sounded like forced nonchalance, as I lifted my head from his shoulder and put my hand there instead. 'Never mind. Come back through to the bar. Actually...' I looked at my watch. 'We should probably go home, it's getting late.'

'You got any cash on you?' He swivelled round to look at me.

I frowned. 'No.'

'You've got your bag though.'

'No, Paul. I don't have any cash. Come on, let's go.'

'It's close to a win though. There was a guy here before me must have put fifty bucks in, so it's due for a pay out.'

I put my hand on my bag, knowing that even while I hesitated that of course I would give him money. But I had to hesitate to show him I didn't approve, and I really didn't, but now that he was here and I was here and the slot machine was full of money and ready to pay out then what was the harm? Part of me wanted to linger too, maybe to win again, when it felt like we'd been struggling to just keep even for so long.

'This is all I have,' I said, taking two ten-dollar notes from my purse and handing them to him. 'Then we have to go.'

He smiled at me. 'Thanks. Do you want to press it? Maybe you're my lucky charm...'

I shrugged and smiled back then stood in front of him. What did it matter? It was only twenty dollars; just a bit of fun. But at the same time, it really wasn't much fun at all.

He wrapped his arms around me and I grinned, wiggled my fingers, and then flattened the first note and fed it into the notes slot.

Five

Paul

'The school emailed me again,' Emily said as she stacked the dishwasher after dinner. She still wore her work uniform, black trousers and a teal coloured polo shirt with the clinic's logo on it. Her feet were bare. Her hair was tied back in a ponytail, though strands had fallen loose, and she'd taken out her contact lenses and put her glasses on.

I filled the kettle and switched it on. 'Why?'

'The paediatrician had asked me to get them to do some classroom observations, remember?'

'Yes, I was there.'

'Alright, no need to be like that.'

I saw her shaking her head. I sighed. 'Sorry, I'm just tired. I'm frustrated with work. It feels like we're going nowhere.' I'd been working with Damian for about six months now. It was harder than I had thought, but I had to keep pretending that I knew what I was doing. Sometimes, I felt like a cute new puppy being led around on a leash. People were keen to meet me, but then I lost track of what they were talking about and they turned away from me.

'It was never going to be easy to start a new business. But hey, they're paying you.' She raised her eyebrows and smiled.

They were. Though it wasn't enough. We were so behind financially from all the time I spent out of work, that I couldn't get ahead. As soon as I earned money, it was gone again, and I hated the feeling that we were just hanging on and any moment, it could all disappear again. The work meetings were often in restaurants, and I had to take out my credit card and contribute, sometimes paying for everything. I had to get taxis – I could hardly walk away from the taxi rank and down into the train station in front of all the clients and bankers. Damian knew what I was being paid – he was the one paying me after all – and sometimes I wondered if he was testing me. I couldn't fail; without him, I really did have nothing. I was probably being too sensitive: he wasn't to know how much we'd lost. Besides, he promised that soon, once we were open, things would change, and I'd get a share of the company.

I sighed and looked at Emily. 'It's just all new to me. I guess before, with soccer, I just did what I was told from the coaches, the managers, and sponsors. Now they talk of capital raising and licences and marketing and I'm a bit lost but have to pretend to know what they're talking about.'

She turned around and looked at me, eyes concerned. 'I know, sweetie. It's a different world. You've never done it before, but don't lose confidence. They asked *you* to join them; you're as important as they are to that business. Don't be afraid to tell them when you feel out of your depth.'

I sighed, then got the teabags out of the pantry cupboard and put one in each mug. 'You're right. I'll just fake it 'til I make it.'

She smiled at me. 'That's my man.'

I smiled back, then sighed again. 'So, what did these school observations show?'

'I don't know yet, I have to go in to meet the school psych to talk about what she thinks, but ultimately we have to wait until the appointment with the paediatrician next month.'

'Cam's doing alright, though, isn't he? He seems more settled.'

She sighed. 'Yes. Maybe. I don't know. Part of me wants them to say there's nothing wrong with him, but the other part wants the paediatrician to give me a diagnosis, to explain it all, maybe to have something we can treat, and simply to be able to say to people, "Hey, he can't help it," you know?'

I looked up from pouring the boiling water in the mugs. 'I do know. But really, I'd rather nothing was wrong.'

'Me too! I know that, it's just... he's just not like the other kids, Paul, and it's hard for him.'

And you, and us, I wanted to say, but there was no need.

I put the kettle back on its stand. 'I just find it frustrating, Em. They've talked about so many things in the past and I thought they said he didn't have any of them. Surely, they've observed him every day at school since Year 1? Here we are in high school and we're still going back and forwards to all the specialists. Honestly, he's seen at least two or three psychologists, an occupational therapist, a speech therapist, the paediatrician heaps of times. How many 'specialists' does it take?'

'It's not as easy as diagnosing a broken leg, Paul. They said that sometimes when the demands of school increase, the symptoms become more of a problem. Now he's expected to organise himself and he just can't do it. He's away with the fairies half the time, and you've seen his grades. Remember when we saw the neuropsychologist—'

I raised my eyebrows and smiled a little. I'd forgotten about that specialist.

She smiled a little but kept going. 'His IQ was above average and yet now, he's barely reaching the standard.'

'Nobody tells us what the standard is. Whatever happened to As, Bs and Cs?'

She sighed. 'He's barely getting Cs then.'

'Neither did I at school,' I said.

She tutted. 'Oh Paul. I know that, and look how amazingly well you've done. I don't care what grades he gets as long as he's reaching his potential. The issue is that along with all the trouble he's getting in, now his grades are slipping and I don't want to let this go on any longer. Look at his social skills, how he interacts, how he copes, how he concentrates. He's so anxious all the time. Kids with an autistic spectrum disorder—'

'I thought they were talking about ADHD? He's not autistic!'

'I know that, Paul, but it's a spectrum, you know. It's not all like *Rainman*. They're linked. They said he might have that when he was little, remember?'

'Yes, then we paid a fortune for all the assessments and tests and then they said he didn't. You also were convinced he had OCD then.' I shook my head, then screwed the lid back on the milk carton and put it back in the fridge.

'Well, help me then, Paul! I'm confused too, I don't know what it is but something's not right, he's not happy and I'm just looking for an answer because if I know what's wrong with him then maybe I can make him better.'

I sighed. 'I'll talk to him.'

'Will you, Paul?' she said, eyes pleading. 'It's just that I don't know how to get through to him. At least you've been a twelve-year-old boy. I know where Tilly's coming from: I can remember how confusing it is when your body changes.'

I screwed up my face. 'That's definitely not my area.' I remembered Tilly pushing away her cereal this morning, hardly touched, and before I could say anything, she had walked out of the kitchen towards the bathroom to do her hair, presumably, which seemed to take an inordinate amount of time.

'Girls' stuff.' Emily smiled, folding up the tea towel then putting her hand on my arm. 'So, you can do the boy's stuff. I thought that boys would be less... moody. Oh, look, I don't even think he's moody. There are no... undulations. He's constantly tense. And everything has to be just right. Jesus. I never thought I'd complain about having a child who was so determined to do everything perfectly. I thought teenagers were meant to be messy and lazy?'

I smiled. 'You trained them too well.'

'It's not funny.'

I sighed. I knew that he hadn't been himself. And I knew how stressed Emily was about this, on top of everything else. She did so much for the family, working – something that she shouldn't have to do – and managing all the things with the kids as I got busier and busier. Since my career ended, now two, three years ago, it was she who had held us all together.

My face flushed with shame as I thought about how hard Emily was trying to keep everything under control. Self-control was something I was finding harder and harder. But I could change; I would try harder. 'Come and sit down, babe. Whatever it is, it is. And we'll deal with it. We'll go to the paediatrician's appointment, we'll find out what the problem is, then we'll sort it out.'

She looked at me, biting her lip, but then she nodded and picked up her mug. I switched off the kitchen lights.

–

'You said you'd be able to come, Paul!'

I cringed as Emily's voice shrieked through the car's hands-free phone system. The appointment with the paediatrician that had seemed so far away when we had talked about it weeks ago was today. But today, every day, I had too much to do, too much to think about.

'I'm sorry, Em. I'm sorry, I know, but there's this meeting with the Board and I have to go. Maybe you could change the appointment—'

She cut me off. 'Paul. I'm trying to be calm, I really am. I've just dropped the kids at school, I'm late for work because, as usual, your work has taken priority, despite the fact that my job is no less important than yours. I've already had to tell Lucy that I'm leaving early and can't see any urgent appointments today, so I'm losing money and she's pissed off at me. It took months to get in to see this doctor, you know that. And it's not fair to delay Cameron's care because of your work. Can't you just explain to them how important it is? Surely, they can do the meeting without you? It'll take, like, an hour or something.'

'I tried—'

'Did you? Really? Have you even mentioned it to them? They have children, I'm certain that they would think that

51

taking your child to a specialist's appointment is more important than a meeting.' I heard the scepticism in her voice; my face burned.

'Yes!' I hadn't. Damian had called me and told me about the meeting. I had thought about Cameron's appointment, but instead of saying something, I had said I'd be there. Damian had a way of talking that didn't allow you to disagree. He was my boss, after all, and he had believed in me when I had almost stopped believing in myself. I knew how much it meant to Emily for me to go to the appointment, but it was also important for me to show Damian that I was serious, that I was dependable. I couldn't lose this job. Not with the way things were. We would go under.

My face reddened as I thought of Cameron when I'd dropped him off yesterday. He'd gotten out at the slipway but left his sports bag in the car. He hadn't turned around when I beeped the horn. There was a queue of four-wheel-drives behind me, so I had driven around the corner and double parked; I'd only be a minute.

I hadn't seen him at first. Then I'd frozen and just watched. It's not that he was doing anything unusual, he wasn't drawing attention to himself other than by being him. Lots of kids were milling around, in pairs or groups, as they waited for the bell to ring. It's so hard to describe what it is that made him stand out – I'm trying to convince myself that actually, he blended in fine and it was just that I was looking for something odd that I noticed it. But he was all alone. It was like he had a force repelling everyone else. I saw a group of boys that he played rugby with, chatting and mucking around, and I watched Cameron go up to them and edge his way into their circle. The boys glanced at him, then turned away and kept walking, leaving him all alone.

Emily's voice filled the car again. 'Did you tell them why you needed some time off? That it's your son's health? What if we were going to meet with a cancer specialist?'

'Emily, come on. That's not a fair comparison.'

'You don't know how serious this might be.'

'I just don't think that saying I wouldn't be there if our child had a life-threatening disease is fair.'

'It is absolutely fair, Paul.' I could hear the tears in her voice.

I wasn't going to win this one. 'Alright, okay. You're right. I'll tell Damian. I'll come,' I said quietly. Damian would understand. But I felt something burning in the pit of my stomach. Why was I so nervous about asking him? I was a grown man, but I felt like a child. I was worried that if I told him I couldn't come, that maybe I would be cast out from his group, that I'd never reach the status of people like Lucas and Tim. He invited them on his boat, they went away for weekends together and to meetings where I wasn't invited, and while I hated myself for it, I found myself hanging around the edges hoping to be included. Shame burned through me. Shame about my sycophantism, and shame about my desire to have the sort of money Damian did. But really, was it so bad to want to decrease the stress on my wife from working so much, or to try and keep up with mortgage payments?

I forced myself to breathe slowly.

Emily hadn't said anything for a moment or two, then she spoke quietly. 'It's fine, Paul. I'll manage it.'

'I said, I'll cancel the meeting,' I said.

'And I said I'll manage it. If it's that important then you need to go.'

'I do want to be there, Emily, it's just—'

'I know, Paul. Look I'm almost at work, I can't talk about this now, it makes me too upset and I don't want to go in there looking like I've been crying.'

'Alright. I'll try.'

'Thank you. I would love you to be there, but I understand if you can't.'

'I'll do my best.' I *would* call Damian and say I'd forgotten that Cameron had a medical appointment, and that I needed to leave early. But with Emily now giving me permission to skip the doctor's meeting, I could use that time to give myself some room to manoeuver. I had to keep Damian onside. I had to show him that I could keep up with him and everyone else, and to do that, I needed to take more risks.

Six

Emily

The months passed, and before we knew it, it was two years since Paul had started working again. Cameron, fourteen now, was no worse than usual: the paediatrician was monitoring him every few months but nothing definite was diagnosed, and we just muddled through, dealing with issues as they arose. Tilly started high school.

I hadn't stopped working; I had learned that the carefree dream life that we had for years was long gone. Life still didn't feel easy though: with the restaurant finally due to open soon, Paul was working more than ever. He had meetings during the day, and in the evenings he was often out late. The dinners and corporate engagements meant that most weekends, he was out until the early hours on at least one night. Other evenings, even though he was at home, he spent hours fiddling with his phone, preoccupied, stressed, taking calls from work and disappearing into the study until I gave up and went to bed alone. I said nothing though: Paul was happiest when he was busy, engrossed in something and feeling useful. That's not to say that I didn't frequently feel a flicker of irritation when he stopped talking to me mid-conversation as he hurried out of the living room to answer his phone, while I waited with our TV show paused. I went to bed exhausted, and woke up tired, but we had a routine and I was, if not in control, then at least on top of things. Paul was being paid and, with the top-ups from speaking at charity lunches and corporate dinners and my wages, we had built a buffer again. The money was trickling in.

And then it wasn't.

–

When the kids were younger, I would go to the park every week or so with a few of the mothers who didn't raise their eyebrows when Cameron misbehaved. One of them, Samira, was from London, and as we pushed our children on the swings, we compared how we were each managing as best we could to raise our children without any family around. Her husband was some sort of engineer, and she was in finance, or had been, before children.

One of those days, a few of us were sitting on picnic blankets in the shade of a fig tree, with tubs of cut up watermelon and packets of crackers in the middle for the kids to share. Their kids were running around; Cameron was sitting alone in the sandpit sifting sand through his fingers. It was chilly in the shade, with a cool breeze coming in off the river. Samira took her wallet out of her baby bag and opened it up, then handed each of us a business card. She was bored being at home with only children to worry about and so had decided to start a new business, she explained. I frowned, both jealous at her initiative, and irritated at her trying to recruit us. I gave out free physio advice to them all the time, especially when Samira and another woman had decided to run a half-marathon. I pushed the feeling away.

'That's fantastic, Samira. Good on you. I don't know where you find the time,' I had said, smiling.

She beamed. 'Thanks! I knew you'd all understand how important it is to me and how it feels to want something just for *me*. Anyway, I want to teach women financial literacy.'

I rolled my eyes as one of the mums groaned, then we laughed.

'I see it all the time,' she continued, smiling, waving her hands around to make us listen. 'We are smart women, we have – or had – careers, and we put it all aside for our kids. Which is great, don't get me wrong, but the problems start when your husband leaves you ten years later for some floozy and you've lost your skills or your registration and you have no idea how much you have in your superannuation, and what shares you own and you're buggered.'

I bit my lip. I had let my physio registration lapse. 'I do all our banking and bills. Paul's useless at that stuff. And then we send it to his accountant at the end of the year and she sorts out all our mistakes.'

'Don't be so sure,' Samira said. 'You'd be surprised. Do you have a company and a trust set up? Income protection? Wills?'

I made a face. 'God, no. It's just money in, money out. I think...'

At that time, I didn't think we had any need for all those things. Why would we need a will? Any money we had would go to each other, and the kids, wouldn't it?

But now, we did have a company and Paul had invested what little money we had in other companies owned by Damian and his group, and a self-managed super account that didn't have anything in it because Paul said that we were better off using the money now, and we each had credit cards. And every month, I sat down to try and make sense of it all.

–

I don't know how I didn't notice sooner. On the first Monday of every month, I dropped the children at school then went home, made a coffee and did our family banking online: I paid the phone and credit card bills and school fees, and filed away things I could claim as a tax rebate. I never really looked at the available balance on the internet banking properly – it was complicated, as it included our business account and self-managed super and credit cards, and I had become secure again, knowing that we were both bringing money in to the family. I never really studied the money coming in: it was never regular, and the money from the speaking gigs was unpredictable and often took a long time to clear through Paul's agent.

I sat at my desk in our home study with my laptop open with the pile of bills and receipts on my left-hand side, ready to work through them. I took a sip of my coffee, but, as I went to put the mug down, my eye stopped on the available balance. '$9356.72 available.' I squinted, thinking I must be reading it wrong and missed a digit. I was sure that the last time I'd checked, or at least recently, we'd had '$39039.39 available' in our account. I remember looking at it and, as well as being so relieved that finally, we had enough to see us through any other brief disasters, also wondering what the chances were of having exactly that pattern of numbers. It felt like good luck. And a lot of money. We still owed over a million on the house, but the Sydney property market had gone up so much that it was worth at least double that, so we could always sell it and move to a cheaper suburb.

I traced the number on the screen with my finger. No, it definitely said nine thousand, not thirty-nine thousand, available. Maybe it had been a couple of months ago that I'd seen that balance. I mustn't have read it properly last month.

Our mortgage, due the following week on the 15th, as always, was almost five thousand a month. My car repayment was $900, and my credit card bill alone was over two grand, just from groceries and day to day things – I put everything on my card, to get the frequent flyer points so Paul could upgrade his flights when he went travelling. So once those were paid, we'd have practically nothing.

I frowned, then clicked on the savings account to open the list of transactions. Paul's salary had been going in as usual. But there was nothing else: no speaking fees. And there were some big withdrawals: $3000 here, $5000 here, $5000 a week ago, from ATMs and transfers into another account that I didn't recognise including $10000 two weeks ago. I scrolled down, holding my breath. These transactions had been going on for the last few months. Where had $30000 gone? I leaned back in my chair, staring at the screen, the house quiet apart from the thumping of my heart and a dog barking in a neighbour's back yard. What was going on?

Tears filled my eyes as I remembered the story of a man who couldn't face the shame of telling his family he'd lost his job, so instead dressed in his work clothes and sat in the public library all day, reading Proust. No, that wasn't it. Paul was still being paid. I'd met Damian and seen the restaurant. But what had happened to the payments for the corporate work? He'd been going out to dozens of functions in the past few months; I'd seen him put his suit on and hurry out the door then come back late at night. I'd been complaining about the amount of time he was out, and he had told me he had to work.

My mouth went dry. An affair.

He must be having an affair.

Strangely, I heard myself start to laugh. I shook my head and groaned. What a bloody cliché. And to be stupid enough to think that I wouldn't notice tens of thousands of dollars disappearing from our account? This is what they do, men who have affairs, isn't it? They want to be caught, and they're too weak to tell their wives so they set up some clues to be found out so that the wife has to bring it up and confront them. Pathetic. It was pathetic to be unable to admit that you're unhappy before you drop your trousers and open your wallet and take food from the mouths of your own children.

I laughed and then I cried because now what would I do? Paul and I were a team. We'd always said we'd be together forever, and we'd remember all the great things about us to counteract anything bad because, we'd promised, we wouldn't be like everyone else. We loved each other.

I wiped away my tears as I heard the engine of the postman's motorbike outside. I was relieved the blinds in my office were still drawn so he didn't see me. I didn't believe it. I couldn't believe it. Paul wouldn't have an affair. Other men that I knew, yes, but I had a good eye for the men who strayed. And Paul wasn't one.

But if he wasn't, where was all our money?

I picked up my phone to call him, then put it down again. My heart was racing and I knew that if I spoke to him now, I'd come across all frantic and I'd look like the crazy one. I needed to calm down and think through this. I needed to be sure before I confronted him.

I would sort out the things I could control first. I sorted the bills into a pile and checked the due dates. I wasn't going to pay them yet, but needed to see what the priorities were. I walked through to the kitchen and made a cup of tea because the coffee would make my nerves worse. And, how could a disaster happen when I was making a cup of tea in my own kitchen? Holding my mug with two hands to save it spilling from my trembling hands, I went back through to the office and sat down again and checked the bank screen again.

It hadn't changed. Had the bank made an error?

I scrolled through all the transactions again to try and work out what was going on. I printed out a calendar page then, with a red pen, began to write down where he'd taken money out, when he'd been paid, looking for a pattern, cross referencing it to my diary, trying to remember what we'd done on each day. Most of the time he'd taken the cash out in big chunks, it was on the weekends, in the evening, when he'd been doing speaking engagements. Or that's what he'd said.

He'd been cagier about where he was going recently; or maybe I'd stopped asking. All this stuff with Cameron, and work – I'd been distracted. Tears welled up in my eyes, then I clenched my fists as rage surged through me. No! I wasn't going to take the blame. I wasn't the one doing God knows what and if I hadn't asked where he was going every night, it was because I trusted him. I screwed my eyes tight: I was going to cry but I hated crying, and I didn't want to let myself break, but as my breath started to come in gasps and I heard myself call out with the fear of it all, I knew that I had to confront him. If he was having an affair, I needed to know, I wanted to know.

Maybe we'd been hacked, his card stolen. That would explain everything.

I took some deep, jittery breaths, until I thought I was calm enough to talk. I picked up my mobile. What had he said he was doing today? I hadn't asked; he hadn't volunteered anything. As I swiped the screen of my phone, my fingers trembled. My face contorted again with the pain of it all and tears spilled over. I didn't trust myself to speak; I texted him.

Are you busy? I need to talk to you urgently.

I dropped the phone on my desk and watched it, noticing the 'delivered' message change to 'read' and then the dots appeared on the screen as he began to type a reply. He must know what it is about. He knew I accessed the bank accounts.

Just in a meeting. Call you soon. Everything okay?

No, I wanted to type, *no it's not and you know it*. I pictured Paul sitting with Damian and all his cronies with their sparkling water and herbal tea and white teeth and nice suits in these meetings, him trying to get into their circle and understand what they were all talking about, how vulnerable he had seemed, how my heart had ached to see how hard he had been trying to forge a new career.

But he'd been lying to me. I typed back.

Call as soon as you can.

Half an hour later, I was still sitting at my desk, glancing at my phone every few moments. I'd checked the banks accounts, again, and again, checked my emails, even Googled 'husband withdrawing large amounts of money' and read forums of women whose husbands had double lives. But I may as well have been reading a novel; I couldn't believe that what these people had experienced really could ever happen to me.

I jumped as the phone rang. My hand shook as I reached for it, seeing a photo of Paul with his arms around Cameron and Tilly on the screen. I'd taken it years ago in Bali. They were all sitting at a pool bar, him with a bottle of beer, the kids with some fizzy drinks concoctions with little umbrellas in them, all grinning. It was so rare to get a good shot like that. That holiday had been great; it was before Paul was injured, and life seemed perfect. Even Cameron had relaxed on the holiday, maybe as there was no pressure on him to do anything. At least that's how I remember it now. I'm sure at the time it wasn't as idyllic; memories of trips are often far better than the reality of the holiday itself. And besides, an all-inclusive resort in Bali with no one working and no one at school wasn't real life. Cameron *did* have to go to school, and one day he'd have to get a job. And so, when the day came to leave Bali, everything went right back to the way it was.

The way it was. Right now, I wished that life was the way it was back then, even the way it was this morning, before I knew about this, when Cameron was the only thing we had to worry about.

I answered the phone, still with no idea what I was going to say.

'Hi. I'm sorry, I was in a meeting. Everything okay?' Paul said, sounding breathless. 'I'm just walking to my car, about to head into the city for another one, though, but your message worried me.'

'I don't have any idea what you do all day. Where are you now?' I know my voice was accusatory; I didn't care.

'What? I'm at work, at the office.'

'You've never invited me to your office.' I could feel myself building and building.

'What's wrong, Emily? You're—'

I spat the words out. 'I checked the bank accounts today, Paul. You tell me what's wrong.'

'Oh.'

'Oh?'

'I was going to—'

'What? What were you going to do? Do you have thirty grand sitting in another bank account somewhere? Is it in a trust for the kids' education? What's going on?'

'I can't talk about it now, Emily. Let me just finish this meeting and I'll come straight home, I promise.'

'Are you having an affair?' As soon as I said it, my voice broke and the tears started.

'No, no, of course not...oh, Emily, I would never...' He sounded frightened. 'It's not that—'

'Then what the hell is going on? Where is all our money? I can't pay the bills, Paul! Where has it all gone?' I was shrieking now, but I couldn't stop. I heard a car door close through the phone.

'I can't talk about it now, Emily. I'm so sorry. I love you. I have to go.'

And then he hung up on me.

I stared at the phone. My tears dried into brittle rage. How dare he hang up on me? I called him again; the phone rang twice then went to voicemail. I rang him again; same. And then when I rang a third time, it went straight to voicemail and I knew he'd turned it off. I threw my phone down on the floor. If there was nothing going on, he'd have told me. I heard myself scream in fury then buried my face in my hands.

I didn't try calling Paul again. He didn't call me back. Eventually, I dried my tears and I piled the bills up neatly on my desk, then I walked out of my office and closed the door. I put on my sneakers and left the house, put on my headphones and listened to Pink very loudly and tried to walk then run then sprint quicker than my thoughts could catch me. And every time a panicked thought scrambled up to the surface and tried to get a foothold, I turned up the music and I ran faster until I had no energy left. I longed for it to be school pick-up time, to have the distraction of the children to keep me busy until Paul came home, and I could get some answers.

By the time I heard the front door open that evening, I had almost resigned myself to the fact that I was on my own from now on. I was going to have to work harder, full-time, and I was going to have to be the one who protected the children. I heard Paul's footsteps in the hallway.

'Kids,' I shouted, over the noise of the music coming from Tilly's bedroom. 'Dinner.'

I got the egg flip from the drawer and scraped the sausage rolls off the oven tray. I picked off the burned pastry from the bottom of them before Cameron could see it. I slid them onto two plates, and took it to the dining table, already set for the kids. 'Dinner, now!'

They came through as I put down a plate of cut carrot sticks, cucumber and capsicum slices in the middle of the table and went to get their glasses of water.

'What are we having?' said Cameron as he skulked through and picked up the TV remote control.

'Sausage rolls.'

'And what?'

'Just what you can see on the table,' I said, shaking my head. 'Tilly!'

'I'm not hungry,' she called through from her room.

'Oh, for God's sake,' I muttered. Where was Paul – hiding in the bedroom? 'Tilly. Get out here now.'

She came through, glaring at me. I felt my eyes fill with tears; Tilly sat down quickly and squeezed tomato sauce onto her plate.

Cameron had switched on the television.

'Cam,' Tilly whined. 'I don't like—'

I slapped my hand down on the bench top. 'You two. Be quiet and eat your dinner or the TV is off and you're in bed.'

They both stared at me; I saw them glance at each other for a moment and then they began eating. I dabbed my finger in the corner of my eye. 'Sorry,' I mumbled. 'Please. Just eat. I need to go speak to Dad.'

I walked out of the kitchen and down the hallway into our bedroom. He was in there, already in his suit trousers, buttoning up his shirt. His work clothes – jeans and a polo shirt – were on the floor. He looked up briefly as I closed the door behind me then he looked down at his hands, trying to fasten his buttons, then began putting his foot into his shoes.

'What are you doing?' I said, incredulous, shaking my head. 'We need to talk.'

'I've got a gig, in an hour, I need to get going.'

'A gig?'

He nodded.

'Don't you think that telling me what is going on is more important right now?'

'I have to go.'

My pulse sped up. I hissed the words out through gritted teeth so that the children wouldn't hear me. 'You are not going anywhere! Why did you hang up on me, and then not call me back when you've had all day to explain what's going on? Now you're off out again?'

I saw his lip quiver, and the sight of that made my own tears fall. My anger drained and I sat next to him on the bed. I could barely get the words out. 'Paul. You need to be honest with me. Are you having an affair?'

His head whipped round to me. 'No! No, of course not. Never! You're the most important thing in the world to me, you and the kids. Oh, babe, it's not…' He covered his face with his hands.

'Paul. This is serious. What is it then?'

'I will tell you, I promise. I just really have to go. It's important, I can't miss this. It's work.' His voice was pleading.

'Are you in trouble?' I said quietly.

He shook his head. 'No, it'll be okay, everything will be okay. Emily, I promise you. It's just cash flow, it's all there but there've been delays with the business, you know. I've had things to pay. I didn't want to tell you as I didn't want to worry you, but

65

you need to believe me when I say that I love you and I'll sort this out, I promise you. You don't need to worry. I'll have the money back in there tomorrow, I promise.'

He took a deep breath, sniffed, then wiped his eyes and stood up. His face was pale, his eyes red-rimmed. His back was hunched and he hung his head. I stared at him, this man who was the other part of me. I trusted him when he said it wasn't an affair. In my heart, I knew he wouldn't do that to me.

I stood too and touched his arm. 'Are you okay?'

He nodded, and spoke quietly, looking at the floor. 'I'm just sick of playing this part.'

'What part, Paul?' I squeezed his arm. My heart was hammering, fear pulsing through me.

He breathed in, trying to puff his frame up with false bravado. 'Nothing, never mind.'

'Just get through the gig tonight. Then come straight home and we'll sort it out. You don't have to fix everything yourself, Paul. You just need to talk to me and tell me what's going on. We're a team.'

He nodded, not catching my eye. 'I love you, Em. And the kids.'

I reached up and straightened his collar then stood on my tiptoes to kiss his cheek. 'We love you too.'

He hesitated for a moment then walked towards the bedroom door. I followed him out.

'You driving?'

'Oh. No, I've ordered an Uber, it'll be here any minute.'

I nodded. He picked up his keys and wallet from the hallway table, put them in his pocket, then walked down the hallway to the front door. His suit jacket hung off him more than it used to and with it, his pride. I watched him as he opened the door, walked out, then closed it without turning around. I waited for a minute or two, holding my breath, confused about what all this meant, then was flooded with a sense of dread.

I ran to the door and opened it, but he was gone.

Seven

Paul

In any city in the world, you can guarantee that there's one place that'll be open all night – the casino. And guess where we usually stayed with the team when we travelled for work? The casino hotels. They were often the most glamorous places to stay, subsidised by the millions they were raking in downstairs from the punters. Also, most of the big functions – the charity balls, the awards nights – were held in the ballrooms of the casino complexes. They rolled out the red carpet for us in front of the busloads of people on the $10 return coach trip – including lunch – that collected and deposited them from the outer suburbs to lose their money.

I had been hired to speak at a fundraising dinner for children's cancer. I had agreed, of course. There hadn't been so many opportunities lately; Jock said it was a problem after you hadn't played for a while, because no one remembered who you were. I'd seen the guests whispering to each other when I was introduced, puzzled looks on their faces while their companions shrugged. I couldn't turn this down. The money was critical now.

I don't know how I got through it, standing in front of a couple of hundred merry middle-class people who were drinking champagne and bidding for signed, framed sports shirts. I was one of them once. I must have said the right things, because no one seemed disappointed in me but as my mouth was opening and closing and words were coming out and everyone was listening to me and laughing at the right places, all I could think about was Emily. Sweet Emily. Even when she had every right to be furious at me, to scream and hit me, she didn't. She offered a hand out to help me. When she said she loved me and kissed me goodbye, I think she knew. I think she knew that this was the last gig, either way.

She said she doesn't know where the money's gone but she must. She must have known that when I came here to the casino, night after night, in my suit, I wasn't earning money. I may as well have burned all our money and with it, our house and everything we own. How could I ever face her again?

There's nothing left. The mortgage and car repayments are due next week, and I don't even know if we can cover them, even after the payment for tonight hits the bank. That would be $3300; $3000 plus GST. That's what three hours of my time is worth. Pretty good, huh? But it's not enough. That and a few glasses of French champagne and a fancy dinner that I couldn't even taste when all I could think about is how I should have plugged my ears with wax against the siren song of the slot machines on the casino floor, just beyond the walls of the function room.

Somehow, after the event had finished, I managed to steer my body away from the casino floor, to one of the bars that surrounded it. I knew I should go home. Emily would be worried. I owed her an explanation. My body burned with shame; I couldn't tell her that the money, our money, was *here*. It was paying this barman's salary, feeding *his* kids and paying *his* mortgage. It was paying the electricity to keep all these lights glaring and the noises blaring around me. It was paying for the plush Egyptian cotton sheets on the hotel beds upstairs. I sat on a stool at the bar, facing away from the casino floor. But I knew it was only a matter of time.

—

I don't recall ordering a beer but soon, I had drained the dregs of one, put the glass down, then raised a finger towards the barman who nodded and started pulling another. That second beer took me down to $3270 for that night's earnings. There was a knot in my chest. I could feel it tightening, just below my throat, until I was sure that I couldn't breathe. My hands started to shake and luckily the barman brought my drink and I cupped my hands around the cold pint glass and managed to bring it to my lips and sipped the beer, then gulped it down to prove to myself that the knot wasn't real, and air and food and drink could still go into me.

I did it again and the shakes started to settle and I felt like calling him over again and ordering a bottle of whisky and downing the whole thing right here, right now and maybe just for a few minutes I could pretend that this might somehow be okay, when I knew that it never would be.

It was too late.

And before I knew it I had taken my phone out of my pocket and reinstalled the app that I deleted only this morning, after Emily had called me, and I didn't even have to think about what I was doing when I transferred $1000 from our joint bank account to the app and I found the next race and I put it all on the nose on the favourite, at four to one. When I tapped the screen to confirm the bet, I was still again. The knot had loosened, for a moment, and there was a tiny buzz in my chest instead. Because maybe, just maybe, it would come in and then I'd have more than $7000 from tonight which would mean that we wouldn't default on the mortgage and Cameron and Tilly wouldn't be out on the street because of me, and I'd have a bit more time to fix everything. All I needed was a little win, just to buy time, which in turn would buy me back Emily's trust, and my family, my life.

But if not, it was all over.

Over and out.

The horse came second.

I closed my eyes to stop the tears from falling, there at that bar, and without a second thought, I went straight to the ATM just outside the gaming floor with my head held high and withdrew the maximum limit – $2500 – and then I logged into my online banking and transferred another $2500 to my second account, and then I withdrew that too. Then, I followed the familiar path through the casino and without allowing myself to think any more about what I was doing, hurried straight to the door to the VIP rooms, and they welcomed me by name and I greeted Nicole and she took my jacket and handed me a drink. They give me free drinks here, and a special room to gamble in.

Here, I'm a VIP.

I sat down at my own private roulette table and I handed over my money to the croupier and he gave me a pile of chips and I put them all on red.

I nodded at the croupier.

'No more bets,' he said, not looking at me even though I was the only one there.

I watched the little ball hurtling around and slowing and slowing and I could hear the scratching of the ball on the wheel and the click click click as it started to skim the serrations of the wheel and at that moment, I imagined that I was magic and I could control it, that I could force it to slow down and then when it had almost stopped I closed my eyes and lay my hands flat on the table and waited for the croupier to call the number.

'RED FIVE.'

Red. He said Red.

You'd think I would have screamed, grinned, cheered, but I wanted to weep. Because now I had to do it all again. Because I knew that as certain as I loved my family, I could not pick up the chips that the croupier had just clinked down on the table in front of me, I could not pick them all up and stand up from this chair and walk across the floor past all the gaming tables and slot machines and lights and noise calling me to them, I could not walk to the cashier and cash my chips in and take the money and be relieved that I could pay the mortgage this month. I blinked back tears as I pushed the chips that he'd just given me straight back onto the red section and downed my drink.

I knew how it would end.

How long had I sat there? I remembered looking at my watch at 4am and thinking of Emily and the kids fast asleep at home and how in a couple of hours they'd wake up thinking it was a normal morning, thinking maybe we'd go out for breakfast. We'd be lucky to have enough now to even buy a box of cereal from the supermarket. I also didn't have enough money left to play the minimum bet in the high roller room, so I took my place on the casino floor with all the other sad souls.

Gradually, people started wandering past me, glancing at me and looking away quickly, fresh faced after a full night's sleep on a king size bed with a pillow menu. There was a time when I looked down with superiority at the bodies slumped over the tables watching the roulette wheel whir round with frantic eyes when I was going down for breakfast. Now, it was me hunched over the table, my back aching, my eyes gritty, my mouth sour. My suit wasn't fooling anyone; I was one of the weak people I used to sneer at. 'Can I get you a tea or a coffee?'

I looked up at the waitress. I could see the pity in her eyes, and I could see how I must look to her. Bloodshot eyes, dark shadows under them, stubble, a suit stained with drops of Scotch, sallow skin oozing the smell of alcohol and desperation. I looked at the glass tumbler in my hand, the ice almost melted away, the water diluting the dregs of caramel-coloured whisky that I'd been drinking all night. I looked up at her, then shook my head.

All I had left was the money for the cab, $50 tucked into my sock so I couldn't reach it without really thinking about it. There was nothing left.

'One more,' I said, pointing at my empty glass. The last one. The last drink for the Very Important Person.

Eight

Emily

I jolted awake as the alarm on my phone went off at 6.30am and my first thought was that Paul was going to tease me, because clearly, I *could* sleep when he stayed out late. Even at the best of times, when I'm not consumed with worry about him, I can never sleep fully until I know that everyone in my family is home and locked up tight with me. So, last night, more than ever, I lay in the dark with my eyes closed like an animal, ears pricked to the sound of every car that drove past, every voice I heard, every creak the timbers of the house made during the night.

Paul had been late home before, many times, especially in the last few months. After everything that happened yesterday, I had expected him to come straight home. I had started calling him at midnight; the events are always done by then. It rang at first, but he didn't answer. I sent a text message, then another, and when I tried ringing again, and again, the call went straight to his voicemail. He'd either run out of batteries, or he'd switched it off.

In the middle of the night, my worries grew and filled the room, and every so often, a wave of rage would build up then crash into tears. I longed for him to stumble in, drunk, so that I could yell at him for worrying me, and then let the relief settle over me.

So, when the alarm woke me, I assumed that Paul had crept in while I had dozed off and simply the sensation of him breathing next to me had been enough to lull me back to a proper, deep sleep. I grabbed my phone to turn off the alarm, then turned over, but even before I had turned, I knew he wasn't there. The duvet was still pulled tight on his side, his pillow undented. My mouth dried; my heart raced. He must have slept in the spare room, that's it. He got in late and hadn't wanted to wake me. The fact that he never slept in the spare room didn't matter. This hadn't been a normal night. I remembered the way he hung his head as he walked out the door as he left; I could barely breathe.

I rubbed my face then sat up, waiting a moment for my head to stop spinning. I sipped the water by my bed and swirled it around my sour tasting mouth, cleared my throat from the dry exhaustion of such little sleep, then walked out of the bedroom in my bare feet. I looked towards the front door. There were no shoes kicked off in the hallway, no keys or wallet or jacket flung on the hallway table.

The door to the spare room was closed. It wasn't really spare: we used it as a TV room for the kids. Tilly practiced her viola in there. I turned the handle and pushed the door open. It creaked, and I peeked in. The sofa bed hadn't been unfolded, and the room was cold and still. My hands began to shake.

I walked on my tiptoes, trying not to wake the kids, towards the back of the house but he wasn't in the living room either. His clothes weren't discarded in the bathroom. I wanted to cry. I went back through to the bedroom and got under the covers, not sure what else to do. My phone was still charging on the bedside table, but there were no missed calls or messages. I tried calling him, but it was still off. Maybe he hadn't been able to call an Uber if he was out of batteries? But surely, he could have flagged down a taxi? I opened Facebook on my phone to see if I could trace his night out through people tagging him, but there was nothing on his page. God, anything could have happened to him. He could have been robbed, mugged, hit by a car. Should I call the hospitals and police? That seemed a bit dramatic. It wasn't even 7am. I forced myself to breathe slowly. He'd probably gone to some club and would stagger in soon, then I would scream at him but at least he'd be safe. Maybe he was avoiding me and crashed out at his brother's, and soon Jane, Alasdair's wife, would call me when she woke up and saw him on her couch. For now, I had to carry on as normal, have a shower, get the kids ready for Saturday morning sports, and when it was a decent hour and the kids were occupied, I'd make some calls.

—

'Where's Dad?' Cameron said, clomping down the hallway towards me, his kit bag slung over his shoulder.

'He had to go out early. He'll be back soon. Are you ready? Let's go.'

I looked over at the clock on the oven. 'Are you ready, Tilly?' I shouted.

'Coming!' Tilly came into the kitchen in her PE gear and bare feet, tying her hair up as she walked.

'Socks? Shoes?' I leaned over the sink and filled up her water bottle.

'Where's Dad?'

'At work. Hopefully he'll make it there.'

'His car's here,' shouted Tilly as she peered out of the window.

'I think he got a taxi,' I said quickly, and shook my head as the tears threatened to fall. 'Just get in the car, would you? I'll have to drop Cameron at rugby today, then get you to hockey. He'll meet us there.'

Paul never missed Cameron's rugby. No matter how late he'd gotten home, no matter how hung over he seemed, he was always there. He took Cameron to his game, and I went with Tilly to her's. He talked to the other dads; I sipped coffee and chatted with the hockey parents. I enjoyed my Saturday mornings; it was a chance to see the mums that I rarely saw any more. When the kids were younger, we'd always chat as we waited at the school gates, but as the children have become older and grown away from us, we mothers have started trickling back to work, and now we just drive through the slipway, and the children and bags and sports gear tumble out. At the end of the day, they bundle themselves back in and we speed off to the next activity.

I knew that Paul enjoyed those mornings on the sports field too. He missed playing, and this was the next best thing, even if Cameron had chosen rugby over soccer. He'd been pretending to be happy with the restaurant, and sometimes he did seem genuinely relaxed, but he'd been distracted, stressed. But when he watched Cameron play, I could see him find himself again. I glanced at my phone on the kitchen bench; still no calls.

'Mum…' I heard Tilly's singsong voice. 'Mum? Mum!'

'What, Tilly? Don't yell at me like that!'

'Aren't we on oranges today?' Tilly said.

'Shit!' I hit the tap with my hand to switch off the running water, then held on to the edge of the sink for a moment and let my head fall. I took some deep breaths and forced myself to relax. 'Just get in the car, please, both of you. With your shoes and socks and shin pads and hockey sticks and mouth guards and whatever else you need. Just help me out today, please, you're old enough to get yourselves ready.'

They walked out quietly, and I could feel them looking at me. Where the hell was Paul? I could kill him for doing this to us. Using all our money, and now disappearing and leaving me to pick up the pieces, without any explanation of where the money had gone, or where he was.

I breathed deeply and slowly for three breaths, to force myself to calm down, then took the bag of oranges that thankfully, I'd bought a couple of days ago, out of the drawer in the fridge, grabbed a kitchen knife, a tea towel, and a chopping board, then shoved them in a bag. I'd have to chop the oranges up

76

on the side of the field. As I hurried to the car, I tried Paul's mobile again. Nothing. Tears sprung to my eyes and my breath shuddered. I couldn't rationalise this anymore. Something was wrong.

Nine

Paul

'Paul, mate...'

There was something heavy on my shoulder, and a deep, sonorous voice in my ear, rising and falling in volume. I tried to open my eyes but I couldn't. Where was I?

I was on my feet somehow, but my legs were so heavy that I just wanted to let them fold at the knees and my neck seemed to have stopped working as my head lolled forwards onto my chest.

'Come on, mate, on your feet... no, no, don't call an ambulance, he's okay, I've got him...'

'Damian?' I tried to say but instead I heard my voice slur, 'Daaaa...' and my tongue and mouth and lips felt thick and numb, the sounds that came out lagging long behind my thoughts.

'You're alright, come on.'

Was I still at the casino? 'Where...?' My head pounded.

'It's Damian. You're at my house. Taxi driver said you passed out in the cab, said you gave him my card just before and told him to call me. He did and dropped you here. Let's get you inside. Can you walk?'

I wanted to say no, that I didn't think I could make it one step further, but somehow, I managed to shuffle a few steps and then fell back onto the soft cushion of a seat.

'You're not going to throw up, are you?'

I shook my head, but I wasn't so sure.

'Anything I need to know, mate?'

'No...' What did he mean?

'You just pissed?'

I don't know, I don't know, I don't know. I must be. I must be. I shook my head.

'That eye looks bad.'

Eye? I managed to lift my hand up to my face; I flinched as I touched it.

'You spoken to Emily? You got your phone?'

I leaned to the side and patted the pocket of my trousers but there was nothing there. I reached across my body to the other side; I felt my wallet but no phone. 'Jacket pocket,' I mumbled.

'You haven't got a jacket.'

I had a vision of it hanging on the back of a chair at the casino.

The casino. The memories erupted, and I let out a wail.

'Mate, come on, it's only a jacket. It's probably in the cab; we'll track it down. At least you've got your wallet.'

I felt him take it from my pocket; I let him.

'Did you have cash? Has someone cleaned you out? You haven't got a dollar in here.'

The skin under my right eye stung as tears dripped into it. This was my best suit. Emily would kill me. 'My jacket...'

'Good job you got him to call me first, Paul, not Emily. You're probably in enough trouble for staying out all night without turning up like this.'

I managed to turn my head enough to look at him. When I forced my eyes to open, the right eye wouldn't oblige. 'You don't know the half of it,' I croaked, and then I slumped forwards and began to cry in complete and utter despair. I wished I was dead. Not in a cry-for-help way; really and truly, I wished that cab driver had thrown me out of the car and run his taxi over the top of me.

But when I peered through my swollen eye, a concrete brick of shame crushing me, I saw Damian. And he wasn't screaming at me, nor looking at me in pity or disgust. He was smiling. 'Right, I'm going to put the kettle on while you have a shower, and then we're going to get you sorted out.'

–

I didn't want to come out of the shower. I turned the water as hot as I could stand it, at full force, until I had managed to stop my hacking sobs. Look at me, I thought. What a disgrace. Why the hell had I called Damian, of all people? He was the last person I wanted to see me like this. My head pounded and nausea racked my body; I couldn't think straight. I considered climbing out of the bathroom window and running off. But I'd probably get stuck and look even more of a fool when he pulled me back through. I had a scrap of dignity left. I would leave by the front door.

I got out of the shower and dried off, then splashed my face with cold water from the sink. My eye was swollen and red, and the rest of my face was puffy. Jesus, what had I done? My breath quickened again, and my body tensed and tensed until I was sure my bones would snap and I smacked my right fist into my left as my face crumpled again.

There was a knock on the door. 'Paul? I've left some clothes for you just outside the door.'

I cleared my throat and gripped the edge of the sink. 'Thanks. Just coming.'

I waited a few moments, trying to compose myself, then opened the door a fraction and took the clothes. Dressed in Damian's shorts and tee-shirt, I felt like a child wearing the spare clothes at school for peeing your pants. What an embarrassment I was. I had to go out and face him. I had to. I couldn't hide. I would go out, say thank you, and sorry, then leave. I shouldn't be here.

I inhaled, then exhaled slowly as I left the bathroom and walked into Damian's living room, views of Sydney harbour visible through the patio doors out onto his balcony. Two mugs were on the glass coffee table, and the smell of mint wafted off the steam rising from them. Damian sat on a black leather armchair, looking concerned. He was in dark blue jeans and a red polo shirt. His thick dark hair was combed with some sort of glossy product in it. He was clean-shaven. He looked bright, healthy. I contrasted him with my own sorry appearance, and the smoky smell of Scotch already oozing from my pores despite the shower. I hovered, my arm on the back of the matching sofa. 'Thanks, Damian. I'm sorry... I'm sorry for calling you and turning up like this. Thanks for your help. I guess... I must have been attacked or mugged or something. I don't know what happened.' I pointed to my eye.

He shook his head slowly. 'I think you do.'

As he stared at me, I felt compelled to sit down. I came around the edge of the sofa and perched on the edge. 'Is that for me?' I nodded towards the mug.

He nodded; I picked it up and sipped at the hot peppermint tea, hoping it would settle my nausea, then put it back on the table.

'Are you okay?' he asked, after a few moments of us sitting in silence.

I swallowed hard, then again, as my chin began to quiver. I stood up. 'Sorry,' I managed to say. 'I need to go. I'll explain everything later.'

He stood too, then reached over and put his hand on my shoulder. 'Stay.'

I closed my eyes and felt my body swaying. Tears began to fall, and I collapsed back down on the sofa. I couldn't stop myself from breaking down again. I covered my face with my hands. All I could hear were my own pathetic sobs and gasps and sniffs. Now I'd lose my job too. What an idiot I was.

'What happened?' he said.

I don't know how long passed before I was able to speak, but Damian waited. I heard a clock ticking somewhere in the room. Such an old-fashioned, comforting sound. It reminded me of sleeping in my grandmother's house as a child.

'I've ruined everything,' I croaked.

He shook his head. 'It's never that bad.'

'It is that bad. You don't understand. I've lost everything. I thought I could fix it but we've been so behind with everything and Emily has been working so hard and I thought that maybe I could just win a little to make things easier and it got out of hand... it's gone, everything has gone, I've lost everything... I... I wish...' I lifted my head as some clarity came over me. 'It's over for me, Damian. My life is over. I'm sorry I've let you down.' I started to stand up again, my legs ready to flee, somewhere, anywhere.

'I know how you feel,' he said, calmly.

I shook my head, then sat back down.

'I know you don't believe me, but we all have a past, Paul. We've all done things we regret.'

Irritation surged up; there was no way that he had been where I was now. 'Not like this. You don't understand what I've done. I've lost it all, Damian, every cent we have and more. There's no coming back from this.'

'You're wrong. There's always a way back.'

'No!' I shouted. 'Emily will leave me. The bank will take my house. My kids will hate me. I have no money, nothing at all. I have tried to beat this but there's something wrong with me, something wrong inside me and they're better off without me, you all are.' I hated the sound of my whining, but I didn't care. It was how I felt, and I had never been so certain of anything but the fact that I was a liability to them all. My family was better off without me.

'I can help you, Paul.'

I sneered. 'It's too late. Nobody can.'

'I can.'

I shook my head quickly, tears blurring the sight of Damian leaning towards me. He sighed, looked around the room, then spoke softly. 'Have you ever heard of Phoenix?'

82

I shrugged. I'd seen it written on some documents at work, heard it mentioned at meetings. I'd assumed it was just one of Damian's numerous companies.

'I don't talk about it to many people, but I know I can trust you. There's a few of us at work who are members – Tim, Lucas; we have members all over the world. We are people who have been where you are, Paul. Not just gambling, but drinking, unhappiness, struggling with life generally. Many of us have been told there's something wrong with us, but we have taken control of our lives back. Back from the doctors who make a career from keeping us sick, from the pharmaceutical companies whose drugs make us worse, from the advertisers who brainwash us with their processed foods ads and make alcohol taste sweet to get us addicted, and the media who fuel it all. Paul, you have no idea how good life can be. Free of all that, you can have this.' He swept his arms around the room. 'The dream, Paul: the house, the boat, travelling the world, a clear mind, a fit body. I don't tell many people about it, only people who I believe are strong enough, and I know you are. You just have to say the word and I'll help you.'

'It's too late.'

'It's never too late. I can get you help, now. Today even. Phoenix has treatment centres all over the world, and there's one just outside of Sydney. One call and I'll get you in there. No doctors, no medicine, just help to see how the world can be.'

'I have to go home, to Emily...' Emily. How could I face her?

'You can go home first, to pack your bag and say goodbye to your family. But look at you. What other choice do you have?'

I did look at me: bare feet, wearing my boss's clothes, crying, penniless, bereft, bruised. Yes, look at me. My face burned, and acid churned in my throat.

'Paul. We can help you. You need proper help. You need to get away from this, until you can see things for what they are again and then, and only then, your life will turn around. I guarantee it.' He was staring at me.

'I've got no money.'

He waved his hand. 'Money is not an issue. You will pay me back when you're back on track. That's how it works when you join us. Phoenix helps people who need it most, and then, when you're better, you help us, and you look out for others who need help. We pass it on. And while you're in the centre, I'll make sure that Emily is okay, and the kids.'

'I don't know how I'll pay you back.'

'We'll sort it out once you're well. You'll see: money will be no concern for you. You just have to say that you want us to help you, and we'll be there for you.'

I hesitated, shaking my head. His words swirled round my head. I wanted to run away, to not have to face up to what I'd done to my family. But as much as I wanted to end it all, clearly, I hadn't wanted that enough: I'd called for help. Maybe this was the help I needed. Maybe if I explained to Emily that I was going to change, then she'd forgive me and I could salvage something. And if not, if it all failed, then I still had the option to leave it all behind.

'What do you say?' he said.

I rubbed my face with both hands. What else could I say? 'Yes.'

Ten

Emily

Alasdair answered straight away; he always did. Even if he was at work, he always answered, unlike his brother, Paul. I didn't call him very much, I never had need to, but being the only family we had in Australia, we looked out for each other. He'd come out to Sydney after we did, after visiting us and seeing the life we had. He was a few years older than Paul. He'd studied mining engineering in Aberdeen, did his time on the rigs and then got sponsored to work out here. He had married an Australian, Jane, and never looked back.

'Emily,' he said, a lilt in his voice. 'How are you?'

'Hey, Al. I'm good.' I tried to match his carefree tone. 'Look, this is probably nothing, and I know you would have called if he was, but is Paul with you?'

'Paul? No. Why?'

I bit my lip as I tried not to let the panic out. The background noise of Alasdair's own kids' sport quietened, and I knew he was moving away from watching Rosie play netball. 'Don't worry. It's nothing. It's just that he went out last night to a function and he didn't come home, I thought maybe he'd stayed at your place.'

As I said it I knew that it was ridiculous. Alasdair lived forty minutes away, over the bridge on the Northern beaches, away from the city and anywhere Paul would have been. Why on earth did I even think that he would have gone there?

'No. I'm assuming you've called his phone?'

'Yeah, it's out of batteries or something. I'm not worried. Just let me know if you hear from him. He probably just got drunk and stayed at a friend's.'

'I'll make some calls.'

'No, it's fine—' Inside, I was chanting, *yes please, please help me, I don't know what to do.*

'This is not like him, Emily.'

I wished I could agree with him. He was right, Paul had never stayed out all night before, but he'd come close to it, getting home in the early hours, sometimes sneaking in not long before the sun rose. I'd stopped asking where he'd been: I just hadn't had the energy to confront it. Stupid, stupid me. But Alasdair, like anyone else looking at us from the outside, had no idea about any of that. To him, and so many other people, we looked perfect.

'I'll keep trying him. He's probably just lost his phone and walking home or something. He'll turn up. I'm just at Nash Oval, the kids, they think...' And before I knew it, I was crying. In front of all the other school mums and dads, and I ducked my head down and wiped my eyes under my sunglasses. 'Sorry, Al. I'll call you back.'

I ended the call then glanced up and saw that Tilly was staring at me and not the ball. I raised my hand and waved, trying to look natural but instead like someone caught in a riptide after swimming outside the flags, just about to go under.

I composed myself, then forced myself to smile as I cut up the oranges on the side of the field, cursing as I realised I'd forgotten a box to put them in. I arranged them on the chopping board and laughed loudly when people told me they wished they'd thought of just taking the knife with them when it was their turn. At half time, as the girls sucked the juice from the segments and discarded the sticky rinds, I texted one of the mums at the rugby pitch whom I'd asked to keep an eye on Cameron. He was okay, but Paul hadn't turned up there yet.

I was walking over to the rubbish bin with the orange skins when my phone rang. In just a fraction of a moment I dropped everything on the ground and pulled my phone out of my jeans' pocket. It was an unknown number. I answered the call. When Paul spoke, I almost collapsed with relief.

'Paul, thank God.' My relief gave way to anger; my worries all seemed so ridiculous now. Of course he was just drunk. 'Where the hell are you?' I hissed, turning my back to the pitch and walking towards the fig trees that lined the park, shading the cars around the perimeter, my feet slipping on the figs that littered the ground amongst the gnarled tree roots.

'I'm sorry,' he croaked.

I froze, my anger transforming into fear in an instant. He was crying. 'Paul. Where are you? What's wrong?'

'I've ruined everything.'

'Paul. You're scaring me. Where are you? I'll come—'

'No, don't come, I'm okay.'

'I'm at hockey. Cameron's at rugby. Are you home? Are you—'

'Emily, please!'

'What? Don't shout at me! You've been out all night, not answering your phone. After everything that happened yesterday… I've called your brother, now he's all worried. Wait, whose phone is this?'

'Stop, just stop. I can't—'

And I did. I stopped talking, and I waited with my heart pounding in my ribcage and my hands shaking and I didn't know if I wanted to hear what he had to say.

'I need to tell you something,' he whispered. 'I've done something awful. It's all gone.'

'What's gone? What are you—'

'I've lost it all. Our money. There's something wrong with me. I'm so sorry. I need to get myself sorted out.'

'For God's sake, Paul. You're not making sense. Are you hurt? I'm coming now to get you. Where are you?'

'I just need to get tidied up and I'll come home soon. We'll talk.'

And then, as my mouth was open and tears were streaming down my cheeks, he hung up, and when I called back the number, it rang out and went to the voicemail of Damian Talbot. What the hell was he doing with him? I rang it again and again until eventually, someone – Paul or Damian – turned the phone off.

Eleven

Paul

Have you ever had to lie to your children? I don't mean little white lies, like telling them that Santa Claus or the Tooth Fairy is real, or that you have a stomach bug when you're retching into the toilet bowl with your head pounding after only stumbling home a few hours ago. I mean a real, fat, ugly lie.

I wish I could say it was horrible to lie to Tilly and Cameron, but to be honest, looking into their big blue eyes and opening my mouth and letting the untruths just slide off my tongue was the kinder thing to do. I'd become so good at it by then, and the alternative – telling my children that I was a failure – was so inconceivably impossible.

The night before I left, I called them through to the living room. Tilly had flounced through from her bedroom, complaining that she was doing her homework and how was she meant to get it done when I kept interrupting her? Cameron had ignored me the first time I called him, and the second time, so finally I went into his room and unplugged his headphones from his iPad. He didn't protest, just followed me out of his room to the couch. The news was on the TV; I paused it, the newsreader's mouth frozen open mid-speech. Emily, in the kitchen overlooking the sitting area, had almost the same expression on her face as she leaned on the dark grey granite bench top, barely moving, waiting to hear how I was going to tell them.

I wanted to tell the children alone, but I didn't have the energy to fight her. Emily was on my side, I knew that. She was trying to support me the best way that she could. But I hadn't been able to stop gambling for her, or for the children. I had to believe that Damian's way would cleanse me of the addiction that had pushed its way into my cells, like an infection after I'd touched the handle of a dirty shopping trolley then brought my fingers to my lips.

The kids sat on the couch against the back wall; I sat opposite them on the armchair. 'So, I need to tell you something,' I said, my voice strong.

Cameron turned his head from me and stared at the TV; I wanted to shake him. Tilly looked straight at me, frowning, looking for a moment like the toddler that she had been all those years ago, except that her face now was long and thin, her high cheekbones replacing the chubby cheeks she had as a little girl. I wanted to scoop her up in my arms. For just a moment, I started to waver, and I considered telling them the truth. Emily was always on about honesty and working as a team, but I couldn't do that to them. Kids should be allowed to be kids, shouldn't they? They don't need to know the problems of adults; my job was to shield them from the hell that goes on in the real world. Was it so wrong to want my children to look up to me, to let them believe for a little while longer that I was a hero?

'I have to go away for a few weeks, for work. It might even be longer. I'm not sure.'

'Where?' Tilly said, and by the way she screwed up her beautiful eyes I knew her too-smart little mind was whirring through the possibilities. 'Why?'

I made myself laugh. 'Don't be so serious, sweetie. It's just work, I'm just touring around a few places.'

'Oh. Where are you going?'

'All over,' I said. 'Melbourne, Adelaide, New Zealand—'

'No way.' Her eyes widened. 'Can you bring me back something from Hobbinton?'

'It's not real, Tilly,' Cameron said in that bored, deadpan way of his that I knew infuriated her.

'I *know* that, Cameron. I'm not stupid—'

'Hey, hey.' I held my hands up. 'I'm not sure I'll be near there. I'm not even sure where it is!'

'The South Island. You can do this Lord of The Rings tour, I saw a video of it.'

I smiled and ruffled her hair. 'I don't know my schedule yet, but I don't think I'll be on the South Island. I'll try though!' See, that wasn't really a lie. 'Cameron, mate, do you have anything you want to say?'

He looked at his knees, scratching at a scab, but said nothing. I could sense Emily trying to catch my eye; I shifted in my seat so that she disappeared from my peripheral vision.

'When are you going?' Tilly said.

'Tomorrow. Early, before you wake up. I'll...' My voice started to quiver; I cleared my throat. 'I'll miss you both. Be good for Mum.'

Both kids looked at me for a moment too long. 'I won't be gone long, I promise, a few weeks,' I said quickly, before they could ask any more questions. I stood up and hugged Tilly, then clapped Cameron on the shoulder. They disappeared back to their rooms.

I sat down on the couch and leaned back, closing my eyes as I listened to their doors closing and Emily's footsteps approaching. She sat beside me, but not too close. She spoke quietly. 'What if they find out?'

'They won't.'

'It would only take one person to talk and it'd be all over the papers.'

'No one will talk, and no one cares. Journos have got more exciting people to write about than me.'

'Why did you say you were only going for a few weeks when it's going to be six? And did you have to say New Zealand? Now they'll expect postcards and—'

I opened my eyes, but couldn't look at her. 'I did my best.'

We sat in silence, our legs almost touching. I looked at my hands, the sunspots on the back of them, the bitten nails. How did I get to this point?

Emily spoke quietly. 'What is it that you want, Paul?'

'What do you mean? I want to get myself sorted out.'

'But what have you been missing? What have you been chasing?'

'I don't know.' I shook my head.

'What more do you need in life? We were happy. We had enough. Weren't we enough?'

'I don't know,' I repeated, my eyes prickling.

'It's like this part of you always wants more. When everyone else is settling down, you want to keep moving up, but at what cost?'

'You used to want it too, Emily. We always spoke about making enough money to have a big house, a boat, go travelling, or have enough to take a year off and live in London or New York.'

She sighed, rubbed her face. 'We did. But that was just a dream, Paul. That's not real life. This is. Kids and a house and dishes to do and lawns to mow and hard work.' She opened her arms up wide. 'We have a family. What would you be happy with? A million dollars? Ten million? What do you want?'

I shrugged. I couldn't tell her what I really thought, that ten million wouldn't even buy us a house on the harbour. I said nothing; I felt her anger decrease again and longed for her to reach out and touch me.

'The kids will be fine,' she finally said. 'They're used to you going away.'

I shook my head.

'You know what I mean, Paul.'

I stood up. 'It'll go quickly.'

She stood too and placed her hand on my arm, just lightly. I stilled, then after a moment, went to pack.

Twelve

Emily

It didn't seem so different, not yet. Tonight, I had eaten sausages with the kids, because it didn't seem worth cooking a tastier meal for just myself, and nagged them both to eat more. I had cleared the table and done the dishes and the children were in their rooms doing their homework, supposedly. I just wanted to put on my pyjamas and make a cup of tea and lie on the couch and watch something easy on Netflix to distract myself from worrying about Paul. But I had to talk to the children first.

I knocked lightly on Tilly's door. 'Can I come in?'

'Hold on.'

I heard a rustle, a drawer closing. Hiding her iPad, no doubt. Another time, I might have insisted that she show me what she was doing, but not today. The door opened. Tilly's face was flushed. 'What?'

I raised my eyebrows. 'Can I come in?'

Tilly shrugged and stepped back a little. 'I'm doing my homework.'

I walked in, stepping around the clothes on the floor, and sat on the bed as Tilly sat back down at her desk. Her books were open.

'What homework do you have today?'

'Maths, English, the usual.'

'Need any help?'

Tilly shook her head. 'I'm fine. Mum, are you okay?'

I smiled a little, sighed. 'Yes, I'm fine. Just missing your dad.'

Tilly nodded.

'How are you going? I know the last day or two has been a bit…'

'Weird.'

'Yes, I suppose it has been weird. I'm sorry. It'll settle down, it's just that going on this trip for Dad has been… difficult.'

'Why?'

I pressed my lips together. I was forgetting who I was talking to. 'Oh, nothing. You know how he gets. He's been working hard. But the three of us, we'll get things back to normal while he's gone and we'll have our routine and the time will fly by. I feel like I don't know what's going on with you, or your brother.'

'I'm fine, Mum.' Tilly looked back at her desk. 'It's just that I need to get this homework done, I have hockey training early before school tomorrow.'

I nodded. I pressed down the part of me that wanted to tell Tilly what was going on, to explain to her that this wasn't *my* fault, that I was trying my best to hold on tight to the edges to pull everything together but I wasn't sure if my hands were strong enough. She'd find out, soon enough. I thought back to my own childhood; parents thought they could hide things but children knew, if not the facts, then at least the mood by the cold stares and the tension in the air. I cleared my throat and stood up. 'Okay, darling, well, I'm here if you need any help. I was pretty good at maths when I was your age, you know.' I smiled, and she sort of smiled back at me.

I had to knock twice on Cameron's door before he answered; his music was playing, the same bloody song I'd heard for weeks and weeks now.

'What?' he called.

'Just me. Mum. You okay?'

'Yes.'

'Can I come in?'

'No,' he called, sounding bored.

94

'I'm coming in.'

The music stopped and a moment later, the door opened. He peered through the crack.

I tilted my head to the side. 'You okay, Cam?'

He nodded, looking at the floor.

'Can I get you anything? A drink? A snack?'

He shook his head.

'Dad won't be gone long, you know.'

'I know.'

I wanted to push the door fully open, but knew better. 'Well, come and get me if you need anything.'

'Okay.' He nodded, flicking his eyes up to meet mine for a moment, then looked away. Did they fill with tears? It was too late; the door had closed and I heard his steps cross his floor then his music came back on. I rested my head on his door and made myself breathe slowly.

Back in the kitchen, as I made my single cup of tea, I felt the absence of Paul all around me like a cold chill. He wouldn't be coming home tonight, even if it was in the middle of the night to find me anxious and angry. I wouldn't see him, or even talk to him, for six weeks. That was how the treatment programme worked, and I had – reluctantly – agreed to it. I could cope without the contact, but I hated having to lie to the children. I only had a vague idea of where he was, but I imagined a big, clinical building, grey carpets, large rooms with chairs in a circle. Was he frightened? I knew how hard it would be for him to admit to weakness. I felt fire in my cheeks as I admitted to myself that I hoped he *was* scared and humiliated. *I* was frightened, and yet I was the one who had to lie to the kids and pick up the pieces, pretending that everything was fine, while *he* got to hide away for six weeks and have someone cook and clean for him, and he could go to bed early and sleep in and take lots of hearty walks and talk about himself. It wasn't Paul who had to stammer to some faux-sympathetic woman at the bank that we couldn't pay the mortgage and beg to defer our payments for two months. Yes, Damian had arranged for his wages to continue, but minus a huge percentage to pay for the treatment, and I couldn't even think about how long it would take to pay back. It wasn't Paul who had called the credit card company to extend our limit and lie about the reason why. It wasn't Paul who would have to take extra shifts at work and clean the house and do all the washing and shopping and cooking and organise the children as well as worrying about him and me and our future. It was all me. So yes, let him feel frightened and judged for what he was doing to our family.

I picked up my mug of tea, gripping the handle. My hand slipped. Hot tea sloshed over the side and onto my hand. 'Shit!' I shouted, then slammed it down again as my tears began to fall. I grabbed a towel and dried my hand then mopped up the spillage, trying not to let it overwhelm me.

I longed to speak to Paul, to yell at him and ask all the questions he kept avoiding, to blame him and shout at him and to tell him that I loved him. But I couldn't, for six weeks. I doubted that he'd need to be there that long, though. Once he'd settled in, surely we'd be able to visit, or at least call.

I stared out of the glass doors to the dusk settling over the back garden, the dark outline of the lemon gum tree, black against the streaked purple sky. When the kids were little, we'd always told them to look at the moon, no matter where Paul was travelling, as he'd be looking at the same moon too. The moon was barely visible but I gazed at it. And as I did, I understood that the worst had happened. I was on my own. We were broke. Now that my worst fears had come true, something inside me switched on. I had to keep control of my family, and of myself. I turned away from the moon, back to my home and my children and stood up a little taller. It was all up to me now.

Thirteen

Paul

It wasn't anything like Hobbinton. As Damian drove the car up the dirt road towards the centre, I made a promise to myself: when I got better, I would take the kids there, to the South Island of New Zealand. We could have done that a hundred times with all the money I'd burned in the casino. I squeezed my hands into fists and felt my nails digging into my palms. I couldn't let myself think about what I'd lost; I couldn't bear it any more. The kids would love it in New Zealand. We could do the cheesy tourist things, dress up in hairy feet and take pictures with swords; we could walk, camp, eat good food, and be far away from the real world that had eaten into me. Cameron would be able to relax without the pressures of school and rules and routines. It had gotten to him too, to all of us. I'd get better, then we could get away, as a family.

But now, I was at Treetops Retreat. There were no Hobbits, but it was almost like another world. The bush around us was thick and muffling. Tall gum trees towered above dense Woolly Bushes, and velvety scarlet Kangaroo Paws lined the dirt driveway. I heard insects chirping – crickets maybe, or cicadas. Or did they only make sounds at night? Why had I never paid attention to all the amazing things around me rather than chasing something that could never be real? Birds screeched above as they swooped around the trees chasing clouds of insects.

I'd read the brochure. I knew this wasn't a typical rehabilitation centre. Unbeknownst to Emily I had tried before to get help. I blurted it out to my GP once when I had gone to get a prescription for more painkillers for my knee, when he had frowned at me and told me that I really had to get off them, that I was becoming dependant. I had laughed, sadly, and told him that the painkillers were nothing because I was gambling, and I couldn't stop, and he sent me to the local Gamblers Anonymous group, which was held in, of all places, the back room of a Retired Serviceman's League Club. In the UK, at least the betting shops weren't in the pubs; in Sydney, they have special little rooms at the back of the bars of clubs and hotels where you can watch the races and put your bets on or play the slot machines with a beer in your hand. I'm all for being strong willed, but making gamblers sit in the same building as alcohol and a betting window, well... it must have been some genius that came up with that idea. At the time, at that meeting, the others there weren't like me. *They* had gambled so much that they'd lost everything – their marriages, their jobs, their houses. I couldn't identify with them. Back then, I still had some control and my gambling had never affected Emily or the kids.

I bit the inside of my cheek. I couldn't deny that, now, I was exactly like one of them.

–

After that god-awful morning when I had found my way to Damian, he had taken me for lunch to meet his friend, Michael, who ran Treetops. I must have looked terrible. I'd had another shower and Damian had loaned me a shirt and a razor to shave, but the alcohol was still seeping from my pores and I had the beginnings of a black eye. I tried to smile at Michael as Damian introduced us but all I could think of was what Emily must be thinking about me after I had called her when she was at the kids' sport. I couldn't keep my foot from tapping or my stomach from churning as terror darted around my head. I immediately ordered a glass of red. Neither Damian nor Michael ordered a drink, and I knew I shouldn't, but I didn't know how else I could bear to even open my mouth to say hello.

I saw the look in Michael's eyes as I grabbed for the wine glass with a shaking hand when the waiter delivered it, and immediately, I understood that he had been where I was. It made sense: he ran a centre for addicts. I knew how hard it would have been for him to resist the pull to pick up his own oversized shiny glass and pour in just a little of the ruby red wine. I knew that he'd be able to smell it like a wolf sniffs out its prey, I knew that his mouth would have filled with saliva and he'd be running his tongue around his mouth, his lips practically able to taste it, and his brain would be thinking, *go on, just one sip*. Because that was the urge I battled with every second: not to drink, but to bet. Michael had been where I had been and had not only survived, but thrived. I saw the Brietling watch on his wrist as he reached for his sparkling mineral water, and the purple silk lining of his Paul Smith jacket, hanging from the back of his chair. And so, I listened to him.

Over lunch, which I didn't eat a morsel of, Michael kept repeating that something had made me call Damian, something in me knew how to get help. He was right.

'We can help you,' Michael had said. 'We know how to help you.'

Damian nodded, leaning forwards and looking me in the eye. 'You just need to believe us. We know how to help you. There is a different way to live.'

'I've got no money,' I had croaked, shaking my head.

'I told you earlier. Don't worry about that. I'll arrange everything. We all donate a percentage of our wages to Phoenix, so we have funds to help you, and then you will do the same when you're better.'

'I have to help Emily, the kids…'

Michael chimed in. 'You're no help to them like this. Look at you. You have no choice. Phoenix is your only way back from this.'

My head was spinning and I couldn't concentrate but they looked at me so intensely that I wanted to clutch onto them because who else did I have to hold onto to stop me from sinking? I signed the paperwork that Michael put on the table.

Damian gave me $200 to see me through the next couple of days while they arranged for me to be admitted to Treetops Retreat.

After that meeting, and three glasses of that glorious cab sav, I walked straight to the pub and I put that $200 in the slot machines without any hesitation. I lost it all in less time than it took to drink one rum and coke. And then, as I stared at the dregs of the drink in the scratched glass, the frosting of someone's lipstick still staining the rim, and felt the furry coating of red wine on my teeth and the beginnings of a headache and a thirst, I felt like shit. Like the worst human being in the world. The worst husband, the worst father. Useless, worthless – a liability. Not simply ineffective, but a monster terrorising my family, trying to take away everything that my children held dear in their lives. Happiness, stability, security. I gripped my hands on each side of the machine and I lowered my head and used every part of me to stop me smashing it into the glass. I walked home, then admitted everything to Emily while she looked at me in silent horror, her face pale and her hands shaking, and two days later, I packed my bags and put any remaining trust and faith in Damian and Michael.

–

The car stopped outside the building. Damian switched off the engine. I didn't undo my seatbelt. My hands were flat on my knees as I took some deep breaths. I had to remember why I was here. This was my last chance.

I unbuckled my seat belt and got out. Damian walked around the car to stand beside me and clapped me on the back. 'I'm proud of you,' he said. 'You've made the right decision. You're one of us now.'

I nodded, then extended the handle of my small suitcase, wheeling it behind me as I walked towards the front door. Damian pressed a button on the intercom, then said his name when a voice crackled through it. Moments later I heard a door inside being unbolted, then footsteps approaching before the front door opened and Michael was there. He greeted me warmly. I briefly shook his hand, unable to look him in the eye, and then walked through the door that he held open for me. My suitcase wheels jarred on the small step; I hoisted it over the bump into the vestibule. I turned around. Damian waited on the threshold.

'Good luck, Paul,' he said.

'You're not coming in?' My pulse sped up at the thought of that door closing.

He shook his head. 'This is something you need to do on your own but when you're ready, I'll be here for you. We'll all be here for you.'

He held out his hand, and I shook it, swallowing down the lump in my throat. Michael closed the door behind me.

'Welcome, Paul. We're so pleased you've made the decision to come here and change your life,' Michael said, smiling. 'Follow me.'

I attempted to smile, then followed him from the small vestibule through an inner door that he unlocked with one of the keys on the lanyard around his neck. It was just for security, I reminded myself. It was to protect me as much as anyone. Damian had assured me that they were very careful here, that they specialised in helping people who had a profile and needed discretion.

'Just leave your bag there,' he said, pointing towards a pale timber desk with silver steel legs, an Eames chair behind it. A small MacBook was open on the otherwise empty desk. I wheeled my bag over and left it near the desk, then put my hands in my jeans pockets and looked around. The floors were pale polished timber, like the desk, and in the middle of the room was a white rug with a teal coloured diamond pattern. Around the edges were three pale blue Featherstone chairs, just like the replica one Emily bought for our bedroom at home. There was a small white round side table with a few leaflets on it between two of the chairs, and a sixties-looking sideboard against the wall with books on top of it. An artichoke light shade above us threw dappled light onto the rug. Two paintings, if you could call them that, of coloured stripes hung on the wall. Emily would like this room. I blinked hard.

He motioned for me to sit down, then Michael sat down too. I placed my hands on my knees, then clasped them and laid them in my lap.

'Oh,' Michael said, standing again. 'Can I get you a drink? Water? Herbal tea?'

'A coffee would be great. I didn't sleep much last night.'

'We don't have coffee here I'm afraid.'

'Oh. Water's fine, then.'

As he left, panic began to rise in me at the thought of no coffee, and as my breath quickened and became shallow I wanted to grab Michael when he came back in and rip the keys from around his neck and open the door and go back to my family. But I also knew enough about myself to know that this was how I always dealt with things, by running away when it got too hard. My fingers started to knead the knuckles on the opposite hand that they were gripping. Stop, I told myself, give it a chance. I had chosen to come here. I could always leave later.

Michael returned a few moments later with two glasses of water. I sipped mine, then put it on the white table next to me. Michael opened a blue binder and began to ask me some questions. I thought back to the children, who'd be at school now, and Emily, at work. We were all such separate people now. Could we ever come back together, or was too late? Tears sprung to my eyes; I blinked them away and kept on talking, and then when Michael handed me a pen, I signed on the dotted line.

'Are you ready?' he said.

I nodded, then rubbed at my eyes, and when I opened them, he was still staring at me, waiting for me to speak.

'I'm ready.'

Fourteen

Emily

I ran my finger down the menu as the waitress stood above us with her pen ready, glancing around the room. 'Umm... the wonton soup, please.'

'Same,' said Ceecee. 'And a glass of the Riesling. And some spring rolls too, to start.'

'Make that two Rieslings,' I said. Bugger it. Paul had only been gone for a fortnight and I was already worn out from working extra shifts, trying to manage the kids and the house, and attempting not to worry about him. When Ceecee had texted and asked if I would like to go to lunch today, the last Friday of term before the chaos of the school holidays, I had pushed away the voice that told me that we couldn't afford it and agreed before I could stop myself. Paul had wasted tens of thousands of dollars, and even now, relaxing in his plush centre, he was costing us thousands and thousands more. I was allowed to spend $50 on lunch.

I used to catch up with Ceecee, and other friends, all the time. Her son, Will, was in Cameron's year, and her daughter, Ruby, was in Tilly's class. We used to have a coffee together after drop-off, or a late lunch before pick-up, then wait in a line of other mothers' cars to get out of the shopping centre's underground car park at 3pm after a glass of wine or two. But after I'd gone back to work, it seemed frivolous. It was frivolous, but it was worth it. I needed to see someone from my life before this nightmare.

'Paul still away?' Ceecee said, as she poured us both some water from the bottle in the centre of the table, then gathered her curly black hair over one shoulder.

'Yeah. He is.'

'Jeez, how long has that been?'

'I don't know, a couple of weeks now.' Two weeks and two days. 'It's fine.'

'I don't know how you do it. When is he back?'

The waitress appeared with the glasses of wine, placed them on the table and walked off without saying anything.

'I don't know, he said that it was for six weeks when he went, but I don't know.' I sipped my wine. Despite myself, I knew my eyes were filling with tears. I shook my head and blinked hard, staring out of the window. 'God, sorry.'

'Don't be silly, don't apologise. It must be bloody hard. You must be exhausted. How are the kids?'

Ceecee knew about the problems we'd had with Cameron; we'd met through our boys being the same year of school. She was a part-time GP and, over the years, I had confided in her and asked for recommendations for the various professionals he'd seen.

I sighed, and looked at her, my voice breaking despite myself when I spoke. 'They're okay. Well, not really. They miss him, you know. And I know that when Paul's not here, well, I need them to step up and Cameron takes up so much energy and before I know it I find myself yelling at them again. He's getting worse. He's hardly said a word to me in the past couple of weeks, and when he does, he seems so angry. I want to tell him that it's not me he should be angry at. I'm trying my best...'

Ceecee leaned back in her chair and tilted her head to the side. 'Of course you are, Em. He knows that. Will said he's been quiet at school.'

'Did he? What else did he say?'

'Oh, I don't know, you know what the kids are like. I never know what to believe, and I didn't even think it was worth mentioning, but he said Cam's been getting a hard time from some of the boys, you know the usual suspects.'

'What kind of a hard time?'

'I don't know, really, Will just said that he looked upset and has been in the library. Nothing physical, I'm sure.'

I looked up and smiled briefly as the waitress plonked down a plate of spring rolls and a little saucer of chilli sauce. I picked one up and pulled off a piece of the pastry, then dropped the roll on my plate. 'I have to tell you something. I haven't told anyone, but I just have to or I'm going to go mad.'

She frowned. 'What is it?'

'Paul's not at work.'

'What do you mean?'

'Please don't tell anyone, if anyone found out…'

Ceecee leaned forward. 'Of course I won't, you know that. Where is he? Has he…' Her eyes widened. 'Has he…'

'Left me? No.' I smiled a little, sadly. 'No, I don't think so anyway. He's gone to a treatment and rehabilitation centre.' I held my fingers up in fake speech marks as I emphasised the words.

'What?' Her hand reached for her wine glass; I saw it pause just before she picked it up.

'Not booze. Gambling.'

'Gambling? You're joking?'

'Nope. Gambling. He lost everything we have.'

'Everything?'

'Every penny.'

'I had no idea that he even…' Her eyes were wide.

'Me neither.' I let out a bitter laugh. 'Clearly.'

'Bloody hell. Are you okay? I mean, the house, the kids…'

'Yeah. We're okay, just. His work has been great, thank God, they're still paying him sick pay, and his boss recommended this centre so they're doing some sort of payment plan from his wages, and at least he's locked up there so he can't gamble. And I'm working. We can manage. It's just so bloody hard because before we had a buffer, you know, in case something was to happen, and now it's all gone. I feel like we're living week to week and I hate that. We've worked too bloody hard for that. I think we'll have to put the house on the market, I can't see how we can get out of this otherwise. I'd rather do that than take the kids out of school, Cameron would be...' I rubbed at my face, unable to continue. I reached for my drink.

'Oh, Em, I'm so sorry. I don't know what to say.' Ceecee's face was pale.

I shook my head. 'No, there's nothing to say. I'm sorry for burdening you with all this, it's just that I haven't told... It makes me so bloody angry, you know. Everyone thinks he's amazing, this famous sportsman, now a restaurateur, the golden boy of his family. His mum's been calling to talk to him, and she's getting snippy with me because he hasn't called back. Sometimes I just want to tell her, tell all the dads at school, that he isn't who he says he is, tell them that *I'm* the one who should be patted on the back and fawned over.'

'You absolutely should be patted on the back. You're amazing.'

I shook my head. 'No. Just doing what I have to. Oh, I know I should be more supportive of him, but it just seems so... unfair. God, sorry for whingeing.'

'Wow, Emily. You have every right to whinge, shout, scream, cry. I'd be furious.'

'Oh, believe me, I've done all of that. I am furious, but what can I do? The kids don't know and so I have to just keep it all in and pretend that everything is normal when I'm terrified that it's all going to come crashing down, or that when he gets out in a month that nothing will have changed. I don't how I can trust him at all after this.'

'How's he going in there? Is it helping? Is he getting better, I mean?'

I gulped my drink and leaned back as our soup arrived. 'Who knows? He's not allowed his phone, the internet – for obvious reasons – and I'm not allowed to contact him. I suppose he's fine.'

'That's crazy! What if something happened to the kids or something?'

'I don't know, I guess maybe they'd make an exception.' I smiled sadly. 'I thought that, you know, he might turn on his phone at night, when no one was looking, and text me or something. I've sent him messages, when I've been feeling a bit overwhelmed – though I've kept them nice. I call his phone every couple of days, just in case it's on. I've called his boss, he's the one who's got some connection to the place, but he tells me that he isn't allowed any contact either.'

'What on earth has his boss got to do with it? That seems a bit odd.'

'I know. Paul told him. Told him before me. Don't ask me why, I've got no idea. Turns out that Damian – that's his boss's name, knows someone who used to be an addict and set up this rehab place and he's involved in running it or something. I've looked it up, but the website is pretty obscure. When I called to see how he was, they said they couldn't give any information about any clients for *confidentiality* reasons.'

'You can't go and visit? Jesus, I think I'd be breaking in and slapping him for doing this to you!'

I laughed. 'God, I've felt like it. I don't know, going there seems a bit extreme. And I'm working all the time anyway and have the kids with me all weekend so when could I do it?'

Ceecee sighed.

I shrugged. 'It's hard. There's part of me that's desperate to see how he is and to confront him, but a huge part of me is saying that I shouldn't be chasing after him when *he's* the one who got me into this position. Paul should be doing everything in his power to see if *I'm* alright, you know?'

'Do you think he is?'

I shrugged, looked away and blinked hard, then reached into my bag for a tissue. Of course he wasn't, otherwise he would have contacted me.

'Enough about Paul. How are *you* coping?' she said quietly.

I shrugged. 'You know me. I cope, I always do.' I smiled wryly. 'In some ways, it's easier: I just do what I need to do, I get up early and I do everything because I know that no one else will. Before, you know, he was always in and out and coming home late and I was never sure how much he'd be around. I was always… uneasy. A bit anxious, never quite sure what to expect. It sounds stupid, but now that he's not here, at least I know what I'm dealing with.'

'You're amazing, Emily, and I can't believe you've been dealing with this all by yourself.' Her voice wavered.

'Now, I don't need you crying too.' I tried to laugh. 'You'll set me off.'

'Sorry. Tell me what I can do to help.'

I shook my head. 'No, nothing.'

She held her hand up. 'No, don't start to say you can do it all. I can pick up Cameron or Tilly from school, take them to ballet or rugby or whatever, or take them home with me, you *must* let me help and don't even think of telling me you don't need it. Or if you just need a gin and tonic and a chat then I'm definitely in.'

I pressed my lips together and picked up my chopsticks. I slowly slid off the paper wrapping and snapped the pair in half, unable to look at her. 'Deal,' I said. 'Now, I need to talk about something else.'

Fifteen

Paul

I woke with the dawn song of the magpies, who sensed the sun rising long before the darkness lifted. I guessed it was about 4am. I had been waking early, spending a couple of hours before the day at Treetops started, fighting back tears and panic as I longed to be home again. With no phone, no internet or computer, not even a piece of paper and envelope, I had no way to contact Emily and the kids. I felt like a prisoner with no control. I counted the days I had been here and how long I had to go, but it filled me with angst and made my legs writhe with the desire to get up, walk out of here and keep walking until I found a main road and made it home.

But, I reminded myself, I wasn't a prisoner. If I really wanted to, I could leave, but I was still here. I came here of my own accord, and I couldn't let myself forget why.

Each day started with a 6am wake up and before breakfast, an hour of 'contemplation' with the other clients. At first, I'd baulked at the idea, assuming it was some kind of praying. I had never prayed in my life, just clasped my hands and mumbled along to the Lord's Prayer when I had to at weddings and funerals, or school assemblies. This was nothing like the school prayers though, and despite myself, I came to enjoy the hour we spent lying in a circle on the floor, our eyes closed, letting our bodies relax, and just listening. During contemplation, Michael played background music, which always made me smile, as it was the type of hippy whale song music that Emily used to listen to when she did yoga. I warmed at the thought of her laughing along with me. Over the music, Michael talked to us in a sonorous voice about how he came to find Phoenix's way of life, and how other clients had beaten their addictions to alcohol, drugs, gambling and sex, or overcome depression and schizophrenia without medications by believing in the power of themselves, by stripping their life back to the basics.

Phoenix, this group that Damian and Michael and Tim and Lucas were part of, was bigger than I'd realised. From talking to the other clients – all men, all successful on the surface but broken beneath – I understood that we'd all been chosen by an existing member to come here because they could see our struggles, but also our potential. Phoenix's matrix spread all over the world and, from what I could gather, it was a network of highly successful people who believed in themselves and in living the life we were meant to: eating real food – no processed, manufactured sludge; no alcohol; no drugs, prescribed or otherwise; living well. And by doing that, Michael reminded us every day, we would reach our amazing potential and would be free of the toxic influences that poisoned our bodies and minds and led to our addictions.

Initially, I wanted to get up from the mat and challenge him – but I had come to realise over the past weeks that he was right. What had the doctors and medicines done for my knee except make me depend on them? Their false promises made me cling onto an unrealistic dream when I could have been moving forwards to other, bigger, opportunities when I was still young.

After the daily group session in the morning, we had breakfast. Vegan, no caffeine. For the first few days I was ravenous, desperate for something sweet or spicy, a coffee. I had a constant headache and stomach cramps for a week. But, like everything, you get used to it. Then, after breakfast, I had my hour alone with Michael every day, bar Sunday, when we had to spend all day in contemplation.

'How are you today?' Michael said when I sat down in his office this morning, settling back into the chair.

'Okay,' I said. 'How are you?'

He nodded. 'Great, thanks. Right, Paul, today, I want to hear about the first time you remember gambling. I want to trace this back and find out where this has come from, what started you down this path.'

I raised my eyebrows.

Michael continued. 'Your first drink, or the first time you get high, or the first win… that experience floods your mind with a drug more powerful than any pharmaceutical you can try, it hardwires your brain. I'm here to help retrain you, break all those connections, and get back to your true self.'

I nodded. I had told the story of my first big win so many times, but always when I was trying to impress people with a tale, over a beer and a bet. I remembered the details as if it happened yesterday, the story of the starting gun shot that flung open the gate and threw me panting after the rabbit that was always just out of reach.

It was in the smoky back corner of the Bondi hotel. Emily and I lived in an apartment near the beach then, only a couple of blocks' walk away. It was a pretty ordinary Australian pub, walls thick with years of smoke, tables scored with indents of bottles and schooner glasses. But in the evenings, all the tourists and the young locals – people like us – came out to drink and dance in the nightclub upstairs.

It was a hot, lazy Saturday. The season must have finished, otherwise I would never have been out drinking on a weekend, so it must have been early autumn. Emily and I flirted with the anticipation of the hours stretching out ahead of us. We'd done our usual Saturday routine: we'd slept in, then gone for a walk along the cliffs, then later, breakfast out at Bronte. Then we'd cleaned the house and paced around, bored. Lunchtime was too early to go out to the pub really, but maybe we could go and just have one drink, maybe pass the time with a bet in the bookies.

So, there we were, cold beers on the wobbly table with condensation dripping down the fogged schooner glass, hands damp and slippery with sweat. Backs of bare thighs sticking to the scratched bar stools. The coasters damp, cardboard peeling at the corners. A group of us perched on bar stools, drinks in hand, the weekend newspapers folded up on the table, the form guides pinned up on the crumbling cork noticeboards, the TVs on the wall showing the races, the sound a low hum. When the Sydney races finished, there were always the Western Australia races, three hours behind us in New South Wales. If you were desperate, there were always the dogs, or the trots, later on. And when you were going to the toilet, you walked past the slot machines and you may as well drop your coins in; it was better than having them weigh down your pockets.

More people started to drift in as the afternoon floated by, smelling of sunscreen, sandy hair still thickened from the salt water, shoulders red. They gathered around bottles of white wine askew in metal ice buckets on the tables. We'd had too much to drink by then to study the form properly, not that we really knew how to do that anyway.

Emily came back to the table, flapping the betting tickets then slapping them down on the table. 'Last race. Three mystery bets. Three bucks each,' she said. 'We've got this one.'

I had raised my glass then lined up the betting slips on the table as the race started, gulping my beer without taking my eyes off the screen in the corner. The sound on the television was turned down as the music played from the main bar. I lost track of which numbers I was meant to be looking for, and the horses were lurching along too fast and I couldn't really see the numbers on them anyway, but I thought at least one had come in. I looked at Emily and shrugged my shoulders.

She nudged me. 'I think you got it,' she whispered, face breaking into a grin.

'Nah,' I said, shaking my head though my body was buzzing with the hope that maybe, just maybe, she was right. As the next race was about to start, the official results flashed up on the screen. Emily whooped, then I checked the tickets and the excitement fizzed up in me. I had it! My heart started to beat faster as I looked at the odds. An old bloke in the bookies was shaking his head as he looked at the screen. 'That's a big trifecta.'

It was a big trifecta. Two thousand, one hundred and forty-six dollars, just like that. From a three-dollar bet. I screamed and we all cheered and stood up and raised our glasses, and others in the bar saw the commotion and joined in. Emily jumped off her stool, threw her arms around me and gave me a huge kiss on the lips. I waved the betting slip in the air and I felt amazing, filled with the certainty that my life was perfect.

–

'That day was going to be so ordinary,' I said to Michael, as I finished telling the story. 'But it became one of the best days ever. We went out, we drank champagne, we went to a club. Even if I won a million dollars now, it wouldn't compare. Holding all that cash in my hand was like nothing I'd ever experienced before. It was the dream, it was the unexpected magic of it all.' I could still feel it.

'That was the first time. What about the next time?'

I nodded, looking at my knees. 'I don't really remember the next time, or the time after that.'

After that, the memories become darker. The glare and deafening din of the casino when I'd lost track of time, my eyes following the little ball as it hurled around the rim of the roulette wheel, also straining to watch the numbers spinning the opposite way; my hands trembling as the wheel and the ball slowed, silently praying to someone for the ball to keep going just a little bit longer and make it to that lucky number; the panic and dread as the ball skipped past my number and the croupier swept away my chips. The compulsion to open my wallet and hand over another $50 because it was just a bit of fun, and the man sitting beside me was winning, so why shouldn't I?

Michael's voice brought me back to reality. 'Can you see how many other influences you had on your brain then? Alcohol, gambling, drugs, friends who encouraged and enabled that lifestyle… Every time you see those friends, have a drink, see Emily, those connections are firing up and making you want to recreate that feeling that you can never have again. Not through gambling. There are other ways to reach those moments of exhilaration. I can teach you. But you need to say goodbye to that part of your life.'

'I have,' I said. 'I've had to because it's all gone, there's nothing left for me to risk.'

He had shaken his head slowly, like a teacher showing his disappointment. 'If you left here today, you'd find something.'

'There is nothing.'

'You'd find something.'

'I would never take things from my kids.'

He said nothing, just nodded a little. I blushed. I had mentioned the kids, not him. At this moment, I was deadly serious, but I also knew that when that urge came over me, when I started to feel restless inside, that the gambling had always won so far. I had to admit that I didn't trust myself. I had already taken a lot from my children. When would I stop? Would I take their phones, their iPads? Emily's engagement ring? It was ridiculous, and yet as I thought it, I felt a deep, dangerous, part of me spark into life again and I knew I had to stay away from them for now, for their sake.

Sixteen

Emily

I was back in the position that had become so familiar: sitting across a desk from Cameron's teacher. I reminded myself that other parents didn't have to do this. But no matter how familiar it was, sitting in this chair pared off my thin skin of adulthood, leaving the core of an anxious child waiting to be told off.

I swallowed down the seed of guilt lodged in my throat and clasped my hands to hold them still. Maybe I shouldn't have kept sending him to school over the past few weeks, maybe I should have listened to him as he begged me not to make him, as I dragged him into the school counsellor's office then stormed away from him as he cowered on the couch with tears brimming in his eyes. I was frustrated, sick of everything about our day and night being consumed with Cameron, and angry with Paul for swanning off and leaving me to handle everything. Cameron had become more withdrawn since Paul left, and at the same time, more chaotic, refusing to go to school, yelling at me, not sleeping. I had tried being calm, tiptoeing around him and giving into what he wanted. I had tried shouting, pleading, crying, threatening, but he just shrugged, his eyes perplexed. He wouldn't explain it to me; or couldn't.

It wasn't a surprise, therefore, that the school had called me to come and collect him. I had to leave work, my receptionist clearly annoyed at having to cancel my clients, who probably wouldn't come back to see me now. But I had no choice: who else was there but me? And now, I sat on the edge of an uncomfortable wooden chair, across the desk from Mrs McCarthy, Cameron's year coordinator, and Miss Da Silva, the school counsellor.

Mrs McCarthy began by making small talk and somehow, I smiled and chatted back. *Get to the point*, I wanted to say. *Just tell me*. They must have had a meeting about this, before, without me, to decide what they'd say. Mrs McCarthy had a Liverpool accent. I had never noticed before. My eyes filled with tears as I realised how much I missed being home, in the UK; I blinked hard and refocused.

'Have there been any changes at home?'

I nodded. 'Paul's been away for a few weeks, for work, and isn't due back for another few weeks. I'm trying to keep everything normal, but...'

She leaned forwards, her eyes kind. 'I understand, Emily. Look, I'll get to the point. There was an incident this morning. In English, he was staring out of the window and kicking his chair, so his teacher asked him to concentrate, and well, things escalated. In the end, Cameron threw his book at the teacher then upturned his chair and ran out.'

I froze.

'It's okay, he didn't go far, he went behind the tennis courts and we managed to calm him down and get him back to class. But he's been more... difficult, recently. He's not able to focus or concentrate, and he's definitely more irritable, and then this.'

'I'm so sorry.' I shook my head slowly. 'I'm not sure what to say. I...'

'Don't apologise, that's for Cameron to do.'

'I don't know really what to do, I am trying.'

She raised her hand. 'I know. Please don't think I'm criticising you, I'm not at all. I can see how hard this has been for you. We just want to make sure that Cameron gets help.'

I nodded and the words tumbled out. 'I think he's missing Paul, and I'm trying my best, but I have to work and look after the kids and, well, you know, do everything at home. And I don't want him to fall behind at school, but I can't seem to get him here on time, he can't get himself ready, he won't listen and at night I hear him pacing around and I worry that he's got no friends…' My hands were shaking now.

Mrs McCarthy continued, her words spoken slowly and carefully. 'When he is here, it's clear that he can't concentrate on his schoolwork. He's not really managing to complete tasks in class, and the quality of his work is going downhill. And it was interesting to hear you mention your worries about his friends. The thing about teenage boys – and you'll remember being a teenager – is that any point of difference between the kids puts a target on their back. We've been watching closely and some of the kids are starting to tease him a bit, and he's reacting to them.'

At that, I wanted to run out of this office straight away and find Cameron, ask him which boys were hassling him and get Paul out of that bloody centre to throttle them. Literally wring their necks.

'Do you think that's why?' I said, my voice lifting. Could it be that simple? They could expel bullies, or we could move school. 'Is that why he's like this? He's being bullied?'

Miss Da Silva glanced at Mrs McCarthy, who nodded a little. Miss Da Silva shook her head and began to speak. 'No, no. I'm sure it's not helping but I think that what we're seeing is more than just a reaction to bullying. As you know, I've been trying to engage him.'

'But maybe we don't know the extent of it. He has a computer in his room, maybe there's cyber bullying. I went to that workshop that you held here last term.' I looked quickly to each of their faces, hopefully.

Miss Da Silva raised her hand. 'Please, let me explain. You know that we have a zero tolerance for any sort of emotional or physical bullying, and the boys in question have been repri-manded and we're watching it very closely. But I don't think that's the only issue.'

'He's never had many friends,' I continued. 'You know, he has the rugby team but they don't really hang out with him outside of training. I've always been worried about that.'

'Yes. Although over the past few weeks, it's definitely gotten worse.' She was using her counselling voice. 'As well as his academic and social decline, he just looks… sad.'

I nodded.

'Have you taken him to see a doctor at all?'

'Yes. He's seen a paediatrician a few times. He said he probably had ADHD, but just mild. But Paul spoke to someone at work whose child had ended up having some kind of psychotic breakdown and another one who knew a kid who'd had a heart attack from the medication, so we decided not to put him on the stimulants. The paediatrician said that was okay, that we didn't have to. Maybe it's that?'

'How about a psychiatrist?' she said, softly.

My body stilled. 'Paul and I have discussed it,' I said slowly. 'But, well, he's – we've – always thought he was just a kid, you know?'

I looked at the teacher and counsellor again, willing them to keep going, to say the things that I couldn't, to take the decision out of my hands so that I had no choice, so that I could tell Paul that we had to do it.

Miss Da Silva leaned forwards. 'I am very concerned that Cameron is ill, and as a psychologist, I strongly recommend that you get him a referral to a psychiatrist. I am happy to recommend a child psychiatrist who I think would be great.'

I needed to talk to Paul.

I couldn't talk to Paul.

I looked up at their concerned faces. 'Yes, please,' I managed to whisper.

–

Driving home in the car, I thought about what Paul would say. I wanted to talk to him about it, so that I didn't have to second-guess myself, but how could I? And I couldn't wait; Cameron needed help now. *I* needed help now. Paul would understand. I owed it to Cameron to take control now, while we still had his trust, before any power we had disappeared as he left gawky, conflicted adolescence for adulthood. I was his parent, and I had to make sure that I had done the best job I could to prepare him for the world outside of the shelter of home and school. If I didn't do something, I was failing my son.

That evening, I sat at the dining table with Cameron and Tilly while we ate home-made burgers. Cameron seemed okay now: he ate two burgers, he bickered with Tilly, who picked at the edges of the cheese and refused to eat the meat, declaring that she was going vegetarian, but Cameron seemed calm. I could barely finish my food; I sipped at a glass of wine and forced myself to swallow the lump of gristly meat.

The kids finished and stood up.

'Hey,' I said. 'Clear the table please.'

They both, wordlessly, picked up their plates and took them to the kitchen. I grabbed my own plate, and the salt and tomato sauce, and walked over too. 'Tilly, could you go outside and take the washing off the line please?'

'Me?'

'Yes, please,' I said, not allowing myself to bite at her petulant tone.

'How do I do that?'

'Are you telling me that you don't know how to take clean washing in?' Although as I said it, I realised that I probably had never asked her to do it before; I ran around them and Paul and did everything in this house. I spoke more softly. 'Just get the washing basket from the laundry and unpeg them. I'll fold them later.'

She made a face like I had asked her to clean the toilets.

'Thank you, darling.' I turned to Cameron. 'Hey buddy, not so fast. You can help me stack the dishwasher.'

He opened his mouth to protest.

'Don't bother, Cam. Remember, your dad's away so you kids have to step up and help me.'

He sighed. 'Okay. Are these in here clean or dirty?'

'Use your eyes! Can't you see? Dirty, just rinse our plates and stick them in too.'

I began scraping the scraps of leftover food into the bin. 'Cameron, while you're here, I wanted to talk to you. School called me in today, about what happened in English.'

'Oh.'

'Yes, oh.' I closed the cupboard door to hide the bin and turned to look at him, leaning back against the bench.

'Mr Singh is rude. I didn't understand what we were meant to be doing.'

'Did you throw something at him?'

'It was hardly throwing! I just got angry because he wasn't listening to what I was saying. I didn't mean to.'

I sighed, looking at my little boy, his eyes downcast. 'Cameron, you can't do that, you know? The school are worried, and so am I.'

'I'm sorry!' He looked at me, his face flushed.

'It's alright, I know it's not like you, but I want us to go and see a doctor.'

'I don't need to see a doctor.'

I swallowed hard. 'I think you do, and I'm your mum.'

'What does Dad say?'

'It doesn't matter. He's away, I'm here.' I stepped towards him. 'Sweetie, you're not in trouble, okay? I just think we need to get you checked over by a doctor to see if we can help you with, well, how you're feeling and why you're not coping as well as you normally do. There are doctors who specialise in that. Remember when we saw Darren, the psychologist?'

'I hated him.'

'Don't be ridiculous. Anyway, this is someone like him, but a doctor.'

I saw his fists clench but could see the panic in his eyes. 'I don't need to see someone.' He lowered his voice. 'I'm sorry. I won't do it again.'

I reached my arm out to touch his. 'Oh darling, it's not a punishment, it's not just because of that, but we need to go for a check-up. Just like we would if you had headaches, or stomach aches. And, if the doctor says you're fine then, that's that. Okay?'

I heard the back door open as Tilly came back in. She walked towards us. 'What's happening?' Her brow was furrowed.

'Nothing,' Cameron said. 'Mum's just overreacting, as usual.' He glared at me and I saw the tension in his muscles. For a moment, I saw his father in him, and realised that a part of me was afraid. He loomed towards me, pushed past and stormed off towards his room, slamming his door behind him.

I rubbed my face and tried to exhale slowly.

'Mum, you okay?' Tilly said, a tremor in her voice.

'Yes,' I said brightly, my voice too high pitched. 'I'm fine. Hey, thanks for doing that.'

'Can I go now?'

I nodded quickly. 'Sure.'

She took a step towards me, gave me a quick hug, then went off to her room.

–

It was easier than I expected. I took him to our GP after school the next day, without any fanfare, and explained what school had said, while Cameron remained silent. The GP gave us a referral, I called up the psychiatrist and I made an appointment. There was a cancellation two days later, and on the day, we just got in the car, and we went.

I had prepared a story about why Paul wasn't there. But it never came up. The doctor, a tall, thin woman who looked to be in her 50s, wearing red-framed glasses, introduced herself as Dr Davidson. She asked us to introduce ourselves, then asked who lived at home – and of course I mentioned Paul then – and what he did for a living, and that was it. She saw Cameron and me together initially, then me on my own, and then she asked to talk with Cameron on his own.

When she asked me to leave the room, my heart sped up. I looked at Cameron.

'Is that okay? I'll be right outside if you need me.'

'He'll be fine,' said Dr Davidson, smiling at him. 'Won't you?'

Cameron nodded, so I slowly walked to the door, waiting for him to protest, but he didn't. I don't know why I felt disappointed. Of course, I wanted him to talk to the doctor so we could work out what was wrong with him, but the other part of me wanted him to act out, so that the psychiatrist could see what I was taking about. But, I could hardly prod him until he screamed at me, so I swallowed and walked out to the waiting room.

When the office door opened again, about twenty minutes later, Dr Davidson invited me back in. Cameron was still sitting in the chair, looking down at his school shoes. Scuffed, I noticed. I should have polished them. I sat down next to him, my mouth dry.

Dr Davidson cleared her throat. 'Thank you both for coming in today and for being so open with me. Cameron, I'm impressed at how well you've spoken with me, even though it must be very frightening coming here.' I put my hand on top of Cameron's and gave it a squeeze. What had he said?

Then the doctor talked about his social difficulties, his high levels of anxiety, how his anxious thoughts get stuck in his head, how he couldn't concentrate properly and wasn't able to enjoy anything. She said some children cope with strong emotions by withdrawing, and others by hitting out. I felt like I was watching a television show, removed from these terms she was using to describe my son. Cameron became more tense beside me as she continued to address me.

'I don't like to label children.' She smiled. Then turned to Cameron. 'Cameron, what I do see is that sometimes it's hard for you to relate to people, and sometimes your worries get too big for you and that makes you unhappy. I know that there are things at school that you struggle with, and some stresses at home.'

I fixed the smile on my face to hold back my tears. What had he said about home? I should have told her about Paul, but then what if she thought this was all to do with that, with what we've gone through recently, and overlooked the fact that we've had problems with Cameron for years?

'Emily,' she said, turning back to me, 'it's clear to me that he has become quite an anxious and sad young man, and we've spoken earlier about some of the reasons why that might be. I've read the documentation from the paediatrician, who thinks he has a degree of ADHD, and the school, as well as the OT and speech therapist and the psychologist.' I had brought my folder of notes – every assessment that I'd taken him to over the years: those that spoke about some of his social difficulties, that queried 'high functioning autism' while others disagreed, his social skills, his sensory processing difficulties and some obsessional interests, hoping that she could make sense of them all and bring all these words together into something that meant something.

She pushed her glasses up on her nose and leaned back. 'It's not unusual to see children who have a mix of lots of issues and we can't always say it's one or the other. ADHD can lead to anxiety, and anxiety can lead to concentration problems. Then of course, as he struggles to cope with his feelings and acts out, or withdraws, he becomes more socially isolated which makes everything even more difficult and can lead to feelings of sadness. I prefer to think of children, or teenagers, or adults, as unique people with their own unique strengths and challenges.'

I wiped a tear away and glanced at Cameron. 'He has so many strengths, Dr Davidson. He's so kind and smart and he's great at sport. He's on the rugby team; did he tell you that? He loves computers.'

She smiled at me. 'Yes, I know that. He told me.' She leaned back and crossed her legs. 'Look. Usually my first step is to recommend that he see a clinical psychologist, to help him learn how to manage his thoughts and feelings, and his behaviours, but I know you've tried that. Also, the fact that your school psychologist asked you to see me is a bit of a red flag to indicate that we might need to try some medication to settle things down.'

I breathed out, only then realising that I'd been holding my breath waiting for her to say that.

'Some families are keen for medication, others are not, and I respect that either way. What are your feelings about it?'

I sighed out a shaky breath, clutching Cameron's hand. 'Look, it's not something I take lightly. His dad... and I,' I added quickly, 'have been against that, when the paediatrician recommended the stimulants. He's just a kid. But, well, things have changed. I feel like we've tried everything we can and he's still... struggling, as you say. Cam, what do you think?' I turned to him.

'It's fine,' he said, not looking me in the eye.

'Cameron and I briefly spoke about it and he said he's willing to try it too.'

I wiped away a tear. If he was willing to take medication, he was admitting that he was unhappy and needed help. That broke my heart.

'Cameron, we'll get you feeling better, sweetie. I promise,' I said quietly.

He nodded.

Dr Davison continued. 'Great, well I'm glad we're all in agreement. I do feel that we've reached that point, and regardless of what label Cameron has, let's try to treat the symptoms.'

And then she told us that she was going to prescribe an antidepressant that could also help anxiety. She thought the anxiety was causing more problems than his inattention at the moment, and he also had some depressive symptoms – a low mood, sleep difficulties, a lack of enjoyment. She would prescribe Fluoxetine – Prozac. My heart sped up. She went through the side effects and even as she did, I knew I'd say yes, because what other choice did I have? It might help, she said. It might take a few weeks to start to work. He might get some headaches or nausea. He might get more agitated, some kids even become suicidal, but it was rare.

I took the prescription, put it in my bag, then we went to the chemist on the way home, I handed it over and we came out with a box of tablets in a white paper bag.

'Hey, Cam,' I said, glancing at him as I turned left, towards school. 'Best not to mention this to Dad for now, you think?'

'Well, I can't, can I? He hasn't even called.'

'He has, I told you, it's just hard for him to call when you're at home because of—'

'Work?' He raised his eyebrows, then turned to look out the window.

'Yes, work,' I said quietly.

'Okay.'

'You know what he's like. Let's just give this a go, and we'll see if it helps you feel better. If it helps, great – then we'll tell your dad. If not, then we'll just stop them, and he'll be none the wiser.'

The next morning, I popped out one of the tablets from the blister pack, cut it in half with a knife, then gave it to Cameron with his breakfast. He swallowed it down with his orange juice, grimacing at the taste, then he went to school, and that was that. For the first time in weeks, I felt my shoulders relax a little, knowing that I was taking some control, and that someone believed me.

Seventeen

Paul

'Tell me what has led you here,' Michael said.

I leaned forwards, elbows on my knees, hands over my face.

'I don't know.'

'You do. People don't end up as gambling addicts for no reason.'

'I don't know,' I snapped. 'If I knew that, maybe I wouldn't be here at all.'

'But you are here. When did it stop being a choice?'

'I don't know when I stopped having a choice. I've thought about this over and over. If I could pinpoint the actual day, one particular event that turned everything in me the wrong way around, then I could understand what caused it.'

'And what would you do?'

I let out an ironic laugh. 'Well, I would just rewind life to that point, and make a different choice.' But this was real life, not a choose your own adventure book. I couldn't go back and change my path. The things I have done have altered the stories of other people too, and it was too late to pull our mixed narratives apart. 'I won't ever go back to gambling. Never again.' I ran my fingers through my hair. It needed a cut. What would the kids be doing now? God, I missed them. And Emily. 'Look, I know I said I'd stay here for six weeks or whatever it was, but it's been a month. I miss my family. I want to go home.'

Michael smiled. 'Everyone does. But this is precisely the time you need to stay.'

I felt my muscles tense. 'You don't understand. Cameron, my son, he has problems. He'll be wondering where I am, and it's not fair on Emily.'

'It's not fair on them to go back when you're not ready. And it's not fair on you, to give up so soon.'

'I'm not giving up. I don't give up. I understand; I get it. I want to get back to work, get fit again, spend more time with my family.'

Michael kept the smile on his face but shook his head condescendingly.

'What are you looking at me like that for?'

'I was like you once. This is only just the start. If you go home now, nothing will have changed.'

'I've changed.'

'Not enough. Not yet. You still need to learn why you're like this.'

If I really wanted to, I could stand up right now and leave. I could demand that Michael give me back my phone, demand that he call Emily to pick me up. And Emily would come. She would drop everything she was doing, and she would be here as soon as she could, with the kids squabbling in the back seat and they'd drive me back to my familiar, warm, chaotic, home, where Emily was at her happiest.

Emily has always been so content with simply being at home, finding such joy in the everyday moments that I hadn't appreciated before: kissing the kids goodnight, having a glass of wine – just one – with dinner, watching a trashy TV show, then going to bed early with a book. Why couldn't I be happy with what I had? All my life I'd been endlessly chasing something: to make the school football team, to be selected by a talent scout, to get signed, to score goals, to be on TV, to make money. I had been far happier chasing my dreams than I ever was when I caught them.

I groaned, looking at Michael. 'I'm just finding it so bloody hard, being away from them.'

'Being disconnected right now is what you need. You need to rid yourself of everything that was happening to you, out there. Here, you are safe, and you are becoming healthier every day in your mind and body. No electronics, no caffeine, no junk food, no alcohol, no temptations to ruin you.'

'I may have been addicted to gambling, but I'm not addicted to any of those other things.' Drinking was never my problem: hangovers always made sure I could never back it up the next day.

'Really? Could you go without your coffee, or your glass of red with dinner?'

I rubbed my face. 'That wasn't causing any trouble.' But I guess I was addicted to work, to soccer. 'Maybe I've just got an addictive personality. A gene that flicked on and started this whole bloody thing.'

Michael looked tense as he spoke vehemently. 'There's nothing wrong with *you*, Paul. All this crap out there about genes and diagnoses and medication for this and that...' He shook his head. 'The problem is not in *you*; the problem is the world out there that you let influence you. Remember what it's like out there? Kids and adults stare at their phones as they're walking down the street, they can't concentrate because emails and messages constantly ping onto their screens, they can't sleep because they're worried that they're missing 'likes' on Facebook or Instagram. When they go out, they take hundreds of photos and don't look at the world through their eyes any more, girls pouting in bikinis taking selfies at the beach instead of swimming.

'This... narcissism, showing the world filtered flattering photos of our holidays, why? To instil *envy*, envy that makes people like you think that everyone else is doing something better than you are, instead of being happy with what you have. We poison ourselves with fake food, with alcohol, with drugs prescribed by doctors as a quick fix, but do they ever work? Do you know how they design those casinos, Paul? They have psychologists – people who are supposedly meant to help us – paid a fortune to help them rig the machines to brainwash you and force you to keep pressing that button, like a rat in a cage getting cocaine. They deliberately set up the place so you have no idea if its night or day, they pump oxygen into the room to keep you awake, give you free drinks to keep you disinhibited…'

'Okay,' I said, the tension in my head building. 'Okay, I get it. Please…'

He raised his voice, his pupils dilated as he stared at me. 'You *don't* get it, Paul, or else you wouldn't want to leave. The world out there is not good for you, not until you've learned how to rise above it. That's what Phoenix will teach you, unless you're too weak and are ready to give up.'

'I don't give up,' I said, irritated. 'I was a professional athlete. I didn't get there by giving up. I'm getting really pissed off by how—'

He pointed a finger at me. 'You *were* an athlete. You're not now. And it sounds to me like giving up was exactly what you did. You gave into all the temptations out there, you lost yourself.'

My eyes were filling with tears. Jesus. 'Alright, I get it.'

'I don't know that you do.'

'I do!' I wiped at my face. Couldn't he see that I'd had enough?

'If you did get it you wouldn't be giving up, wouldn't be trying to walk out of here after, what, four weeks? You've had years and years building up to this and you think you can fix it in a few weeks? There's so much more you have to learn about yourself, about the world out there, and how to heal yourself.'

My breath quickened, and my lip quivered. I tried to slow my breathing. 'I understand,' I said, my voice tense.

'No, you don't!' he shouted.

My fists clenched; how dare he? I was here by choice. Yes, I was indebted to Damian for helping to arrange this and lending me the money, but he was withholding a percentage of my wages until I'd paid him back the fees here, and for the time off work I'd taken. So, that meant that Michael worked for me, and I had been working damn hard to get myself better, doing everything they had asked of me. I sat forward, my legs ready to spring. I stared at Michael. He stared back. I held his gaze, but then my vision blurred and I looked away. This was humiliating enough; I didn't want to cry in front of him too. No matter how much you hurt, you get up and you keep going. That's how I survived the housing estates in Scotland, that's how I got myself out of that and into soccer.

I pursed my lips and let out a slow breath, looking at the worn-out toes of my sneakers. If I left now, before my treatment was finished, would Damian still let me work for him? Would he trust me enough, knowing that I had turned up on his doorstep, begged him to help me, then thrown it back in his face? And what if I did stuff up, and gamble again? Without Damian employing me, what else would I do for an income? It was already going to take months and months to pay back what I owed him, and then once I was out of here, I'd need ongoing help to keep me away from gambling, and I'd have to pay for that too. After paying Damian and Phoenix, Emily and I would still struggle to make ends meet. Damian had promised that when I was better, if I could prove myself worthy of joining them, that I would be rewarded. So, this really was my only way out of this. My life – my family – depended on me getting better. Michael was right. A month was nothing. This had been going on for years. I had no choice. 'I do understand.'

'I'm not sure I believe you, Paul.' His voice was strong.

'I do. I'm not going anywhere.'

I heard him sigh and I looked up. Michael was leaning forwards now, a kind smile on his face. 'Mate, we've all been there. *I've* been there. We can change your life. You just have to trust us.'

'I do.' I nodded.

'Alright. I trust you too, Paul. You've made the right choice.'

It didn't feel like I had a choice.

Eighteen

Emily

The traffic was barely moving as I neared the school. The rain was pelting down as I peered through the brief clear patches of the windscreen as the wipers worked furiously to clear the rain. I had a headache from working straight through without any lunch, again, so I could be there to pick the kids up from school. I glanced at the clock on the dashboard; I was five minutes later than usual which meant that even if the weather had been great, I would still be stuck in a long line of traffic waiting for the older kids to come out of school, with the odd perplexed driver unwittingly dropped in the chaos of school pick up. The radio show paused as my phone rang over the Bluetooth through the car stereo. Paul's name appeared on the screen.

'Jesus!' I muttered as I jabbed at the screen several times to answer the call. 'Paul? Paul, can you hear me?'

'Hi Emily. How are you?'

His voice filled the car and my eyes blurred with tears. I had hoped he would call any day, now that his six weeks was up. I had called Treetops again and again, but they wouldn't tell me when he'd be released, or even confirm that he was there. Damian had been evasive, saying he didn't know much but that he had heard Paul was doing well.

'It's you. It's really you. Good, good, we're fine. How are you? I haven't heard from you in so long. I tried calling you every day, but your phone...'

'I'm sorry. They don't allow phones.'

133

'I know that, but it's just ridiculous.'

'I'm sorry.'

'It's been over six weeks! Was there was no way to call me? No payphone or email or even a letter?' I knew I was shouting now, partly against the noise of the pouring rain on the car roof, but mainly because now that I heard his voice and he sounded like my old Paul, I realised I was furious at him, for putting us through this.

'Sorry. It's just… it wasn't allowed.'

I sniffed. 'You're a grown man. Even prisoners get a phone call.'

The traffic began to move slowly forward as I saw children empty out of the school building and run, blazers over their head, to shelter under the edge of the school building as teachers with umbrellas called their names out as the cars moved forwards.

'I'm just picking the kids up. They'll be in the car soon. They want to talk to you, they've been asking all these questions about why you haven't phoned, and I've had to pretend you have called during the day. They know, Paul, they know I'm lying to them. Can you hold on for another few minutes to talk to them? They really miss you.'

'Emily, I'm coming home.'

'Oh, thank God. When?'

'Now.'

'Now? But—' My mind raced as my stomach began to churn.

'I thought you'd be happy.'

'Oh Paul, I am, I am happy. It's just that I've heard nothing from you for so long and now you tell me you're on your way home. I just assumed there would be some, well, meeting, to plan it all. Are you okay?'

What I wanted to ask was, are you safe to come home? Have you stopped gambling? Because I had worked too hard to try and hold everyone steady to have him tip us over again.

'Yes, I'm great. I've changed, and I know that sounds like something in a movie, Em, but I have. I've opened my eyes to so much about myself, about the world, and I'm positive that we will be great. I can't wait to share it all with you.'

I closed my eyes briefly, then opened them. It was good to hear him sound so positive, so enthusiastic. 'Okay, well, that's great, Paul. What time will you be home? Can I pick you up?'

'No, I'm good. I have a lift, I'll be home in a couple of hours.'

'Why don't we just come to where you are? Tilly won't mind missing dancing, they'd love to see you…'

'No, they'll drive me.'

'Okay.' My breath was shaky as I spoke. 'The kids will be so pleased to see you.' Would I be pleased to see him? Already I felt uneasy, like he was intruding back onto the life that I'd had to make for the kids and me since he left us.

'I've missed you all,' he said. 'I can't wait to see you.'

I steadied my voice. 'Me too. I love you.'

—

I cut up some watermelon and put it on the kitchen table, then opened a packet of crackers for the kids' afternoon tea. Tilly had skipped dancing once I told her that Paul was coming home so she was in her room doing stretches instead. 'Kids!' I called, 'come and get a snack.'

Tilly came, grabbed a piece of watermelon, took one bite then walked back towards her room.

'Hey,' I said. 'That's not enough.'

'I'm not hungry,' she said. 'I ate everything in my lunchbox today.'

I had been packing a couple of extra things for her. She was doing so much dancing, as well as hockey and cross-country running, and she'd been looking thin. 'Okay, darling. Maybe Dad will want to go out for dinner to celebrate being home.'

Cameron wandered out, his shirt hanging out, in his socks. 'Come and eat something, Cam.'

He sat down at the table. I looked at the pile of lunchboxes and water bottles and school diaries and notes and iPads on the breakfast bar. I wanted the house to look nice when Paul came back, to show him I'd been coping. Or perhaps it was better to show him how it had really been for me, having to do everything by myself for all this time. But then I looked at Cameron, his eyes downcast, nibbling on a cracker. I went over and sat opposite him.

'I think I'll have some afternoon tea with you. I didn't have lunch today.'

'That was silly,' he said.

I nodded. 'Yes, it was.'

'Imagine if I told you I hadn't had lunch.'

'True, Cameron. I'd tell you that was silly.' He smiled, just a little.

'Hey, how are you feeling? You've been on the tablets almost a month now. Are they doing anything?'

He shook his head.

'Anything good at all? Or anything bad? You can be honest with me.'

'I don't feel any different.'

'Okay. Dr Davidson said that we could increase the dose to a full tablet, so we'll do that from tomorrow, okay? I'll just give it to you with your juice tomorrow morning.'

'Won't Dad see?'

I had thought the same thing. 'Don't you worry about your dad, I'll talk to him.'

'You know what he'll say. He'll just tell me to get on with it.'

'Oh, Cam.' I reached across the table. 'He won't. The doctor said you're ill and it's no different to having a broken leg or diabetes, okay? This is not something that you can do anything about, you need medicine. Hey, why don't we just *not* tell him for now? I'll bring it to you in your room in the morning, you just swallow it down. If he sees, we'll say its paracetamol. But it's not a secret, Cam, you have nothing to be ashamed of.'

I bit into the piece of melon, then wiped my chin with my finger. 'How was school today?'

He shrugged. 'Fine.'

'Who did you hang out with at lunch?'

'Nobody. I went to the library.'

'You okay, Cam?'

He didn't look me in the eye. 'I'm fine.'

I watched him eating, and waited, but I knew better than to push him. 'Okay, sweetie. I'm going to clean up before your dad gets home. Show him how well we've managed while he's been off gallivanting around the world!'

I had just finished washing up the lunchboxes and plastic tubs when I heard a loud voice bellow down the hallway. 'Guess who's home?'

'Daddy!' shrieked Tilly as she ran out of her room. I smiled; as grown up as she tried to be as she moved closer to being a teenager, she was still a little girl at heart. I followed her as she ran down the hallway towards Paul, both of them with their arms wide open. I was trying to be calm but I found my feet began to run of their own accord towards him too. Tilly shifted over to his left and he put his right arm around me and squeezed hard. I leaned into his chest. 'Welcome home,' I murmured.

'You smell different, Dad,' Tilly said.

'Must be the different washing powder,' he said. 'Hotels, hey?' He relaxed his grip on me and looked down the hallway. 'G'day, Cameron,' he beamed.

Cameron stepped forward and gave him a hug too. 'Group hug!' I joked, feeling a weight drop off me as I realised we were all back together.

'Did you bring me any presents, Dad?'

'Tilly!' I said sharply.

'Of course I did,' he said. 'Though I didn't see any Hobbits in New Zealand, I'm sorry. But something weird has happened to my feet and they've gone a bit hairy...'

'Dad!' Tilly was delighted, and I saw Cameron smile too.

She and Cameron watched as he unzipped his suitcase. My stomach churned. What did he bring them from a rehab centre?

He handed each of them a carrier bag. I saw them pull out a magazine each: some teenage girl one for Tilly, a computer one for Cameron, and a notepad and one of those pens with multiple colours at the top that you can click down. He must have stopped at the newsagent on the way home. My heart smiled.

'Thanks, Dad,' Cameron said. 'This has got some Minecraft codes in it. Mum, can I play on my iPad?'

'Have you done your homework?'

'Haven't got any.' He raked his fingers through his hair.

I raised my eyebrows, paused, then smiled. 'Yes, go on then.'

'Me too?' said Tilly.

I laughed. 'Only because you've caught me in a good mood.'

They both came past me, and as they did, I grabbed them both and gave them a big hug before they wriggled free and went off to their rooms.

Paul zipped up his case again. As he stood up, I put my arms around his waist and hugged him again. 'You do smell different,' I mumbled. 'And you feel different too.'

He held me and kissed the top of my head. 'You've just forgotten what I feel like.'

'I missed you.'

'Me too.'

I breathed deeply. He did feel different. He'd lost weight, but in a good way. He looked leaner, fitter. I let go and stepped back, looking him up and down. He was wearing a white T-shirt and jeans. The sleeves were tight on his arms and I could see muscles there again, and his waist was slimmer. I smiled. 'Have you been working out?' I said in a mock American accent.

He laughed. 'A little. They had a small gym. Not much else to do in there.'

I sighed then spoke quietly. 'Are you okay?'

He nodded, then looked me in the eye. 'Yes. I'm great.'

'Really?'

'Really. I promise you, everything is going to be great. This is the turning point. I'm back.'

—

We went out for dinner. The kids wanted pizza, so we drove to an Italian restaurant, a small place where they made their own pasta and had a wood fired oven. I ordered a Prosecco. 'You want one? To celebrate?' I asked Paul as the waiter hovered.

He shook his head. 'Just a sparkling mineral water.'

I felt a surge of irritation. 'Really?'

'Just don't feel like it,' he said, glancing at the children and then back to me.

'Actually,' I said to the waiter, my face blushing. 'I'll have the same.' Of course, they wouldn't have allowed him any alcohol in an addiction centre. I should be happy; how many times had I told him that he was drinking too much? But I was also disappointed. I wanted a drink, and now I felt awkward. I pushed it out of my mind.

'So, how's school been going?' Paul asked the kids.

'It's fine,' said Tilly. 'I'm running in the interschool cross-country next week. Only the top ten of the year got in.'

'You were in the top ten?' he said, grinning. 'That's fantastic!'

'She ran so well,' I added.

'It was raining so hard, Dad, you should have seen it, everyone was like mud monsters by the end of it, but now we have to train three times a week.'

'Well done, I'm sorry I missed it.'

I heard the regret in his voice.

'How about you, Cam? How's rugby going?'

'It's okay,' he said. 'We've won a couple and drawn a couple, but we haven't lost for a few weeks.'

'I can't wait to see you play this weekend.'

Cameron nodded.

'And how's school?' Paul prodded. I held my breath; Cameron glanced at me and realised that I hadn't said anything to his dad. I saw him relax a little.

'You know, just the same. Too much homework.'

Paul smiled and they continued chatting away. Maybe Cameron *was* a bit better from the tablets. He seemed more chatty and relaxed than I'd seen for a while, or was that just because Paul was home? I also felt more relaxed than I had in weeks.

'So, have you decided what you're going to have to eat?' I asked as the waiter approached with our drinks.

'Ummm... meat lovers,' Cameron said.

'Tilly?'

'I'm not that hungry.'

'Don't be silly. You had running this morning and you have hockey tomorrow before school, you need to eat a big dinner.'

'Small margherita, then.'

'Please...' I said, raising my eyebrows.

'Please,' she snapped.

I ignored her and ran my finger down the menu. 'What to have, what to have... What are you having, Paul?'

He looked up at the waiter. 'Do you have gluten-free dough?'

I turned to look at him. Gluten-free?

The waiter shook his head. I could only imagine what he was thinking.

'Okay, I'll just have the Caprese salad, please, with the cheese on the side.'

I frowned, then smiled a little too broadly at the waiter. 'Spaghetti vongole for me. And we'll have a margherita, a meat lovers, both small, and some garlic bread too.'

When the waiter left, I cocked my head as I looked at Paul.

'I told you I've made some changes,' he said, defensively.

I smiled. 'Remember what you used to say about people on gluten-free diets?'

He didn't smile back. 'Things have changed.'

I hesitated, then nodded. If he wasn't gambling away every cent we had, what right did I have to complain?

—

Later, after the kids were asleep, we both lay in bed looking at the ceiling.

'How was it in there?' I said.

'It was good,' he said. 'I learned a lot.'

I nodded, waiting. He said nothing. The anger that I'd suppressed all through dinner flared up. 'Is that all you're going to say?'

'I don't know what to say.'

'Well, what did you do in there? What treatment did you do? What has changed? What have you *learned*?'

'Not now, Emily. I'm just glad to be home. I'm tired.'

I clenched my jaw. 'I've been pretty tired too, Paul.'

He turned his head to look at me. 'I'm sorry. You've done a great job.'

'Don't condescend me,' I hissed, propping myself up on one shoulder. 'You owe me an explanation, Paul. I need to know what on earth was going on in there, and what the hell went on before that. I'm trying to be supportive, you know, I didn't say a word when you left, when I've been managing everything here with the kids and the house and work, worried sick about money and the kids and you.'

'I'm sorry,' he said, blinking hard.

I sighed, lying back down. 'I just can't believe that anyone thinks that it's okay to lock a husband and father away from their family, like a prison. I can't believe that you think it's acceptable...' My voice broke. 'Why didn't you contact us, to let us know how you were? I tried you almost every day. I called your phone, I sent messages, I called the centre, I called Damian.'

He sighed, sounding exasperated. 'Don't blame Damian. He's the only one who's helped me.'

My heart sped up. 'The only one who has help you? Are you serious?'

'Oh, Emily, I didn't mean that. You have done so much. It's just that I don't want to upset him.'

'But it's fine to upset me?'

'Emily, you're putting words in my mouth. I'm exhausted and feeling overwhelmed and so glad to see you and the kids. I've missed you so much. I'll explain more, but not right now. I just want to be here with you now and get used to being home. I'm… I'm scared of what happened and I need to process it and take it slowly. I need you, Emily. Please don't be angry with me. I'm sorry.'

He reached over and touched my shoulder. Hot tears spilled from my eyes and I tensed as he pulled me towards him, but let him. As I lay my head on his chest, crying quietly, I wished I could laugh with the joy of having him back but, really, I wanted to scream with the anger I held towards him, and the fear of what would happen now.

Nineteen

Emily

Even at the higher dose, the medication didn't give Cameron a headache, or nausea, or make him agitated, or suicidal. Nothing happened.

I took him back to the psychiatrist for a review, and she increased it again, but still, after another month, there was no change. Dr Davidson tried to do some therapy with him, but eventually, she told me that he wasn't 'engaging' with her. He wasn't trying, but whether it was because he wasn't able to, or just didn't want to, I didn't know.

'I'm starting to think that maybe there's more to this,' she said to me one day, while Cameron was in the waiting room playing on my phone.

'Okay...' I said, stomach clenching.

'The problem is that I can't get through to him psychologically, with therapy. He's difficult to connect with...'

Yes, I wanted to say. *That's what I've been saying since he was a baby.*

'I note that he doesn't seem to be able to concentrate very long, and the school psychologist called me during the week to discuss how they've noticed at school he's still very distracted. I'm wondering about revisiting the idea of using some medication for his attention and concentration.'

I nodded. I would agree to anything at this point. 'Yes, if you think... I just need something to change. To see him like this... he's impossible at home, I ask him to get ready and I find him staring out the window with one sock on, and his grades are getting worse, especially this year.' I pursed my lips and exhaled slowly.

'I do think he's still anxious, and that's one thing that's really blocking him. But I don't know how much of that anxiety is because he can't focus and plan and organise and he knows he's falling behind as the demands of school increase. He's trying to juggle multiple subjects and homework tasks, classrooms to get to, and because of his long-standing social issues, he's trying to manage that too. He's a unique, complex young man but I think if we can target one part of that complexity by addressing his ADHD, then it should have a flow on effect onto his worries and his self-esteem,. Being a fourteen-year-old boy is complicated.'

'Yes. I agree. What medication are you thinking of? I don't know much about them.' That wasn't true, of course. I knew pretty much everything about psychiatric medications in kids. I'd spent enough time on the internet, reading blogs and forums and health websites.

I thought about Paul, the way he'd react. I didn't know why I hadn't told him yet about Cameron's medication or even the fact he was seeing a psychiatrist. I was struck by a feeling of loneliness that I hadn't felt, or allowed myself to feel, since he'd left. I longed to have someone to talk to about this. Once, on a trip to Singapore for a physiotherapy conference, I remember strolling through the Botanical Gardens on my own, aware of how beautiful they were, but feeling disconnected, like I was looking at a photograph on the wall because I had no one to share it with. Just as I wanted to share that with Paul, I wanted to share this decision, to talk about the pros and the cons and have someone back me up. But Paul had been busy, distant. I couldn't talk to him about this.

Dr Davidson smiled, cocking her head to the side sympathetically. 'I do need to go through the side effects with you – there are a few that are common, but manageable, and others that are rare but potentially serious.'

She explained that he'd probably lose his appetite and might not gain weight or grow, but that she'd monitor that. He might get more anxious, and that was one of her biggest concerns, given that he already *was* anxious. And there are rare but serious 'events' of psychosis or heart problems.

I thought of Paul; I *knew* what he'd say. There would be no discussion, and for as long as I could remember, he had had the final say. And now, well, it was even less likely. I blinked hard. He had proven that when *he* took charge of the decisions for our family, we almost lost everything. I was the one coming here with Cameron, and if there was nothing wrong with him, then a psychiatrist wouldn't be telling him to take medication.

'Okay, I'm happy to try them.'

'You don't have to decide today: it's something you might want to talk through with your husband? Cameron told me he's back,' she said gently.

I sat up straight. I nodded. 'He's been back for a while now.'

'It would be good to meet Paul, answer any questions he has.'

I shook my head. 'He finds it hard to get time off work. But I'll talk to him, of course, and to Cameron. But my feeling is that we must try. We can just try, can't we? Then if this medication doesn't work, we could stop it?'

'Yes, yes, of course. Look, why don't I give you the prescription today and you can think about it. Call me if you have any other questions, and I'll give you some information to take home with you to read. I'll talk about it now with Cameron too, and let's review it in a few weeks at our next appointment.'

I sighed, then reached down for my handbag. 'Sounds great. Thank you, doctor, I really appreciate everything you're doing to try and help us.'

'That's why I'm here,' she smiled.

Outside, Cameron looked up from the phone in the waiting room, then stood up. 'My turn?'

I nodded, then as he walked past me, I put my arm around his shoulders and gave him a hug. 'Your turn. I'll be right here.'

A few weeks later, I waved at Ceecee as I swung the car round into a spot parallel to the beach. I took some cash out of my purse and tucked it into the pocket of my yoga pants, then hid my purse in the glove compartment. I grabbed my cap from the passenger seat, hurried out and locked the car behind me.

'Sorry,' I called as I approached her.

'Don't apologise,' Ceecee said. 'I've only just arrived myself. Cameron?'

I laughed. 'Not this time. He's been, better… It was Paul this time.'

'Oh God,' she laughed. 'Which way do you want to walk?'

I pointed south. 'Less people this way.'

We set off at a brisk pace. When Paul was away, I had spent every ounce of my energy, if it could be weighed like an ingredient, trying to keep the kids and myself afloat. Now he was back, and even though he spent most of his time at work, or at his nightly meetings and *contemplations*, I needed to make time for myself again. I'd been swallowing down my protests every time he went out to a 'meeting'; he wasn't gambling, and I couldn't complain about him going to work, or his treatment. We had money coming in steadily, even though it was never enough. He was healthy, he wasn't drinking, he wasn't going out all night, he looked amazing. But underneath such a dramatic change, I felt uneasy about how much of himself had been lost in that transition too.

'How are things with you?' I asked, and listened as Ceecee told me about her patients, and her kids. I smiled and sympathised until she asked me how things were with me.

'Have you heard anything from Will about Cameron at school?'

'No,' she said. 'But maybe that's a good thing?'

I looked at her and nodded. 'He's doing well,' I said, then laughed. 'I should explain that: he's still difficult, he's still rigid,

146

but he can focus now, he's doing better at school, according to the teachers, and that means he's happier.'

'The medication?'

'Yep, has to be. Look, don't get me wrong, I still think there's more to it all, but for now, things have improved.'

'Paul's back too,' she said gently.

'I know,' I said. 'I know that makes me less stressed and I know that means that we're all more settled, but he was like this before Paul...' My voice trailed off as we both jumped at the sound of a bicycle bell behind us. We moved over to the left. 'I don't know why they can't go on the road.' I shook my head.

'Have you told Paul yet?'

'About the medication?'

'Yes, the medication!' she laughed.

I looked at her, then shook my head. I'd been meaning to tell him, but I just never seemed to get the chance, and it seemed easier to avoid that conversation.

She raised her eyebrows.

'I know, I know. I will. It's just that he won't even let the kids have a fizzy drink any more, never mind stimulant drugs!'

We both laughed, but I was uneasy. I needed to tell him.

'How is he, anyway?'

'Good, good,' I said brightly. 'He's not gambling, he's working hard, he's not drinking, he's not eating meat...'

'Wowsers,' she laughed. 'Sounds like he's given up all the good stuff.'

'Yeah, it's a bit weird. I mean, I can't complain, right? How many times did I nag him about drinking too much? But I don't know, I just wish that maybe he wouldn't gamble but could still be himself. He's not letting the kids watch the TV when he's home, and when we eat together it's all this healthy stuff.'

Ceecee laughed. 'That's what we're all meant to be doing, isn't it?'

I forced myself to laugh. 'You're right.'

But when I thought back to how the kids had jumped when they heard his car in the driveway, and ran to turn the TV off, and how Cameron had asked me if he could sneak in a burger when I picked him up from school so that his father wouldn't know, I felt apprehensive.

'Anyway, he's off caffeine too. Which means I need a double shot when we finish this walk.'

'Let's make it a triple,' she said. 'Let's walk faster so we get to the coffee and muffin sooner.'

–

The auditorium was full of parents and siblings and grandparents, chattering. Tilly was so excited about the dance show, after hours and hours of rehearsals and costumes and hair and make-up. I had tried to help her this afternoon with her stage make-up, drawing wings on her eyes and using a brush to get the red lipstick on her. Paul and Cameron had stayed out of our way, playing Yahtzee in the front room. I had dropped her off a couple of hours ago to get ready for the show, and now, here we were to watch her. I felt restless, wondering if she was nervous backstage, if she'd eaten the snacks I had given her and gone to the loo. And I was also restless because since my walk this morning with Ceecee, I knew that I had to tell Paul about Cameron seeing a psychiatrist and his medication. He deserved to know.

'Looking forward to this?' I smiled at Paul as he squeezed past an older couple – grandparents, I assumed – and took his seat next to me. He raised his eyebrows. He waved at some of the other parents he knew a few rows behind us.

'Maybe you should have stayed home with Cameron.' Cameron had jumped at the chance to stay home and I knew he'd have whipped out his iPad as soon as the car had driven off.

He laughed. 'Yes, I think I'll probably wish I had as soon as this starts. Modern dance is not my thing…'

'She's doing jazz and hip-hop too,' I said with a smile. 'Not just contemporary.' I sat down and arranged my jacket over my lap. I settled in the chair, waved at a few other people then spoke, casually. 'Cameron seems good recently, doesn't he?'

'Yeah, he does,' he said, flicking through the programme. 'They both do.'

'He really struggled when you were away,' I said. I wanted to tell myself to be quiet, to not go any further, to leave it. Why was I talking about it now? But I had started and I had to keep going.

'It was hard for us all,' Paul said.

I put my arm on his. 'Oh sweetie, I know. I didn't mean that. It's just that, when you were gone, he really struggled, and the school called me in again because there was a huge incident when he got violent, and, well, they said I had to take him for some help, to a doctor, a psychiatrist.'

'What?' he swivelled round to look at me, then glanced around him and spoke quietly, his eyes accusing. 'And you're telling me now, here?'

'Ssh, Paul. I'm sorry, you're right, this isn't the right place.' What was I thinking? Telling him here? But I knew exactly what I was thinking: that I could quickly tell him, and he wouldn't be able to get angry because all these people were around to protect me and soon the curtains would open and the lights would dim and we wouldn't be able to talk about it at all. 'It's not a big deal.'

'It *is* a big deal!' he hissed. 'I have spent months learning about myself, and one thing I've learned is that our behaviour is not something that can be fixed by going to see so-called specialists, when all they want to do is hand out pills. Do you know what that shit does to your brain? Tell me you haven't—'

I knew that under my make-up, my face was drained of colour. My heart pounded. 'No, no, of course not, I'm just saying...' What the hell was I saying? I shouldn't have said anything, now I was ruining Tilly's special night because I wouldn't be able to concentrate, and she would know when she saw us afterwards that we'd had a fight no matter how much we tried to hide it from her.

I took a deep breath and spoke quietly. 'I just mean… But haven't you noticed how much calmer he is now in the mornings? I'm not shouting at him to hurry up and he's not storming off to his room—'

'That's because we're all different now. I'm different, I understand myself so much better, and you've changed too. Everyone is happier, because we're getting back to who we are, Emily.'

'It might also be that I'm not yelling anymore *because* he's better. It works both ways, you know?'

'No, it's because we have stopped putting terrible things into our bodies and our brains. We've gone back to what's important: real food, real relationships, no YouTube and Facebook and all the crap that the screens do to their brains. That's why he's different.'

There was a hush coming over the theatre now and people turned to face the front. 'I just meant to say that he struggled but now you're back, everything seems so much better,' I whispered.

'If he needs help, he can stop putting all that crap into his body and he can come with me to the Phoenix meetings and learn about himself. No doctors. Seriously, Emily. I don't want him near a psychiatrist. He's just a kid.'

I nodded. 'I know, I know, I'm sorry, I just wanted to let you know.'

My face flushed with the lies that were tripping off my tongue, as I knew that now, there was absolutely no way that I could tell him about the medication. I should stop it.

I should.

Twenty

Paul

Alasdair was already waiting for me when I arrived. He was sitting at a small round table in the back corner of the café, wearing dark blue jeans and a business shirt, open at the collar, his sunglasses on his head. I had planned to be early, to give myself a chance to settle my nerves. Damian had said it would be hard to see people from my old life for the first time. He wasn't sure I was ready yet, but Alasdair had been calling me for weeks and I couldn't fob him off. He knew where I had been, and why; Emily had told me that she'd had to tell him after that night at the casino. Besides, how could I ever prove to myself, never mind Damian, that I could cope unless I tried? Alasdair had suggested a drink; I told him I couldn't do that yet. He had paused and then suggested breakfast. Safe. Yes.

I had an odd sense when I saw him out of the corner of my eye that Alasdair was a stranger. It had been months now since I'd seen him, but it was more than that. Everyone seemed different to me since the change; I supposed I did to them, too. I could see things around me that I never noticed before, the things placed there to tempt and trick me. But I knew I could resist those things now, see them for what they were.

Alasdair scraped his chair back and half stood up as he saw me approach. I raised a hand in a wave, then walked towards him, squeezing past the other full tables on my way. He held his hand out, which threw me a little. We didn't usually shake hands, but I clasped it, gave a half-hearted shake then clasped my other arm on his shoulder. I kind of patted his back; he cleared his throat, pulled away from me and we sat down.

'You're looking good,' he said.

'Cheers. You too. You haven't taken up cycling, have you? You got some lycra shorts under those jeans?' Alasdair had always hated sport; he was the smart one.

He shrugged and smiled. 'Jane was on at me to join her gym, so I've been going to these boxing classes. It's good. Nothing like you used to do...'

I shook my head. 'That was a long time ago.'

We both sat in silence, looking at the menu. A bearded waiter appeared, with one of those holes in his ear with a black plastic disc in it. Alasdair ordered a flat white. My mouth watered at the thought of coffee, but I knew that giving into one craving could only lead to other things far more dangerous than caffeine. I ordered a peppermint tea.

'Interesting.' Alasdair smiled.

'The tea or that ridiculous hole in his ear?'

'Both are... unusual.'

I smiled. 'Gaping holes in wobbly earlobes is perhaps a little stranger than my choice of beverage.'

'Fair call.'

'It's part of my treatment,' I said. 'Like a whole life transformation, you know. No caffeine, no alcohol, no gluten, no dairy...'

He nodded slowly. 'No taste...'

I forced a stiff laugh and swiped at him with the menu. He ducked and put his hands in front of his face like a boxer. He was always such a dweeb.

We both looked at our menus again. There was hardly anything on here I could eat, and I knew Alasdair would comment on what I ordered. I started to feel my face heat up.

The coffee and my tea arrived. Alasdair spoke seriously. 'How are you doing, Paul?'

'Yeah, you know. I'm working lots now, trying to exercise, when my knee is up to it, meditating, working on myself.' I looked down, swirling the tea bag around in my cup by the string.

He was nodding slowly. 'Emily told me about... Well, you know she called me that day you disappeared.'

'Yeah. I was a dickhead. But I'm better now. I've learned so much about myself, and the world. It's all clearer now.' I couldn't look up. 'Have you spoken to Mum?'

'No. Well, I have to speak to Mum almost every bloody day – now she's worked out how to use Facetime – about some complaint she has about the neighbours, or the BBC, or the Tories in London, but not about you. No point.'

'No, no point. I've spoken to her a few times, but not about this. It would only worry her.'

'That's what I thought. Anyway, Paul, it sounds like you've got it under control. So, I think if you need to drink herbal tea and eat rabbit food to get yourself back on track, then that's a pretty good compromise.'

'Thanks.' My voice was quiet, and I only just got the words out.

'So,' Alasdair said loudly in a cheery voice. 'They got any tofu and sprouts on the menu?'

I smiled, relieved at his humour, and managed to look up at him. 'I reckon I can find something tasteless here. Bit of extra Tabasco on it and anything tastes good.'

After breakfast, I walked out of the café lighter, with the relief that it had gone well. My brother was fine with me changing my life, and that meant a lot. I was fine with it too, more than fine, but doubts still crept up every so often, a little voice asking me what harm a coffee would do. The voice was soothing, familiar, persuasive, seductive. I'd heard it many times before.

Later that afternoon, I fixed a smile on with the camera pointing at my face. The photographer had already barked at me to point at the menu, to shake Damian's hand, to sit at one of the outdoor tables with a slice of pizza in my hand gazing into the distance with a glass of red to my lips. I knew that my face was frozen into my media grin, but I had done this so many times that I felt like me again.

All the doubts I had before meeting Alasdair vanished. These past few months had been amazing; there is no other word for it. Everything that they'd told me while I was in Treetops, everything they had told me about how my life would turn around if only I believed in Phoenix, had come true. I was as fit and healthy as I'd ever been, I was not only working, but the restaurant was ready to open and couldn't be going better. Damian had given me a pay rise, and so even after paying a percentage to him and to Phoenix, some of the financial pressure was off. People looked up to me, and I held my back straight now. My mind was bright, and life couldn't be better.

Even my relationship with the children, and Emily, had improved. I could sense Emily was a little wary of me, by the way she hesitated when I said things about the way she still chose to live, but she was changing, and I knew she'd come round, as would the kids. I didn't blame her; I had been wary too, I had resisted initially. But now, she's at least respecting what I say about not filling our home with negativity and poisons, allowing us to get back to the way we were always meant to live. We are all going to be amazing.

I stretched subtly as the photographer asked me to stand in front of the glass doors of the restaurant, just to the side of the lettering on the glass door: 'PAULIE'S'.

'You're the man, Paul,' Damian had said when he told me. 'It's perfect. You're the face of this, you're the reason why it's going to be a huge success because I've seen what you can do when you believe in something.'

'Just need to make me a bit Italian, though, eh?'

He had shrugged and laughed. 'They'll love your Scottish accent, but the Scots aren't famous for their pasta and pizza, eh?'

I had felt my chest puff out like I'd just scored the deciding goal in extra time. God, I missed this feeling. Success, pride.

I put my hands in the pockets of my new grey suit, trying to look like I was slouching naturally, my head cocked to the side and smiling, and I could see in the photographer's eyes that I looked good. It had been worth every penny to go into the centre.

I would never go back to how things were before. I was in control of my life now, and Damian and all the others at Phoenix were there to make sure that I would never fall again.

Twenty-One

Emily

Mornings became normal for the first time I can remember in our lives. It was because Cameron was on medication, and that reduced everyone's stress. Paul bumbled around with his rabbit food and hot water with lemon, and Cameron would just... eat breakfast. No arguing, no delaying, no spending hours in the shower, no inspecting each spoonful to make sure that it was just right. He was just eating breakfast.

And so, it was even more heartbreaking when his decline began again.

–

I didn't notice his slide back down at first; it wasn't dramatic. I noticed some hesitation, he began to get stuck in his own thoughts, then more preoccupied, irritable, impulsive. I told myself that maybe it was just a blip. Maybe he'd grown, and he needed a higher dose of medication, or maybe he was becoming resistant to them and, just like an alcoholic, he needed more and more to get the same effect. Or maybe it was just a bad night's sleep, a bad day, a bad week.

One morning, at breakfast time, I watched him staring at his Weet-Bix, muttering to himself. 'Cameron,' I said.

His eyes shifted towards me and his lips stopped.

'You eating?'

'I'm not hungry.'

'You can't go to school without breakfast,' I tried to say it light heartedly though the strain it took to make my voice sound light was immense.

His eyes darted around and knew his anxiety was flooding him and me talking to him was making him sink into it. 'I said I'm not hungry, Mum,' he said, looking down.

As my muscles tensed with the strain of keeping calm, a jolt of déjà vu punched me in the chest. Except it wasn't the trick of déjà vu, this was reality. We were back to where we started.

I looked away, grabbed a sponge, and began wiping the island bench top. 'Off you go, then. Take a piece of fruit with you at least.'

I wiped the bench again, then dried it with a tea towel, then wiped it again until I heard his room door close. Only then did I let out the breath I'd been holding and clutch the edge of the kitchen bench. Can you imagine if your child had cancer, and you thought he was in remission, and then one day you saw a spatter of bruises on his skin and inside, you just knew it was back? That's how I felt. This illness was killing him. It was taking away every possibility he had in life: for relationships, for education, for work, family, for happiness. It would kill him.

On the drive to school, I chattered on about rubbish the whole way there, aware that I was taking corners too quickly in my hurry to get him there before he was so late that he'd be in trouble, because that would set him off even more.

'Did you take your tablets this morning, Cam?' I said, casually, or so I hoped.

He replied almost instantly. 'Yes.'

'Are you sure? I know it can be hard to remember every day.'

'Come on Cameron, own up,' said Tilly from the back seat, in a teasing voice.

'Tilly, not now,' I said sharply.

Cameron turned his body away from mine and looked out of the window of the car.

Tilly kept niggling at him. 'Cameron, Mum asked you a question...'

'Shut up!' he shouted, turning around in his seat. 'I don't see you taking tablets every day.'

'I don't need to,' she said, 'I'm not—'

'Hey!' I shouted before she could finish her sentence. 'That's enough. Tilly, you're lucky that you're healthy. Some people, like your brother, have an illness, and a mental illness is no different to—'

'Diabetes. I know, Mum...' I knew without needing to look in the rear-view mirror that she'd be rolling her eyes by the way she drawled her words. I squeezed the steering wheel.

'Both of you need to stop this. Cameron, I expect you to be honest with me. You're turning fifteen soon; you need to start taking some responsibility and stop acting like a child.'

'Stop treating me like one, then.'

I exhaled slowly. 'Fine,' I said. 'I trust you.'

'No, you don't! Or you wouldn't be constantly asking me about them.'

I glanced at him then back at the road in front of me. 'Okay, darling, let's talk about this later.'

'There's nothing to talk about.'

I shook my head and exhaled slowly to stop myself reacting. I drummed my fingers on the steering wheel. Some days I wished I could drop them off and just keeping on driving.

I dropped Tilly off at her school first, then Cameron, and then I parked around the corner from school and called Dr Davidson's office. Her secretary took a message and said she would return my call the following week, when she was back in the office. That was too late. I needed her now. I ended the call then threw the phone down on the passenger seat. Where was she when I really needed her? It was times like this that I realised how far apart Paul and I had grown. In any normal relationship, in this situation, a wife would call her husband, wouldn't she? But he didn't know. It was impossible to think that he hadn't noticed the difference in Cameron. But then again, he'd been spending so much time out of the house at his meetings or whatever the hell he did that his life seemed to be moving in a different direction to ours.

–

Paul didn't get home until after ten that night; I was watching a re-run of a renovation show, wishing I could go to bed, but unable to calm myself enough to sleep until I knew Paul was home, pushing away the fear that he was lying to me and he was back at the casino. I focused on the show: the tinkly music and the deep voice of the presenter were soothing, and I loved to see other people's lives go wrong when they went over budget and had to live in a caravan, but it always ended up good at the end. The house was always built, in the end.

Paul's keys grated in the lock. The door closed, and I heard the two thuds as Paul took his shoes off, then he walked through to the living room.

I forced myself to smile. 'If you'd headed straight for the shower, I was going to check your phone for messages from your girlfriend.'

He frowned, scanning my face to work out if I was joking, then smiled too. 'Can't think of anything worse. Who would have the energy to start dating again?'

'And you'd have to have her kids. Think of that – nappies, sleepless nights, toddler tantrums. Best to stick with what you know, yes?'

He was still making himself smile. 'I couldn't do much better.'

I tried to smile. 'How was it?'

'Good,' he said, nodding. 'Good.'

'Still can't tell me anything?'

'There's nothing to tell.'

I nodded now, sighed, then followed his gaze to the television. 'Oh, for God's sake, it's a reno show.' But I switched it off.

I stood up, picked up my mug and the biscuit jar from my feet and walked towards the kitchen. As I poured the cold tea down the sink and put the mug in the dishwasher, he went into the bathroom. When he came out, his face was shiny and clean looking. He looked younger, like when we'd first met. I had to admit, being a teetotaller suited him. I thought back to the couple of glasses of wine I'd had with my reheated curry from the back of the freezer. Maybe I should give it up too. But I had needed it today. And it was Paul who became addicted to things, not me.

I reached up to touch his cheek and held it there for a moment. 'I love you.'

'Me too.'

I smiled. 'You love you too?'

He smiled a tired smile. 'I'm just going to read before bed.'

'Me too. I've been waiting up for you. I wanted to chat with you about Cameron.'

He sighed. 'What about him?'

'Don't be like that, Paul!' I snapped. I stopped myself from saying that I'd been to work too, picked up and fed the kids, checked their homework, tidied up, folded the washing and left it in little piles outside the respective bedrooms while worrying about the fact that Cameron's light was still shining beneath his door, and then waited up for him. 'I'm worried...'

'Emily.' He rubbed his eyes. 'I'm really tired, it's been a long day. Is it anything new, or can we talk about it tomorrow?'

'Never mind, then,' I said, then stormed off to the bedroom. While I waited for the doctor to call me back and Paul to have enough energy to talk to me about our children, Cameron was getting sicker. And I could not stand by and watch that happen when I knew exactly what he needed.

I tapped on Cameron's door before I went to bed. 'Just me,' I said, waiting for him to answer. I wasn't silly enough to just barge into an adolescent boy's room. But there was no answer; I knocked louder. I knew he'd be sitting on his bed, headphones on, doing something on his computer. I used to insist that the two of them only went online if they were in the family room, where I could keep an eye on them, but, like a lot of other things, I gave up on that. Paul didn't know they were on the internet in there, when they said they were doing their homework, but I did, and at the moment, I didn't care.

'What?' I heard him say. I slowly pushed the door open and spoke through the gap, keeping my eyes down.

'Can I come in?'

'Yeah.'

I opened the door further and slowly walked in as he closed his lap top and took off his headphones. I sat on the end of his bed. 'It's really late.'

He nodded. 'I can't sleep. I'm just watching a movie.'

'I'm sorry about earlier. In the car. I've been thinking about what you said, and maybe you're right. When Dad was your age, he wasn't far off leaving school to play professional sport. There's only a couple more years of school then you'll be off to uni.'

'Maybe,' he said quietly.

I nodded, smoothing the blankets with my hand. 'Yeah, maybe. If you want to. Anyway, I just wanted to say that I know you're becoming older. But I still think of you as my little boy, and I worry about you.' I looked up at him. 'Are you listening?'

'Yeah.'

'So how about this? I'll still look after the tablets – they're strong and I need to keep hold of them. But if you promise me you will take them every morning, I won't ask or hassle you, I'll just leave them outside your room, and you will take them yourself. What do you think?'

'Okay.'

'Cameron, you know how important it is for you to take them, yes?'

'They make me too skinny,' he mumbled, head down. 'It's hard for rugby.'

I closed my eyes for a moment. Of course, he'd noticed that he'd lost his appetite and maybe a little bit of weight. But what was a bit of weight loss compared to being ill? I hadn't thought he'd care. Tilly was always going on about her weight but that's what girls do. But I supposed being skinny wasn't good for a boy like Cameron, when all the other guys were trying to bulk up.

'How about I ask your dad to take you to the gym with him to do some weights? Maybe get you some protein shakes and I'll make you extra smoothies? I've seen how much better you are, Cameron, with the tablets. But if it keeps on being a problem, then we'll talk to the doctor again, see if there's a different one. What do you think?'

'Okay,' he mumbled, looking down at his hands. His cheeks were flushed. I reached out and touched his arms and had to trust that he would do the right thing.

'Promise?' I said.

He nodded. 'Promise.'

—

I tried to trust Cameron and let him take some control. I brought his tablets to him on a little plate and left them outside his door with his glass of orange juice first thing, and they disappeared. But nothing changed, and I knew he was lying to me. A mother's instincts are always right. A mother bear doesn't just let her cubs figure things out for themselves when the risks are immense; she watches them every moment, ready to clamp onto the scruff of their necks and drag them back home to safety if they're in danger. So, I had to break my promise.

—

He could have thought of a better hiding place. Flushed them down the toilet maybe, or put them in the bin outside, but then again, he hated the smell of the sun-warmed old rubbish and the thought of touching a redback when he put his fingers under the rim of the lid.

Really, Cameron, I thought as I opened his desk drawer and saw a little white pill roll towards me, and, when I felt in the back corner of the drawer, there were dozens, of both his antidepressant and his ADHD capsules. *You're smarter than this.*

I held the pills in my hand and sat down on his bed. This is what our relationship had come to. Him lying to me; me checking up on him because in my bones, in the marrow where a mother's instincts sit, I knew that something was wrong.

I called Dr Davidson again and said it was urgent. She called me back. The kids were at home, but they were only too happy to lock themselves away in their rooms when I went out into the garden to take the call, shouting to them that it was a work call. I told her what had happened. As I waited for her to speak, I pulled some dead leaves off the lemon tree and dropped them into the vegetable patch, overgrown with twiggy parsley that had gone to seed.

'Is he still eating and sleeping?' she asked.

'Well, yes, he's eating better than he was on them. I don't think he's sleeping so well, his light was on late last night, after I went to bed. He seems tired.'

'Are *you* sleeping?'

I froze for a moment, and then realised that I had begun to cry. I wiped quickly at my eyes and gathered myself. 'A little.'

Her voice was calm and quiet. 'Do you have any concerns that he might have thoughts of self-harm?'

'No, no.' That had never been a symptom of Cameron's – thank God. But I knew why she was asking and what she was going to say next.

'The problem is, Emily, that we can't force him to take medication, unless he's a risk to himself or—'

'Others. I know. I know that! But why do I have to wait until my son is about to jump in front of a train before I can help him? You know as well as I do that he's not well. He's been doing so much better on the tablets, and I *know* it won't change who he is and he's always going to have... challenges... but at least he'd been vaguely happy, going to school, not tortured!' I kicked at a lump of some yucca that had put down roots after being blown into our yard.

'I know, Emily. I know. But what can we do? Force him to swallow tablets he doesn't want to? All we can do is keep trying to persuade him, and let him know we're there for him.'

'When he gets like this he can't be persuaded.'

'He was before, Emily. He did take them of his own accord, remember? Can you bring him in to see me tomorrow, I've got a spot at 3.30?'

'I can't tell him that I was snooping in his room.' I glanced back towards the house.

'You don't have to. Let's just go down the path that we've noticed that he doesn't seem so well, give him a chance to explain. There might be a simple reason for this. Can I ask about—'

'His dad? Best not to. We'll come in tomorrow afternoon.'

I hung up the phone and as Dr Davidson went back to her own family, who would never have any problems like this, I walked back down the garden to my own. I couldn't wait for Cameron to make that decision. A good mother doesn't let their children go. She knows when her child is in danger, and she does everything she can to keep him safe.

––

It was as easy as getting two spoons, putting the antidepressant between them and crushing it until it became a powder. The stimulant was easier: I just opened up the little capsule, poured the powder out and mixed it all up together. I mixed them in his juice, next to the couple of pills that he would hide in his drawer. He always drank the juice. I wondered if he'd notice the taste – he was so sensitive about things like that – but he never did. I suspected he knew, and he was happy for me to do it, to save face. Sometimes it's harder to admit that you've been wrong, and to go along with the pretence. Dr Davidson must have known what I was doing too; she must have seen the steady improvement in him. I knew that when he got better, Cameron would agree that it had been the right thing to do.

Twenty-Two

Emily

'I've done something awful, Ceecee.'

Ceecee's eyes widened and she pushed my glass of wine nearer to me. She'd picked up Tilly with her daughter, Ruby, from orchestra after school and taken her back to her place. The girls were upstairs supposedly doing their homework but no doubt taking selfies or sending messages to boys. I caught myself as I had that thought; I loved that she was upstairs with a friend pretending to be doing her homework. That's what normal, healthy, teenage kids do, isn't it? If only Cameron was hanging out with his friends, sending messages to girls. Paul was picking him up from school for some father-son time, which probably meant they were back at home with Cameron sitting in his room and Paul reading a pamphlet or finding a new thing to reject.

'What? Tell me?' She was frowning.

'It's about Cameron's medication.'

She sipped her wine and nodded. 'Go on.'

'He's stopped taking it.'

'Oh no, why?'

'Who knows? Because he can.' I sighed and picked up a crumb from the granite bench top. 'I'm being unfair. I know he doesn't like the side effects. But he'd been getting so much better.'

'So, what's the awful thing that you've done?'

I took a deep breath. 'Okay, I haven't told anyone this. I crushed up his tablet and put it in his juice.'

Ceecee laughed; I stared at her, my heart racing. This wasn't what I'd expected her to do. 'What's funny?' I said, making myself smile.

'Oh, sorry, Emily, I don't mean to laugh. Is that all? It's just like telling your kids that the worm tablets are chocolate. Who cares?'

'These aren't just worming tablets though, they're psychostimulants. And he's growing up, it should be his decision,' I said, feebly.

'Oh, what rubbish.' She waved her hand in the air. 'You're his mother, he's a child and he's ill. They're prescribed by a doctor. What else are you meant to do? And as he gets better, you'll be able to tell him because then he'll be able to see what a difference it's made and make the right decision.'

'I haven't told Paul yet.'

She raised her eyebrows.

'Don't look at me like that, Ceecee, you know what he's like… He's getting worse, you know, the more time he spends at this centre surrendering himself to higher powers or contemplations or whatever.'

'Sounds a bit bizarre, Em.'

'Oh God, it bloody is!' I laughed. 'I can't quite believe that I'm sitting here telling you I'm tricking my kid into taking medication and my husband has turned into some freak. It's like a bad soap opera.' I smiled but my eyes were wet.

She frowned at me.

I took a sip of my wine to give myself a moment. I had tried to find out more about Phoenix. There was hardly anything online, but I had found a forum where some people who had left it spoke about how much money they'd given the organisation, about how they'd been pressured to recruit more people to join, and the hypocrisies they'd seen with the group taking money from people to fund lifestyles that seemed to rely very heavily on modern conveniences: holidays, boats, expensive clothes and houses. I was uneasy about it all but didn't know how to tackle it with Paul. 'I don't know, really, it all sounds like nonsense to me. Not that being healthy is nonsense, but it's taking it too far, and there's something about the money involved that makes me worry. He doesn't talk much to me about it; he knows what I'd say. But on the other hand, it works, you know? He's looking well, he's not gambling, he's working again, earning money and he seems happy.'

'But are you?'

'Happy?'

'Of course.' I looked down.

'Really?'

'I don't know. He's changed. And I know he had to change, or something did – we were so close to being ruined. But I suppose part of what I loved about him was his edge, you know, the fun and the risk taking. That was Paul. And now I'm married to a vegan, teetotal, anti-TV, anti-internet hippy. Me!' I laughed as I picked up the bottle of wine and topped up our glasses. 'God, I need another glass, we can't have it in the house anymore.'

She shook her head slowly. 'Who would have imagined? Can't imagine you ever putting that in your list of wants in a man.'

My cheeks burned; it must have been the alcohol. I had hoped this was just a phase, and that after he'd been out of Treetops for a while, he'd relax a little bit. But the opposite had happened, and doubts started to creep into my mind about our future. My skin tingled, and this time I knew it was the shame of thinking like that. Paul was my husband. But he was so different to how he'd been before that I didn't know how we could build a life around him.

'You don't think Paul would understand, if you told him about the medication?'

I shook my head quickly. 'Not a chance. I tried bringing it up and he shot me down.' I put my hand into the shape of a gun in the air. 'He got all worked up about our brains being poisoned by medicine and how doctors are just part of the problem and don't know what they're talking about. Honestly, he'd be furious.'

Ceecee hesitated, wiping at a drop of wine on the bench top. 'Emily, are you sure Paul is okay? He's not, I don't know, ill? This all sounds pretty crazy.'

I rubbed my face. 'I guess it does.'

Ceecee spoke quietly. 'Does Paul need to know about Cam's medication?'

I sipped my wine again and pictured Cameron, how he was when he was on the medication, when everything was just calm, and even if he wasn't swinging from the roof in glee, he had relaxed. I was not willing to go back to the way things were. 'No. I don't see why Paul needs to know. Not yet.'

'Okay, here's my two cents, for what it's worth. You are Cameron's mum and it's you who has dealt with him day in day out. *You* know what's best. You must trust yourself. If it was me, I wouldn't give it another thought.'

And so, I didn't.

–

I was more nervous about going to dinner with Damian now than I had been when I first met him almost three years ago, when he had first offered Paul the job. So much had happened in that time. I had lunch with his wife, Shona, once or twice before Paul went to rehab, but it had always felt awkward and forced as we had little in common except for our husbands' jobs. And, after he came out, I was too busy. Yes, I could have made time, but I felt ashamed that she and Damian knew more about my husband's problems than I did. At least I'd had a couple of glasses of wine at Ceecee's this afternoon to relax me, because there would be none at the dinner.

Paul seemed relaxed about tonight at least. He hummed as he dressed and after we'd said goodbye to the kids and babysitter, he tapped his fingers in time to the classical music CD he'd put on as he drove.

I was determined to make an effort tonight. After talking with Ceecee, I still couldn't shake the guilt about not telling Paul about the medication, never mind the fact that I was also deceiving Cameron. Her words about Paul's ideas sounding crazy still echoed through me, but if this was his life now, I had to try to meet him half way.

I hadn't been to Damian's home before, but of course, Paul had. We drove up to the gates of a beautiful, white art deco house. My eyes widened.

'Wow,' I said. 'Look at those views of the harbour. You can even see the Opera House over there.'

'Wait until you see them from the balconies.'

I followed Paul to the front door, which opened before we'd even knocked. Damian greeted us with a big smile. He wore a pale pink polo shirt and navy chinos, and grey deck shoes, and his hair, as always, looked thick and glossy. A small white dog yapped around his ankles until he shooed it away with his feet. He shook Paul's hand, then clasped both my shoulders and kissed me on each cheek. 'You look beautiful, Emily. Welcome, please.' He stepped back. 'Please come in.'

We weren't late, but already the others were there, and looked settled. I had the sense of turning up to a surprise party. I blushed as everyone stood up and started to greet us. It was the same group that I'd first met at that dinner at the casino: Lucas and Amina, and Tim and Sam. Shona appeared from beside me and surprised me with a warm hug. I handed her the flowers I'd brought, a bunch of Australian natives, and blushed even more as she gushed over them. I wished I was handing over a bottle of champagne that we could open. It felt strange; I don't think I'd ever been to a gathering in someone's house where we didn't start with an alcoholic drink. I scolded myself. My husband was a recovering addict, and he had told me that Damian was, too. And the others, all those in Phoenix, had been addicted to something or had some problems. It was selfish of me to crave a drink; I could cope for one evening.

With a glass of sparkling water, with a slice of lemon, in my hand, we sat outside on the balcony. The views were magnificent, looking out over the harbour as dusk set in over Sydney. Below us, in the terraced garden, there was a swimming pool and wooden deck. No wonder Paul envied Damian so much: this house would have cost millions of dollars.

'You have a beautiful home,' I directed to Damian and Shona, as we all sat down on the balcony.

'Oh,' Shona waved a hand in the air. 'We've had it for ages, way before the property boom.'

'Lucky.' I smiled, although I knew that even before Sydney's house prices began to rise exponentially, this house would never have been inexpensive.

'Not luck. Hard work, that's what got us here. We've got high hopes for Paul – and you,' Damian said. 'He's a hard worker, just like I was.'

'He is,' I nodded, realising how true it was, although I resented their assumption that I was envious of their house. Maybe I was being too sensitive; I *was* envious of this house. But Damian was right: for all Paul's faults, he always gave one hundred per cent to everything he did. He had never been lazy, or even content with what he had. While it had frustrated me at times, I knew it gave him the drive to always strive for excellence. Would he be content with a house like this? I wasn't sure that he would ever be satisfied, but perhaps that was why I loved him. I felt heat in my cheeks; I did love him.

'We're very proud of him,' Lucas said, sitting forward.

Paul laughed a little too loudly and I turned to him, watching him shift in his seat and shrug.

My back stiffened. 'Yes, me too.'

Damian continued. 'I don't know what Paul's told you about us, and our involvement with Phoenix, but we've all been where he was. We...' he waved his hand around the table 'were all addicted to alcohol.'

Shona laughed. 'Hey, not us! Just the men.' Sam and Amina laughed too, and I joined in, though it didn't seem that funny.

'No, but you ladies were a huge part of our recoveries, and still are.'

I nodded, blinking hard as I realised that my eyes were filling with tears. Paul put his hand on my leg and squeezed gently.

'Emily, I wanted to have this dinner to acknowledge everything you have done for Paul, because even though it's been an awful journey for him, and you, we're so glad that he found Phoenix.'

Did everyone here know about his gambling? I knew Damian did, and therefore assumed Shona was aware, but the others too? My face burned.

Amina leaned forwards now, tucking her long black hair behind her ears. 'Emily, if you ever need to talk to anyone about what you've gone through, come and talk to me, or Sam, or Shona of course. We understand.'

'Thank you,' I said quickly, 'that's very kind. But I'm fine. *We're* fine. And thank you again, Shona and Damian, for having us tonight. It's very kind of you.' My mind raced as I tried to think of a way to steer the conversation away from my dirty laundry. 'So, Damian, how is the restaurant going? It looks fantastic!'

He leaned back in his chair. 'It's great. Thanks to the hard work of everyone here, especially your husband.'

Paul shook his head. 'Not me. I've hardly done anything.'

They continued to congratulate and flatter each other as I felt more and more disconnected from my surroundings and wished I was back in my own house, or in Ceecee's messy kitchen. My breath had quickened; I felt trapped. Sweat beaded on my upper lip despite the breeze blowing off the dark waters of the harbour below us. My vision began to waver and panic started to take hold. What was wrong with me? I clutched Paul's arm. Everyone turned to me. 'Sorry,' I said. 'Can I use the bathroom?'

'I'll show you,' Sam said. She got up, and I excused myself and followed her.

After a few minutes running cold water over my wrists and drinking water from the tap, I made myself breathe slowly and deeply. I was making a fool of myself. Everyone was being lovely, but I couldn't shake my uneasiness. I closed my eyes for a moment, then cleared my throat, pulled my shoulders back then stepped outside.

Sam was still there.

'Oh,' I said, jumping. 'Sorry, I didn't realise you were waiting too. I just felt a bit faint all of a sudden.' I held the door open.

She smiled and shook her head. 'I was waiting for you. Come and sit down.'

I frowned, glancing out to the balcony, then back to Sam, who had sat on the couch.

'Okay,' I said, hesitantly, sitting on an armchair opposite her.

'I just wanted to talk to you in private. They can get pretty intense.'

I shook my head. 'No, no, they're just being supportive.'

She reached for my hand; I let her take it though wanted to snatch it away. 'Tim told me, about Paul.'

'Oh.' So they did know. My cheeks burned.

'Don't be embarrassed. I know how you're feeling. It was the same for me when Tim used to drink. I tried to hide it from everyone, I was ashamed. But, once I realised that he wasn't doing it to escape from me, but that he was like that because *we* had been living the wrong way, it made us stronger. I know that right now, it seems like Paul's growing away from you.'

'No, no, he's just...' my voice trailed off. I wanted to go outside and sit with Paul. I could hear him laughing at something. 'He's working hard, and I know he needs to go to the meetings to stay well.'

She smiled sympathetically, staring at me. 'Emily. I have been where you are. I understand.'

'That's good to know. I appreciate you reaching out to me.' Maybe I could stand up quicker if I just went along with her.

She leaned forward and lowered her voice, glancing over at the balcony where I could hear the men's voices. 'Look, I wanted to talk to you tonight to ask you to come along to a meeting.'

'Me? Oh, no, I—'

She squeezed my hand; it felt like a handcuff tightening. 'I know you don't have an addiction, not like Paul, or our husbands did, but when I joined Phoenix, it helped me to understand more about what had happened to Tim, and we were able to move forwards in our relationship. And even if you don't think that you have a problem, I guarantee that your life will change for the better when you join us.'

The faintness had returned. 'Look, I'll think about it. Thanks.' I made to stand up, then noticed Shona and Amina were coming towards the living room too, leaving the men outside. I swallowed hard as they approached, then sat next to Sam on the couch.

'I've just been telling Emily that we have all been where she is now, and suggesting that she comes to one of our meetings and thinks about joining Phoenix.'

'We'd love that, Emily. You must,' said Amina. 'For me, it not only gave me support, but it opened my eyes. Not to mention the opportunities it has given us...' she giggled.

My cheeks hurt from the smile fixed on my face as the women all laughed. I felt like I was locked in a resort trying to sell me a timeshare, or with friends pushing their latest Tupperware or pyramid scheme onto me. What opportunities were they talking about? Money? My heart raced as I thought of the money that was debited every month from our account to Phoenix. That was just paying back the rehab, wasn't it?

I stood up quickly, pulling my hand back from Sam. The women all stood too. Shona put her hand on my shoulder. 'Come back outside. We can talk more about it later.'

I nodded and let her steer me back to the balcony. My legs were weak. I found my way back to the seat beside Paul and

174

moved my chair closer to him. I don't know how I managed to get through the rest of dinner but finally, the evening ended.

–

In the car, as soon as I closed the door and sat down, the tears began to fall.

'Emily,' Paul said, his eyes wide. 'What's wrong?'

'Just drive, Paul, let's go home.'

'What's—'

'Just drive!' I shouted.

He started the car and began driving.

'What was that, Paul?' I accused once we were a few minutes away and I felt sure that no one from dinner could see or hear me.

'What was what?'

'You know,' I shook my head. '*That* was some sort of attempt to, what, recruit me?'

'Recruit you? No, Emily, it was just my friends having us over for dinner. You're overreacting.'

I glanced at him; he was frowning and looking straight ahead at the road as we wound along towards Bondi. The sight of normal people milling around the streets made me want to jump out of the car and join them.

'Did you know that they were going to corner me and tell me I had to come to meetings and join them, and promising the world?'

'No, and I don't think you're reading the situation correctly, Emily. They're nice people, and if they *cornered* you, I'm sure that they were just trying to be friendly and welcoming, as I'd have hoped you'd do with them.'

'You didn't hear what they were saying. They surrounded me and kept going on and on about it and I just want things to get back to normal, Paul.' My voice broke. I stopped, taking a few deep breaths and looked out of the passenger window.

'This is our normal now, Emily.'

'It's not normal, Paul. You're out all the time, and all these restrictions on everything, it's just getting too much.' I wiped at my eyes.

Paul spoke quietly. 'Would you rather I was gambling?'

I sighed. 'You know that's not a fair question.'

'I need to do this, Emily. Otherwise I am finished.'

'That's not true, Paul. You are the one who has stopped gambling, it wasn't Damian, or Phoenix or whatever.'

'I owe him everything, I owe Phoenix everything.'

'We'll pay them back, as you said you would.'

'It's not just the money. They saved my life.'

I shook my head. 'It feels like you believe you owe them more than you owe your family.'

He slowed the car and indicated to turn right at the traffic lights. 'Emily, don't put me on the spot. It doesn't have to be one or the other. I owe you and the kids so much too.' I glanced at him as his voice broke. Fresh tears brimmed in my own eyes. He cleared his throat and composed himself. 'But I have to pay them back, yes, the money, but Damian also kept my job open, arranged everything for me. Who else would employ me? How else would we pay them back and support our family?'

'We'd manage. Don't feel that you have to do what they say. That's not like you, Paul, you're losing yourself in all this... stuff. I'd rather lose the house and see you and the kids happy in a crappy rental in the outer suburbs than have their fancy waterfront mansion—'

He raised his voice. 'Then what has everything been for, Emily? Why have I worked so hard to build up my career, why did we move to Australia if not to have a good life? Is it so wrong for me to want to give you and the kids a house, a good education, and nice holidays?'

I shook my head and spoke quietly. 'That's not important, Paul.'

'I don't want to have to sell our house and struggle for money. That's not the life I want for my kids. That's not a nice way to grow up.'

Well, you shouldn't have given it all to the casino, I want to say, but I didn't need to.

Twenty-Three

Paul

'How was training today, Cam?' I said as we both sprawled on the couch watching the rugby.

I'd had to relax the 'no television' rule: Cam's big game was tomorrow and watching others was the best way for him to learn. The people at my Phoenix meetings didn't need to know. After Emily had come with me to Damian's for dinner, she had refused to engage any more with me around Phoenix's philosophy and we'd reached a stalemate over the past few months where we each did our own thing and tried not to bring up our beliefs. I knew she had some points, even if I didn't admit it to her, and I was trying to give the kids some leeway. Besides, it was so important for Cameron to see how the professionals played. When I was playing soccer as a teenager, I'd taped the games on our VHS and watched them over and over, studying the plays, memorising the tactics. I hadn't watched a soccer game since I'd left Treetops though – it took my mind to places I couldn't let it go.

But I could handle watching Union. It was Cameron's thing. Back in Scotland, when I was a kid, Union was the domain of the private schools, so I never had the opportunity. I would never have been big enough to play anyway. Cameron was just big enough to be a fly half. They didn't play soccer at his school, and despite me doing everything to get him to play it outside of school, he had resisted, feigned illness, stomped around the pitch. Emily said it was his way of rebelling against me, and so, I had let him as long as he chose another sport. He didn't love rugby either, but it kept him connected to the other kids and gave him a group, even if he was on the periphery of it. His school's rugby team was good, and tomorrow, they were playing in the finals of the private boys' interschool competition.

He shrugged. 'It was fine. Saunders worked us pretty hard.'

'Not too hard, I hope – got to keep fresh legs for tomorrow.'

'Yeah, all good. It was more like tactics and things. We didn't run too much.'

I nodded then leaned down and picked up my water. I had a sudden craving to be picking up a beer; I pushed it away even though I could almost taste the hops on the back of my tongue. They had warned me that this would happen; so many connections had been welded into my brain that it was hard wired to temptation. Sport to Beer to Betting. I had to be vigilant.

'Arrgh!' Cameron hit his forehead with his palm as the Force scored a drop-goal. Before I could look away, the TV suddenly cut to the adverts and my mouth went dry. My breathing started to speed up as I forced myself to look away from the Sportsbet ad, to block out the familiar voice.

'Did you see that, Dad? They gave it away! Where's our defence?'

'I know, Cam. What a disgrace.' My voice was flat, but my mind was oscillating. 'What's the score now?' I tried to level my eyes on Cameron but the game was back on now and across the bottom of the screen was a banner and it was telling me to pick up my phone and put on a bet, and all the combinations I could do and how much I would win and just like that craving to pick up a bottle of beer, I wanted to reach for my phone and reinstall the app and gamble.

I had been wrong to let myself relax, to think that I could resist. This is why we couldn't watch the television. My heart raced. Cameron was being bombarded with these little flashes of adverts shooting into his brain and settling there, until one day he'd be a little bit curious and maybe he would open an account and put his first bet on based on their phoney promises.

'Dad?' Cameron was looking at me, his brow furrowed.

'Sorry, Cam, what is it?' How much did he know? My face reddened as I tried to smile at him, then looked back at the TV, keeping my eyes focused on the game, even though behind the players I could still see the banners around the edge of the pitch advertising all the different ways that I could place a bet. I grabbed the remote and pressed the power button, jumping up from the couch as I did so.

'Hey! I was watching that.'

'It's all over, Cam. Come on, let's go practice some kicks for your game tomorrow.'

He screwed up his face. 'You said I needed fresh legs. It's getting dark.'

I looked out the window, saw the twilight shading the garden, dulling the green of the grass and the blue of the pool, heard the distant barking of a dog. My head was swirling with thoughts, and my eyes prickled with tears with the knowledge that I couldn't even watch a sports game with my son. Phoenix was right: temptation was everywhere, and I had been stupid enough to think that I was strong, that I could relax a little bit back into my life, but as I saw my reflection in the glass patio door, with Cameron sitting on the couch beside me, looking up with confusion on his face, I knew that I couldn't. I had to be even stronger. I had to remove all of this from our lives.

'Dad!'

I rubbed my face and sat down again next to him. 'Sorry, Cam. It's just… do you want to…?' What else could we do though? Our life was based around activities that involved technology: television, internet, games consoles. I felt myself slump as I realised that Cam and I had little else in common. We didn't talk, not really. We chatted in front of the TV while both of our focus was on the screen. I swallowed down the guilt. 'A board game?'

He raised his eyebrows. 'I want to watch the end of the match.'

'I know, but it's over.'

'No, it's not, there's still ten minutes to go. There's only a try and a conversion in it. Dad, what's wrong with you?'

'I just don't want to watch it now. I don't want you to watch it.'

He tried to take the remote from me; I pulled my hand back and glared. 'Don't, Cameron, I'm warning you.'

'You're warning me? What are you going to do? Take away television? It's just a rugby game!'

I kept my voice steady though my muscles were tensing. 'Don't raise your voice at me, Cameron.'

'Why not? You're never even here! You're always working and then you come in here and make all these rules and it doesn't make sense!'

'That's not true!'

'It is! We got used to life without you here and then you come in and make it all crazy again and won't even sit down and watch the game with me!' His voice was wavering.

'It's not good for you, for us, Cameron, watching that. It's not just the game, the game is fine, but look at the adverts, their strips, it's all designed to get into your mind...'

'You were a sportsman! You make me play sport even though I hate it and—'

'Oh, don't be ridiculous. You don't hate it!'

'I do. You've never asked, Dad. It's the only thing you ever talk to me about and now we can't even watch the game.' He stood up, shaking his head.

'Cameron, sit down mate,' I pleaded. 'Let's talk—'

'I'm going to my room to play a *boardgame*,' he sneered.

Now I shouted. 'Cameron, that's enough! Don't talk to me like that. I'm just offering to spend some time with you—'

He pushed past me, out of the room then I heard his bedroom door slam. I sat on the couch, hands shaking. I was glad Emily was out, picking up Tilly from a friend's house.

Where had all that come from? As my anger settled, I realised that he sounded exactly like Emily. All those ideas, they weren't his; it was exactly what his mother had said to me over and over. He'd heard her ideas about me so many times that he believed them too.

That night, I didn't tell Emily what had happened, and I guessed Cameron wouldn't either.

—

I'd set my alarm for 6am. It was as if I was playing today; I was excited, nervous. I went for a quick walk. No one was up when I got home; I emptied the dishwasher and began making breakfast.

Emily came through in her pyjamas. 'You'll wake the house with all that clattering,' she yawned.

'It's time to get up. Cameron's big game,' I retorted. How about, *thanks for making breakfast, Paul*?

Emily pressed her lips together and I knew she was trying to stop herself from saying something. I didn't ask. She squeezed behind me and began filling the kettle. 'Do you want some tea?'

I said nothing. She knew I couldn't drink tea.

I whisked up some eggs, from our own backyard chooks, so I was reasonably okay with the others eating them, added a tablespoon of water, then poured the mixture in the pan. I added the herbs I'd chopped from the garden, some tomato and spring onion and while that started to cook, began slicing up some fruit.

Emily got out a box of cereal and put in down on the bench top right next to me. I bristled.

'Would you like some omelette?' I said pleasantly.

'No, thanks. I'm fine with cereal.'

'It's not good for you.'

'It's Weet-Bix and milk. There's nothing wrong with it. Please don't comment on my choices and I won't comment on yours.'

I closed my eyes for a moment. Michael had given me suggestions of things we could say in this situation, ways to explain, but I also knew Emily well enough to know that this wasn't the time. Maybe Cameron had said something to her about last night. She was itching for a fight and I wasn't going to give it to her, not this morning. 'Cameron, Tilly!' I called.

'Let Tilly sleep in.'

'Isn't she coming to watch?'

'I don't know. I doubt it.'

'She should.'

'Jesus, Paul,' she hissed, turning to face me. 'What's wrong with you today? Stop acting like you're the authority in this house. She never comes to the games, let her rest, it's the weekend.'

'There's nothing wrong with me.' I forced a smile then turned away from her as I heard footsteps.

'Morning, Cam,' I said brightly. He glared at me too. He hadn't forgotten about last night yet then. 'I'm making you an omelette,' I said. 'Give you energy for today.'

He sat at the table and I saw him smile past my shoulder at Emily. I kept looking at him until he met my eyes, then he looked down at the table. I turned around to Emily. 'Your mum and I are excited about today. You nervous?'

'No, I'm okay.'

'Before a big game, I used to have this funny feeling, it was like I was nervous, but I was also ready, you know, sometimes it was almost like I was in a dream, like it wasn't real.'

'Dad, he's playing against Scotch, not the All Blacks.' Tilly smiled as she walked in. Her hair was tangled in waves over her shoulders, her face pale. She had a thick dressing gown over her pyjamas as she walked over to the kitchen. 'What are you making?'

'A veggie omelette... very healthy.'

'Cheese in it?'

'Nope,' I said. 'Dairy free.'

'Good,' she said. 'I'll have a little bit.'

'Finally,' I smiled, letting a laugh out. 'Someone who appreciates my cooking.'

Tilly rolled her eyes as she folded her leg under herself and sat at the table. I let out the breath I was holding, and turned back to the pan.

Twenty-Four

Emily

'He's doing well, isn't he?' I said, smiling at Paul as we stood on the sidelines.

Paul raised his eyebrows and nodded. 'He's is. We just need to get some points on the board though...'

'Come on, Cam!' I shouted as Cam ran towards a tackle, then clapped my hand over my mouth and laughed as I nudged Paul. We weren't meant to cheer these days: parents were meant to stand quietly to stop the obsessed parents having meltdowns on the side of the pitch. Cameron was good; he had inherited Paul's athletic skill. But perhaps it wasn't genetics, perhaps it was just that even before he was born, it was assumed and expected that he would be an athlete of some description. Even when I was pregnant, every time he'd kicked inside my taut belly streaked by jagged red scars, Paul joked about his left footer. He was given a Scotland soccer strip when he was born, a ball for his first birthday, a cricket set when he was two, rugby balls, a footy, a skateboard. He went to Auskick and Nippers and Little Athletics and rugby training and swimming squad. The only choice he really had was which sport he was going to dedicate himself to.

But I never felt bad about pushing him in sport. Team sports were good for him, the psychologists had told me that. It was a way to make him part of something, to understand rules and boundaries, a way to socialise in a healthy way. And when Cameron fixed his mind to something, then it became his life.

I unashamedly tried to focus his attention on something that everyone applauded, so that he would be admired by friends, parents, the school. Who doesn't love a kid who is great at sport?

Just then, Paul's phone rang. He took it out of his pocket, glanced at the screen and then answered it, stepping back from the field. 'Damian,' he said brightly. I shook my head and pointed at the field, but Paul turned and walked away. Bloody Damian. Checking up on him on a weekend, no doubt telling him he should be at another meeting. I still saw Paul struggle not to drink, not to grab a packet of chips, not to go out and, presumably, gamble. I saw it when he looked off into the distance, when he was distracted and his muscles tensed; I could see him battling against himself. And then he would pick up his keys and go out. I bit my tongue as I saw that all these guys in Phoenix denigrated the modern world when it suited them – the TV, internet, alcohol – and yet they were happy to drive around in expensive cars and have a website for their addiction centre and make money by selling pizzas and alcohol to the public in their restaurants as well as taking payments every month from people who were vulnerable and at their lowest points. But how could I complain when I had Paul back? At least he was here at the game.

–

Last week, it was Tilly's last hockey game. Paul had some work to do, he had said, even thought it was a Saturday morning. He would meet us there. I had driven the car up onto the verge underneath a sprawling fig tree next to the oval. Before I'd even switched off the engine, Tilly had opened her door and jumped out, her hockey stick clattering out of the car behind her.

'I don't see him,' she said, glaring at me.

'He said he'll be here.'

'There's Ruby and Naomi over there,' she said, shading her eyes and peering into the distance. 'I'm going to go and warm up.'

'He's probably just parked somewhere else and is already there. Go get started and I'll look out for him.'

Tilly had slammed the car door and hoisted her sports bag on her back, carrying the stick in the other hand. As the engine cooled, I watched her walk further away from me. Her legs looked so thin as the wind blew the fabric of her tracksuit trousers around them, and I felt a physical pull towards her that I hadn't felt for so long. She was so grown up now, and yet so vulnerable. Throughout all this with Cameron, she hadn't complained. She'd done her homework, organised herself, never complained about anything, and I'd just let her do that, been relieved and grateful that she was so good. What went on in her mind? Of course this was affecting her; how could it not?

I swung my legs out of the car then reached back for my coffee. I looked around the cars parked on the grass, those across the street, and I couldn't see Paul's car. I wouldn't call him. I would not call him.

Just as the whistle went to start the game, just as Tilly had glanced around the crowd again with a frown on her face, the game started. Now she wouldn't be able to concentrate on the game because she'd be wondering where he was, if he'd come. Paul couldn't see how anxious she was under that front.

And then I heard his voice in my ear, and I could almost feel the thick smugness sliding through my ear canal as he mumbled, 'Good morning.'

I turned around. He was holding a take away cup with a chamomile teabag string hanging out of it. Plenty time, obviously, to stop off at the cafe. 'They've started.'

'Yes, I can see that.' He managed to catch Tilly's eye and waved wildly at her; she grinned and raised her stick for a moment, then ran off after the ball.

'Don't distract her.'

He sighed, then nodded and smiled at a few of the other parents milling around who still treated him like a star. Look at the athlete, and look how he's passed his athletic prowess onto his daughter, and how he's given up his Saturday morning to watch and cheer her school team on. I've been here to see her every single week since she was kid, without fail, and no one gives me a medal.

We both stood and watched, cheering at the right times and if you saw us from a distance, you'd assume we were just another married couple.

–

At least he was on time today for Cameron's game, I suppose, even if he had gone off to answer his phone. I watched Cameron run down the wing, waiting for a pass, but then the other team kicked it out.

'How long 'til half time?' I said to Max, one of the dads standing next to me.

He looked at his watch. 'Just a few minutes I think. We need to get a try before half time.'

'I know! I'm so nervous for them!' I said.

We chatted while I tried to watch for Paul out of the corner of my eye. I was not going to give him the satisfaction of turning around to look for him. Cameron glanced over; I gave him a thumbs-up and a little wave. He was looking thin too. I had to make more of an effort to get extra calories into him, as well as Tilly. Between the tablets and Paul's obsession with healthy eating and no added anything, Cameron had lost some of his bulk.

'Turn around,' I mouthed as I waved my finger to get him to turn around again and concentrate. He was scanning the crowd, I knew, looking for Paul. Part of me wanted to protect Cameron from knowing his dad had gone to take a phone call, but a part of me wanted to tell him, *your dad's on the phone. Your biggest game and he's gone to talk to his crazy mates.* My fists were clenched and rage surged up in me. I turned around to see where Paul was, to tell him to get off the bloody phone and pay attention. And then I heard it.

A crunch. A snap like bones breaking. An exhalation of air. A piercing whistle. A gasp. A scream.

Someone grabbed onto my arm. From my peripheral vision, I saw hands go to mouths, faces grimace, and heads snap towards me. Before I even registered what I was looking at, I was sprinting onto the pitch.

Cameron was on his back, spread-eagled, eyes fluttering behind his lids as if insects were crawling around trying to pierce through the paper-thin skin.

'Oh my God, Cammie!' I dropped to my knees on the grass next to him.

A hand on my shoulder held me firmly back. 'Don't move him. It could be his neck.'

I pushed the hand off my shoulder and looked up. All the players stood around us, staring at Cameron, faces frozen. One boy – no, he was bigger than that – a young man, wearing the maroon strip of the opposing team, was pale, his eyes wide and staring. It had been him.

'What happened?' I said to him, quietly, forcefully, as I took the limp hand of my son.

'I didn't mean it.'

'Tell me. Quick! I need to know what happened.'

'It was just a tackle…' He looked around at his teammates, then up to their coach who was running towards him and steering him away.

I looked up. 'Where's Paul? Paul!' I shouted, wildly looking around me, and now he was sprinting across the pitch towards me, his face aghast.

'Emily, don't move him,' Saunders, our coach, said.

My voice was higher pitched now. 'What happened?'

Paul arrived and was down on his knees too, but I couldn't hear what anyone was saying for the ringing in my ears. 'Cameron, it's Mum, can you open your eyes?' I looked up. 'He's unconscious, Paul.'

'He'll be okay, Em. Come on mate, Cam, wake up.' Paul's voice was trembling.

'He can't hear you!' I hissed. 'He was looking for you! He wasn't paying attention because he was looking for you! Where were you?'

'We've called an ambulance,' someone said behind me. I ignored them.

My heart was racing and my voice was piercing. 'What happened? This is a schoolboy game of rugby. What the hell happened?'

'I didn't mean it!' That boy again, trembling now, eyes wet.

Suddenly, Cameron's limp hand that I held in my own squeezed my fingers tight. The breath I'd been holding escaped.

But, before I could talk, Cameron's hand went limp again, then squeezed with such force that I thought my fingers would break. My heart seemed to stop as I looked down at his body as it started to convulse. His hand slackened again, and I withdrew my own and held it to my mouth as his arms curled into his body, then splayed out so straight that I was sure his elbows would snap, then his whole body jerked and convulsed as if something was inside him throwing him around on the muddy spot where he lay like a marionette. I screamed. His face was contorted in pain, the muscles around his jaw tense and tight, and then a streak of blood ran out of the corner of his mouth and down his chin.

'His tongue,' I shouted, though there may as well have been no one else there as the circle around him stretched thinly and moved away from him as if he was something to fear. But my words seemed to break the spell, as suddenly everyone wanted to help and came forward, hesitantly. 'His neck,' I wailed. They had said not to move him, but now his body was convulsing and his neck and head were lolling around and all I could picture were the hard, little bones of his cervical spine splitting and grinding together and snapping his spinal cord. But his arms and legs were still moving, so surely that meant that the signals were still travelling from his brain down that thick white spinal cord to the nerves of his hands and feet.

'Shit!' Paul shouted. 'Where's the bloody ambulance?' He rocked back and punched the ground beside him, crying now. 'Shit!'

'Stop, Paul! Please, stop.' I looked at the crowd around me. 'Where is the ambulance?'

What should I do? You were meant to put people fitting in the recovery position so they didn't choke on their tongue, but what if they might have broken their neck? But how could moving him be even worse than this? His tongue would be swollen, the blood that had surely come from his teeth grinding down on it would be pooling now in his throat. 'Get a collar,' I screamed. 'Don't we have a collar? Who's on first aid?'

As the coach ran off to get the first aid bag, which probably only had an ice pack in it, Cameron's convulsions eased, and then a few seconds later, it was over. I watched as a dark stain on his shorts spread and I wanted to cover him with a blanket, to save him the indignity of having dozens of people watch him not only fitting, but losing control of his bladder. I leaned over him and laid my body on his, crying, and stayed there as I heard a siren in the distance, thankful that I could feel the rapid beat of his heart under my cheek.

Twenty-Five

Emily

I steadied myself with my hand on the wall of the ambulance as I jostled around on the fold-down seat in the back. Paul followed in his car. There was nothing I could do as I watched the paramedic strap an oxygen mask to Cameron's face, stick ECG leads on his bare chest and connect a bag of fluids to the cannula in the back of his hand and another lead to his finger. I could barely see him beneath it all. I answered all their questions as best I could, but I hadn't seen him fall. They asked if he was normally well, and if he was on any medication. He must have had a knock to the head – that was the only explanation.

As I watched his face, his eyes fluttered then opened.

I breathed out and spoke in a wavering voice. 'Oh, thank God. Cameron, it's Mum, we're in an ambulance. You're fine, though, you're fine, darling, it's all going to be okay.'

His eyes flitted rapidly; I could tell he was still out of it. A few moments later, he opened them again and he seemed to focus for a second. He began to sit up and at the same time, his hands reached for the oxygen mask, pulling it off his face.

'No, sweetie,' I said quickly, looking at the paramedic as she put her hand on him to gently push him back down. 'We're in an ambulance. You were knocked out at rugby. We'll be at the hospital soon.'

'I've got to…' his voice sounded slurred and muffled beneath the mask. Then his eyes closed again.

My heart sped up and I looked at the paramedic. 'What's happening?'

'It's not uncommon,' she said. 'Don't worry, we're almost at the hospital. We'll be there any minute.'

I nodded and looked back at my son, and before long, I felt the ambulance slow and the doors opened.

Paul appeared as Cameron's trolley was unloaded from the ambulance and he was pushed through the sliding glass doors of the emergency department.

'Oh Paul,' I clutched his arm. 'He woke up but he didn't make sense and now he's unconscious again.' I started to cry as I saw Paul's eyes fill with tears too. He pulled me towards him.

'He'll be okay,' he said quietly.

'Yes. He will.' I nodded and bit my bottom lip as I listened to the paramedics handing over to the hospital staff in low voices as, without even looking at Cameron, they put new leads and masks and tubes on him. Cameron started to struggle. 'Paul,' I said, pulling away from him. 'He's waking up.'

I hurried over, trying to get to him between the doctors and nurses that surrounded him in different colours of scrubs. I had no idea who was who. There was a man in green scrubs, with balding dark hair and black-framed glasses holding a clipboard, and by the way the others moved around him, I guessed he was in charge.

'You're Mum?' he said. 'And Dad?'

I nodded as Paul answered 'Yes. Paul Napier,' he said confidently and held out his hand.

'Brad Eaton,' he said. 'I'm the senior registrar here in ED.'

'He's waking up,' I said, reaching over to put my hand on Cameron's shoulder as he began to wriggle. 'Cam, it's okay, it's Mum, I'm here,' I said, trying to calm the shrillness in my voice.

'Hey, mate,' said Paul, and I could hear his voice wavering and knew that he too was barely holding it together. 'Cam, it's okay, mate.'

Cameron was moaning now and pulling at the leads on his chest. The doctor turned away from us and said something to the nurses and one of them hurried off while the other one held Cameron around the wrists.

'We need to give him something to calm him down, just a little. We need to get some blood tests and a CT scan to check his head.'

I felt faint; I grabbed the edge of the bed as the nurse reappeared with a syringe and began to unscrew a little cap on the line going into his hand.

'Don't worry,' Dr Eaton said. 'It's not uncommon for people to be confused or agitated after being knocked out. It's not necessarily bad.' He smiled a little, but I could see by the way he turned around again to watch the nurse inject the medication that he was concerned.

'Now, I need to double-check his medical history. So, no other illnesses?'

'No,' said Paul. 'None at all.'

'So just the anxiety and ADHD? And he's on Prozac and dexamphetamine.'

Paul stiffened beside me.

'Yes,' I said quickly. 'That's all.'

'Any problems with the medication?'

Paul was staring at me; my face went hot and the world around me slowed and stilled like I was in a dream. *Be quiet*, I wanted to say to the doctor. *Not now*. I could feel Paul's confusion then anger radiating from his body, but he said nothing.

I tried to speak; my voice was croaky. 'No. Just some loss of appetite. Maybe some headaches.'

'Has he been complaining of headaches for a while?'

'No, not really... I...' I began to see speckles in front of my eyes and my ears were ringing. 'I'm sorry, I think I'm going to faint.' I took a step back and looked around, trying to see a chair.

'Go outside, Emily,' Paul said to me in an even voice. 'Go and get some fresh air. Then sort out Tilly. I'll stay with him.'

I nodded, already backing towards the door.

Twenty-Six

Paul

Cameron was asleep again, despite the noise and chaos of the emergency department being held at bay only by a flimsy green curtain drawn around us. I rested my head in my hands, my elbows on my knees in the plastic chair by his bed. My head was spinning. How could Emily do this, and, even worse, keep it from me?

I heard the grating of the curtain rings on the rod above the bed, and looked up as Emily tiptoed in. She came over, then sat down on the edge of the chair next to me. She put her hand on my knee. 'I'm sorry,' she whispered.

I looked up at her, then turned my gaze to Cameron. 'Em, I… I honestly don't know what to say. I can't believe you'd do this without telling me, after we'd discussed it.' I shook my head.

'He was so much better,' she said, swivelling her body round to face me. 'You were away, Paul, and I was on my own and things were getting worse and worse and the school called me in and said he had to see someone. I tried, but I couldn't get in touch with you. I didn't know what else to do!'

I held my hand up. 'You already told me that, at Tilly's dance show, and then you told me that you wouldn't see a psychiatrist or give him medication. You lied to me, Emily. Don't blame me! You've had plenty other opportunities to discuss this with me.'

'I'm not blaming you, I blame myself!' Cameron's bed creaked as he turned his head, then settled again. I lowered my voice. 'All I can say is I'm sorry, but this isn't the place to talk about it. It's not important now.'

'Of course it's important now,' I hissed. 'He's here because of you! The medications can give you seizures. They damage your brain.'

She screwed up her face and leaned forwards. 'What? That's ridiculous. He was knocked out in a rugby game, Paul. This has nothing to do with the medication. They *help* your brain.'

I took my phone out of my pocket; my hands shook as I typed in 'dexamphetamine'. 'Just look, Emily: Psychosis. Tics. Chest pain. Seizures. Sudden death.' I turned the phone around and put it in Emily's view. She batted it away. I continued. 'He had a seizure. You said yourself you didn't see the tackle, the young lad said it was just a normal tackle and he wasn't near his head. God knows what happened to him!'

'This,' she waved her hands over Cameron, 'has nothing to do with the medication.'

'You don't know that, Emily! Do you know what this stuff does to you? You've been giving him *speed*. You've been giving our son a drug, two drugs! I've told you a thousand times, these doctors don't know what they're talking about and they prescribe this crap because the drug companies buy them dinner and fly them to conferences. It's snake oil… no, it's worse than that because it can kill you!' I was shaking. I turned away from her, then stood up and paced, breathing deeply. I looked back at Cameron, his chest rising and falling with the hiss of the oxygen machine. I slowed my breathing to match his and my anger drained away, leaving just the fear.

'Paul, I—'

I held my hand up. 'Just don't talk to me. All I care about right now is Cameron.'

She nodded. I sat again and we both stared at our son.

Emily and I barely spoke as we waited for the doctor to come back and tell us the results. I asked where Tilly was; she told me that Alasdair and Jane had picked her up, and her car. After the scan, they let the sedative medication wear off. Cameron had woken up, seemed more like his old self, then had dozed off again. I itched to call Damian. I was frightened of my anger at Emily, at my reaction and the way that feeling so scared and enraged made me want to shout and scream or have a drink or find something to lose myself in. I wanted to tell someone who would understand why I felt like this.

I glanced up at Emily — she was staring at Cameron, biting her thumbnail. I forced myself to stay where I was. This wasn't the time to flee. I had learned that I used to run away when the pressures at home become too high. Emily was right, partially, when she said I had always left her to deal with Cameron. I had. I know that. I ran off to work, where everyone propped me up and flattered me, and then later, I ran to gamble, to give myself the thrill that I just couldn't feel at home any more. And where had it led me? Right here, with my son in hospital. By running away, I allowed Emily to make decisions, and this was what had happened.

A doctor poked her head through the curtain. Dr Eaton had gone off shift and she was his replacement, she explained. She looked tiny in scrubs that were clearly too big for her. She reminded me of Tilly. Tilly; we must call her. She must be frantic.

'Everything okay in here?' the doctor said as she stepped through.

Emily sat up straight and nodded. 'Have you got the results?'

'Yes, all good,' she said brightly. 'The CT scan is normal so there's no bleed or fracture or anything like that to worry about.'

'Oh, thank God,' Emily said.

I let out a breath. 'That's great. Great.' My head was reeling. 'So, it's just a concussion?' Emily said.

The doctor cocked her head to the side. 'That's most likely, yes. But we need to keep him in for a day or two. I want the neurologists to see him, to investigate other causes of the seizure. And we need to observe him for at least twenty-four hours, he was pretty confused for a while there.'

'Mum? Dad?' Cameron's voice croaked from the bed.

'Hey, mate,' I said, reaching over to take his hand. 'You've woken up.'

'Cam,' Emily said softly. 'This doctor just told us some great news, that your head scan was normal, but they need to just keep an eye on you for a night or two, okay?'

'Okay,' he said.

'I'll leave you to it. We'll transfer him to the ward in a couple of hours. I'll talk to you later.' The doctor went back through the curtain.

'You alright, Cameron?' Emily said. 'Did it make sense, what the doctor just said?'

He shrugged, opened his eyes. 'I'm tired.'

'I know, sweetie,' Emily said, her voice breaking. She swept his hair back and left her hand gently on his forehead. 'Just go back to sleep, darling, it's been a big day.'

'You hungry, mate? I'll pop out soon to get something to eat. Can I bring you something back? Some hot chips?' I knew he liked them, despite the fat and salt. Now, I would make an exception.

'Thanks,' he said, then his eyes closed.

We sat in silence for another few minutes until it was obvious he was asleep. 'Come with me to get some food,' I said, standing up.

'No, you go, he might wake up—'

'You need to eat. We need to talk. Let's go. We'll tell the nurse and she can call us if he stirs. We won't be long.' Shame shivered through me at the tone of my voice, but this was serious.

Emily's eyes lingered on me and I sensed her apprehension, but I wasn't going to run from this anymore. She stood up and picked up her bag. I put my hand on the small of her back, steering her out.

We exited the emergency department into the car park where the ambulance had entered. There was a bench next to a slip lane for taxis and people being dropped off, but a man with his leg in a cast sat there. Emily turned and started walking towards the main hospital building.

'Emily. This way.'

'He wants hot chips. There's a café in there.'

I walked in the other direction, towards the main road; she followed. We fell into step beside each other, she clutching the strap of her bag, me with my hands in my pockets.

'I don't want to talk in front of Cameron,' I started, my voice calm. 'But I'm really struggling to understand why you'd do that and I need to talk about now or I swear I'll explode.'

She said nothing. I waited.

She sighed. 'I told you Paul. You were away, and things reached a crisis point, the school said I had to take him to a psychiatrist. And then… I tried to tell you, I really did, but I don't know how to talk to you now, you think a lot of… things now, Paul. If you'd come with me to the doctor you would have had some say in it.'

'Did Cameron get a say in it?'

'He's a kid. He's ill.'

'He's not ill, he's fine, and he's his own person. You can't just poison him.'

'For God's sake, Paul, stop saying it's poison! You're sounding like a crazy person! That's why I couldn't talk to you about it, you're impossible to talk to, you don't think logically!'

'You deliberately excluded me from making a decision about our son.'

'Because you made it quite clear that you were happy with the way he was.'

'He was born like this! It's not like we had a different child who suddenly caught a virus!'

'He's unhappy. Why don't you want him to be happy?'

I stared at her, then dropped my eyes. 'It's you who's unhappy, Emily.'

199

'No, I'm...' Her voice trailed off. 'I'm only unhappy because he is.'

We both knew what I was thinking: that if she wasn't spending all day worrying about Cameron, what would she do? The children were growing up, growing away from us, and she didn't know any other way to be than an anxious mother. 'Emily, maybe it's you who should be getting some help. Why don't you come with me—'

'Piss off, Paul.'

I whipped my head round to look at her, but she was storming off. My eyes focused on her silver flats walking one after the other along the pavement.

'Emily, stop.' I ran to catch up to her. She had to understand. 'That stuff can give you heart attacks, high blood pressure, make you hallucinate, stop you growing.'

'That didn't happen to him!' She stopped and turned to me, at the edge of a side street, her eyes wide and blazing.

'You don't know that!' I hissed through gritted teeth. 'You're not listening to me! What do you think I learned in all that time I was away from you? I hated being away from the kids, but I had to because something had to change. I learned about our minds, and how we are poisoned by all the crap in the world, in our food, in the television and above all, these so-called medications! You see what state I was in, and I didn't need medication; I just needed to learn about myself. Cameron doesn't need medication, he never did, he does not need to see some pseudo-doctor—'

'Dr Davidson isn't a *pseudo* doctor, she's a *real* doctor. She's been to medical school and done her specialist training for years, which is more than you have! You can't learn about medicine from a month or two in some rehab run by loonies!'

I shook my head. 'That rehab saved my life.'

'I know, I know,' she said quickly. 'I'm sorry, I didn't mean—'

'And why didn't Cameron tell me?'

She frowned. 'He—'

'Did you ask him to lie to me too?'

'No, no...'

I started to step off the kerb. A car sped past us; I stuck my middle finger up at him. 'What does that dickhead think he's doing? Speeding along like that next to a hospital where there are kids!' I shook my head then strode out behind the car. I heard Emily hurrying after me.

Emily put her hand gently on my arm as we reached the other kerb. 'Paul, slow down, stop, please.'

I stopped and spun around to see her, my head pounding. Her eyes were full of tears. 'Listen, don't be angry at Cameron, don't blame him. It's not his fault. I thought I was doing the right thing. He was getting better, so much better...'

My heart was racing. 'What?'

She spoke rapidly, eyes flitting from the ground to me and back again. 'Look, I had to make sure he was taking his tablets. Maybe he started taking them too.'

'Emily. You're not making sense.'

She wiped at her eyes and stepped towards me and took my hands in hers, speaking in barely more than a whisper. 'Don't blame him. He didn't want to take them. He doesn't know.'

'What?'

'I was giving them to him. He didn't know. He did take them then he stopped them. He didn't want to take them. He was hiding them, I found them all, so I was giving them to him in his juice, but he didn't know, and maybe he started taking them too, I don't know!'

My heart almost stopped. 'You are kidding me.'

She was silent; I glanced over and saw her wipe away a tear.

I couldn't keep all the thoughts in my head in any coherent order. 'Let me get this straight. You were sneaking them into his food but still pretending that you didn't know he wasn't taking them. So, he could have been taking double the dose?'

'He wasn't though, he wasn't taking them, I know it. Paul, I'm sorry.' She started sobbing, in the middle of the street, with people walking around us hiding their glances at us.

201

'Shh. Stop crying.' I looked around us. A middle-aged man walking an Alsatian stared at me; I glared at him. I let her sniffle for a while then held her shoulders and stepped back so I could look at her. 'You need to tell them. You need to admit what you've done. It could be critical.'

'He just got knocked out, Paul! Don't say it like I did this,' she said, waving her hand back towards the hospital. 'I was trying to help. I knew that when he got better, he's understand.'

'You can't make those decisions for him, Emily.'

'Yes. I. Can.' Her eyes flashed. 'Someone had to. You weren't there.'

'Yes, I was. I've been there every day—'

'No, you haven't.'

I just shook my head. 'I can't talk to you right now. Let's go back.' We had turned left again, heading back towards the hospital.

'I shouldn't have let him play,' she said, tears streaming down her face. 'He's just trying to get your attention, he's not even interested in—'

I groaned. 'Why do you keep going on about that? I never forced him. I never wanted another me. Why would I?' Even when I was at my peak, I was miserable, propped up by people telling me how wonderful I was but torn up with doubt. I breathed deeply. I would not give her the satisfaction. 'Emily. Not everything in our life is my fault. Him being in that hospital bed is not my fault.'

There was nothing more to say. Emily said that I couldn't think logically but neither could she. I was no more willing to change my view that my son did not need psychiatric treatment any more than Emily wouldn't change her view that he did. Our argument was so familiar that our brains didn't even need to register it. Our mouths and bodies just went through the motions, like riding a bike.

We bought the hot chips, walked back to Cameron's room, and both pretended to him that nothing was wrong, the same way we'd been pretending for our entire marriage.

Emily wanted to spend the night at the hospital; I couldn't persuade her otherwise. There was only one recliner chair to enforce their rule of only one parent staying the night. I needed to get away from her anyway; I needed to think. Feelings of rage kept peaking, then ebbing as sorrow and regret took over, a depthless sadness that Cameron was the one lying in a hospital bed, not me. How could we move forward from this?

Cameron was in the shower in the bathroom adjoining his room. Emily was moving around the room, smoothing his sheets, folding up the gown he'd been wearing. She blinked several times as she lined up his muddy rugby boots at the end of his bed.

'I'll go and pick up Tilly,' I said. 'Take her home to her own bed.'

'She's okay. Ceecee texted me. Your brother dropped her there for the party after they left here this afternoon. She and Ruby are already in their pyjamas and watching a movie in bed, just let her have a sleepover.' Emily's voice was hoarse, her eyes rimmed with dark shadows.

I nodded. 'Okay.'

'Cameron seems better,' she said.

He did – groggy but coherent. 'Yes. Let's see what the EEG tomorrow shows.' They wanted to check for epilepsy and have a review with the neurologist. They also wanted to talk to the hospital's psychiatrist; I was not going to miss that.

I kissed Cameron goodnight, promising to be back in the morning, and nodded at Emily then left the hospital.

–

It was dark outside. I walked to the multi-storey car park where I'd parked this morning and as I closed the car door behind me, I folded my arms on the steering wheel and lay my head down. My mouth was dry. I wished Tilly was home. The house was going to be empty and my own company was always the most dangerous when I was upset. My mouth began to salivate with

203

the thought of the taste of a gin and tonic: slightly bitter, cold liquid sliding down my throat. It would take away some of this tension, let me relax and think clearly. And before I knew it, my mind had jumped forward and I could feel the relaxation and exhilaration and excitement of hitting that button, spinning that wheel, feeling like a winner even just for the briefest of time.

It took all my strength not to turn onto the highway that would lead me where I wanted to go. My hands were pulling the steering wheel round to the left as I approached the turn off and I desperately wanted to let them. I almost cried out with the strength it took to keep it straight and stay on the road. I should go back to the hospital, even if they won't let me stay. I should be with Cameron. I should pick up Tilly from Ceecee. I should go home. But then, I knew that at home, the pull to open up my laptop, or reload the app on my phone to make a bet was too strong. There was only one other place that I could go.

I knocked on his door. My stomach was churning; maybe he wouldn't answer. I heard the scrape of his dog's claws on a wooden floor as it ran towards the door, the thud of footsteps behind him. The door opened.

'Damian, I—'

He frowned, then opened the door wider and I stepped inside.

'I'm sorry to come unannounced, I... Cameron's in hospital.'

'Shona,' he called into the back of the house. 'Paul's here. We're just going into the study.'

Shona came towards the doorway, wiping her hands on a tea towel. 'Hi, Paul. Good to see you. Is everything okay?'

'I'm sorry to barge in like this, I just—' I felt my eyes glisten.

She smiled and shook her head. 'Don't apologise. Our door is always open.'

Twenty-Seven

Emily

It had been impossible to sleep. It wasn't just the recliner that didn't recline any more than an economy airline seat would, or the stuffiness of the room, or the nurses coming in every hour to wake Cameron and shine a light in his eyes, or the beeps and chatter outside the room, it was the gut-felt guilt that churned inside me that kept me lying with my eyes wide open as the dawn light crept into the room.

The door opened and Paul walked in with two takeaway coffee cups. He handed me one. 'You back on coffee?' I tried to joke, speaking softly so as not to wake Cameron.

He shook his head. 'Just a black tea. I'm allowing myself a little bit of caffeine today.'

My eyes filled with tears at his small smile.

'How is he?' he said, turning his gaze towards Cameron.

'He's sound asleep now. They woke him every hour last night with all the observations they had to do.'

'The doctors been in yet?'

I shook my head. 'Not even they are silly enough to be at work this early.'

Paul was staring at Cameron, his lips pressed together.

'Here,' I patted the recliner next to me. 'Come and sit down.'

He shook his head then picked up the straight-backed plastic chair in the corner and moved it quietly nearer the bed.

'I'm sorry, Paul,' I said in a barely audible voice.

He didn't look at me, but I knew he heard as he nodded, just a little.

'I thought it was the right thing to do.'

'It wasn't.'

I stilled; it was as if he'd slapped me. What had I expected? That he'd reassure me? I let the sting of his words slowly settle and something else began buzzing though me. I gritted my teeth to stop myself from responding. I was sick of feeling this guilt. I'd spent years being questioned about my role in Cameron's behaviour; I'd lost count of how many people had asked me if I'd had trouble bonding with him, how I'd coped with two young children when Paul was away, how I disciplined him. No one asked *Paul* what he did to parent Cameron, how *he'd* coped with sleepless nights and tantrums, and that was because he never had to. And every time they questioned me, I smiled and told them that I coped just fine, but inside I was seething at their questions, but couldn't tell them how unhappy I was, or how I resented Paul for being able to walk out the door every day while he went out to a normal adult life, and how sometimes I wanted to throttle the kids for not giving me any time to just eat a bowl of cereal or have a shower or make a phone call without constant interruptions or go for a walk, anything but get them another glass of milk or mop up a spill or break up a fight or shout at them to get their bloody shoes on for school.

I exhaled. Paul still hadn't looked at me, still had no idea that every time he left it to me, I tried my absolute best and yet still, *still*, I was the one getting the blame.

I look down at the smattering of freckles across Cameron's nose, the same reddish-brown as the short curls on his head. If it wasn't for the cannula in the back of his hand and the clear fluid dripping into his veins, the hiss and beeps of the machinery around him, I could imagine he was in his bed at home. He needed a haircut. When he was a toddler, I used to cut his hair when he was like this, asleep. I couldn't bear the tears and the pleading and bribing that I had to do to get him to sit still with a hairdresser trying to get a Wiggles cape on him. It was much easier to use the kitchen scissors when he finally gave up and crashed into angry sleep after hours of being in and out of his room, laughing and running from me and refusing to sleep. And then he'd wake Tilly and I'd cry because it was all I could do to stop myself from walking out of that house and slamming the door behind me. Later, I'd drag myself through the house picking up detritus from every room and folding laundry and washing the dishes and by the time Paul came home, Cameron would be like he is now, looking like a sweet, innocent little boy and then I'd start to blame myself too because how could one little boy cause me to feel so unhinged?

Cameron would be okay. I was sure he would be. The neurologist would come today, and the psychiatrist, and Paul could direct his questions at them, not me. The doctors would know what to do; they had to. Because if they didn't, then I really didn't know where I fit in the world any more.

Paul used to be like that, uncertain. Even when he was at the height of his soccer career, he was never quite sure of himself. And that drew me in: only I knew the real him, his vulnerability and insecurity. Only I could help him. To everyone else he was Paul Napier, the star, someone they cheered on, bet their money on, and he never let them down. He was confident physically; he was meticulous about his training, his diet, his sleep. And I loved that about him, but I also loved that I was the only one he would ever tell when he was struggling. When the doubts crept in and I'd wake to find his side of the bed empty at 5am, when I'd tip-toe out to find him doing sit ups on the living room floor, with wild eyes and a grimace on his face, beads of sweat on his forehead, it was me whom he allowed to just sit with him, as he kept going and going until he lay back, panting. Only then did I know that he was back in control again, that he'd forced that doubt away as his blood pulsed and his muscle fibres tore. And sometimes, he'd lay his head afterwards on my chest, in the hollow beneath my shoulder and hold me while I stroked his head. And then he'd be okay again, and off to score goals.

But as his body couldn't keep up, that uncertainty grew, and what had been a twinge of anxiety, like his niggling knee pain, became a constant ache. But he refused to give in. He kept getting up even though I knew he wanted to crawl away. He wouldn't listen to the doctors until he had to.

Looking back, that was when it all went wrong. When Paul admitted to himself, and then me, that it was all over, he floundered as I tried to keep him tethered to me with a slowly fraying rope of love. But gambling with our money, our family, our future, and now Cameron's health, meant that I was ready to pull that last thread until it snapped.

Since coming back from Treetops, he had been surer about things than he had ever been, but he wouldn't let me past that swagger of confidence, or admit to the doubts that he *must* have.

And I have been complicit. I haven't challenged him enough on his obsession with pulling back to the simple life, or his conspiracy theories. I went along with it. Why, when it meant that I had to lie to him all this time? He was so sure that there was no room for any uncertainty anymore; he'd shut off that part of himself, leaving all the doubts to me. And I *had* doubted: doubted that I would manage the kids without him, doubted that I could support us all financially on my own, and yes, doubted that the decisions I was making for the kids were the right ones.

I looked down at Cameron again. My certainty that he'd be okay flickered a little, threatened to go out, but then reignited.

I spoke clearly. 'Paul. I'm sorry for not talking to you about this. I don't know how many times I can say it.'

'Things are going to change, Emily.'

I stared at him. Was that a threat? 'I know that. I've been saying that for a long time.' I leaned towards him. 'Paul, I love that you're better. But you're still… absent from us. I still feel like I'm doing all the parenting on my own.'

He raised his eyebrows.

Here we were again, hurling our words at each other.

'Emily,' he sighed. 'This is not about me.'

He shook his head, then took Cameron's hand. A nurse walked in. *Good timing, Paul. What a beautiful picture of father and son.*

The nurse greeted us and I moved away as she checked Cameron's pulse and blood pressure, waking him up. She shone her torch in his eyes. 'All fine,' she said then wrote on his chart and walked out.

The silence was thick around us. I smiled. 'Hey, Cam, how are you feeling?'

'I'm okay,' he said. 'Sore head.'

I nodded, then glanced up at Paul who was ruffling Cam's hair. 'Good job you've got a thick noggin.'

'Do you remember it, Cam? The game?'

He shrugged. 'Not this,' he pointed to his head. 'I remember running on. That's it.'

I glanced up at Paul, frowning. 'That's okay, darling. The doctors said that sometimes you can't remember when you get a knock to the head. It won't affect anything else.'

'No rugby for a while, eh?' Paul said. 'When I was your age, they just sent us back on.'

'And look where that got your dad.' I smiled, not taking my eyes off Cameron.

'You did alright, Dad.'

'Do you need a drink, Cam? Your throat sounds dry. It's the air conditioning in here, it's so stuffy.' I walked over to the table at the end of the bed and poured him some water from the plastic jug.

'Is it cold water?' he said.

'It's cold enough.'

'I only like it from the fridge. That's been sitting there for ages.'

I closed my eyes for a moment and breathed in, then slowly out. 'I'll go and get you a bottle from the cafe downstairs in a minute. Anything else you want?'

'Nah, don't Emily, this water is fine, isn't it mate?' Paul said, reaching to take the glass from me.

'He won't drink it,' I said, forcing myself to talk sweetly.

'It's just water…'

'Paul…'

'Here, Cam.' He grabbed the glass from me and thrust it towards Cameron.

I held my breath.

'It's not cold,' Cam said, his voice rising and his eyes darting towards me. Take his blood pressure now, I wanted to say to the nurse. See how fast his heart rate is. This is what I'd been talking about.

'Come on, Cam. Your mum doesn't have to go downstairs and buy a plastic bottle of water when you've got some here…'

'Mum…' his eyes were wide.

'I'm going, Cam, I'm going. I'll be back in a minute.' I stood up, grabbed my bag and left Paul to calm him down.

–

When I got back to the room, there were two doctors there – one had a stethoscope draped around her neck like a scarf, her long light brown hair tucked under the rubber tubing, and the other, a male, hovered behind her carrying a manila file. My heart sped up.

'Hi,' I said quickly, putting the bottle of water down on the table over Cameron's bed. 'I was just getting some water.' I forced myself to smile at Paul. 'Have I missed anything?'

'These are the neurology doctors,' Paul said, then smiled a boyish grin at them. I glared at him. 'They just got here.'

'Yes. Good.' I glanced at Cameron; he was staring at the television with the little speaker lying beside him on the pillow.

'Should we…?' I cocked my head towards Cameron then looked at the door.

'If you want to. Though this won't take long,' the more senior looking doctor said, although she can't have been older than forty.

I nodded.

'Cameron,' Paul said. 'Can you turn that down, mate? The doctors are here to talk to you.'

His eyes flickered towards us, but he didn't move.

'Doesn't matter, Paul,' I said, then looked to the doctor. 'Is the EEG today?'

She nodded. 'Yes, just to be sure we're not missing anything. As you know, the CT was all clear. No bleeds, no fractures. And his obs have been fine, with no more seizures so I'm hopeful it's just a concussion.'

I let out a big breath. 'Great. Great.'

'Great news,' Paul said, and I saw him blink hard. I hadn't realised he'd been close to tears. I reached out and touched his shoulder, then dropped my arm back by my side.

'He took a big knock to the head though. I want to keep him in today, for the EEG, and for the psychiatrist to review his medications, and then you can take him home tomorrow morning as long as you're comfortable keeping an eye on him, monitoring him for any bad headaches, vomiting, confusion.'

'Of course,' I said, at the same time as Paul said 'Yes'. We looked at each other and smiled.

'He'll be so much happier at home.' I nodded.

The doctor handed me a leaflet about concussion and told us what to look out for.

'And when can he play again?' Paul said. I opened my mouth, but he beat me to it. 'Not that I want him to rush back into it, I just want to know what he can and can't do.'

'Nothing for a week, at least. Then, if he's up to it, he can do some non-contact stuff with the team. You know, running, sprints. But no contact until you're sure he's doing okay with that. Talk to his coach too. Don't rush into it. He's been knocked out, he's only young.'

'So, with concussion – is there likely to be any long-term damage?'

She shook her head. 'No, there shouldn't be. Just make sure you look out for him over the next couple of days, and he'll be fine.' She turned to Cameron. 'Just try to keep that head of yours out of tackles, okay?'

He looked up, smiled, and looked just like his father. 'Okay.'

I forced myself to laugh to make up for Cameron's lack of reaction. 'Alright, that sounds like a plan. So, if all goes well, home tomorrow?'

'Yes, I'll get the nurses to reduce the frequency of his neuro obs so you can get a bit more sleep tonight.' She smiled, nodding at my coffee. 'We can meet briefly tomorrow morning to finalise everything and then he can go home.'

'Thank you, Doctor.' Paul shook her hand.

After they left the room, I sat on the end of the bed and put my hand over Cameron's foot under the blankets. 'Great news, yeah? Did you understand what she was saying?'

'Yes,' he said, not looking at me. He sniffed, blinked hard then rolled onto his side.

–

I stared at the tiny television mounted from the ceiling above Cameron's bed. He'd been for his EEG, eaten a little watery soup for lunch with white bread and butter. Some daytime show was on, with breaks for news and infomercials for strange fitness equipment and blenders. My back ached from leaning towards Cameron's pillow to hear the sound. Paul was making a point of not looking at it, although at least he wasn't making a fuss about Cameron watching it. Paul tapped on his phone every so often, his jaw set. He looked tired. The fluorescent light made us all look sallow. It was too warm; there were no windows to open. I felt my eyelids grow heavy and I didn't realise that

I had dozed off until I heard a knock on the door. My eyes snapped open and I blinked hard, trying to orientate myself. I smoothed down my hair and licked at my dry lips. Paul stood up; Cameron wriggled up on the bed.

'Good afternoon,' a woman said. She was brightly dressed in a royal blue pleated chiffon skirt and kitten heels, a white blouse and blonde hair loose around her shoulders. 'I'm Dr Karina, from the psychiatry team. Your doctors have asked me to come and have a chat to you. Is that okay?'

I nodded. 'Yes, yes, of course.'

Paul hesitated. She smiled at him, and he seemed to take a long time to answer. 'I'm Cameron's father, Paul,' he said.

'Good to meet you, Paul, and...' she looked at me.

'Emily,' I said quickly. 'Cameron's mum.'

'Dr Karina,' Paul said. 'Before you start, I just want to let you know that I have decided that he will not be going on any more medication. We will be managing this ourselves.'

She closed the door behind her and pulled up a chair from the back corner of the room. She sat, her knees turned to the side so as not to hit the bed. 'That's fine. At this point I've just been asked by your team to come and see if I can offer any help. I understand that Cameron has been seeing a private psychiatrist, Dr Davidson, and was on medication...' she looked at her file. 'Dexamphetamine and fluoxetine?'

Paul remained standing. I could see his chest expanding and contracting more quickly.

'Yes, that's right, dexamphetamine, for ADHD, and the fluoxetine, for anxiety and depression. That's right, isn't it, Cameron?'

He shrugged.

'And then he stopped them, and he got worse, and we just restarted them a couple of weeks ago and he was getting better but now this...' I waved my hand around the room and tried to keep talking so that I didn't cry.

'Okay,' she said, writing something down on her clipboard. She glanced at Cameron, then turned back to me. 'I understand there might have been a mix up with the dosing? Are you happy for us all to talk together? What I usually like to do is to talk to the parents first, and then to the child separately, if that's okay with you?'

'No,' said Paul, and took Cameron's hand. His face was red. My heart pounded. 'Cameron is old enough to hear everything that we all have to say about this. Look, I'm sorry doctor, but we don't need your help. We will sort this out.'

'Paul, she's just—'

'No!' his voice boomed.

'Dad, it's okay, I don't mind…' Cameron had sat up straight and put his arm on Paul's. His eyes were wide; I moved towards him.

Paul closed his eyes for a moment. 'I mind, though, Cam. Mate, we will sort this out. You don't need to see a psychiatrist, you don't need any of the medication that Mum's been hiding in your drink.'

Dr Karina frowned.

'Oh, Paul, for God's sake—' I tried not to shout.

'No, Emily, I've had enough. I've had enough of all this crap. No more. No more!' The muscles in his neck were tense. I looked away.

'If you'd just like to sit down, Mr Napier.' Dr Karina was standing now, though she was barely as tall as Paul's shoulders. Her head was tilted to the side and she spoke quietly, calmly. I noticed that she had moved slightly towards the door.

Paul shook his head. 'No, I'm sorry, I do appreciate your time, but we'll be fine. Please let them know that we don't need a psychiatrist. We will handle this ourselves.'

Dr Karina looked at me and I could sense that she was checking that I was okay with this. Was I? No, not really, but what could I do? I glanced at Cameron; his eyes were darting between the three adults in the room and I felt myself deflate. He didn't need this. He didn't need the people who loved him pulling him in half. He was not simply a young man cleaved from off-cuts of us. He is himself; he is so much more than us.

I swallowed down my protests and nodded slightly at the psychiatrist.

She nodded too, then sighed. 'Well, if you change your mind...' She pulled open the door to the room and walked outside. The door closed behind her.

—

By the time I picked up Tilly from Ceecee's and drove back to the hospital, I could barely stand up. My muscles felt depleted, and I could barely muster the energy to talk. I fixed a smile on my face as Tilly chatted to Cameron about how everyone was talking about the tackle and it was all over Snapchat and that even though he had gone off to hospital, his school had still won the final. Cameron asked what else they were saying. Tilly shrugged and her face reddened. I gestured to Paul to follow me outside the room.

We stood in the corridor. 'What will we do tonight?' I said, quietly. 'I need to get some food soon, but I can stay again. Tilly has school tomorrow.'

'I'll stay,' he said. 'You're exhausted.'

I was. I had lost track of when I had last slept and longed for a hot shower and change of clothes, a proper meal that didn't come from the hospital canteen. I felt my eyes fill with tears. 'I want to stay.'

'You go home,' he said. 'Please, you stayed last night. Go and get some sleep.'

I sighed, nodded. 'Okay. Thank you.' Suddenly I couldn't wait to get into my bed, to pull the blankets up around my neck and close my eyes. 'I'll come back straight after I drop Tilly at school in the morning. I'll be here by 9.30 for the meeting with the doctors then we'll take him home.'

Paul looked at his feet for a moment, then straight into my eyes. 'I promise I'll look after him.' He turned to Cameron. 'Say goodbye to your mum, Cam.'

The next morning, after a deep and restful sleep, I didn't bother calling the ward to see how Cameron was as I was heading straight in as soon as I'd dropped Tilly off.

In the car, I felt light. Cameron was coming home, and everything was out in the open now. But Till was sullen. She threw her bag and viola case into the car.

'Why can't I come too, Mum?'

'Darling, he's fine. You need to go to school. You'll see him this afternoon.'

'Why do I have to go? I don't think the teachers are going to complain when my brother's in hospital and coming home.'

'Is everything okay at school?'

'Fine.'

'What are the kids saying?'

'Nothing. I haven't seen them.'

I raised my eyebrows.

'Nothing. I don't know. Just some stuff on Facebook.'

My heart wrenched. I thought of his body convulsing, the stain on his shorts. Surely no one would laugh about it? I swallowed, pursed my lips and tried to get the image out of my mind. Tilly staying away from school would fuel the whispers. Part of me wanted to insulate her from the licks of tongues hot with gossip. It would blow over, but I also knew that Tilly's quiet, uncomplaining nature that I'd taken as stoicism was really self-preservation. She took it all in and locked those feelings tight inside.

I chatted away as we drove, anxious to keep her distracted and to hurry to school so I could get to the hospital. Everything would be alright once we got home later today. After I dropped Tilly, I pulled into a café on the way and bought one coffee and one black tea, and three fresh muffins, then drove into the hospital car park.

In the lift, I watched the red numbers on the lift display change from G to 1 to 2 to 3. There was a ping as the elevator slowed. Oncology. I nodded slightly to the woman who took a deep breath and stepped out, blinking back my own tears. This is what I'd been trying to explain to Paul: it could be so much worse. I couldn't imagine the horror of the parents walking onto Floor Three. They clung to each other for survival; they didn't let their child's illness pull them apart.

The lift ascended again. It pinged at Floor 4, then it stopped. My stomach twisted a little as the doors hissed open. A woman pushing the breakfast trolley waited while I turned myself side-ways and squeezed out into the corridor onto the Kookaburra ward. Neurology.

I walked straight along the corridor towards Cameron's room.

There was no one at the nurses' station on my left: nothing unusual. I glanced at my watch; I was right on time. I'd hoped to be here earlier, but Tilly wouldn't finish her breakfast and had been difficult, and then the slipway queue at school had been busy, and then I'd slowed in the sludge of the Monday morning traffic. I snapped an imaginary elastic band on my wrist; I was here now. I wasn't late; I wouldn't look like the bad parent after Paul had spent the whole night here.

I walked past the shared ward and turned right off the corridor into the Cameron's room. I rubbed my hands with the sanitiser mounted on the wall outside of his room, hoping the alcohol rub would dry up the sweat on my palms. Taking a deep breath, and fixing my smile on my face, I pushed open the door.

I stopped. His bed was empty. Had they gone for the meeting already?

But the bed wasn't just empty: it was stripped back to the mattress. The bedside table was bare, with no signs of his iPad or magazines or water bottle or bag of jelly snakes. My heart beat faster. Had he been taken to another ward? For a moment, I wondered if I was in the wrong ward, that I'd walked out of the lift on the incorrect floor, overconfident that I knew where I was going, and instead had emerged into a carbon copy ward a floor higher or lower. But no: the small whiteboard above the bed still read 'Cameron Napier', but otherwise, the room was empty.

I entered the room, letting the door swing closed behind me, then walked into the ensuite bathroom, hoping I'd find him in there packing up his toiletries, but it was empty except for a damp hospital towel crumpled at the bottom of a laundry bin.

I hurried back out into the corridor. The muffled quiet of the room gave way to the sound of distant coughs and chatter, cries and chirps of machinery. I paused and listened hard, but couldn't hear Cameron's voice, or any sounds of him that I'd been hearing every day for almost fifteen years, not his footsteps, his breathing, his presence. He wasn't here.

I sensed someone stop behind me; I turned around to see one of the young nurses, Jasmine, her frown matching the one that I knew was on my face.

'Oh,' she said. 'I thought…' She stopped, her eyes darting towards the door of Cameron's room.

I followed her gaze, but the door remained closed. I looked back at her pale face, tilted my head to the side, and waited for her to speak.

'I thought you…' Her voice trailed off and as it did, my heart beat faster.

'Where's Cameron?' I said, trying to keep my voice steady.

'Paul said…'

'Have you moved him already? Where's the meeting? I'm here for the meeting.'

Her eyes widened, and she looked at the floor as dread crept through my bones.

'Jasmine, what's going on?'

'Come with me,' she said, turning around and heading back towards the nursing station.

I followed quickly. 'Where is he? Is he okay?'

Jasmine paused at the nurses' desk and murmured to another nurse whose name I didn't know. This woman raised her eyebrows and opened her mouth in a way that could only be interpreted as alarm, then saw me looking at her and closed her mouth again. She nodded, then bowed her head and Jasmine turned back to me. 'We're just paging Dr Chan to come and have a chat. He'll be here as soon as possible.'

'I'm just here for the meeting. Wasn't it at nine-thirty?'

Jasmine bit her lip then spoke. 'The meeting was cancelled.'

'Cancelled? But no one told me. Why?'

Jasmine stepped towards me, gently, her hand raised towards my shoulder. 'I'm sorry, Emily, we need to wait for Dr Chan, he'll be here in a few minutes and explain everything.'

I stepped back, my hands starting to tremble. 'Jasmine. Where's Cameron? Is he okay? Has something—'

'Oh, Emily, Cameron's fine, I promise. I thought you… Paul said you knew.'

'Knew what?' My chin began to quiver as I understood what had happened, who had cancelled the meeting, and why. I reached for the back of a chair. Paul. 'When—'

Jasmine was almost whispering. 'First thing this morning. About two hours ago.'

I had always thought, despite everything, that Paul loved Cameron and wanted the best for him. But now, for the first time, I no longer knew who Paul was, and I no longer knew what he was capable of. He had gone, and he had taken Cameron with him.

I turned around and I ran.

Twenty-Eight

Paul

When Cameron was newly born, I held his tiny body and looked into his eyes beneath his frown. 'Hello, little mate,' I whispered and silently, I promised that I'd do anything to keep him safe.

Until you have kids, it's hard to explain that clarity when you understand that it's not about you anymore. *You* as an individual don't matter, you only matter in terms of what you can do for your child, how well you can protect him and help him grow to become happy and fulfilled and independent.

Until I went to Treetops and found Phoenix, I'd forgotten that. I had allowed myself to be pushed and pulled and put on a pedestal, poisoned by the modern world. But I've relearned that my life is insignificant. My mission is to teach my son – and my daughter – that there is another way to live.

–

Before we left the hospital, I turned off the bloody television that he was hypnotised by and leaned in to him.

'Mate, I'm sorry that I haven't been there for you.'

'You have, Dad.'

'No, I haven't. Not enough. But we're going to change that. I know you didn't want to take the tablets and I'm sorry that your mum tricked you. That should never have happened. We just need to get away from this.'

'It's okay, Dad, Mum didn't mean—'

'Shh, mate, don't make excuses. You don't need to. You're just a kid.' I smiled and ruffled his hair. 'Well, not quite, almost a man. I think we need to get away from here, take a bit of a holiday. I thought we could go somewhere remote, go camping. We can live off the land, catch our own food. How would you like to get away from all of this for a while?'

He shrugged. 'I guess… but what about school?'

'Don't worry. Doesn't matter if you miss a few weeks of school. Cam, when you get to my age, you realise that what they tell you is important – getting the best grades at school, exams, uni – it means nothing. Nothing. You'll find your path, and all that is important to me is that you are happy. I'm sick of people telling you that there's something wrong with you because you can't concentrate when you have to sit in a hot classroom for eight hours. Mate, I hated school.'

'Where will we go?'

'It's a surprise! I've found somewhere perfect. We're going on an adventure.'

'But Mum's not here yet.'

'It's alright, I've spoken to her. She has to go to work and Tilly has some things at school to finish. They'll hopefully join us soon but we're going to have time together first, just the two of us. It's going to be brilliant.'

'But—'

I held my hand up. 'It's all decided. We'll be out of here in ten minutes and we'll be on our way.' In the car downstairs, I had packed us both a bag, and our passports were in my pocket. I'd drop the car at Damian's holiday house up the coast where she wouldn't look, jump in a taxi and by the end of the day, we'd be on the plane.

I neither wanted nor needed Emily's agreement. She had a made huge decision about him without me, and now it was my turn to try things my way. I knew my son too; I knew him just as well as she did. Cameron was no longer a child. He just needed to come away with me and we would work this out.

Twenty-Nine

Emily

I paced outside the hospital and called Paul's phone from my mobile: it rang out three times, then it went straight to his message service. Bastard. He'd switched it off. There was no point leaving a message; he knew why I was calling.

I hurried back into the main foyer of the hospital found a payphone in the corridor of the hospital. Maybe he'd answer an unknown number. I searched in my purse for coins. Jesus, who carried coins for payphones these days? I slotted in a $2 coin, then pressed the silver buttons with a shaking finger to dial his number, but again, it went straight to voicemail.

The doctors looked sheepish when it had become clear that I knew nothing about his discharge. They had no reason to stop him, of course. Cameron was medically well, and they didn't feel he was a risk to himself or others, and he was with his father. They said I should have told them if I was worried. My fault again.

I hadn't been worried. I hadn't imagined that he would take Cameron.

Tilly. My stomach dropped with dread and I heard myself gasping and calling out her name.

I took a sharp intake of breath and called her phone. It was off too. But they had to be off during the teaching time at school, that was the rule. And she'd be in class, quietly doing her maths or science, oblivious to all of this, wouldn't she? Oh God, why hadn't I let her come with me to the hospital today?

I quickly scrolled through my contacts for the school reception number. Thankfully, the receptionist answered straight away.

'Deb, hi, this is Tilly Napier's mum, I'm sorry to call during the day, but I need to talk to her urgently. There's been a family emergency. Would you be able to get her out of class for five minutes? I need to speak to her immediately. Her mobile's off.'

'Of course, Emily. Hold the line and I'll get her straight away.'

I heard the clatter of the phone being placed back on the desk. I tried to count slowly as I pictured Deb checking the timetable to see where she'd be then leaving the reception area and walking along the corridor or up the stairs and finding Tilly. It was taking too long. My breathing was quickening and I tried to slow it down as I felt my fingertips and lips tingle. Where was she? I stepped outside of the foyer, not taking the phone away from my ear. I needed some fresh air and I didn't want everyone to see me when she came back on the phone to tell me that she'd gone.

I heard Tilly's voice on the phone. 'Mum?' Her voice was shaking.

I managed to breathe again. 'Darling, sorry. I didn't want to scare you.'

'What is it? What's wrong? Is it Cameron? Is he okay?'

I was starting to cry; I couldn't let Tilly hear me like this. I sighed and tried to level my voice. 'He's fine, really, don't worry. I just... have you heard from your dad?'

'Dad? No, why? What's going on?'

'It's hard to explain. Look, I'm going to come and get you. But listen to me: if your dad calls you or turns up at school before I get there, do *not* go with him, okay? Please, please, just wait at school and I'll be there in twenty minutes.' I realised I was already running towards my car.

'Mum, you're scaring me. What's wrong with Dad?'

'I'll explain everything. Please don't worry – I know that's impossible but we're all okay. It's just that your dad has discharged Cameron from the hospital and I'm sure it's just a misunderstanding. I'm certain that they're both okay, you just know how your dad feels about hospitals…'

'Where are they?'

'Just put Deb back on, okay? Then go straight back to the classroom and get your stuff and wait at the office, I'll be there really soon. I love you, darling. Just wait for me.'

'I love you too, Mum…' I could hear that she was crying, and I hated myself for upsetting her. No, I hated *Paul* for upsetting her. Maybe I shouldn't have disturbed Tilly, left her at school with her friends, but what if he wanted her too? I caught myself in the instant that I thought that. Paul wasn't a bad person; he wouldn't kidnap his own daughter. Or would he? I never thought that he'd take Cameron without telling me, but he had.

—

Tilly was sitting behind the reception desk with Deb, the school counsellor, and the head teacher of the high school surrounding her. They all stood when I ran in the front door. Tilly began crying and ran out to hug me. I tried to stop myself from sobbing as I held her to me and smoothed down her long ponytail.

'What's going on, Mum?' she cried.

'Oh sweetie, I didn't mean to scare you. I'm sure it's just a misunderstanding and Dad thought that he was meant to pick up Cameron.'

'Well, why aren't they at home then?'

'They probably are! I haven't even been home yet. You're right, darling. It was just… unexpected.' They weren't at home. I'd called the home phone too. 'Have you got everything?'

'Can we do anything?' the head teacher asked. 'Can we call the police?'

I stared at her, then glanced at Tilly's face. 'No, no, there's no need. I'm sure it's all a misunderstanding. But if he comes here, can you… let me know?'

She nodded. They understood without speaking that something was terribly wrong.

Thirty

Emily

I slowed the car as I looked for the turn off. I had never visited Paul while he was here of course: we had an agreement. I'd never been exactly sure where it was, but he'd later told me that it was off the highway just past Thirroul, and that was enough for me to go on today. It would have been easy to miss the small wooden sign next to a dirt road off the highway; the bush around it was overgrown but I saw the words 'Treetops Retreat'. I braked heavily, thankful that there was no one behind me, then turned the car onto the track, forcing myself to slow down as the stones flicked up from the ground onto the silver metal work of the car. I wanted to floor the accelerator as we rumbled up the dirt road, my head shaking around on my neck, but I didn't want to alarm Tilly any more.

'Good job we have a four-wheel drive, isn't it, Tilly?' I tried to speak calmly.

She smiled, for a fleeting moment, then went back to chewing her lip.

Once I'd understood that Paul wasn't going to answer my calls, and really had gone, I was sure that this would be where he'd take Cameron. We had driven home from school to find an empty house, then straight here. On the way, everything I knew about Phoenix swirled round in my mind. Their extreme views, their secrecy, the way they were taking money from Paul every month for his 'treatment'... it was no more than a cult. These people weren't doctors, or psychologists, and probably not even qualified counsellors. They'd brainwashed Paul and were taking money from him – from *us* – to fund their mansions on the harbour – and now they were going to try to do the same to my son.

Treetops Retreat. It almost made me laugh. They must have put a lot of thought into the name, all sitting around a table scribbling names on a whiteboard, trying to make it sound like somewhere beautiful, all healthy fresh air and hikes through the bush and hearty meals, somewhere to rest and recover. What sort of treatment facility takes tens of thousands of dollars from a husband and father, and doesn't let his wife or children visit or even talk on the phone? Well, they *would* let me see my son.

I swallowed as I turned the corner and saw an old, white farmstead flash between the thickets of gum trees and woolly bushes. I could smell the sickly-sweet wattle flowers. I tried not to think about what it meant that there weren't any guards; the whole time Paul was here, he could have walked out and come home to us at any time. But, that also meant that Cameron could walk out too. Cameron could only have been here for a couple of hours maximum, if Paul had come straight here from the hospital, and he would have no idea what was going on. He'd had a head injury. He was just a kid. Or, maybe the building itself was locked, or maybe they'd drugged him. I bit my lip. I was being ridiculous. We were here now. I'd talk to Paul and take Cameron home. Nowhere would ever be as good for Cameron as being with me.

There were only three cars and a Ute in the area in front of the building. I frowned; Paul's car wasn't here. I gripped the steering wheel to stop my hands from shaking, turned into a flat area near the Ute, then took a deep breath and turned off the engine.

I unclipped my seatbelt and opened the door. 'You stay here,' I said to Tilly.

'No,' she said, already opening her door. 'I'm not staying here by myself.'

'Darling—' I paused. Maybe she was safer with me. 'Alright, but stay next to me.'

Outside, a soft breeze rustled the trees around me. It was cool in the shade, away from the wide flat road with the sun bouncing off the red dirt. Birds called in a high-pitched chattering. I breathed in deeply, then out through pursed lips.

'Mum? Where are we?'

I jumped. 'Sorry, sorry, Tilly. I think Cameron's here. It's just like a hospital, a clinic. Let's go.'

I walked up to the front door. It was solid, thick wood. Next to it was an intercom, and a gold plaque simply saying, 'Treetops Retreat'. I tried the door handle. It was locked.

I stepped back and looked at the windows, wondering if they were locked too. I shook my head: who was I kidding? This wasn't some action movie where I could slip in unseen, unchain him then take him far away from here in a high-speed car chase. This was a clinic. In Australia. It must be registered. Yes, it was run by people who had strange ideas, but they were people I knew and had met and who worked with my husband, and who had been guests in my home.

I pressed the intercom button, hearing a buzzing inside. I waited, heart thumping. I heard footsteps and my stomach churned. I took Tilly's trembling hand.

A man opened the door and as he did, I pulled my shoulders back and tried to make myself look tall. I needed to look like I was in control, not allow him to smell my desperation.

I smiled at the man. 'Good morning. I'm here to see my son, Cameron.'

The man frowned for a split second, then stepped out onto the doorstep and closed the door behind him. I heard the latch close. I saw the keys on a lanyard around his neck.

I stepped back a little, then tucked my hair behind my ears.

'I'm sorry. I think you're mistaken,' he said.

'I'm his mother.'

'I'm sorry, I think you've made a mistake.'

'Is Paul here? Paul Napier. You know him. He's been here; he was a patient. Now, he's part of your… group. Of Phoenix I mean.'

Tilly squeezed my hand. She didn't know her father had been here. I shouldn't have brought her. I should have made her stay in the car. I should have left her at school.

'I'm sorry, Mrs Napier, but I can't help you. You'll need to talk to your husband.'

I put my professional voice on to hide my intimidation. 'As I am sure you know, I have been unable to contact Paul.' I blinked a few times to compose myself, amazed that I was still smiling, though my cheeks were starting to ache with the effort. 'Could you just tell him I'm here? He won't mind.'

'I can't release any information about our clients. You'll have to talk to your husband and son yourself.'

'You're not listening to me.' I wasn't smiling now. 'My son is in here. He's a minor. I'm not asking you to break any confidentiality, because I know he's in there, because my husband, is a member of your… your group. I just need to see that he's okay.'

This man, face set, stepped forwards towards me again. I didn't move this time. He was taller than me, though I held myself as high as I could despite my muscles trembling. I stepped to the side and moved towards the door, even though I knew it was locked. What was I doing?

'Mrs Napier…' He blocked me with his arm.

'Mum, don't.' I could hear Tilly's tears in her voice as she grabbed my arm. I let her pull me back, then ran towards the window further along the wall of the building. There was a white venetian blind pulled down, but I cupped my hands around my eyes and tried to see through.

'Cameron,' I said loudly.

'Mum, let's go,' Tilly said, her voice high pitched. 'Please, Mum.'

'Cameron! It's Mum!' I shouted, and before I knew it I was banging on the window with my fist. The man had taken his phone out of his pocket and I began running around the building, shouting out my son's name, sure that he could hear me and would raise one of the blinds and I had a vision like a movie where we would press palms through the glass, crying, and, somehow, I'd get him out of here. I shouted and shouted, and realised that I was crying too and I staggered as I slid on a gumnut around the back of the house. And then the man was in front of me again, with another man, and Tilly was running up behind me and pulling at my arms and I could no longer hold myself up high because my face was streaked with tears and my voice was cracking and my ankle hurt where I twisted it. They marched towards me, telling me I was on private property and they were going to call the police if I didn't leave, and then a woman appeared and told them to wait, and she put her arm around my shoulders and led me back to my car, with my other hand clutching Tilly's. Tilly was sobbing now.

I opened the car door and sat on the driver's seat, my legs on the ground, and tried to compose myself. Tilly was staring at me, her eyes wide and her face pale.

'Mrs Napier,' the woman said, quietly, glancing back at the man. 'Cameron's okay.'

'So, he is in there?' I tried to stand up again, but she put a hand on my shoulder and seated me back down again. 'Are you a mother?' I hissed. 'Do you have kids? Have you any idea what this is like for me?'

'Cameron is safe. I promise you. That's all I can say. But you need to go.'

'You don't understand,' I pleaded. 'I need to see him. He was in hospital a few hours ago. He's ill, I just need to see for myself, and let him know that I'm here.'

'He's not here.'

'He is. He must be.' He must be, because if he isn't then where else is he? Was this some horrible misunderstanding and he was just at the café with Paul or down the shops? No, no, because then Paul would answer his phone.

I stared at her, then looked back up to the building where the two men stood sentry in front of it, arms crossed. I looked back at the woman. She had curly auburn hair. Freckles on her nose. She looked like some part of her must be kind.

'He's not here.'

I swung my legs back into the car. Tilly was sitting in the passenger seat, her face covered with her hands. I took a deep breath and looked at this woman's hazel eyes, hoping that woman to woman, she'd help me. 'He only likes cold water. From the fridge, not the tap.'

She nodded a little then stood up and walked back towards the men at the door. They stood there in a line, the men's arms folded, the woman's arms holding her cardigan closed around her body. I closed the car door then leaned over and pulled Tilly towards me.

'What's going on, Mum?' she cried.

'I don't know, darling. Have you got your phone?'

'Yes.' She leaned down into her school bag, beneath her feet and began rummaging around. If Paul wouldn't answer me, surely he would answer his daughter's call?

'Can you call your dad's number? Then give me the phone.'

She nodded, pressed a few buttons then handed me the phone. Straight to voicemail.

'Goddammit!' I shouted. 'Find Cameron's number,' I said, pushing it back towards her. 'Sorry, darling, I don't mean to get upset.'

She rang Cameron's, held it to her ear then shook her head.

I held my hand out and I took it from her and heard the end of his voicemail message.

'Cameron, darling,' I said, trying to stop my voice from shaking. 'It's Mum. And Tilly. Call us any time. Any time at all. We're coming to get you.'

I handed the phone back to Tilly, then started the engine. 'Sorry, sweetie. I don't mean to worry you. I'm sure there's an explanation for this.'

She nodded but was looking away from me. I reversed the car, slowly, then started to drive back down the dirt path. We were going to the police.

Thirty-One

Paul

As I drove along the highway, I glanced at my phone even though it was switched off. Emily would be frantic. I pushed the thought of her away. Cameron was more important right now. I would call her soon. I glanced at Cameron; clenching my teeth at the squeaking of the leather seat as he rocked back and forth.

'Cameron, mate,' I said, in a light voice. 'Can you stop doing that?'

He said nothing, shook his head then stopped moving.

'That's better,' I said. The radio announcers chatted inanely to callers about things they'd done by text message that they should have done in person. Resigned, fired people, broken up with partners. Maybe I should send a text message at least. Maybe I should just call her. No, not yet. Not until we were on our way; I wasn't sure she couldn't talk me out of this and there were still hours to go before the flight. 'Cameron, do you want to choose some music? This is crap.'

He reached for my phone.

'No.' I snatched it from him. 'Not from my phone.'

'How then, when I'm not allowed to use my phone either?'

'I've told you mate, you're too young to have that thing near your beautiful brain.'

'You do.'

'I'm fully grown, mate. My brain is ruined as it is.' I laughed loudly, flatly. He didn't. 'Just try to find something on the radio.

I know that's a foreign concept to kids like you. When I was a kid, we had to turn a little dial through all the crackling sound to try and find a song. Jeez, I remember when my dad first got a tape player in the car.'

Cameron was biting at his fingers now, turning his thumb sideways and gnawing at it, looking out of the window. 'Cam, your hands.'

He sighed, shifted around in the car seat then began pressing the screen on the car through all the radio stations. I couldn't wait to get away from all of this. I thought about those Sunday family car trips when I was a kid. The Sunday run, my dad had called it. We used to protest but we'd load up into the family car, books in hand for the journey, and drive through the countryside. We'd sometimes go to a hill, walk up to the top to a cairn and huddle against the rocks drinking tomato soup from a thermos. We listened to a tape in the car on the way home. Just one singer or group, none of this chopping and changing from song to song. We'd let the tape play the way it was designed. It'd always start with a catchy song, then slow down a little until we'd settled in and then, as we'd speed over the country hills giggling as our stomachs lurched when we descended, the river rushing along the side of us and rabbits darting across the road, the songs would speed up.

Cameron switched again and again to new radio stations after hearing only moments of a song. Everything that Phoenix taught was true. How could we expect him to learn, to succeed, when a thousand times an hour his attention was shifting from this to that, discarding things he doesn't like on a whim, swiping here and there and checking his phone to see who has updated Facebook or Instagram or Snapchat in the last few minutes in case he misses out. How did he have any chance?

'Just pick something, Cam,' I said, hearing the strain in my voice. 'Just leave one thing on and give it a chance. We're almost there.'

He pressed the screen again, then sat heavily back in the seat. He began drumming his hands on his thighs. I tried to focus on the song. I swallowed. I *would* call Emily, but not yet.

—

'Damian.' I reached my hand out to shake his and he pulled me into a hug. I let myself relax a bit. It seemed easier when I wasn't battling alone with my own doubts.

'Paul. And young Cameron!' he said warmly, holding his hand out to Cameron.

Cameron paused for a moment then shook his hand. 'Hi.'

'How are you feeling? I heard you had a nasty knock to the head.'

'I'm okay now, thanks,' Cameron said, glancing at me. I nodded and put my hand on his back and guided him forwards, into the hallway.

'He's going to have a bit of a black eye for a few more days I think.' I smiled, closing the door behind me.

'Just like your old man in his day, eh?' Damian said, laughing. 'Come through. You hungry? Thirsty?' he said to Cameron.

Cameron shook his head. 'No thank you.'

'I'll get you some water. We'll have lunch soon. You need to eat well today.'

We followed Damian through as he chatted about the house. 'We used to come up here all the time when the kids were young, every long weekend and school holidays. But now that it's the two of us, we don't use it as much even though it's only an hour away from the city, really. I really should rent it out, but I don't like the idea of strangers using it.'

He turned on the tap and poured two glasses of water and handed one to each of us. I saw Cameron look at it, then slowly bring it to his mouth and pretend to sip it. I shook my head, feeling my tension rise. How had we allowed him to get like this?

Cameron and I sat on a saggy black leather couch in the living area adjacent to the kitchen; Damian settled in a matching armchair. There was a wooden coffee table in the middle of the room with some old, hardback books piled on it. No magazines. No TV. Damian drove the conversation, asking Cameron questions about school, and I chatted about the drive up, the weather, anything to pass the time.

'Dad? Can I call Mum?' Cameron said while Damian had gone to use the bathroom.

'I'll call her soon,' I said brightly.

'I want to talk to her.'

Damian's voice boomed into the room. 'No mobile reception here, Cameron,' he laughed as he came back through. 'That's the way I like it. Now, young man, I need to have a private talk with your dad. I've got some old sports gear in the shed out there, would you like to go have a look, see if you can find a ball to kick around? I'd love to see it get some use.'

Cameron looked at me, his eyes pleading with me to rescue him. This is why we were here: he'd forgotten how to play, how to just be. I nodded at him and gestured towards the back yard. He glared at me and stomped off.

I forced down a surge of irritation at his sulky behaviour. I reminded myself that soon, I could teach him the value of hard work and self-reliance, far away from all the things and people who had made him sick.

Damian closed the door and sat back down in the armchair. 'How did it go with Emily yesterday?'

'Oh, mate. Don't suppose I'm allowed a drink?' I smiled.

He shrugged. 'We don't tell you what to do. You have to be the one to make the right choices.'

'I was joking.' Sometimes I wished that Damian could be more relaxed around me. I saw him as a friend as well as a mentor, but it seemed that he still didn't trust me enough to let his guard down around me.

'Did the psychiatrist come?'

I stopped smiling, I nodded then filled him in. When I finished and look up at him, he was sitting up straight, his jaw set.

'I'm proud of you, Paul, for standing up to the psychiatrist, and to Emily. They all want to give him drugs, Paul. *You* are the one who is going to save Cameron from them; look what's happened already. She'll do it again, you know.'

'I know. I just…' I couldn't help but want to defend Emily; I knew what she did was wrong, and I was furious for her deception. But I wasn't ready to completely demonise her either.

'Paul. Look at me.' I looked up at him, staring intensely at me. 'You're a clever man, Paul, well read.'

I smirked. 'Not really—'

He pointed his finger at me. 'Stop. You're putting yourself down again. You are an extremely intelligent man. Now, tell me, when you think about great literature, or great men in the history books, did you ever read about them having a mental illness? No, you didn't. Did people have ADHD when they were fighting for survival? Did people have problems with gambling, or sex addictions, or multiple personalities when they were working hard and being self-reliant and improving themselves? No: those so-called mental illnesses didn't exist. Mental illness still *doesn't* exist.'

I felt hot. I glanced out the window at Cameron, kicking at the dirt.

Damian continued. 'I'm not denying that sometimes we feel sad; I've felt sad many times. But being sad is not an illness. And if someone, in the history of the human race, was a bit different to others, they weren't put on brain-altering medication and given an hour of therapy every week and government handouts. They were accepted into their village and given a different job. Maybe they weren't ever going to be the leader of the group, but they'd be given a role. Maybe they'd be the cook, or the one who tended to the animals. They were still important, no, *crucial* to their village. They were integrated and genuinely needed.'

'I know, I know. You're right.'

'And this is what happens, Paul. This is what happens when they get their hands on our children.' He pointed his finger outside towards where Cameron was.

'She does love him, though.'

'I have no doubt she does, and so do you. But she doesn't understand. She has refused to listen to you. You need to get him away from her, from the doctors.'

'I know. You're right, I'm just worried—'

'There is nothing to worry about. He would never have been in this situation, Paul, if it wasn't for the medication. I've alerted the Phoenix team in Scotland and they're ready to work with Cameron.'

He stood up and went over to the bookshelf and took down a thick hardback book. He handed it to me.

'DSM five,' he said, disdainfully.

I looked at the cover, then flicked through the pages. 'Yes. The psychiatry book.'

'This book is how the psychiatrists have falsely diagnosed your son, Paul, and how they would have diagnosed you if you had been weak enough to let them. The Diagnostic and Statistical Manual. Instructions, Paul, step by step tick boxes. You could train a monkey to use this.'

I nodded.

'They used to have homosexuality in there Paul, as an illness. It's dangerous, Paul. Just look at psychiatry's history: torture, genocide, forced sterilisations, locking people away for being disabled. They're little better than alchemists, trying to turn the misery of others into gold for themselves.'

I took the thick book and began to flick through the hundreds and hundreds of pages, scanning the titles on each. Major depression, reactive depression, persistent depressive disorder, generalised anxiety, unspecified anxiety, ADHD, ADD, social communication disorder, autistic spectrum disorder, conduct disorder, oppositional defiant disorder, intermittent explosive disorder, Bipolar 1 disorder, Bipolar 2 disorder… During my time at Treetops, and in the many meetings I'd attended afterwards, we had discussed how our society expects excellence. We tell our children that if they work hard enough, they can be a sports star, an academic genius, slim, popular. And when our children are not brilliant, what do we do? We pay huge sums of money to a doctor to give them an excuse for not living up to society's expectations, and if you're extra lucky, some toxic medication that gives you diabetes and stunts your growth or makes you fat and fries your brain.

I had heard of the DSM-5 diagnostic book before I had become involved with Phoenix. It was a few years ago. I'd had a long day at work, and when I put my key in the front door lock, I paused for a moment, not sure what I'd find when I stepped in. Often, I'd walk into a mess, Emily red-faced and slamming things around; other times, she'd smile at me and ask how my day was, and the place would be spotless.

I turned the key, and stepped inside. Emily was sitting at the kitchen table with her laptop open, a notepad beside her.

'Hey,' I said.

Emily swivelled round, grinning, and beckoned me over. 'Come and read this.'

I put my keys and phone on the kitchen bench and leaned over her shoulder. 'What is it?'

'So, there's a new diagnostic system about to come out. DSM-5. They've updated it from DSM-4 – they change it every so often, you know, to make sure that it's up to date with all the mental illnesses.' She went on to explain while scrolling through webpages and pointing at the notes she'd been scribbling on a notepad. 'I'm just trying to find all the details, this could be just what we need…'

'What do you mean?'

She patted the seat next to her and slid the laptop over towards it so it was half way between her and the other seat. I sat down. 'They're changing the way they make a diagnosis. The psychiatrists. So maybe we'll get some answers now.'

'But how does that change things for us?'

'Well,' she continued. 'They can never figure out what's wrong with Cammie. So maybe now he'll finally fit something, maybe now he'll get a diagnosis.'

'Emily,' I groaned. 'That's ridiculous.'

She turned to me, frowning. 'It's not ridiculous, Paul. If he had a diagnosis, then we could get some help.'

'He's got lots of diagnoses, Emily – you've told me at various times he has autism, bipolar, ADHD, OCD, anxiety... am I missing any?'

She tutted. 'Paul. Don't be horrible. He doesn't have *any* diagnosis, that's the point. These things have been thrown around him for so long and everyone disagrees. Don't you see, Paul? If he fits into one of these new diagnoses, it'll help him. Once he gets a diagnosis, he can get help at school, and maybe there's a treatment that can help him.'

I pressed on my temples. We'd been through this so many times and neither of us would say what I knew she was thinking: that if Cameron had a *diagnosis* then people would stop looking at her as if she was a bad mother. Because she'd told me before, in tears, that it was what she feared, that every time he acted up, she felt blamed.

'Emily,' I said softly. 'I understand why you're excited, but doesn't this seem ludicrous? That one day a kid is fine and the next day he has a mental illness.'

'They discover new physical illnesses all the time.'

'That's different.'

'It's not different at all.'

'What about kids who had a mental illness yesterday and now don't?'

'Then their parents would be ecstatic. To be told that their child is fine.'

I sighed. 'We've been told Cameron's fine, and you're not ecstatic.'

She was silent then, and I watched her eyes fill with tears. She shook her head just a little. 'Is it so bad to want him to be happy?'

'He is. In his own way.'

She her fingers on the table and shook her head harder. 'He's *not*. You know he's not.'

'Okay, okay...' It wasn't worth another fight. I knew he wasn't completely happy. But what boy is? I wasn't when I was his age. Everyone thought I was happy because I was good at sport, but I still thought I wasn't good enough. 'Emily. Sometimes I just wonder if we're losing sight of *him*, you know? There are so many labels flapping around him that we can't see his face anymore. Maybe it's better if he doesn't *have* something. Think about it – every school, every uni application, every job, every insurance policy, he'll have to say he has a mental illness that might not even exist in a couple of years' time because they might change the book again!'

I took a deep breath and looked at Emily. She was staring at the screen, her lips tight, but I knew she was listening. I was glad she didn't respond. We were just trampling over the same old ground, and none of this was helping Cameron. Or us.

–

I looked up from the book, back at Damian. I felt sick at the thought of how frantic Emily must be. 'Am I doing the right thing?'

He nodded. 'You are. You have to help Cameron.'

He was right; I knew that. Cameron had no way here to avoid the influences that were making him sick. It was everywhere – television, magazines, social media, music videos that told my daughter she had to grind her body at a misogynistic man if she wanted to be loved. We feed them over-processed food full of sugar and wheat that our body was never designed to digest, making their bodies sluggish as their liver and kidneys work overtime to try and clear it all from the body. They spend their days stooped over screens forgetting how to connect to the outside world while their cervical spines curve and parents pay quack chiropractors to help them straighten up as they would be if they were outside all day. Mobile phone signals are mutating their brain cells, vaccinations are assaulting their immune system and then we turn around and expect them to be miniature versions of what we ourselves wish we'd become. We've all known for so long that there's something wrong with the way we live our lives. And my children are paying the price.

Not anymore.

I nodded back to Damian. The only thing I was unsure about was leaving Emily and Tilly. I *was* doing the right thing for Cameron.

'I don't even blame her, Damian,' I said.

'She doesn't understand. But she will.'

'I'm sure she'll come around too, once she sees the difference in Cameron. She's a good person.'

'Of course, she is. But right now, she doesn't understand. This is the only way to help her see that you – that *we* – are right. You're going back to where you grew up, when life was simpler. Sometimes you need space and a change of scenery, and you'll have plenty of support. There's no time to waste for Cameron, though. You can't wait.'

'I know.' I stood up, thanked him, and shook his hand. 'I'll see if he'd like a nap before the flight this evening.'

Soon, we'd be on our way.

Thirty-Two

Emily

The police were sympathetic, but disinterested. He was with his father, they said, and when they asked if I thought that Paul might harm Cameron, I shook my head. 'No,' I had said, quietly. 'He wouldn't hurt him.' In my heart, I knew that.

Back at home, I allowed Tilly to go into her room with her laptop. I had her phone near me, as well as my own. We had a home phone, and though Paul and Cameron wouldn't even know the number, I checked the voicemail anyway. I searched Cameron's room for any notes, or anything obviously missing, but it was so hard to tell. In our bedroom, I looked up on top of our wardrobes, where we kept our suitcases. I dragged a dining chair through from the kitchen and stood on it, stretched up, then pulled the cases down. I screamed as one of them caught the corner of my head. The cases clattered to the floor. I felt myself teeter sideways, then jumped down onto the wooden floors and let my tears fall. How many cases did he have? Was there one missing? Maybe he was coming home, maybe it was all a misunderstanding? But it was the afternoon now; they'd been gone all day. If there was nothing to worry about, he'd have called me by now.

Suddenly, my phone rang.

In an instant, I was on my feet, flying along the hallway to the kitchen. I grabbed for the phone. Tilly ran towards me from her room, then stopped as I picked it up.

'Paul,' I said. 'Where the hell are you? Where's Cameron?'

243

'He's fine, Emily. He's with me.'

'Jesus, Paul. Where are you? Put him on, I need to—'

'Emily, he's here, he's fine.'

'I, I...' I didn't know what to say. I had so many questions to ask but it all just seemed so bizarre that I couldn't formulate the right sentences. 'Where are you? When are you coming home? Is he okay?'

'Emily. He's perfectly fine. We... we're just going to go away for a while.'

My heart almost stopped. 'Away? Away where? He's got school tomorrow.'

'Please, Emily, you have to trust me.'

I was aware of Tilly gripping the edge of the benchtop, staring at me. I turned my back to her and walked back towards my room. 'Trust you? I – Put him on, Paul. I need to talk to Cameron. Now.'

'Emily—'

'Now!' I screamed. 'This is not a joke.'

Paul's voice was strained. 'Emily, I'm just taking him home for a while. To Scotland. I want to spend some time with him, get him away from all of this for a while.'

'All of *what*? Me? His sister? And what do you mean, home? I'm at home, Tilly is at home, and we're terrified and we're watching the door and waiting for the phone to ring and I just want to speak to him.' I started to cry. The firmness in Paul's voice scared me. My anger drained away, replaced by something far more terrible. 'Paul, please, please, let me talk to him.'

Paul hesitated.

'Please, Paul. Don't do this to me. You're scaring me, and Tilly. She's here now. She's listening.' I whispered.

'Mum?' Cameron's voice came on the line.

I almost sank to the floor. 'Oh. Cameron. Cameron, thank God. Darling, where are you? Are you Okay?'

'I'm not sure, we're at one of Dad's friend's places, Damian's, in the bush. We're going to the airport soon.'

244

I tried to keep my voice light. Damian. I started to feel dizzy; I made myself slow down my breathing. 'The airport? Where are you going, sweetie?'

'Scotland,' his voice wavered. 'Didn't Dad tell you? We're going to see Grandma and then we're going on a camping trip. Dad?' I heard Cameron and Paul mumbling but couldn't make out what they were saying.

'We have to go, Mum. Dad said that you and Tilly will come and join us in the school holidays after we have some time together. Are you coming?'

'Oh darling, that sounds wonderful. We will come. We'll come very soon. Cameron, do you remember my phone number? Off by heart, I mean, not just from your phone.'

'Yeah.'

I hoped he understood what I was trying to say. 'Make sure you write it down, okay, in case you don't get mobile reception out there, so you can call me from a payphone or something when you get there, okay? Just call the operator and reverse the charges.' Can you even do that these days?

'Sure.'

'Cameron, I'll see you really soon, okay. I love you.' My voice broke.

'I have to go, Mum.'

'I love you, Cameron. I'll be there as soon as I can.' I spoke lightly. 'Can you put your dad back on?'

'Okay, bye, Mum.'

I heard mumbles again as the phone got passed over to Paul.

I hissed at him. 'Paul, do not dare go anywhere. What the hell are you doing?'

'I'll contact you when we get there. Please don't be angry. I just need some time with him, I just want to reconnect with him. I've been away for so long.'

'Paul, don't you dare turn his head with all that—'

'Emily. I just want to show him a simple life.'

I was losing him; I knew he was trying to end the conversation. 'Please, please—'

'Em. I love him. I love you all. I promise it's all going to be okay. I'll be in touch soon.'

And then he hung up.

–

That evening, Tilly and I sat opposite each other in the café. She ordered the Thai beef salad, me the duck and lychee red curry. Cameron usually had the burger; Paul usually had the nasi goreng. Now that we were here, I realised how silly it had been of me to come, but I didn't really know what to do and I needed something to be familiar. I waved as a woman I knew from school bustled in with her kids trailing behind. Maybe I'd thought that no one would think anything was wrong if they saw Tilly and me out together, or maybe I just needed to see life going on as normal because then, my fears seemed silly. Fathers and sons went on trips all the time, didn't they?

I ordered my second glass of wine. 'Isn't that Sasha, from school, over there?'

Tilly turned and looked over her shoulder. She nodded. 'Yep.'

I nodded too. 'You hungry?'

'Not really,' she sighed. She hadn't touched the beef.

I bit at my nail. My leg was jiggling up and down. What was he doing now? I had looked up all the flights to Scotland. Only a few airlines, either via Dubai or Doha, flew tonight. I guessed they'd fly to Glasgow or Edinburgh, like we usually did. Or maybe they'd fly through London and go straight to Aberdeen. Most of the flights left about 10pm, so they'd have checked in and be waiting to board.

'We should have gone to the airport.' Tilly spoke quietly.

I looked at her; she was staring at her glass of water. I looked down at the table and rubbed my eyes. Of course, she was right: we should have gone to the airport. Why hadn't I gone to the airport? I almost jumped out of my chair, already calculating how long it would take to drive out there, park, and then find them. But they'd be through security already, hidden away in the lounge. I didn't have a ticket, our passports. And that would mean admitting that something was wrong, when Paul was just taking him on a holiday, wasn't he?

'There's no need for us to go chasing them through the airport, darling. They're just… going to have some bonding time. A boys' trip.' I tried to grin; it felt like a grimace.

She looked up at me briefly, then shook her head.

I reached over and placed my hand on hers. 'Don't worry, sweetie. There's nothing to worry about. It's just Dad, they've just gone on a holiday.' The more I said, the more I believed it. How could it be anything else when we were in our usual café for an early dinner surrounded by our usual friends?

I couldn't sleep that night. I had managed to get Tilly to have a bath and get into bed, and she was finally asleep. I had reached into the cupboard above the oven where we kept the spirits, back in the days when Paul enjoyed a drink, and found a bottle of Hendricks, quarter full. There was a plastic bottle of tonic in the beer fridge out on the back patio, and lemons on the tree, so I made myself a large G&T.

As I drank it, I thought about them on the plane, what they'd be eating, watching, thinking, doing. I wondered how Paul's no TV rule would go when he was stuck on a plane half way around the world with nothing to do. I imagined he'd have had to break his no alcohol, no caffeine rule too. And what about the plane food? It almost made me smile; I imagined teasing him about it later. When they landed, they would call me. By the time I had finished my third G&T, my fear had faded. They'd just gone camping. They'd call me tomorrow when they landed.

Thirty-Three

Emily

I could hear my phone ringing through the pounding in my head. I opened my eyes then closed them again at the morning light shining in the room. I'd forgotten to close the blinds. Paul usually did that.

Paul. Paul must be calling.

I grabbed the phone from the bedside table, and almost knocked over my glass of water with the cord that attached it to the charger. I deflated when I saw it was Ceecee. I thought briefly about ignoring it, that maybe if I didn't answer it, I could pretend that this hadn't happened.

'Emily,' she said slowly, though she didn't sound upset. 'Have you seen it?'

'Seen what?'

'Okay,' she sighed. 'So, you haven't seen it. You might want to sit down.'

'I'm in bed, Ceecee, I'm barely sitting up.'

'God, sorry, I thought you'd be up getting Tilly ready for morning hockey practice by now.' I glanced at the time. Shit.

Ceecee continued. 'Well, I woke up and as usual, the first thing I did was check the news online, and I was scrolling down, and it's not the head story, not by any means, but there's a story.'

'A story?'

'Emily. It's not all bad. It's a tiny story, the lead is some other political gaff which will take up everyone's attention this morning and then it'll drop off the page and no one will care.'

'What kind of story?' What was she talking about?

'Do not read it, Emily, just ignore it.'

I shook my head and sat up properly. 'Ceecee, you can't call me and make some cryptic comments about a story that I shouldn't read. You're scaring me. Now I have to read it. I need to go—' I hated feeling annoyed with Ceecee, as she was the only one who knew what had been going on with Paul and I needed her support. It wasn't her fault; she didn't know that Cameron and Paul had gone to Scotland.

'It's fine. It doesn't even mention names.'

My bottom lip began to quiver and my face burned. 'Names?'

'Look, it's obviously about Cameron but it doesn't say that. It just mentions him going to hospital, and his medication and all this rubbish about side effects.'

'Oh my God! Are you serious? Jesus. Why the hell is that in the papers? I need to go. It must have been Paul.'

'Of course it wasn't Paul, Emily. He wouldn't want to expose you or the kids to this.'

'But who else knows about this apart from you and me? You have no idea what Paul is capable of.'

'What do you mean? Emily, are you okay? Is he there?'

The fear flared up inside me again, starting deep inside me and burning every nerve to my fingertips. 'No. They've...' How could I explain this? I didn't want to lie to Ceecee but I had to believe that there was only one explanation. 'Paul's taken him on a trip to Scotland. Just to get some rest.'

'Are you serious? He was just in hospital. That was quick.'

I didn't know how to explain it; I didn't want her to judge me. 'I have to go.'

I ended the call and immediately opened my news app on my phone. My stomach was churning, still hoping that Ceecee was wrong. The news site flashed up. The top story was about the finance minister and some taxi vouchers. Then a horrific refugee story. Then a story about the airport being evacuated because of a sprinkler going off, and then there it was:

Boy, 15, hospitalised with life threatening side effects to psychiatric medication.

The 15-year-old son of a prominent Sydney sportsman was critically ill with a life-threatening reaction to psychiatric medication after collapsing at a school sports game. A source told The Daily Mail that the teenager was being treated for severe side effects to psychiatric medication which had been administered by the child's mother, without the consent of the child or his father.

The prescription of psychotropic medication to children has rapidly increased over the past 4 years, despite being unlicensed for use in children, with little evidence of efficacy, and potentially severe side effects including permanent neurological disorders, diabetes, tics, suicidal thoughts and sudden death. The diagnosis of mental illness in children has reached epidemic proportions...

I put the phone down. I didn't need to read any more. I lay back on the bed, blinking away tears, then picked up my phone again and checked the other local news sites, but it wasn't on there yet. Yet. My chin quivered. Who the hell did this? I bet that one of the nurses or doctors or cleaners got a bit loose after a glass of wine and couldn't resist blurting out the gossip to their partner, who was mates with a journalist who had some space to fill. I wiped my eyes and gritted my teeth. They'd pay for this; they would lose their job once I find out who it was.

But the phrases in the article sounded familiar. Could it have been Paul? No, he wouldn't want this in the papers either; he was so wary of journalists and their inflammatory headlines. He wouldn't want his name in the papers, and besides, Ceecee was right: he wouldn't expose the children to this. I shook my head, sniffing and trying to compose myself before Tilly woke up. I knew exactly where this had come from: the phrases sounded exactly like something that Phoenix would spout. Damian. This was exactly like something he and his cronies would do.

I wished I had some way of hacking in to the site and deleting the story. I just had to ignore it, like Ceecee said, and hope that no one noticed until something else more outrageous hit the news and it was bumped further down the page. For now, all I could do was get up and pretend that everything was normal, and hope that one of Tilly's friends hadn't heard their mother and fathers gossip about it over breakfast.

But it was like trying to ignore a mosquito bite on your ankle that begins to itch and you know that scratching it won't work, not for more than a moment, it'll just inflame your ankle until it's red and swollen and the bite is weeping, and the cycle will repeat. I had to stop looking. I put my phone down and went to have my shower, hoping the noise of the running water would start to rouse Tilly. She could just miss hockey practice today.

As I dried myself, I could only think of that news story and how many people would be reading it right now. I quickly dressed then went into the kitchen, clattering cutlery as I emptied the clean dishes from the dishwasher, bashing plates down. I heard Tilly stir and head for her bathroom as I clasped my hand to my mouth. Would it be in the print newspapers? I rushed to the front door and flung it open. I was in my bare feet but ignored the pain as I hobbled down the garden path over loose twigs and gumnuts that had fallen from our gumtree, through the gate and onto the front verge. I picked up our two newspapers, curled up and wrapped in plastic: my paper – the local – and Paul's *Financial Review*. I opened the recycling bin and threw his in. The story wouldn't be in there; it was hardly of national significance.

I hurried back inside and unrolled the newspaper, flattened it on the breakfast bar, then licked my index finger and flicked through the pages. I knew it was hardly front-page news but maybe there would be a little article further in. I sighed and put my hands flat on the bench top for a moment as I realised that there was nothing in there.

Tilly walked in, wearing her pyjamas, yawning.

I closed the pantry door then leaned against it with my back. My hands were shaking like I'd been caught stealing. She looked at me for a moment, then walked to the fridge and opened it.

'What do you want for breakfast?' I said, trying to sound normal. I could tell she hadn't heard anything about the story; she was her usual morning self. The itch subsided for a moment. Maybe no one else in her class would have looked either, after all, all the kids and parents were too busy making lunches, packing bags and driving through rush hour traffic. 'Do you want a lunch order today?'

'It's not Friday.'

'Well, I thought you might like a treat. I can order you some sushi? A sausage roll?'

'Can you just give me the money and I'll see what they have in the canteen?'

She braced herself for my usual answer, my usual explanation that I want to make sure she's having something healthy and not just spending the money on hot chocolate and chips or ice cream, but I just nodded. 'Okay.'

As I was waiting for her toast to pop, I walked back to the bedroom and looked at my phone from the doorway. Then I quickly walked over to it and swiped it to turn it on. No messages or calls – that was good, wasn't it? Then I quickly opened the newspaper app again. The story was still there. It was too early to relax about it. What if someone shared it on Facebook or Twitter? My heart began to speed up again and my eyes filled with tears and I threw it back down on the bed just as I heard Tilly shouting at me that she couldn't find a clean shirt, and I was so relieved to have something else to think about that I wanted to run to her and give her the kind of hugs I did when she was four and all she wanted to do was be by my side all day long. Maybe she should stay home today. No: that would look suspicious. I had to keep things normal while I figured out what to do. My mind went around and around and she shouted again, 'Mum!' and I closed my bedroom door as if somehow, I could shut the phone and all it contained in that room.

Half an hour later, we were in the car. 'I've got a surprise for you,' I said as I reversed out of the driveway.

'What?'

'You can choose the music today.'

I smiled and looked at her, but she was biting her lip. 'It's okay, the radio's fine.'

'No, go on, connect your Bluetooth or whatever it's called and we'll listen to what you want.'

She was silent but didn't move. I crossed a roundabout then glanced at her. She was looking out the window but her shoulders were slumped.

'What is it, darling? I don't mind—'

'You don't have to do this, Mum.'

I felt sick. 'I'm not doing anything, I'm—'

'Lunch order today, my music in the car. You don't have to try and be extra nice just because of Cameron and Dad. I'm not going anywhere.'

I heard myself gasp as I sucked in the air and I started to shake my head. We were stuck on the highway now, two lanes of barely moving SUVs on the morning school run. 'That's not why. I'm not trying to—'

'Leave it, Mum. I just want everything to be normal.'

I blinked hard. 'Me too, I'm sorry,' I managed in a small voice. 'Me too.'

So, we listened to the radio and as the 8am news came on we were already in the school slipway and I stopped the car, and Tilly got out as always and walked towards the school gates. And as I watched her I pleaded with someone, anyone, that today would just be normal for her and that no one would say anything to her. None of this was her fault; none of it had anything to do with her, and everything to do with Paul and me.

I called in sick to work. I parked around the corner from school, annoyed at myself for feeling so anxious about the next call I needed to make. I tried Paul and Cameron, of course, but there was no answer. I would call Paul's mum as soon as it was a decent hour in the UK. I left a message with Alasdair, and with Dr Davidson. And then, I called Damian.

It rang out. I hated that part of me was relieved. Why did he intimidate me so much? Perhaps he could manipulate Paul, but I owed him nothing. I called again, and again it rang out. This time I left a message.

'Damian. It's Emily. Paul's wife. Can you please call me?'

Why was I being so nice? Did I really doubt that he was responsible? I took a deep breath in and spoke quickly. 'I know your part in this. I know they were with you yesterday and I know what you're trying to do with your newspaper stories. It won't work. If you've got something to say to me, then pick up the phone and stop being such a coward.' I hung up, hands shaking. I waited in the car with the engine running. Sure enough, within moments, my phone rang.

'Emily,' his voice purred, 'I'm sorry I missed your calls, I was just driving to work.'

'I left you a message.'

'Oh, I haven't listened. How can I help?'

The hell he hadn't listened. I must remain calm, in control. 'Damian. I know they were at your place yesterday. Cameron told me.'

He sighed. 'Look Emily, I don't want to get in the middle of your family issues.'

'My family issues? The only issue in my family is *you*, and all that crap that you tell Paul. And the news story today? I suppose you're going to tell me that was nothing to do with you?'

'I don't know what you're talking about, Emily. Listen, you sound upset—'

My eyes widened with rage. 'Upset? Upset? Oh my God. Am I meant to believe that my husband and teenage son have taken off to Scotland behind my back after being at your house, *and* there's an article in the paper all about how evil medications are, and that you had nothing to do with it? You're an idiot if you think I'm that stupid.'

His voice was smooth, patronising. 'Emily, these are issues between you and your husband. All I have done is support my friend.'

'You're not his friend,' I spat.

'Paul's a grown man, Emily.'

'He wouldn't do anything to hurt his children.'

'No, *he* wouldn't.'

If he was standing in front of me, I'd have slapped him. 'Oh, but I would. Is that what you're saying? Do you know what, Damian? You're a disgrace. A disgrace of a man.'

I couldn't bear to talk to him anymore. I felt dizzy, I couldn't catch my breath. I hung up the phone, furious at him, and at myself for letting him get to me. I had no doubt any more that he was the one who had fed the journalists. I gripped the steering wheel and closed my eyes, willing myself to calm down so I could drive back home again.

It took me hours to calm down. I made it back home, then went for a walk but I imagined that everyone was looking at me and could see my swollen eyes beneath my sunglasses or know that it was me who had tricked my son into taking medications that the papers say threatened his life. It wasn't true, any of it.

–

Later that morning, I made myself a coffee, then sat down at the computer. I had to think clearly. I splayed my fingers out, the muscles on the back of my forearms tightening as they pulled back my wrists. I looked at the ridges of tendons fanning out from my wrist, over the fine wrinkles and the sunspots. I let my fingers relax and curl down back towards the keyboard. I stared for a moment at the black keys, each with a white letter shining on it, the silver casing of my laptop grubby in between them, and I rested my fingers down on them. Thumbs on the space bar, my pinkie ready to reach out for the delete key, wishing that I could press it and delete Damian and Phoenix out of our story.

For a moment, I stilled with the amazement of the power of words, whether they're accurate or not. The story of everything that has happened to our family could be written by a simple combination of those twenty-six letters, just like every person's body and mind is built from the unique combination of just four basic building blocks of DNA. And, just as Cameron is made from a combination of DNA from me, and from Paul, *his* story has been cleaved in two. My version and his father's version.

I must speak for Cameron; I can't allow these people to shout over the top of me anymore.

I clicked on the story again. The text was the same. How could they publish lies like this? They had it all wrong – weren't there journalism laws about that? I scrolled to the bottom. There was a generic stock photo of a teenage boy holding his head in his hands, with a little by-line with the phone number of Lifeline at the bottom. Beneath that was a section saying '34 comments'. I clicked on the comments link.

The comments sections in newspapers are clearly for people who have nothing better to do at work. In fact, I bet these people don't have a job, because who else would waste so much time and energy writing ignorant comments about my choices and my son, a boy whom they have never met? Not only do they think they're experts in the treatment of mental health, this *Fred of Willoughby* and *Margaret of Cremorne* who say that I'm a 'despicable' and 'devious' mother, they also appeared to be qualified experts in psychology, vaccinations, parenting, medicine and police work. Geniuses.

I focused my rage into my fingers. I clicked reply. I created a profile. I created several. I became *Julie of Bondi*, and *Graham of St Leonards*, and *Michael of Botany*. Throughout the morning, I replied to all the ignorant, judgemental comments, which made me feel better for a moment, but they always came back with something else. I knew that by responding, I was feeding them, fuelling a burning argument I could never win, but I didn't want anyone to read those comments and think that there wasn't another side to this story. There was *my* side of the story, and I needed people to understand what happened, otherwise they'd think I was a terrible mother to do this to my child. I'm not.

I'm not.

–

I'd managed to get an appointment before school pick up with Dr Davidson. My stomach churned as I sat in the waiting room. I hadn't been able to eat all day. I felt bile rise up in me at the thought of food. I was dressed in running pants and trainers, a baggy T-shirt, and my hair was pulled back in a ponytail. I looked a mess. I was a mess.

Dr Davidson's door opened, and she looked around the waiting room, empty except for me. 'Cameron not here today?' she said.

I shook my head, my eyes immediately filling with tears.

She nodded. 'No problem. Come straight through.'

In her room, the absence of Cameron seemed bigger than the physical size of him.

'How are you, Emily?' Dr Davidson said as I sat in my usual blue armchair.

She was wearing a tight dress today, striped like a zebra. I could almost see Paul raising his eyebrows. It almost made me smile. Almost.

I rearranged the cushions behind my back. 'I'm okay. Thanks for fitting me in this afternoon.'

Dr Davidson frowned. 'It's fine, I had a cancellation, and I know Cameron's been in hospital over the weekend, so I was keen to see him.'

'Oh, so you knew?'

'Yes. I had a message from the neurologist on my answering machine saying he was in there and they'd get the consultation-liaison psychiatrist to see him, but that's the last I heard. He got knocked out playing rugby?'

'Yes. He got tackled and next thing I knew he was on the ground and he was having a seizure.'

'Oh, Emily, that's awful. How frightening for you. How is he now?'

I started to speak, then paused to compose myself. 'I don't know... Paul discharged him, without me, I mean.'

'What do you mean?' She sat up straight, frowning.

'I know. It's ridiculous, isn't it? Yesterday, first thing, when I went to pick him up, they'd gone. And, this sounds ridiculous, but they flew out last night to Scotland.'

She shook her head a little, and hesitated.

'I was probably overreacting, but I even went to the police. They won't do anything. They say he's with his father, so in their eyes he's safe.' I held up my phone, in my hand. 'They'll still be flying. I'm hoping they call late tonight, or early tomorrow morning...' I covered my face with my hands.

When I took them away again, Dr Davidson held out a box of tissues.

I took a few, blew my nose and continued. 'I've spoken to Paul's mum, he's spoken to her, she's picking them up from the airport and I know she'll let me know when they're there. I haven't really told you before, but he's very anti...' I waved my arms around the room. 'This. Psychiatry. Medication. So, he's taken him away from it all, I guess. Said he wants to get some space. He thinks he knows better. I haven't told you before but he's part of this group, he went to rehab when he was gambling and they seem to hate doctors...' I rubbed my face with my hands.

She shook her head, a sympathetic smile on her face. Then she leaned back in her office chair and twirled her pen in her fingers. 'Are you worried?'

My chin quivered. I nodded. 'Cameron's not on his medication. Paul won't give it to him. He thinks it caused the seizure and he's angry at me for not telling him about it.'

'Emily, don't worry about the medication. You and I know that it has helped him enormously, but he'll be okay without it too. Are you worried about him in any other way, his safety, being with Paul I mean?'

I shrugged. 'The police asked that too and really, I know Paul wouldn't hurt him. I'm not worried from that point of view, but I'm worried... he's not here with me, I can't see what's going on for him and I'm worried that I lose him to...'

'Paul?'

'Yes.' My voice was small.

'He can't belong to both of you?'

I said nothing.

'How's Tilly taking this?'

'Oh. She's... well, I guess she's okay. She's worried about him, about me and her dad. I hate to think of her lying awake at night thinking about all this, but I know she is. She's like me, always has been.'

'You identify a lot with her.'

I shrugged. That's the way it's meant to be, isn't it? Mothers and daughters, fathers and sons.

'Does she talk to you?'

'We talk.'

Now it was Dr Davidson's turn to nod. 'I'm sure it's very hard for her, too.'

'Yes.'

'She's probably confused and frightened. Like you are.'

'I'm not...' Yes. I was.

'You can bring her in next time, if you like.'

I nodded, laughed in a forced way. 'Paul would have a heart attack. Look what he's done to Cameron. I don't want him to take her too.'

I blinked hard, then grabbed another tissue from the box.

'I know it sounds like some crazy movie, I just can't quite believe that this is happening. Paul has such fixed ideas about things, and I'm worried that he gets to Cameron. Paul now is so rigid in his... beliefs, but Cameron is so complex and Paul can't understand that and he doesn't know how to deal with him like I do.' I looked up at her, my eyes pleading with her to take my point of view. 'I thought it was harmless, you know, Paul not having alcohol or caffeine, or processed foods or whatever, but now he's on about vaccinations and doctors and medications being the cause of it all. It's like a... cult.'

'What's this group called?' she asked. 'That he's part of?'

'Phoenix. The rehab centre he was in was called Treetops Retreat.'

She nodded slowly.

'Do you know them?'

'I know *of* them.'

My heart sped up. 'Should I be worried?'

'Cameron's not in one of their centres though, is he?'

'No, they're on their way to Scotland, for a holiday. I think they're just getting away from it all and going to the country, or something. I think...' That's what they said, wasn't it?

'Emily, it's not for me to say, but Cameron is vulnerable. I can't say that all their beliefs are wrong, but I know that their views are... extreme. I guess I just have my concerns about Cameron getting caught up in all of that.'

'But he's with his dad.'

She sighed and nodded. 'Yes, he is. I'm sure you're right. I'd just be careful.'

I drove from Dr Davidson's office to Tilly's school. She usually got the bus home on Tuesdays but I had to see her. The spring sun made the red flowers of the bottlebrush trees that lined the street glow. What was Cameron doing now? Was he tired? Had he managed to get any sleep on the plane? I knew he was going to Aberdeen; Paul's mum had been surprised that I didn't know. She was sensible. He was just going to his grandmother's house with his Scottish family. But still, Dr Davidson's reaction when I had mentioned Phoenix worried me.

'Mum, what are you doing here?' hissed Tilly, looking over her shoulder back towards the school gates where her friends were milling around.

'I thought I'd pick you up today, save you getting the bus. I thought we could go for a smoothie.'

'Why didn't you just do slipway then?'

'It was last minute, Tilly, I was early so I parked. You could say, "*thanks Mum, for thinking of me!*"' I reached out to ruffle her hair.

'Mum…' She ducked out of my way.

'Oh, I'm only teasing, come on.'

'I'll meet you over there,' she said, pointing to the school car park. 'I've just got to say bye to a few people first.'

I raised my eyebrows then strolled back towards the car, my head down, my sunglasses on so that people couldn't see my puffy eyes after crying in Dr Davidson's office.

'Emily, how are you?' I looked up and saw one of the school mums, Tess, leaning from the driver's seat of her car, queued in the slipway, towards her open passenger window. The queue wasn't moving. I wiggled my fingers in a little wave then looked away, but out of the corner of my eye I could see her beckoning towards me. I pretended I hadn't seen her, then felt a pang of guilt. Tess was a friend. Our girls had been at school together since Year 1. So often, I'd told Cameron the importance of friends, of social connectedness instead of sitting alone on his bloody computer all the time, and here I was, the most alone I'd ever been, blocking my friends. I stepped towards her car. 'Sorry, Tess. I'm just trying to avoid a few people, you know?'

She rolled her eyes dramatically. 'Oh God, do I understand that! How are you holding up? I read…'

'Don't.' I held my hand up. 'Sorry, I just can't talk about it here. I'll start crying again.' I tried to smile and to my horror, a tear escaped. 'Shit.' I fumbled in my bag for tissues, hoping that Tilly didn't choose this moment to catch up with me.

'I just wanted to say that I understand why you did what you did. I know that a lot of the mums are judging, but I know how difficult Cameron was for you to manage.'

'He wasn't difficult. He was ill.' My face was contorting as I tried to keep calm.

'Oh, Emily, that's what I meant! And he needed it. Just ignore anyone who says otherwise, and I have already told them to stop talking about it.'

'Thanks,' I mumbled. They were talking about it? All the mums at school were calling each other for a salacious gossip? I wanted to sink down into the ground. 'I have to go.' I didn't care if she thought I was rude; I had to get back to the car. Just then, Tilly shuffled up beside me. 'I'm ready.'

In the car, Tilly slumped in the front seat. I indicated and pulled out onto the road. I tried to keep my voice casual. 'How was your day?'

I know that's not what you're meant to say to kids any more – the school psychologist had said we should ask about something that made them smile or feel proud, but it always sounded so unnatural coming out of my mouth that they knew it was forced.

Tilly responded, as suspected, with 'Fine.'

'Just fine?'

'Yup,' she said, but by the way she bit the inside of her cheek, I knew that something had happened.

I just nodded and kept driving.

'Did Dad call?' she said, eventually, not taking her eyes away from the window.

'Not yet,' I said. 'They're probably not off the plane yet.'

'It's not fair that he gets to go away and miss school and I don't.'

I sighed, gripping the steering wheel. 'Did you have a bad day?'

262

'No worse than usual.'

I nodded a little, and waited for her to say more.

'Everybody knows, Mum.'

My heart almost stopped. I kept looking straight ahead, keeping my voice light. 'There's nothing to know.'

'It was in the papers. I know it was about him. They said that he was psycho and you were hiding pills in his food.'

'Oh darling—'

'Were you?'

'Don't use that word, psycho, you know your brother had some difficulties but it's just an illness like any other.'

'You didn't answer me.'

'That article was rubbish, Tilly, rubbish.' My voice was shrill and I knew I should pull over but if I only kept driving this conversation would be over sooner. 'The tablets aren't dangerous, they were helping him, sweetie. You know that, he was so much better. He just got knocked out.'

'You could have warned me. Everybody was teasing me.'

I wanted to sob at the thought of Tilly struggling through the day with the little stuck-up princesses at school teasing her. 'I'm sorry you had to go through that. It's got nothing to do with you, Tilly.'

'It's got everything to do with me, Mum! It's my family too, and they've gone and we're just sitting here doing nothing.'

'I'll sort it out.'

She sniffed and turned away from me, looking out the passenger window, her shoulders heaving. I bit my lip and blinked back my tears, then reached out and put my left hand on her knee. She tensed, but didn't turn back. We drove home in silence. When we reached home, she kicked her shoes off in the hallway then stomped off to her room and slammed the door.

Thirty-Four

Paul

Mum's face broke into a grin as she spotted us walking out of customs at Aberdeen Airport. She waved, waved again, then clasped her hand over her mouth. She looked smaller than I remembered, greyer, a bit plumper. I smiled and waved back and put my arms around Cameron's shoulders as we neared her.

She hugged me. She barely came up to my chest but still managed to make me feel protected. She would look after us. She looked up and I kissed her cheek. Her skin was chamois-soft, slack and smooth. She turned and hugged Cameron, then held him at arm's length. 'Let me get a good look at you, son. You're so grown up now, Cameron. So handsome!'

'You must need new glasses, Grandma,' he said with a smile.

She swatted at him, smiling. 'Oh, away with ye. You're cheeky like your dad. Well, what are ye both waiting for, come on.'

I pushed the trolley with our luggage as we followed Mum to the car. It had been raining; the ground was wet with a few puddles remaining. I inhaled; the air was cool, fresh. Dusk was already setting in. We'd left Sydney well over twenty-four hours ago and I had no idea what time of day it was here or in Australia. If it was evening here, it must be early morning in Sydney; I wondered if Tilly was off to school and what Emily would be doing. Cameron ducked into the back seat. As we stuffed our bags into the boot of Mum's small hatchback, she muttered, 'Emily phoned me. What's going on?'

I couldn't look at her. 'What did she say?'

She spoke quietly. 'It's what she didn't say, Paul. Have you had a tiff?'

I shrugged as I managed to click the car boot closed. 'Something like that.'

She raised her eyebrows and put her arm on my hand to stop me. 'Paul. I'm chuffed to see you, and Cammie, you know that. But ye canna run away from your problems.'

'I'm not, Mum. Cameron and I just need a holiday. I'll explain it all later.'

She let go of my arm. 'Aye. Well, I'm just saying. Your father and I had our differences, but we always went to sleep wi' a kiss. And I'm glad we did, or I'd have never forgiven myself.'

Despite myself, I felt tears well in my eyes. My dad had died in his sleep, years ago now, when his heart gave out suddenly. 'Mum, not now. I'm worn out.'

She stared up at me through her glasses. I could see the smudges on the lenses of them. Her hair was either grey or bleached blonde, I couldn't tell, and she wore it cut short, framing her pale face, though her cheeks were pink. She had a dark purple scarf wound around her neck and tucked under her black woollen coat. I sighed. 'Do you want me to drive?'

'Drive? You've been travelling for days. Away with ye. I'll drive.'

–

Mum put the kettle on while I had a shower. Cameron had already had one and was getting changed in one of the bedrooms that Mum now used as a craft room. Mum's house felt small, even though as a kid it had seemed huge. Three bedrooms, one bathroom, a living room and a kitchen. That was all we'd had, all we needed. I thought back to our house in Sydney, the scale of it, my complaints about how we only had two bathrooms, or that there wasn't enough separation and we woke Tilly when we got up early to read the weekend papers when she was trying to have a lie in. How had I lost sight of what was important?

I left my clothes in the corner of the bathroom and turned the water on, wincing as the pipes shuddered and knocked. As I waited for the water to warm up, I took off my watch and put it next to Mum's candles and pot pourri on the glass shelf above the sink. I could hear her chattering away to Cameron. I knew he'd be exhausted, like I was, but I could hear him reply and laugh at something she said. Then I heard the doorbell and a high-pitched squeal that could only be my sister. I smiled.

I took my time, savouring the sting of the hot water on my back, and giving myself a few minutes more before I faced Fiona's questions. I stepped out over the edge of the bath, peeling the shower curtain off me, then tied a towel around my waist, bundled up my clothes and hurried through to my old bedroom. My childhood medals and felt-based trophies of footballers still lined the shelves on the wall. The wallpaper was the same textured cream colour, with a frieze of green with black and white footballs. I used to share this room with Alasdair. We'd always been close, only eighteen months' difference and one year of school between us. It'd been great when he'd decided to move his own family out to Australia too. He'd have called Mum, I was sure. Emily would have contacted him. I'd kept my mobile switched off but had no doubt that by now, my voicemail would be full of messages. I wasn't ready to turn it back on yet.

I took a deep breath and walked out of the bedroom. I could hear Fiona chattering away to Cameron, though he wasn't saying much in return. Mum saw me coming down the hallway, quickly stood up from the sofa and hurried into the kitchen. 'I made you a cup of tea. Fiona's here, come through the house!'

I took the cup of tea. There was no way Mum would have herbal tea and I couldn't face her questions right now. Besides, here, back at home where life seemed so ordinary, the idea of a cup of tea being dangerous seemed ludicrous. In the living room, Fiona leapt up and screeched again as she hurtled over to me and hugged me. 'Paul! You might have given us some more warning! You daftie!' She was giggling and hugged me again.

I couldn't help but laugh back. 'Thanks for the welcome! How's you?'

'Wow, you sound like someone off *Neighbours* now! Doesn't he, Ma? And Cammie, well, what a handsome Aussie.'

'Can you understand anything she says, Cameron?' I smiled to Cameron, who was staring at her with a half-smile on his face.

'Just a little bit.' He smiled.

'A *wee* bit!' Fiona laughed. 'We'll get ye' talking the proper way again,' she said. 'Sit down, Paul.' She picked up the plate of biscuits on the table. 'Have one. Mum's got in all your favourites.'

I picked up a piece of shortbread shaped like a Scottie dog, sat down next to Cameron and put it on the arm of the sofa beside me. Mum's dog, Dougall, sat beside me, shifting her eyes from me to the biscuit.

'Mum tells me that you've come for a wee holiday? That was last minute!'

'Yep,' I said, averting my eyes. She didn't push it. 'How have you been? Phil offshore?'

'Aye, he is. It's a pain having him away, but he's lucky to have a job, you know? So many people have been laid off. The oil's not what it was any more.'

'Yeah, it's the same in Australia,' I said, glad that the subject had changed.

'How's Emily? And Tilly? Where are they?'

I sipped at the tea. Mum had put sugar in it. 'They're good. Tilly has a lot on at school, so they might come later, in the holidays, we'll see. But Cam needed to take time off school anyway, he had a bad knock to the head playing rugby, so we thought we'd have some father-son time.'

'Ah, did ye now?' Fiona said, raising her eyebrows as she looked at Cameron. 'Well, it'll do you well to have a wee break. How long are ye staying?'

'I'm not sure at this stage,' I said. 'It was a bit of an impulse trip. A few weeks, maybe longer. We thought we'd go into the hills and do some hiking, camping maybe.'

Fiona peered at me, nodding slowly. I felt my cheeks heat up; I looked away. I knew how sudden this was. The truth was, I didn't really know what we were going to do now we were here. My instinct had been to get away from Sydney and keep Cameron with me. Damian had contacted the local Phoenix group for us, and I had promised Cameron we'd go camping but that was about it. It had all happened so quickly.

Mum glanced at us both. 'You'd better call your ma, Cameron, let her know ye got here safely. She'll be worried.'

He looked at me, and they all waited for my reply. I looked at my watch. 'It's still early in Australia.'

'She won't mind, Paul. She's waiting,' Mum said.

The room seemed to still for a moment. 'Yeah, Cameron, go on. Tell her I'll call her later.'

–

I did call Emily later. I owed her that, and Cameron knew she wanted to talk to me. I waited until he had collapsed, exhausted, into bed so that he wouldn't overhear me. I tried to reassure her that he was okay, and that there was nothing to worry about, while she sobbed and yelled down the phone. There was nothing else to say. My voice was hoarse and my thoughts were slow so I promised her that we would talk every day before hanging up, then I too, fell into a heavy sleep.

Thirty-Five

Emily

Cameron had called in the early hours of the morning. He had apologised for waking me, but of course, I hadn't been asleep. How could I sleep after everything that had happened yesterday? Knowing my child was on a plane, knowing that he was ill, worrying about Tilly and the newspaper article and the call with Damian and Dr Davidson's warnings about Phoenix.

Cameron had sounded tired, but well. I could hear in his voice that he was missing me. Paul called later too, but that went nowhere: I was too upset. Paul's mum sent me messages too, reassuring me that Cameron was fine.

I waited for Tilly to wake. I hoped she had slept. She had barely spoken to me last night, just retreated to her room without any dinner, and I had let her be. She had every right to be angry with me, though I wished that she understood that it was her father she should be angry at. I was the stable one, and yet I knew that as a mother, it was my job to contain her feelings.

It was 7.30am. I had no intention of sending her to school today, but I also knew that if I made the decision for her, she would most likely scream at me. I needed to wake her, and give her the choice.

Her door was ajar. Her light was off and it was quiet, so I pushed open the door slightly. Her bed was against the wall opposite the door, and she lay curled up on her side, with her back towards me. She was in her underwear: knickers and a black singlet that had ridden up her back in her sleep.

I stopped as I looked at her. I mean, really looked at her. Not the way I usually did as I pandered to Cameron, with a cursory glance to check she'd done her hair or scanning the crowd for her at the school pick up. It was like someone had slapped me.

I didn't recognise the girl I saw. How had I missed it? Her skin was pale. Her vertebrae looked like craggy boulders that were going to burst through her paper-thin skin. Her ribs curled around her chest in prominent ridges, crevasses deepening as she sucked air into her lungs. I took a step towards her, holding my breath as I stood above my sleeping daughter. I looked at her beautiful face, with downy soft hair around her sharp jawline. I could see the striations of her throat, the taut tendons in her neck. Her hands looked like those of an elderly woman, with bruises, some poorly healed cuts, the muscle-wasting on the back of her hand leaving her knuckles jutting out like rocks.

I took a quick, sharp breath in and I might have even whimpered at my stupidity, and a moment later, almost cried out with fear. Not her too. I didn't think I could cope with this too.

As quickly as the thought was in my mind, it fizzled out again, and was replaced by all the feelings a mother should have when facing the reality that her child looks like she's starving. Terror, love, guilt. So much guilt.

I backed out of her room, then, from the kitchen, called her name as I always did. 'Tilly, time to get up.'

She staggered through a few minutes later, now wearing baggy pyjama bottoms and a long-sleeved top.

With a shaking hand, I spread some extra jam on the toast I was making for her and put it down in front of her.

'Oh, Mum. We're late, I'll just take a muesli bar.'

'Not today. You're not going to school today. There's too much happening. Have this.' I put it down in front of her.

'I need to go to school. There's PE this afternoon and I need—'

'Not today, sweetie.' I forced myself to smile. 'Just eat your breakfast.'

'Mum! I'm not hungry.'

'Tilly, just eat your bloody breakfast!' I shouted.

She stared at me; I stared back, and my eyes filled with tears as I saw her face fall. 'I want to go to school.'

My head was swimming and the room seemed to spin around me. 'Fine!' I said, in a shaking voice. 'Get dressed.' I picked up the plate of toast and walked back to the kitchen, opening the bin and dropping it in. She watched me, then retreated out of the kitchen back to her room.

–

I had to force myself to shut my computer down after three hours of reading everything I could about eating disorders. A part of me of clung to the hope that maybe there was a physical cause for the weight loss. Maybe a thyroid problem, or coeliac disease. This couldn't be happening to my gorgeous, smart and stoic daughter.

I went out into the hallway and put the latch on the front door, just in case somehow Tilly came home from school by herself. I went into her room. Her laptop was with her at school of course, but her iPad was charging next to her bed. I knew her passcode; mothers know things like that. I opened the web browser and started to type in 'www.f' and immediately, the space at the top of the screen automatically filled with the Facebook log in page and by some miracle, when I tapped my finger on the little blue 'Go' button in the bottom right hand corner of the screen, it did indeed 'go'. Straight to her Facebook page, the login and password details autofilled. Too easy.

I sat on her bed. I hesitated when her Facebook news feed popped up, and my fingers froze as they hovered above the screen. Should I do this? What was I looking for anyway? What if she found out? It felt wrong to be breaching her trust.

But I knew, from everything that had happened, that things slowly sneak up on you. Like Paul's gambling problem: it wasn't like he woke up one day and went from everything being completely normal to full on addiction. It was insidious. And Cameron's problems too were always on the sidelines waiting for their time to be the star attraction. So how long had Tilly been losing weight, and, more importantly, why hadn't I noticed?

I scrolled through her news feed.

There were things on there that I hadn't seen in my own feed, so she obviously filtered which photos she posted for different people. There were photos of her in places I didn't recognise, with a bit too much pouting and make-up for my liking, but forgivable. I looked over to the left to her list of groups. And there was one that caught my eye. Ana and Mia. I clicked on it. And then I wanted to vomit.

Saying that I wanted to vomit was an inappropriate choice of words because if I wanted to vomit, then it wouldn't take me long on this page to learn about a hundred different ways to do it. Horror filled me as I saw pictures of skinny celebrities for 'thinspiration', with thighs like bows and arms like arrows, ways to binge, to purge, to trick your parents and your doctors. By the time I closed the browser and put the iPad back on the charger, tears were streaming down my face. I stood up and smoothed the bedclothes back where I'd been sitting and I walked out.

I'm not sure how long I sat at the dining table. I wiped my eyes and breathed deeply, then when my tears dried, just sat staring into space trying to fit all the pieces together. How stupid I'd been to miss it. It felt so clichéd: an emotionally neglected girl starving herself to get her parents to notice her. The daughter who'd always aimed to be perfect not under-standing that to her mother – and father – she was the very image of perfection no matter what she did. I thought about all the times I'd criticised her, for not tidying up after herself, for biting her nails, for not brushing her hair properly. I should have praised her more, made her understand that when I nit-picked over the small things, it was rarely about her and usually about me and how I was feeling: tired, underappreciated, worried. She must have been feeling like that too. She had always looked out for Cameron, always stood up for him, always tried to protect him. And yet she hadn't said anything about her feelings. She'd always said she was doing fine. But I couldn't remember the last time I'd asked her.

I felt dizzy. I was breathing too fast and the pressure of gravity had doubled, stopping me from expanding my chest and getting oxygen to my lungs. This was serious. This was an emergency. People died from anorexia.

I looked at my watch. It was still the middle of the night in the UK; damn this time difference. I could call but then his mum and Cameron would wake up and everyone would panic and I still didn't know what I was dealing with. Maybe she was just thin. I would make a GP appointment for Tilly after school to see how bad it was, and what we had to do. Than I would call Paul tonight, armed with all the evidence. I had to believe that his heart would scream as loud as mine was now.

Thirty-Six

Paul

'Come on, mate,' I said as Cameron sat in the car the next morning, staring out of the window as the rain coursed down the glass. 'Don't be like this.'

'Like what?'

'Like a child. Difficult.'

'I am a child and I'm not being difficult. I just don't want to go. I'm tired. We only got here a couple of days ago.'

'Cammie, come on.' I looked at him, but he turned his face away from me. He still hadn't taken his seatbelt off.

'We've just driven for half an hour.' I drummed my fingers on the steering wheel.

'I told you I didn't want to come.'

'You can just try it. What's the harm?'

We'd driven north-west from Aberdeen, the city giving way within ten minutes to farmland and villages until, following the instructions Damian had given me, I saw the old stone church. Phoenix held a group here three mornings a week, and they were expecting Cameron today. He was younger than their usual members, but given that Cameron was out of school anyway, they would take him on Damian's recommendation.

My head throbbed. Despite sleeping so heavily on the night we arrived, yesterday, my eyes were gritty and anchor-heavy and, as they dragged down, my whole head and chest sank down with them until I had to just collapse into bed in the middle of the day, swearing that it would only be for an hour. Then, last night, I tossed and turned on the sagging mattress of my old single bed. The rain had pattered on the roof, but instead of soothing me, it had roared in my ears. I was too hot, then too cold. Waves of dread had surged over me then receded briefly only to swell up again as I felt myself drifting off. What was I doing? How on earth could this work? I reminded myself that I always felt like this when I was jet lagged, wound up with anxious thoughts that darted around my body with the certainty that I'd never sleep again. The only other time I'd felt like this was in the slow, long hours after the thrill of gambling skulked away to be replaced by self-loathing.

But today, I had sworn, would be different. Today, I – and Cameron – would be better rested, and we would be able to regroup and move forward.

But Cameron didn't want to be helped. I had expected some resistance, but I was worn out. I sighed. 'Cameron. This is why we're here.'

'I thought we were having some *family* time.' He lifted his fingers up in imaginary speech marks when he said 'family'.

'Don't be a smart arse, Cam.'

He spun around to glare at me. 'Me? What am I doing? You're the one who's dragged me here saying we're going on a camping trip and we've barely landed and you're sending me off to this place with complete strangers, when I don't even know anyone and you told Grandma that I'm here to rest and I want to rest!'

'Don't talk to me like—'

'Like what?' he shouted, staring at me with such hatred that I felt myself shrink back from him. 'Fine!' he yelled, fumbling for his seat belt lock, yanking it off his body then opening the car door. 'Go and have a nap, Dad, and I'll see you later.'

'Stop, Cam…'

He slammed the door and I watched him storm off, wiping at his eyes. He headed for the door of the church hall. I should go with him. But, I knew, he didn't want me. I remembered how I had felt when I went to Treetops on that first day. I too had been full of anger, but that loathing was a symptom, the reason *why* I needed help, just like Cameron. But, like me, he had ultimately chosen to walk through those doors. He needed this.

I waited in the car for another few minutes, then I started the engine and drove off. I didn't have to pick him up for another four hours. I headed back to Mum's.

—

As I closed the front door, my head pounding, Mum started gesturing and waving to me from the kitchen. She held the phone to her ear. 'Hi, darlin'! How are you? Yes, yes, he's here now. I told you he'd be back soon. Hold on and I'll get him for you… Paul!'

I sighed. It must be Emily. I took off my wet shoes and left them at the door, then padded down the narrow hallway towards Mum, my socks slipping a little on the laminate floor.

'It's Emily,' she whispered, her hand over the mouthpiece of the cordless telephone handset.

'Thanks, Ma.' I took the phone from her. I held it to my ear; Mum hesitated before walking into the living room and closing the door.

'It's me,' she said her voice thick. 'I've been calling all morning. How's Cameron?'

'I haven't been out long. Anyway. He's good. He's out now.'

'Out? Out where?' I could hear the confusion in her voice.

'Just to a youth group.'

'Oh my God. Are you kidding me? Is this your nonsense?'

'Emily, don't start. He's just going for the morning, it's his choice—'

'Paul. Stop. I can't stand your constant justifications about this rubbish. Listen to me for a change. I need to tell you something.'

'What?'

276

'It's Tilly.'

My heart started to race. 'What's happened?'

'There's no easy way to say this, but I think…' she sniffed. 'I think she has an eating disorder.'

I was glad she couldn't see me as I rolled my eyes. 'Oh, Emily. When will this stop?'

'I'm serious, Paul. She's so skinny, you should see her.'

'We've only been gone a few days! She was fine when we left!'

'She was clearly like this before you left, we just didn't see it because we've all been so focused on other things. Look, Paul, I'm not just making this up. Honestly, she looks terrible and I looked on her iPad and she's been on these eating disorder websites and she's not eating.'

'I told you not to let her on the internet! Haven't you heard anything I've said? This is why—'

'Paul, don't shout at me.'

I stopped, cradling the phone between my neck and my shoulder.

'I just… I can't do this on my own any more. I took her to the doctor after school today. She's underweight, but she's stable, medically. Tilly just said that she's been forgetting to eat sometimes because she's busy, so I went along with it and said we were just having a check-up, but I know it's more than that. I didn't know what to say to her, I don't want to accuse her of doing this deliberately, especially when it's been so hard for her this week with you and Cameron.'

I said nothing; my eyes welled up.

Emily continued, barely pausing for breath. 'The GP didn't confront her either, but she called me later and said we have to watch her closely. The GP wants to refer her to a psychologist, and we need to weigh her every week and see if she's still losing weight, and if she is, then she needs to have all sorts of medical tests…' She paused. 'Why aren't you saying anything?'

'I don't know what to say.'

'I give up, Paul. We need you. I don't know any more what I think, what I believe. Now Tilly...' I heard her sigh before she spoke forcefully. 'I don't know why I've waited so long. If you refuse to come home, then we're coming to you. I'm booking the flights now and we're coming.'

She hung up and I stared at the receiver, stunned.

'Paul,' Mum said softly, behind me.

I placed the handset down gently on the glass table and turned around, blinking a few times.

'Everything okay?'

I shrugged. 'It's all fine, Ma.'

She said nothing, just held my gaze.

'Oh, it's just a bit of a mess at the moment, you know? Now she thinks Tilly has an eating disorder.' I tried to laugh but it sounded like a strangled cry.

'An eating disorder?'

'That's what she said.'

'You don't believe her?'

I shook my head and pulled out one of the dining chairs then sat down. Mum did too. 'I don't know any more. It's just the same as what happened with Cameron, you know, her obsession with finding something wrong with them.'

'You haven't told me much about what happened with Cameron. Is he okay?'

'He's fine.'

'So, why's he going off to this group?'

'You don't understand, Ma,' I said, rubbing my eyes.

'Maybe not,' she agreed, and we sat in silence for a few moments.

I looked up at her. She was fiddling with the lace doily on the table. 'Mum, do *you* think he's okay?'

'Cameron?'

I nodded, holding my breath.

She shrugged. 'He's just a lad. He seems a bit sad.'

I looked out of the kitchen window, saw the gulls circling in the heavy sky. 'She's looking for the answers in all the wrong places. She spends hours on those health websites chatting to people and getting herself all worked up about imaginary symptoms. I don't know, I wouldn't be surprised if it's just a way to drag me back, you know? She doesn't want us to be here, she never wanted me to take Cameron away from her.'

'Do you blame her?'

I shrugged, sighed. How could I explain it to someone who hadn't been through it?

'Is she imagining the stuff about an eating disorder too?'

'I have no idea.'

'You wouldn't want to miss that, you know.'

'We'll see. She and Tilly are coming here.'

Mum nodded slowly. 'I think that's a good idea.'

'I don't know if Cameron's ready to see her.'

'Of course he's ready. She's his mother, he misses her terribly. Paul, maybe it's you who's not ready.'

'I—'

She held her hand up to stop me. 'I don't know what's been going on, Paul. But I know you. You're a good man, like your father. I can see that something's been happening and it's your business what it is. But just watch your kids, you know. Don't lose them to... well, to whatever it is you're doing.'

'I'm not doing anything, Ma! Cameron is getting help, the right help!'

She stood up and smoothed down her shirt. 'You said yersel', Paul, that you don't think there's anything wrong with him. Just be careful. When I was a kid, the Wee Free kirk was everywhere, telling us what we could and couldn't do.'

'It's not like that, Ma. It's just a group, a clinic. It's not a church.'

'All these rules and silly beliefs. Kids are vulnerable.'

'I'm not a kid.'

'No, you're not, son. You're an adult and I know you can make your own decisions for your own family.'

My face was burning. 'Aye.' I stood up too. 'I think I'll go for a walk.'

At the sound of 'walk', Dougall pricked his ears up from where he was lying on the kitchen floor, then began wagging his tail while looking up at me with his brown eyes.

She nodded. 'Alright, Paul. I'll put the kettle on for when you get back.'

Thirty-Seven

Emily

'Put your hoodie on, Tilly,' I said as we waited at the baggage carousel.

Even though we had yet to set a foot outside, the dampness of the external air seeped into the terminal. Those people who clearly lived here in Scotland had their anoraks and coats on. Others, like us, were less well prepared, with only tracksuit tops or hoodies to keep them warm.

'You tired, sweetie?' I put my arms round Tilly's shoulders. She felt tiny. I squeezed her tighter, alarmed at how frail she felt.

'I didn't sleep at all,' she said, looking teary.

'You did,' I laughed. 'You were snoring.'

She looked up at me then swatted at me; I laughed again.

I know she had slept because I hadn't. I had tried to watch a movie, but it had made me cry and I knew that once I started, I would not be able to stop, so I switched it off. I had watched a documentary about people climbing Everest until that too made my chin quiver and even watching a live Adele concert made me well up. I had instead laid back as much as I could and tried to relax, watching Tilly. She had eaten some food: the salad, a small piece of chicken, a few spoonfuls of rice. The food was awful; I probably hadn't eaten much more so maybe I *was* overreacting. While she slept, I had stared at the screen on the back of the seat in front of me at the image of the aeroplane crossing the world and counting the endless time until we arrived.

Now, we had arrived. I pulled my shoulders back and slung my handbag over my shoulder and with the other hand, held my computer bag and tried to look like I knew what I was doing. My mouth was dry. My eyes were gritty, my skin desiccated. The airport was smaller than I remembered, but at least the queuing, checking, and stamping was quick.

And then, before I knew it, we were walking through a glass automatic door and Paul was standing there. But he was alone.

It had only been a week since I'd seen him, but he had let a short beard grow, peppered with grey; it suited him. His cheeks were pale with a blush from the cold air. He had a fleece jacket on that I'd never seen before, and hiking boots under his faded jeans. He grinned at Tilly; I couldn't help but break into a smile as I watched her run to him and into his arms. I hurried forwards too, and when he looked at me, and he and Tilly broke their embrace to include me, I had no choice but to hug them both, for Tilly's sake. I sniffed and squeezed my eyes tight then opened them and stepped back from him. I saw Paul looking carefully at her, looking for signs that I'd been wrong.

'Where's Cameron?' I said, looking behind him.

'It was a long way for him to come so early in the morning, I let him sleep.'

I dropped my eyes and shook my head. 'Paul—' I was aware that my voice was pleading with him. Still, he was playing games, showing me who was in control. 'Why wouldn't he be here? Don't you think that he wants to see us?'

'I got up in the pitch black. He was fast asleep. He'll be there when we get back to Mum's.'

I wiped at my face, shaking my head. 'I can't believe this,' I muttered.

'Let's go.' Tilly tugged at my hand, took Paul's in the other. 'Come on. I want to see Grandma.'

'Yes, let's go,' I said, unable to keep the bite out of my voice. 'I want to see Cameron.'

Paul began pushing the trolley with the luggage. I clutched his arm and spoke quietly. 'How is he?'

'Good. He's really good.'

I nodded and followed him outside into the crisp air.

I struggled to stay awake in the car, lulled by the warm heater blowing on my face and the bright green hills outside in a clear air that seemed so far away from the yellowing, dry fields of Australia. Everything seemed shrunken here: the roads narrower, the buildings compressed together, the cars smaller with oversized number plates, like children wearing new blazers that they've yet to grow in to. And when I peered through the exhaustion, I thought that maybe I was in a dream as I saw the snow-capped mountains in the distance, with purple around the bases of the hills. I wanted to stay awake, I wanted to make demands of Paul, but my eyes were so tired and finally, after a week of fear sapping my energy, at least I was here. Cameron was only kilometres away from me now. And despite myself, despite hating Paul for what he'd done, just being back together, in this warm car, far away from the place where the problems all started, made me feel that maybe I could afford to let myself rest for a moment.

Something in me sensed when we approached the familiar streets near Paul's mum's house. I forced my eyes open and looked out of the window at the grey granite buildings, beautiful when the sun was shining, but on a damp day like today, cold-looking. Suddenly it seemed like there wasn't enough air in the car. My face started to burn and sweat prickled my skin. I pressed the button to wind down the window a little and the cold wind blasted in.

'Mum!' Tilly whined from the back seat. 'Close your window.'

I leaned my head against the cold glass, letting the chilled air blow across the top of my head from the gap. I felt the glass slide up and glared over at Paul. His finger was on the button beneath his own window.

'Do you mind?' I said.

He ignored me and tapped on his window. 'Hey, Tilly, there's the high school that your mum and I went to.'

'Looks like a prison,' she mumbled, then went quiet.

My teeth were clenched but I had to keep calm, for Tilly. 'It was a bit stricter than your school, Tilly,' I tried to say lightly. She was right; it did look like a fortified penitentiary.

'We used to get the cane,' Paul said, in a deep voice. 'If we spoke back the teachers would put a piece of chalk on the desk and whack it with their belt and we'd watch it disintegrate into a cloud of white dust. That used to shut us up. Imagine if they did that at your school.' He turned around to look at her, grinning, then turned back to face the road.

'I never get in trouble, Dad. They'd run out of chalk for Cameron though.'

'Tilly, that's not true,' I said.

'It is,' she replied, haughty.

'Your dad used to get in trouble at school too, and look at him now,' I said. I saw his eyes dart towards me and his fingers blanched on the steering wheel. I spoke more softly. 'He runs businesses, was a world class athlete. So, behaving at school isn't everything, Tilly. Your brother will be fine.'

'He'll be great,' said Paul.

'Whatever,' said Tilly.

I almost let myself smile.

—

The car had only just stopped when I saw the blinds at the front of the bungalow twitch. I threw open the car door and ran down the gravel drive way to the door on the side of the house, which led straight into the kitchen. The door opened as I put my hand up to pull down the handle and then, like magic, Cameron reappeared back into my life. I broke into a grin then grabbed hold of him as the tears streamed down my face and from the heaving of his body, which already seemed to have stretched taller, I knew that he was crying too.

'I missed you, Cammie. I'm sorry. I'm so sorry I left you in the hospital,' I mumbled into his ear.

'Me too, Mum,' he sniffed.

I broke our hug for a moment, and held him at arm's length to consider his face. Paler, certainly. But unharmed. He looked just like himself. I wished I could pat down his limbs, look at his arms and legs and back and chest as I once had when he was a baby to check for bruises, cuts, lumps or rashes that shouldn't be there. He was whole, he was safe. He was here.

Thirty-Eight

Paul

The local pub was quiet. We used to come here all the time, when Emily was back from university and I was a young football player. It felt like we were back in a time before the dream of our life in Australia. Sitting here, in the warm fug of nostalgia, everything we'd been through recently in Sydney seemed faded in the harsh haze. Had it really happened?

Without saying anything, Emily sat down at a table near the window. You couldn't smoke here anymore but it still reeked of it. I was glad it hadn't yet been taken over by a chain brewery with a standard fancy menu and fake relics on the wall. I went to the bar. I could see the blinking lights of the bandits winking at me from the far wall of the pub. I walked up to the bar. God. I'd love a pint. It almost felt like it would be safe here, like I was protected from everything that had happened in Australia now that I was back home. I ordered Emily a gin and tonic. I hesitated, then ordered a soda water with lime.

Tilly had already crashed out on the blow-up mattress; Cameron had agreed to stay home as I'd let him watch TV with Mum. I figured that a few quiz shows couldn't do him any harm. Since they'd arrived yesterday, Emily and I hadn't had a chance to talk alone. Mum had been hovering around us, and the kids followed Emily any time she tried to step away from them.

I walked back to the table, carrying a drink in each hand. Emily's eyes were bloodshot above dark shadows. Her elbow was on the table, her hand propping up her head.

I sat down opposite her and slid her drink over to her. She picked it up, sipped it, and put it on the coaster. 'Thanks,' she said.

'They had Hendricks.'

'Tempted?'

I bristled, then started to smile, but Emily wasn't smiling, just staring at her drink with her shoulders slumped.

'A little,' I said quietly.

'Have you noticed?'

'Tilly?'

She nodded.

'She's thin.'

'Have you seen her eat?'

'She had some fruit, some toast.' I had watched her, trying not to look like I was watching her: she had eaten, only half a piece of toast, but the jet lag throws your appetite all over the place, doesn't it?

'Hardly any.'

'It's enough. She's tired. From the journey.'

'We're all tired. She's… there's nothing left of her anymore.'

'Maybe she's just over-exercising and needs some extra calories. It can creep up on you.'

She laughed, looking at me through watery eyes. 'You're unbelievable, Paul. Your inability to see exactly what is in front of your face, this… this… denial of yours is insane! Do you think I'm making this up?' She shook her head. 'Oh. You think that I'm doing this somehow, don't you? It's not just that you think I'm making it up, you think that somehow, I'm actually making these things happen to our children. What am I doing, starving my own daughter?'

'That's not…' I shook my head.

'Oh yes, it is. *It is*. You think I'm the problem. Well I'll tell you something, Paul. *You* are her father. *You* are Cameron's father.' She pointed at me.

'Don't point your finger at me like that.' I looked round us, but the few people dotted around the bar weren't interested. The football was playing at a low volume on the TV screens above the bar, and at the bar, two old men sat staring into their beer.

'Doesn't feel good, does it? I'm not taking the blame for Tilly too. Jesus, Paul, I am trying my best. I am the one trying to hold this family together and make up for the space where you should be, while you just run away from it all.'

'I've been trying to make things better too, Emily.'

'Well, it's not working, is it?'

'Cameron—'

'Oh, bugger off, Paul.' She slammed her drink down.

'Well, that's helpful.' I shook my head and looked away.

'Cameron is the same way that he always was. He's probably worse as he's had the trauma of you taking him away to the other side of the world to deal with. He's a mess. Stop kidding yourself that you're helping him. The only reason you might think he's better is that you've taken him away from all the pressures of life. As soon as he's back to school, he'll fail again.'

'You are not the judge of the pass mark, Emily.'

'Tilly has an eating disorder. What are you going to do about it? She's a kid. She could die.'

'Emily, don't be so dramatic.'

She stared at me, her jaw clenched, then she seemed to deflate. 'I can't talk to you. I thought that coming here, that...' she wiped away a tear. 'That things would be different. I'll deal with this myself then.'

'I'll talk to her.'

She rubbed at her forehead. 'Paul. You need to wake up to this. Both of our children are really struggling, and you just sit there and refuse to do anything about it. I won't let you do to Tilly what you did to Cameron.'

'I didn't do anything.'

She stared at me for a moment before speaking. 'That's the point.'

I swallowed. The anger fizzled out and I met her stare. She was wrong.

She was wrong.

Thirty-Nine

Emily

After we got home from the pub, barely speaking to each other, I stayed up for a while, watching TV with Cameron. Paul said he was tired and immediately went to bed; I didn't argue. I couldn't stop glancing at Cameron, trying to reassure myself that now, both my children were with me. He fell asleep in front of the TV; I woke him gently and helped him to bed.

I undressed and put my pyjamas on in the bathroom. In the bedroom, Paul was curled up on his side under the blankets. The light was out but the lamp by my side of the bed was on.

'You sleeping?' I had said, louder than I knew was appropriate. How could he just get into bed and sleep like he didn't have a care in the world?

'I was,' he said, curtly, without opening his eyes.

I sighed, put my pile of clothes on the top of my suitcase in the corner of the room, then dug around in my handbag for my Kindle. My eyelids were like sandbags; my eyes stung like grains of sand had trickled out to scratch them, but I hoped that reading would settle my mind and distract me from my feelings about Paul. Even being in the bed next to him felt wrong, especially after that argument in the pub. I didn't know what stage our relationship was at. I felt the edge of my e-reader in my bag, pulled it out then got into bed.

As soon as I lay down, my body seemed to give up and I sank down into the soft mattress, heavy as a boulder sinking to the bottom of the cold river. Paul was so still that I knew he

290

was waiting to see what I would do. If he thought I was going to reach for him, he was deluded.

I pressed the power switch on my Kindle and a text box appeared with a picture of a power cord and an empty battery. I screwed up my eyes as my breath became shallow. Of course, I had no idea where the charger was and if I did, I needed a power adaptor for the UK sockets. I dropped it on the carpeted floor, turned out the light then lay on my back and pulled the blankets up to my chin. My shoulders heaved as I tried not to let the tears escape because then they might flood me.

Despite my exhaustion, I couldn't fall asleep. It was pitch black outside, but it felt oppressive instead of comforting. I felt sick, and underneath my nausea, my stomach tightened with hunger, my appetite still confused by jet lag. Eventually, Paul's breathing deepened: obviously, *he* could relax enough to sleep. I began to turn onto my side but the worn old springs creaked with every movement. Marjorie had insisted on us having her room while she slept on a sofa bed in the third bedroom. I would have rather not, but it would have caused more trouble to refuse.

–

I must have fallen asleep because when my eyes pinged open, I felt rested. I wondered if last night had been a dream. But as my senses all stirred, I knew it was exactly as I had feared. I wondered If Tilly had slept. I slipped out of bed, and the room. I checked on both children, still asleep, then used the bathroom.

There was no point going back to bed. I felt the urge to go for a run, to sprint until my lungs ached and burned, to force out all the old, stale air that I had breathed in during this nightmare and fill it with clean, crisp oxygen. But my running shoes were somewhere in my suitcase along with everything else.

I tiptoed down the hallway into the kitchen area and filled the kettle, wincing at the roaring of the water. As it began to boil, I slowly pulled open the top kitchen drawer and got a teaspoon out, the metal grating as the cutlery moved. The tea bags were in a tin on the bench top. I made a cup of tea, then went through to the living room and closed the door.

I sipped my tea, flicking through yesterday's paper, which was still sitting on the arm of the sofa. There were so many articles about soccer in the sports pages. I'd forgotten how huge it was here.

After a while, the central heating clunked on, and the living room door creaked open. I jumped.

'Marjorie! You frightened me,' I said in a loud whisper as I saw Paul's mum entering, with a quilted pink dressing gown on.

She smiled. 'Sorry.'

'I'm so sorry if I woke you, I couldn't sleep.'

'Ach, no. I'm up at half five most days. That's the thing when you get older, you don't need so much sleep. I used to think I'd sleep in every day when the kids left home but since they were bairns, I've got in the habit of being an early riser.'

'Catches the worms, eh?' I smiled.

'Aye.' She nodded. 'Did ye sleep okay?'

I nodded. 'Great. Took me a while to fall asleep but then I slept well, except for waking up so early! My body still thinks I'm in Australia. It'll take a couple more days until I adjust.'

'You must be hungry.'

I was starving. 'I'm okay. I'll wait until the others are up, I don't want to wake the kids.'

She nodded, then sat down on an armchair. 'Is Cameron off to his group today?'

I sighed. 'He told me about that. I haven't had much say in it to be honest. Paul... he's arranged it all.'

'Cameron's gone a few times. Paul drops him off and picks him up.'

I sat forwards. I knew I shouldn't be getting information from Marjorie but I could tell that she wanted to talk. 'What does Paul do?'

'I don't know. He's usually out too, he doesn't say much. You know, I don't know what you think about it, but all this mumbo jumbo about food and TV seems a bit much.'

I leaned back on the couch and looked at the swirling Artex patterns on the ceiling, 'Oh Marge, I just don't know what to do about it. It seemed harmless in one way, you know, but now, I don't think it's sustainable. When Paul first started it, I thought he'd go crazy over it for a while, but that he'd come to his senses. Like going on the Atkins diet or something. But now, with Cameron, I don't know.' I did know what I thought, but I wasn't sure if I could confide yet in Marjorie.

'But you've never believed in any of that stuff. Neither has Paul. Neither have I, and I grew up in a generation where people still went to church. This is…' She shook her head. 'I've told him, I think it's a load of rubbish and he's not to spout any of that stuff in my house. He needs to face his problems and deal with them himself. I've told him that! I'm his ma, and I know that's what he's doing.'

'You're right. But these groups, they did help Paul a lot. I don't know what he's told you, but he was struggling a bit, when he had to give up soccer.' Why was I defending him? I felt exactly the same way she did, and it was such a relief to know that she was on my side. She was right: Paul was running away from having to do the hard work and face what was wrong. I wondered if Marjorie knew about the gambling. Had he told her? Or had Alasdair? 'He went through a pretty rough time.'

I looked at her, giving her every opportunity to ask me more. Marjorie paused, and gazed back at me. Her eyes were sad. I could tell that she knew, or at least, knew enough. I didn't need to hurt her any more by telling her all the sordid details.

'Football was everything to him,' she said, quietly.

I nodded. 'It was.'

'And now…' Her voice trailed off. I looked over at her; she was slowly shaking her head. 'He's a good man, Emily. You and those kids are everything to him now. It's all he's got.'

'I know.' But we weren't all he had. Phoenix had replaced us; he looked to them to support him and give him advice, not us. But I didn't know if I had the energy to fight our way back in, or even whether I wanted to.

As the morning light crept up, Cameron padded through to the living room. He was wearing shorts and a T-shirt, his hair ruffled and his face puffy with sleep. I stood up as he entered and opened my arms to him, and he melted into me.

'I missed you when you were sleeping,' I mumbled into his shoulder.

'Me too.'

We sat on the sofa and I pulled him into me. It was like he was a child again, the cuddly little boy who, when he wasn't raging, was so dependent on me. I should never have let the conflict and the clashes overshadow the quiet, unremarkable, times that really should have been the most remarkable of all.

'You hungry?' I said. 'I can make you some toast.'

'Grandma's been buying butteries for me.'

'Butteries! I haven't had those since I was a kid. An Aberdeen special.'

'They taste like a flat croissant!'

I smiled and laughed quietly. 'Not very good for you, but yummy. Has your dad been letting you eat them?'

I felt his head nod on my shoulder. 'I think he's scared of telling Grandma he doesn't agree with unhealthy food.'

'Maybe we should get your sister to eat some.' I regretted it as soon as I said it.

'Mum,' he said, sitting up and looking at me. 'Can I stay with you today?'

'Of course you can, darling. That's why I'm here.'

'I'm meant to go to the group.'

'How's it been going there? What do you do?'

He shrugged.

'You can tell me. I won't tell Dad. I think I know already.'

He looked down at his lap. 'They go on and on about all the bad things in the world. It's hard, Mum, because it's all the things that are normal for me. We need the internet for school, and I thought we did eat healthy, and everyone watches TV.'

'Oh sweetie, those things *are* normal. It's Phoenix that's not normal.'

'Then why is Dad making me go?'

'I guess they just helped him at a time when he needed it.'

'They say that people who don't believe in Phoenix can't be trusted.'

My heart sped up. I forced a laugh. 'What, like me?'

He shrugged again. 'I said you weren't like that.'

I hugged him tight, holding back my fury at Paul, and Damian and all those idiots in Phoenix. 'Cameron. I love you more than anything. You can completely trust me.'

He pulled out of my grip, then glanced at the door. 'They said that medication is bad, too. But I didn't stop them because of dad, or anything like that, I just didn't like how they were making me feel and I hated feeling like there was something wrong with me...' He blinked rapidly; I looked away to allow him to wipe his eyes.

When he was composed, I put a hand on each of his shoulders and looked into his eyes. 'Cameron. I am so sorry that I betrayed that when I gave you your medication without telling you. I shouldn't have done that, even though I did it because I thought you needed it. It was wrong, and I breached your trust. I promise that from now on, we'll talk about everything. You *can* trust me, completely. And, as for that group, you're not going today. You're not going back there ever again.'

'But Dad—'

'Do you want to go?'

'No. I want to stay here.'

'Then that's what you'll do. Leave your dad to me. You're old enough to start making your own decisions now.'

'He said we were going camping. When we came. He said we were going camping together. He didn't say I had to go to

Phoenix. I wouldn't have come otherwise.' His voice wavered and I felt my own tears well up.

'I know, sweetie.' Oh, how I had to hold myself back. I had let Paul get away with this for too long. 'I think maybe Dad had planned that, but then you got here and were probably both a bit tired.'

'Yeah,' he said, hesitating. 'Maybe.'

He knew.

'What would you like to do today? We can do anything you want to.'

'Can we go to a movie?'

'Definitely. I might fall asleep, I've been up for hours and this jet lag will hit me, so as long as you don't mind me snoring.' I hugged him again and went to make breakfast and prepare myself for Paul.

When everyone was up, we sat around the glass dining table in the small dining area off the kitchen. I had another cup of tea, though I craved a flat white. Marjorie had instant coffee but I couldn't bring myself to drink it. We'd go for a drive soon and find a decent coffee. I felt strangely disconnected from the chatter around the table. I ate some toast: white bread with strawberry jam, and watched as Tilly had a few spoons of Rice Krispies and a sip of her orange juice. At least Marjorie only had full-fat milk in the house. Tilly was eating enough, just.

I drained my cup. 'Kids, I'm going to go for a quick walk to stretch my legs.' I turned to Paul, smiling. 'Would you like to come?'

He looked at his watch, then at Cameron, and was about to open his mouth.

'Och, Paul,' said Marjorie. 'Let him have a day off, his mum and sister have just arrived.'

I smiled at her, then looked back at Paul, who said nothing but narrowed his eyes. 'Cammie's not going to that group any more, Paul. I said I'll take him to a movie. I'm just going to get my shoes on, are you coming?'

His jaw was set. 'Yes,' he said. 'Wait for me.'

–

We walked behind the housing estate, one of many that had sprung up in the eighties with the oil boom in the North-East of Scotland, then past the old stone cottages squatting atop the cliff from the time this was a fishing village. Beneath us, down a winding path, slippery with scree, was a bay, the boats pulled up on the shelly beach, with a mosaic of mussels covering their warped woods. A net was strewn along the sand, and small buoys bobbed in the grey water. The wind hurtled past us. I zipped up my running top and pulled the sleeves down over my hands before putting them in my pockets. Paul was better dressed, in a puffed vest over his tracksuit top.

Neither of us spoke as we followed the worn path, the long grass tickling my ankles as we walked, then whipping as the wind gusts picked up. I waited for him to say something. He didn't.

'I don't want to fight, Paul,' I said.

'I'm not fighting.'

'I don't think it's unreasonable for him to spend some time with me today. Do you? He never even got to say goodbye.'

'He's part of a programme. He has to go three times a week. It's helping him.'

'Really?' I tried to keep the sarcasm out of my voice. 'What differences have you noticed?'

He shrugged. 'I thought you didn't want to fight.'

I shook my head and kept walking. He walked ahead of me. 'Why I am the enemy, Paul? What have I done that's so wrong? You are the one who kidnapped him—'

'Don't be dramatic. I hardly kidnapped him.' He turned back to look at me, then shook his head and walked even faster.

I ran a few steps then grabbed his arm. He stopped and turned around. 'Paul, what else would you call it when you take a child out of the hospital without telling me, then fly to the other side of the world with him?'

'I did tell you.'

'Afterwards, Paul! Only when I had called you a hundred times and searched for him and gone to the police! You terrified me! Have you any idea what that was like for me? Have you? Or for him?' My voice broke and I quickly wiped away my tears, hoping he'd think it was just spray from the waves crashing below us. I was having to shout just to be heard. When I looked up again, he was looking at me and for a moment, I saw doubt in his face. I looked into his eyes, those eyes that had looked into mine a hundred times and spoke more softly.

'He's not going back there, Paul. He doesn't want to. You tricked him. You told him you were going camping. He wants *you*, not some strangers. They've taken you away from us, Paul.'

'No.' He was looking down now, shaking his head.

I rubbed at my face. I was so tired of this conversation. When I looked at Paul, I could see he was too. His cheeks sagged and he hung his head. I wanted to reach out and touch him, make a joke, laugh. That's what we would have done before if our arguments got to this point: rehashed, automatic. We would have laughed and then it would have all been forgotten.

'Paul, what I believe is the same as almost everyone else in the world.'

'Not everyone—'

I waved my hand at him. 'Fine, fine, not *absolutely* everyone in the entire world. But in *our* world. The normal, everyday, boring world we lived in before you… well, before you chose to leave it.'

'It doesn't mean that they're right. Look at the people in North Korea or in China, they all thought the same thing but they weren't right.'

'You'll be bringing up the Nazis next. Don't be ridiculous, it's not the same at all.'

'We are destroying ourselves, our children with—'

I let out a groan of exasperation. 'Oh, for God's sake, Paul. I can't listen to this. If you could hear yourself… Remember how you used to react if some religious nutter came to the door? That's what you're like now. There's no point arguing because you're not using logic. That's the difference between you and me. I can see your point of view, I can understand your philosophy and even agree with some of it but—'

He jabbed at his chest with his finger. 'I'm still wrong. That's what you were going to say. I don't see how that's seeing my point of view at all.' He shook his head.

I sighed, let go of his arm then walked over to some rocks and sat down. My legs were tired. I was tired of arguing about this. All we were doing was tramping over old ground, along the well-worn path between us that was all too easy to follow. And it led nowhere.

'We just need to find some middle ground, Paul. For the kids. I'm willing to—'

'Oh, don't start all that about how you can compromise – you're prepared to stop them watching TV but not to make the changes that would matter the most. To accept that we have to do something radical to fix this.'

'You've done some pretty radical things already.'

He narrowed his eyes. 'So have you.'

I closed my eyes. No more tangling ourselves up in the same old knots; those knots were so tight that it was time to cut through them. I opened my eyes again and looked into Paul's.

'I can't do this anymore. We, as a couple, can't go on like this.'

His shoulders dropped. 'I know.'

We both sat in silence. I wanted Paul to be the one who either made that final cut, or to fight for us. He said nothing but I could see by the way his lips were drawn into a thin, tight line, that he was torn too. He was looking down at his knees, his right leg tapping.

'Paul,' I whispered, wanting him to look up at me. He did, his eyes glistening. And then he put his arm around my shoulders and pulled me towards him, and surprising myself, I leaned into him.

He spoke quietly. 'Let's all go away, go camping like I promised Cameron. All of us.'

If I said yes, was I some battered wife going back again for more punches? His hand trembled on my arm as I considered how to reply.

The only other option I had was to cleave our family in two, force the children to choose between us and get back on that plane. Cameron was old enough to decide, but Tilly was still a child and maybe we'd have to get lawyers, go to court. I'd seen so many friends go through that, and it tore them and their children to pieces. Cameron and Tilly were suffering already. If we had to go down that path, I needed to satisfy myself that I'd done *everything* I could to save us. He wasn't a bad man. He hadn't cheated on me. He hadn't hit me, or been unkind. He loved me, he loved Cameron and Tilly. The thought of a life alone seemed bleak, and I didn't know which side my children would fall on if they were forced to pick teams.

I looked up at him.

'Give me one more chance,' he said. 'Please.'

I nodded.

Forty

Paul

The warmth of the central heating hit me as I opened the kitchen door and stepped in, then bent down to take off my muddy shoes. Emily was behind me, doing the same.

'Kids,' I shouted into the house.

'What?' they shouted in unison from the living room, where I could hear the inane sounds of breakfast TV. I walked through and stood in the doorway to the living room. They were both lying on the couch, heads resting on Mum's red furry cushions on either end, just like I used to when I was a kid. I saw Tilly glance at Cameron, then Mum, and reach for the remote.

It didn't matter about the TV, not now. I smiled. 'So, Cameron, you're not going to a movie today after all.'

Mum got up from her chair. 'I think I'll go and have a shower.' She walked out of the room.

Cameron sat up and glared at me. 'What? Mum said—'

I laughed. 'Okay, you can go to a movie but then you'll miss out...' I said in a sing-song voice.

'Miss out on what?' Tilly said as she too sat up, smiling at me.

'We have to get ready for a trip.'

'A trip?' Cameron frowned.

'Where are we going?' Tilly said.

'Well, you know how I promised that we would go on a bit of an adventure, Cammie? Now that Mum and Tilly have arrived, it's time for us to do that. So today, we have to go and get the gear we need and some supplies, start packing.'

'We're going camping?' Cameron grinned.

'Ugh,' Tilly groaned. 'I hate camping.'

'You've never been camping, Tilly,' Emily said, as she came up behind me and stood next to me in the doorway to the living room. Emily was physically closer to me than she had been for weeks, and I was grateful she was making the effort to at least show the kids that we were giving this a try. I missed the days when we were at ease with each other; they felt like so long ago. But so much had happened that filled the space between us. While part of me would love to lean into her, I just couldn't. If I slipped back into intimacy so easily with her, then I could just as quickly slip back into my past too. But I was grateful that Emily was willing to give my way of life a chance; it gave me hope that maybe we could salvage something of our marriage. But if she still couldn't admit that she's been wrong, then I didn't think that we had a future.

'I have been camping,' Tilly said to Emily. 'Remember, the Year Six camp?'

'That was two nights at the river, you could practically see our house!' Emily teased.

Tilly's eyes widened. 'How long are we going for?'

Emily paused and glanced at me. 'We still have to work out the details. Your dad and I have only just decided.'

'We'll see how we go,' I said, my voice bright. 'It's fun sometimes to just see how things turn out and not know all the answers.' I didn't want to put a timeframe on it. It would take as long as it would take to show them that there was a different way to live, and that we could be happy away from all the temptations of our life in Sydney. I didn't want them to see this as a brief holiday, a weekend of roughing it before we went back to the way things were. This could be life-changing.

'Well, *where* are we going? You must know that at least?'

'Well, when I was a kid, your grandma and granddad once took me, Aunt Fiona and Uncle Alasdair on holiday to a bothy on the West Coast. I've been thinking about it since we got here. I've even looked it up, and it's still there. So that's where we're going.'

I sensed Emily looking at me.

'What's a bothy?' Cameron said.

'It's like a hut,' I said. 'A small cottage. But it's basic: no power, no running water. We'll have to catch fish for dinner and cook over a fire that we make ourselves. Just like people used to, in fact, just like many people in the world still *do*. How does that sound?'

Tilly shook her head. 'Sounds terrible.'

I tensed. 'Tilly! Give it a chance. You've never had to do anything hard in your life. I'm just saying that I'm taking you on a family adventure, and you're being rude.'

Emily touched me gently on the arm. 'Paul,' she said quietly.

I took a deep breath and focused on my memories of the stone cottage, surrounded by mountains, green fields, and the sensation of icy cold water as I paddled barefoot in streams until my toes were white and numb. Tilly may think it sounded terrible now, but she'd change her mind when we got there. To me, it sounded perfect.

Damian had emailed me overnight, asking how Cameron's treatment was going. I had replied briefly this morning, saying that he was going well. He would find out that wasn't true, of course, but he wouldn't be able to contact me once we'd gone and I would finally have some space to do things my *own* way. This is the only way I could show Emily and the children that I wasn't crazy for wanting to keep my family away from the internet and TV and advertising and music videos and pressure at school and medication. If Tilly isn't bombarded with images of stick thin women with puffed up chests and lips, she will realise that she is perfect and she will eat when she is hungry. If Cameron doesn't have to deal with all those entitled boys teasing him about being a little different, or worry about completing exams in a set time and get a perfect score, then he will relax. If

Emily can get away from the internet forums, from the parents at school competing about who has the best children or cars or hair or Botox, she will stop comparing our life and our children to everyone else, and let them be who they are. And if I can get away from the constant temptation to gamble, and the need to prove myself to Damian and Phoenix, to be at work earlier and later than everyone else because they remind me every day that I owe them, then I will finally be happy.

'Everyone get dressed,' I said. 'We've got some shopping to do.'

Forty-One

Emily

Paul drummed his fingers on the steering wheel as we drove along a winding road next to the rushing river. We were only twenty minutes or so from the city, but the granite buildings had quickly been left behind for cottages, farmland, and glimpses of turrets from stately homes. I turned my head to try to read the words on a small handmade cross by the side of the road with an Aberdeen football top laid out beneath it, a dried bunch of flowers and a big rock holding it down. In winter, this road could be treacherous. The window was open, and the air seemed to chill a little as we drove higher into the hills.

I turned briefly to look at Cameron; he was staring out of the window behind me. Tilly had her knees tucked up and was resting her head on them, her eyes closed. She wore a baggy hooded top and jeans. Despite Paul's protests, I had packed the backpack with food for her, high calorie drinks and powders, rice, tins of tuna. I had made her stand on Marjorie's scales before we left: her weight was only a couple of hundred grams less than it had been when we left Australia. At least she hadn't lost anything significant. While the GP in Australia before we left had said she was medically well, I knew she couldn't afford to lose any more weight. I still wondered if I had done the right thing in bringing her here, away from her home but, as Paul had said, that's where the problems had begun. Somehow, despite my best intentions there was where she had stopped eating. We were all together now and she had nowhere to hide. And if she didn't eat, we would leave. This was her last chance. This was the last chance for all of us.

–

As we neared Fort William, Paul called out cheerfully, 'Almost there!'

I had been drifting off; the jet lag had still not fully passed. I looked out of the window and saw two red Highland cattle contemplating us through a wooden fence and some squat Shetland ponies wandering in a field behind them. And beyond that, a mountain dominated the sky, its peak white with snow.

'Ben Nevis,' Paul said. 'The highest mountain in the UK, kids.'

'It's beautiful,' I mumbled, then opened the window a little more to try and wake myself up. The air was freezing. I gasped with the sensation, then laughed.

'You okay?' Paul said.

I kept laughing and didn't know why I was until I was in tears. And when Paul started smiling and laughing too, and the kids laughed uneasily, and then with hilarity, I told myself that maybe this is what we needed after all, and after this, everything could go back to normal.

–

'Can we have some lunch?' Cameron said.

'I'd love a pub lunch,' I said, looking at Paul.

He glanced at the clock on the dashboard. 'We've got time.'

'Are you hungry, Tilly?' I said, trying to keep my voice light.

'Not really,' she said.

I pushed down the swell of frustration in my chest. 'Well, we'd better eat as many chips as we can because once your dad takes us to this top-secret location, who knows what we'll be getting to eat.'

'If you catch it, you can eat it,' he said, grinning. I saw a look pass between Cameron and Tilly. They were not impressed.

It wasn't hard to find the local hotel; every town and village in Scotland had at least one. I ate a basket of scampi and chips, the taste reminding me of a hundred pub lunches I'd had like this as a child. Paul had lentil soup and crusty bread, the only vegetarian thing on the menu. I don't think he dared ask if it was vegan, though he didn't spread the butter on his bread. While I really wanted to order a white wine, I had a diet coke. Cameron wolfed down his meal and I smiled; it was so satisfying to see your child eating. Tilly nibbled on some chips, peeled the crumb off a chicken goujon, and had a few small bites of the meat. Before we'd even finished eating, she went off to the toilet. I nudged Paul as she stood up and nodded my head in her direction. He ignored me. I didn't chase after her.

'Right,' Paul said when we'd all finished eating. 'We've got one more short drive then we'd better go and get everything unpacked from the car.'

Cameron frowned. 'Where's the campsite?'

'We're not there yet,' he said. 'I've got a surprise for you.'

-

I couldn't help but squeal along with the kids when we parked at the train station and I saw the shiny black engine of a steam train, a guard shovelling coal onto it.

'Oh. My. God!' Tilly screamed. 'The Hogwart's Express. Is it? Is it, Dad?'

Paul laughed. 'Sure is. Well, the Jacobite. We're going on it, onto our next stop.'

It was impossible not to laugh along with Tilly; even Cameron looked impressed.

'I wish I had my iPad, Mum, my friends are going to be so jealous. Have you got your phone? I need a photo.'

We took photos, after waiting for a few people dressed in Harry Potter costumes to finish posing at the front of the train.

While the kids were looking at the photos to check they were good enough, I leaned into Paul. 'What a great surprise, thank you.'

He smiled back at me.

After we lugged our rucksacks onto the train and showed our tickets, we settled into the cabin. The kids chattered about scenes from the movies that might have been filmed where we sat, and the train slowly chugged off. The scenery was beautiful and the kids were convinced that they knew exactly where we were as they'd seen it in the films, especially when we crossed the arches of the Glenfinnan viaduct.

'You like it?' Paul said. I could sense his need for me to agree.

'Love it,' I said.

When we alighted at a small village on the edge of a bay, we stood with our bags at our feet in a huddle.

'Now,' said Paul. 'I've booked a B&B tonight. Enjoy being in a bed. Because tomorrow, we're going there.'

He pointed into the hills behind us. There was nothing to see beyond the stone buildings of the village. The children looked concerned, but I felt a thrum of hope in my bones.

Forty-Two

Paul

My knee ached as we tramped parallel to the fence of a field. We had been walking for about an hour, I guessed. Were we going in the right direction? I glanced round at Emily and the kids, heads down, trudging in single file behind me. They'd stopped asking me how long it would take to get there. I was hungry. The kids must have been hungry. I felt we should stop but I didn't want to stop until we got there. It couldn't be far now. I pulled my water bottle from the side pocket of my backpack and drank some more, then kept walking.

I lost track of time. Maybe half an hour had passed, maybe an hour, when I heard Cameron shout, 'Dad! Look!'

I raised my head, the top of my back tight from being hunched forward with the weight of my pack, then grinned. We had just come out of the cool of a glade of trees, dark green moss making the rocks slick underfoot, into the late morning sun which was finally warming up the air from the night-time chill. I punched my fist in the air as I saw the glint of the edge of the silver water of the glassy river, and in front of it, the shadow of a small building.

'That's it,' I called back to them. 'Come on, that's the bothy! That's where we're staying.'

We walked faster and as we came closer, I was relieved to see that there was no sign of anyone staying there. It wasn't the right season for the hillwalkers trying to tackle the Munroes; it was autumn now and the snowline on the mountains was descending, and this old farmer's croft was far enough away from a village that few tourists would venture here. Above us, I saw gulls circling; we weren't too far from the shore, from the islands of the Hebrides.

'It's beautiful,' Emily said, stopping beside me.

I put my arm around her shoulders and hugged her.

'Are we staying there?' Tilly said.

I grinned. 'Yes, we are.'

I saw her looking around with a frown on her face.

'That's right, Tilly. There's no one else here,' I said. 'No shops, no TV, no phones.' I took my phone out of my pocket and held it up. One bar of signal flicked up, then disappeared. I switched it off.

'What are we going to eat?' Cameron said.

'We have hand lines for fishing, Cam, and the reason our bags are so heavy is that we have some basics. There are rabbits out there, heaps of them.' A bird of prey, maybe a buzzard, hovered above purple heather at the foot of the hillside.

'I thought you were vegan,' Tilly said.

I ignored her. That would be impossible here. 'Let's go and have a look inside, get unpacked.' I looked at Emily, and she was smiling. Her cheeks were flushed, her eyes sparkled, and strands of her hair had fallen out of her ponytail and blew around her face. Could this work after all? I let her lead the way down to the bothy.

Inside, there were two rooms, each with bunk bed frames, but no mattresses, off a main room with a wooden table and four chairs. There was an open fireplace in the main room, with a small pile of branches beside it. Someone had left a battered book on the table, its pages swollen and rippled: the complete works of Shakespeare. I smiled. A shelf on one wall had a dusty bottle of vegetable oil, a plastic tub of sugar, and a jar of pal, solidified instant coffee. There was no sink, no bathroom. I swallowed down a small flare of anxiety as I thought about all the things we should have brought. No, this was why we were here: this was my way to prove to Emily that we could be happy without everything we had come to depend upon.

'Who's coming to collect heather to make ourselves a mattress to put under our sleeping bags?' I said.

'Me!' the children shouted in unison and the three of us headed out while Emily stayed behind to find the makings of lunch.

Forty-Three

Emily

It had been well over a week since we'd arrived. While we had
solid walls around us and more room than a tent, we were dirty,
often cold, and I was starting to worry about food. Tilly and I
had tried to beautify the bothy. We had picked purple heather
and hung it around the roof, but it soon lost its colour. We'd
pulled logs inside for chairs. But Tilly, in the last few days,
had started to pace around the perimeter of the building like
a prisoner; Cameron sat on a rock for hours on end throwing
pebbles into the river. We had some rice, biscuits, and some
tins of tuna, but our potatoes had been used up and we'd eaten
the apples before they spoiled.

I could see Paul was concerned too, as he came back
one day with berries that we all refused to eat in case they
were poisonous. After a lunch of some rice and baked beans
heated over our little camping stove, washed down with water
collected from the stream that ran down the hillside, and puri-
fied with iodine tablets that we'd brought, Paul spoke with a
strained cheer.

'It's beautiful here,' he said.

'It is gorgeous,' I agreed. 'Don't you think, Tilly? It's so
different to Australia.'

'And the air,' Paul said. 'You can smell how clean it is, you
can imagine that we were living here all those years ago when
William Wallace was here.'

'And got hung, drawn and quartered and his head put on a
stick,' Tilly said, glaring at him.

'How about Bonnie Prince Charlie then?'

'What did he eat?' mumbled Cameron as he scraped the last few pieces of rice from the melamine bowl.

'Well, this afternoon, we're going to try again to catch some fish. They were great the other night, weren't they? If it was spring, we'd plant vegetables, potatoes, carrots.'

'They'd need months to grow, Dad. And sun,' said Tilly.

I was glad that at least she was talking about food; perhaps this meant she was feeling hungry, wanting to eat. She still hadn't eaten much, but then again, none of us had. I knew I had lost weight this week, but I had no way to weigh Tilly out here.

'Maybe we could catch rabbits too. Or venison. Yum!' I knew I was talking in a voice that I'd only ever used when the children were toddlers, while I arranged their slices of carrot and tomato into a smiley face on their plates when we both knew that they were going to spit it out. I'm not sure who I was trying to convince. How would we catch a deer? We didn't have a gun. It was only an hour or two's walk back to the village and I decided that I'd go there tomorrow, just for some vegetables, maybe some sausages. And a bar of chocolate.

I glanced at Paul, in his faded jeans and hiking boots, his fleece, his hands and face red with cold, dirt under his fingernails, his hair sticking up at his double crown. I blinked back my tears. 'Come on, Tilly, let's go find some firewood and let the boys catch our dinner.'

—

The next morning, the children insisted on coming into the village with me, despite me warning them that it would take us all day to walk there and back again. Paul refused, saying he had work to do. I knew he was disappointed in us going to get more provisions, but what choice did we have? And besides, we all needed a change of scenery. After more than a week of talking only to each other, I needed to see other humans, to reassure me that normal life was still going on.

The children were quiet as we walked. I was worried about the energy it must be using up in Tilly. Did she look thinner? I didn't trust my own opinion any more. I'd let them buy whatever they wanted once we got to the village, and if she ate that, I'd be reassured.

It didn't seem to take as long to reach the village as it had a week ago when we had started out for the bothy. We didn't have our packs on to slow us down. I had taken one rucksack with us, empty except from our water bottles, so that I could carry the shopping back. We were all more eager too. With every step we took, the life at the bothy seemed like a game.

The small shop also served as the post office and newsagent. I pushed open the door, and a bell above it rang. The three of us entered the shop and greeted the elderly lady who popped her head out from a door behind the counter. The shop sold groceries, but also magazines, tourist trinkets, basic camping gear, and even had a pie warmer on the counter. My mouth watered at the thought of hot meat.

'Mum,' Cameron shouted. 'Can I have one of these rods?'

'Hasn't Dad got some?'

'No, just those hand lines. They're annoying.'

I walked over to him. Surely a rod would be easier, and more likely to catch fish if we could throw the line out further? 'You'd have to carry it all the way back,' I warned.

'I will.'

'Without complaining?' I laughed and ruffled his hair. That reminded me: we needed shampoo. Our hair was disgusting. He picked two rods, then started looking at the lures and bait. I left him to it. Tilly was looking at magazines.

'Come and help me choose some food,' I said. 'You can have anything you want. We can have a mini feast for lunch before we go back and see Dad.' I raised my eyebrows and she smiled faintly. 'Come on,' I said, and she followed me.

We filled a basket with bread, potatoes, carrots, a couple of turnips, pasta, jars of bolognaise sauce, some mince. I saw Tilly looking at the biscuits. Thank God.

'Go on,' I said. 'Get a few packets.'

Tilly hesitated, then picked up some chocolate digestives; they used to be her favourite but I realised that I hadn't seen her eat a biscuit in months. I picked up another packet, then two packets of shortbread. The basket was full, and heavy. I had to carry it all back. We had enough for now; we could come back in a few days if we had to.

At the counter, we also ordered three steak pies and chips. I wondered if I should get one for Paul. It would be cold by the time we got back to the bothy. Would he eat it? I bought an extra three. If he didn't want them, we would eat them.

I put the basket on the counter as the woman used tongs to put the pies in white paper bags, and Cameron lay down the fishing gear he had chosen. We took the pies, and the woman began lifting things out of the basket and pressing buttons on the till.

'Div ye hae a licence?' she asked in her soft Scottish lilt as she looked for the price ticket on a packet of bait.

'A licence?'

She nodded towards the rods and lures. 'The laird owns the river.'

'I don't know. My husband might have one I suppose.'

'Did he buy it fae me?'

'Um.' The kids were looking at me. Paul hadn't been into the shop without me. He clearly hadn't. 'I don't know. Probably not, I'm sorry. Can I buy a licence too then?' I said.

'Fit stretch ye fishin'?'

'We're staying at the bothy. So, they'll be fishing in the river near there.'

'Fit ye catching?'

I frowned at the woman. She wore an olive-green Barbour jacket, her greying hair curled close to her hair though her skin was pale and far smoother than any Australian women would be that age. Her hands looked soft, the knuckles swollen and red. 'What is there? Salmon? Trout?'

'Canna fish on Sundays.'

I closed my eyes for a moment. 'That's fine. We won't fish on Sundays.'

She went through more rules about where we were allowed to fish, what I could catch, where I could scale the fish, and that we absolutely must put back any fish that we weren't going to eat.

'That's the plan,' I said.

She raised her eyebrows. 'The winter'll be here soon though. There'll be sna' before lang.'

Snow. I saw the kids look at each other and grimace.

'Yes, I know that.' I forced myself to smile. 'I grew up here. Anyway, we'll be long gone before then.'

She nodded slowly and I knew she didn't consider me a local. I pushed the things on the counter towards her a bit. 'Anyway, we'd better get going, it's a bit of a walk back there.'

'The rain's forecast. Watch the streams dinna go into spate. You'll get cut off.'

'Yes. I know. Thank you.' My cheeks were aching from forced cheer.

'And here's yer fishing licence,' she said, sliding a slip of paper across the desk. She totalled up the purchases then took my cash and gave me change.

I thanked her, put the remaining groceries into my rucksack, then handed out the pies and chips to the children and walked towards the door, the little cardboard tags dangling from the new rods that Cameron held over his shoulder as we left the shop.

We walked away from the buildings to a small patch of grass across the road and sat at a faded wooden picnic table. I ripped open my paper bag and lay it flat on the table, then shook out some chips from the box. Tilly and Cameron did the same. We ate in silence. I was ravenous. I glanced at Tilly and let myself relax as she bit into her pie too, then ate her chips. Relief and happiness flooded me. There was something to be said for Paul's

316

ideas: Tilly was eating. I reached down and undid the top of my rucksack and pulled out a large bag of crisps. 'We'll buy another packet if we can face that woman in the shop again!'

The kids laughed and devoured the salty crisps too. This trip had done us good; I could see that.

'I'm going to the toilet, Mum,' Cameron said, pointing towards the wooden building near the picnic area.

'Hold on,' I said. I rummaged in the bag and found the shampoo and shower gel I'd bought. 'Do your best at washing your filthy hair in the sink in there before we have to go back to living in the wild with no running water.' I smiled.

As he walked off, I kept smiling as I looked at Tilly. 'It's so good to see you've got your appetite back,' I said.

She froze.

'Sweetie, I just mean that when we were back in Sydney, we were all a bit worried that you hadn't been eating enough.'

'I had been.'

'Tilly, don't get defensive, darling. Remember the GP said you'd gotten quite thin, but I know it was because you'd been so busy and active, and maybe a little stressed with everything that was going on at home? Anyway, I'm so glad you're feeling better.'

She looked down at the paper bag in front of her, then grabbed it and crumped it up, and walked over to the rubbish bins. I sighed, and gathered up my own stuff. I shouldn't have said anything to her. As I passed by her, I took her hand; she pulled away. 'Tilly!' I said. 'I was trying to be nice. I love you.'

She paused. 'I love you too,' she murmured. I sighed.

Just then, Cameron came out of the bathrooms, his hair dripping wet. I laughed, and even Tilly smiled. 'I need a towel, Mum!'

'I haven't got a towel! Aren't there paper towels in there?'

'No, they're all finished.'

'Here,' I took the long-sleeved top from around my waist. 'Use this. I don't need it and it'll dry soon enough.'

He rubbed at his hair.

'Your turn,' I said to Tilly. 'Take this shirt to dry it off with, or stick your head under the hand drier.'

When she had gone, I turned to Cameron. 'I'm glad Dad didn't come today, it's been nice to hang out with you and Tilly on your own. How are you finding everything?'

He shrugged. 'It's fine.'

'How's your head?' I reached up to touch where the yellow tint of the bruise on his forehead was still visible in the daylight.

'It's fine. Doesn't hurt.'

'You seem happy. Are you having a good time?'

He shrugged again. 'I guess.'

I bit back my frustration. 'Are you worried about anything?'

'I'm worried about missing school. I'll be really behind when we get back.'

I was too, but I couldn't tell him that. 'No, you've only missed the last couple of weeks of term. It's still school holidays.'

'Yeah but it goes back next week.'

I sighed and nodded. 'I know.'

'When are we going back?'

'Soon, I promise.'

Tilly came back out. 'I'm not washing my hair in there. It's gross. I'll do it in the stream back at the bothy.'

I sighed. 'Fair enough. If you don't mind rinsing it with sandy water. Anyway, I was just saying to Cameron that I'll talk to Dad and we can make a plan for when to leave. School starts in a week, and I don't want you missing any more than the first few days of that. How about I'll tell Dad that he's got us for another week, then we're out of here? Can you put up with it until then, for Dad?'

'Okay,' they both sighed.

I had a sudden pang of fear that maybe they wouldn't want to come with me. 'You do want to go home, with me, don't you?'

'Yes,' they both agreed.

318

'I love you both very much.' I hugged them, then we packed up and prepared for the long trudge back to the bothy.

–

I didn't get a chance to talk to Paul alone that night. It was ironic: there was so much space around us, and not another soul for miles, yet none of us moved far out of the vicinity of the others. The next night, as the sky darkened, the four of us huddled around the fire eating baked potatoes and carrots roasted over the fire in tin foil.

Paul's voice rose above the crackling of the fire and the rustle of the foil. 'The nights are drawing in. We'll need to stockpile food.'

I forced myself to laugh as the children both snapped their head to look at me with wide eyes. 'I don't think we can do this over the winter, Paul. Doesn't it snow? What do you reckon, kids?'

Tilly glanced at me with a nervous smile on her face. 'It's pretty cold now.'

'Lots of people have done it before us,' he said.

'And many people have frozen to death out here too, Paul. Your dad used to talk about it all the time.' I turned to the kids. 'Your granddad used to volunteer to rescue people on the mountains. He would get really angry with the tourists who came here to Scotland with only a flask of soup and a pair of running shoes.'

'We're not tourists and they weren't prepared.'

'Neither are we, Dad,' Tilly said.

I reached over and rubbed her knee. It felt like I was touching bare bone. 'Don't worry, Tilly. We're not staying here over winter. We'll be going home soon.'

'Dad,' Cameron said. 'When are we going home? We've been here for ages.'

Paul's face glowed red in the shadows from the fire. 'It hasn't even been two weeks, everyone. We can't give up as soon as we're a bit uncomfortable. This is what it's all about. Can you imagine how proud we'll be to make it through a winter? In the meantime, there's fish and rabbits.'

'Rabbits hibernate over winter,' Tilly said.

'And the river will freeze, won't it?'

'Don't worry,' I said with forced cheer. 'Dad's only joking'. He was joking, wasn't he? I glanced at Tilly and Cameron, trying to reassure them.

—

The next morning, as usual, Paul rose early, before the sun, and pulled on his fleece and jacket and headed down to the shores of the river with his new rod. Later, once the sun came up and he tired of swatting at the midges, he headed up the slopes of the hill and come back carrying stones with his face set.

I asked the children to tidy up around the camp, then wandered over to Paul with a flask of black tea in my hand. He had a pile of rocks now, and was trying to stack them on top of each other. I handed him the flask; he nodded and took it from me. His hands were red and cracked.

'What are you doing?' I asked lightly.

'I climbed up to that cairn up there, it's amazing. I thought maybe we could build something down here. I've been looking at the drystone walls over past those fields, it's brilliant really, no cement or mortar. I'm just trying to see if I can do it. Something to leave our mark, you know?'

'Paul, what's the point?' I said quietly. 'We have to go home soon. Very soon.'

It was as if he hadn't heard me. 'I need more stones though, the ones I have won't fit.'

I put my hand on his arm; he looked at it. 'Paul, listen to me. We can't stay here. The dark's coming in about 5pm now, it's getting cold, freezing at night. It's not safe. I'm worried about Tilly, I need to get her weighed and eating decent food. The kids need to go home.' I paused. 'I need to go home.'

He didn't look at me.

'Maybe we could relocate to the South of France?' I tried to joke. 'Rent an old farmhouse or chateau. We can still grow vegetables and catch fish there.'

He smiled sadly. 'You still don't get it, Emily, this isn't a holiday, not for me.'

'I don't think any of us have seen this as a holiday, like lying around a pool in Bali, but we have to go home sometime. Soon. The kids are tired. They need to go back to school. I said there was a family emergency when we left Australia so that got them out of the last two weeks of term, but the school holidays are almost done now, and they need to get back. I'll lose all my clients at work. If I lose my job, and you're not working, how will we pay the mortgage? We'll lose the house. If it hasn't been robbed already. I didn't even have time to redirect the mail or cancel the papers!'

He rubbed at his face. 'You're still worrying about things that don't matter.'

'Don't matter? Our home? Our jobs? The kids' education doesn't matter?'

'You've never really taken this seriously. I'm not talking about two weeks, I'm talking about changing our lives.'

'Are you honestly saying that we could stay here, what, over winter? Forever?' I clasped my hand to my mouth. 'Oh wow. You are, aren't you? You honestly think that we could live like this? Oh, Paul...' I stared at him, disbelieving. This wasn't real life. Maybe a few families, those on documentaries, managed to live on a desert island and grow up in a supposedly idyllic way, but I know that wouldn't be the whole truth. All sorts of resentments and fears would bubble below the surface of the warm waves lapping on their beach. And the waves here were icy cold and murky. Humans are social creatures, even Cameron. He needed peers; he needed to see how the world worked because that's the world that he must live in. As must Paul.

He kicked at the ground then stared at me. 'Why can't you understand that I can't go back to the way things were? I can't gamble again, I can't see my kids struggling. I can't see Damian and let him tell me that I've failed again.'

'To hell with Damian, Paul! I don't care about him!'

Paul looked away, blinking away the tears that I knew were threatening to fall. I sighed. Nothing had changed. I knew that Paul so desperately wanted this to work, and I knew that his heart was in the right place. He had made this decision, and I had gone along with it. For him, to go home now was to admit failure.

I spoke more softly, though my voice was tinged with sadness as the realisation that this might be the conversation where it all ends. 'I do love this way of life, Paul. I do. And I can see how it has been good for the kids. But not forever. Maybe you can do this forever, but I can't. The children can't. You know that, don't you?'

He didn't answer me as he turned a granite boulder around in his hands, his arms trembling with the weight of it and tried to wedge it in between the space between the rows he'd already built.

'One more week, Paul, and we're leaving. With you or without you.'

I spun around and walked off before he could see the tears falling down my face.

Forty-Four

Paul

'Cameron, you've got a bite,' I said as his line twitched. Instead of flicking his rod to try and pull the hook through the fish's mouth, he was holding it with one arm while he was scuffing his feet back and forth, back and forth in the sand. He jumped at my voice, then went to grab his line but I already had. I jerked it, but the line went slack. I gritted my teeth.

'Sorry, Dad,' he mumbled.

'You need to pay attention, mate. I've told you. This is important.'

I was tired. I hadn't been sleeping and since yesterday, when Emily had told me that she had decided to give up and go home, thoughts and questions and worries were hurtling around my mind. I no longer had the energy to try to persuade her, and I knew that meant that if I didn't go with her, the marriage was over. The children were on her side and it was pointless to try and force them to stay. I knew we had to go. But I didn't know what I would do when I went back. I didn't know if I could continue to live with my family when Emily and I were so opposed. I didn't know if I could trust myself to live a normal life any more. I didn't know if I could survive if I had to live on my own, without my family.

Cameron and I stood by the river, flicking our rods as our feather flies skimmed the top of the water. Midges swarmed around us. My hands were freezing in the rough, fingerless woollen gloves. I looked over at Cameron as he rhythmically flicked his rod. 'Come on, mate, put some energy into it. Real insects don't hop up and down in the same place. Think like a fly, or the fish.'

He glanced at me, then looked back towards the water. I sighed. He'd understand, one day, why we were doing this. I jerked the line out of the water again. Nothing. I'd never been good at fishing. Emily said I didn't have the patience for it, that I could never just relax. I tried to think like a fish, but all I could see was my shadow and Cameron's bright red jacket through the clear water of the river and a cheap lure.

The sun was setting, even though it was barely 5pm, and heavy clouds were blowing in from the west. I looked up at the twilight sky, darkening by the minute. The days were drawing in. Some days the sun barely seemed to climb up above the hills before it sank down again, and the wind grew icy. Soon, the nights would turn bitter, and the heavy grey clouds would burst with flurries of snow. We had grown used to living in the rhythm of the days, rising as the sun did and sleeping as the night fell. As winter drew closer I could almost feel my heart rate slow, conserving my energy, as if I were a creature getting ready for hibernation. I knew what the winter would be like, the almost perpetual darkness, the snow, the freezing temperatures, and even in the city, we'd spend our time cooped up indoors. I thought of our home in Sydney, and the long warm days filled with friends before the gambling ruined everything. Here we were, fingers red with the cold air, stomachs rumbling, exposed skin smarting as the sun slowly disappeared behind us. The midges swarmed around my face. Cameron pulled his beanie down over his ears and huddled down into the neck of his fleece, zipped up to his chin. The rain began to spit.

'Maybe the fish will come out now, at dusk,' I said. 'To eat those midges.'

'I hope so. Stop them biting me.'

'Not as bad as mozzies though, eh?'

'No, Dad,' he said automatically. My shoulders fell a little.

We both turned back to the river and flicked our rods.

I said nothing for a minute or two, then quietly. 'How are you going? You feeling okay?'

I looked towards him and saw him shrug slightly.

'You're looking better.'

'I'm fine.'

I nodded.

'Dad, don't get angry, but are you coming home with us?'

'Of course, I am.' He knew I was lying.

'Don't blame Mum. It's just that we need to go. I've got exams. If I miss them, I might have to repeat the year or something.'

'Cam, I don't want you to worry about exams. It's not important.'

'What about Mum's job? And yours?'

'Mate, don't worry about adult stuff. We're completely fine.'

'Tilly's not well.'

I sighed. 'She's okay.'

He spoke quietly. 'She's been sick.'

I stopped flicking my rod. 'What do you mean?'

'I hear her, she goes outside when you and Mum are in bed.'

'She's probably just going to the toilet.'

He shook his head. 'It's more than that.'

My heart was hammering in my chest. 'Thanks for telling me, mate. She'll be fine. I'll sort it out.'

–

By the time we packed up and walked back to the light of the campfire, the rain that had started as a patter was soon a steady pour. The fire went out, and even if it hadn't, none of us wanted to stand outside in it trying to cook. Inside, we ate tins of cold baked beans and a raw, soft, carrot each. I could feel the kids' resentment towards me for bringing them here filling up the cottage with every exhalation until I wanted to scream. I wanted to cry. I wanted to run away. I wanted to tell Emily about what Cameron said about Tilly but there was no privacy and I was sick of it all. I had only tried to do the right thing for my children and, yet again, I had failed. The damp air crowding the bothy felt heavy with moisture and blame.

There were no gutters on the building and after dinner, I sat on the edge of my bed looking outside and watched the water flow like a waterfall in front of the window. Emily was using the torch to read 'Romeo and Juliet' to the children. Above her voice, I could hear drips on the floor of the main room where the roof was leaking. In Australia, the downpours were always heavy but then they would just stop. Here, this rain was relentless.

Soon, everyone went to bed. There was nothing else to do, and it was bitterly cold. I couldn't sleep, though. Emily was in the bunk above me and I knew she was awake. I couldn't talk to her about Tilly now without the children hearing. I could hear Tilly and Cameron's voices talking to each other from the other room. I must have drifted off at some point, but woke in the black of night to the noise of the wind howling outside and rain crashing against the windows.

The dripping from the main room got faster and louder. My mouth was dry as I realised that this bothy was the only thing protecting us from the elements. But, I told myself, it had been here for how long? At least a hundred years. Longer. It was built to withstand this weather. It was strong.

I swung my legs over the side of the bunk bed, my hip aching from lying on the wooden platform. The cushioning from the heather wore out in hours and even though we tried to replace it every day, it was like lying on twigs. I unzipped the sleeping bag and peeled it off me. I was dressed, to ward off the cold, in socks and tracksuit pants, and a long-sleeved top. I felt on the floor for the head torch I kept there and walked out of the room into the main area to investigate the leak.

I don't know what it was that made me decide to go outside. I knew I wouldn't be able to sleep, and I did need to empty my bladder. I also wanted to feel the force of the storm, just for a moment, so that I could reassure myself how warm and dry it really was in here. I opened the front door, grabbing it as the wind almost wrenched it from me, then stepped outside and pushed it closed behind me before the weather could invade the space.

Outside, the chill hit me and I was soaked through within moments. It was dark; I had the sensation that I was stepping into a cloud.

I switched the head torch on and heard a gasp beside me. Adrenaline surged through me and I quickly turned towards the noise. There, in the circle of light from my torch, Tilly was standing with one hand on the stone wall, staring at me with wide eyes, her hair dripping wet, as she wiped her hand with her mouth. I looked at her feet; the rain had yet to wash away a puddle of her vomit.

'Tilly,' I said, stepping towards her.

But before I could reach her, she turned around and fled.

Forty-Five

Emily

I jumped as I heard the front door of the bothy slam, then Paul's voice shouting above the roar of the rain outside.

'Emily,' he said, loudly. 'Wake up.'

Before I could come to, his cold, wet, hand touched my leg. I jumped.

'Paul,' I said, sitting up and trying not to bump my head on the roof. 'You're soaking.'

'I've been outside looking for Tilly.'

'Tilly?' My heart almost stopped. 'What do you mean? Looking where?'

'She ran off.'

He wasn't making sense. 'It's the middle of the night!'

'I know. I caught her outside, she was vomiting, then I startled her, and she ran off. I tried to run after her, but I couldn't find her.'

I jumped down from the top bunk, and grabbed my fleece that was draped over the end of the bed. 'But it's pouring out there. It's been pouring for hours. It's dark!'

'Yes, I know that. I need your help, I can't find her.'

The panic in his voice cut through my own. 'Let's go.'

Cameron called through. 'Mum? Dad? What's happening?'

'Cameron. Where would your sister go? If she was upset? Dad said she's run off.'

'He knows, Emily, about the vomiting.'

'Why the hell does everyone know about this except for me?! I take it that she hasn't just eaten something that's upset her? I take it that you knew about this and didn't tell me? Do you know what can happen when people make themselves vomit? It's so dangerous, Paul, you should have told me!'

'I'm sorry, Mum,' Cameron whimpered. 'I'll help.'

'No way, Cam. You're not going out in that. You need to stay here. Promise me!'

He nodded, his face white in the torchlight. I stepped towards him and gave him a quick hug. 'I'm sorry, Cammie, it's just… we've got to find Tilly.'

'The river,' he said. 'She likes to sit under the trees on the edge of the river. When she's sad.'

'Which trees?' I said, staring at him. 'Where?'

'There's a big fallen tree, it's hollowed out and she crouches in there.'

'I know where that is,' Paul said.

'Cameron, please do not move. We'll be back.'

Stepping outside was like falling into an underwater crevasse. I couldn't see my hand in front of my face, and the torchlight from Paul's headlamp did little to help illuminate the pitch of the night. The rain was pouring and the river was thundering. Gradually, my eyes adjusted, and Paul and I held hands as we braced ourselves against the wind and moved towards the river, our shoes squelching through the sodden ground.

'This way,' Paul shouted, pointing towards the left.

I started to shiver as rain water trickled down the back of my neck. 'Paul,' I shouted. 'What was she wearing? Please tell me she had a jacket on!'

He turned back to me and shook his head. 'Just her pyjamas.'

'Shoes?'

'I don't know.'

'Oh my God. She'll freeze out here. We've got to find her.'

Paul held my gaze for a moment, then took off at a faster pace. As we neared the river's edge, I recognised the stone dyke.

But something was wrong. 'Stop, Paul,' I said as my eyes made sense of what was happening. I looked in horror. The low wall, usually a couple of metres away from the banks of the river, appeared to be arising from the river itself. All around it, the water seethed and swirled. I looked to my left, upstream, to where the trees were. To where we thought Tilly was. They too were sticking up from the middle of the spate river.

Paul stared at me with wild eyes, then dropped my hand and took off towards them. 'Paul!' I screamed after him. 'Wait for me!'

'Stay here! It's too dangerous,' he yelled, and then he disappeared.

I started to follow him, but within moments the light from his torch had been consumed by the night. My breath was coming in rapid, shallow gasps. I turned around, the thin beam of my torchlight showing me only more darkness sliced by rain.

Suddenly, from somewhere around me, I heard a voice calling me. 'Mum! Mum!'

Tilly?

'Mum!'

'Cameron!' I screamed. 'Go back! Where are you? Don't come out here!'

'Mum!'

Why couldn't he just listen to me for once and do what I said? It was hard to tell which direction his voice was coming from but I made myself take a couple of deep breaths. I had to stay in control of myself, otherwise I couldn't help anyone. I turned around until the river was on my left again and waded my way through the muddy ground back towards the bothy until in the distance, I heard his voice a little clearer and then glimpsed a faint beam of light. 'Cameron!' I shouted. 'Don't move. Stay there! I'm coming!'

It seemed like minutes until I reached him. He was sodden but I could see that he was crying. I couldn't stop myself screaming at him. 'Jesus, Cameron. I told you to stay there.'

'The roof, Mum.' His voice was thick.

'What?'

He pointed back towards the cottage. 'In the kitchen, the roof collapsed. There's stuff everywhere, I didn't know what to do. I didn't know if I should stay in there or not, I didn't know if it was safe.' He was sobbing in between getting the words out and I grabbed on tight to him. He was taller than me, but still my little boy. My hands were shaking with cold and fear. Where were Paul and Tilly?

'Are you hurt?'

He shook his head. 'Did you find Tilly?'

It was my turn to shake my head. 'Not yet.'

Forty-Six

Paul

The water was pulling at my legs as I waded towards the tree, grabbing me like hundreds of hands reaching up from Hades to drag me down. I knew the area where Cameron had thought Tilly might be, but it all looked so different in the storm, and so many of the landmarks I'd become used to had been swallowed up by the swollen river. My voice was hoarse as I continued to scream Tilly's name. Surely she couldn't be out here? But how long had it taken the river to burst its banks? I had searched for her initially for at least half an hour, then gone back to the bothy to get Emily, then we'd trekked out here again. If she'd come straight here, it may have been before the water poured off the mountain streams into the river, already high from hours of drenching rain. Would it have happened gradually, so she'd have had some warning, or all of a sudden?

I thought back to her face when she saw that I'd seen her vomiting. My poor little girl. The shame and fear on her face danced in front of my eyes. She would be weak, she wouldn't have as much energy as me. She wasn't eating properly, I knew that, and surely she'd be dehydrated and dizzy after vomiting. She had no fat on her to keep her warm. She was only in her pyjamas. I clenched my fists and punched my hand into my temple. What an idiot I'd been to take them here, to take this risk. We didn't even have phone reception. No one knew we were here. I screamed again, 'Tilly!'

And then I heard something.

Had I imagined it?

A high pitched sound, above the storm, reached my ears. I stopped for a moment, trying to let the sounds of the rain fade into background noise. I heard it again. 'Help!'

'Tilly! Tilly! I'm coming.'

I took the torch off my head and held it in my hand instead, moving it towards the direction it sounded like it had come from, but I didn't trust that the wind wasn't teasing me, swirling the sound all around me.

'Help! Mum! Dad!'

This time I saw her, standing atop the wall, a tiny, stick figure waving her hands, screaming. There was water either side of her, but I could reach her. I would reach her.

I staggered towards the bothy, carrying Tilly, who clung onto my neck with a strength I have never felt from her. I could feel the bones of her back digging into my arms. My legs were as heavy as the boulders sunken under the river. The rain seemed to ease a little as I walked. I could barely see for the water in my eyes and they stung every time I blinked, but I still knew where I was going. It had been so dark for so long that I was sure that I could have walked blindfolded; terror turns every sense into its sharpest form.

I blinked. Up ahead, towards where I thought the bothy was, I saw two lights. I closed my eyes and turned away from them. Was I hallucinating?

'What's that, Dad?' Tilly croaked, her neck turned to look at the lights too.

'I don't know, sweetie.'

'I think it's a car.'

It did look like the headlights of a car, but how could that be? I kept walking, and saw that it was. I heard a long, loud beep through the patter of the rain. It was the horn of a car.

Then I saw two figures running towards us and I didn't need to see their faces to know that it was Emily and Cameron. I began to run too, then Tilly let go of my neck and clambered down and ran towards her Mum. We were all racked with sobs.

After hugging Tilly, Emily turned to me and held me tight. 'Thank you. Thank you. Thank God you're both okay.'

I clung to her.

When we let go of each other, I pointed back towards the car, which I could see was an old, boxy silver Land Rover. 'Where did that come from?'

'The ceiling in the main room, it collapsed. Cameron came to get me but when we got back, Jim was here.'

'Jim?'

'He's from the village. Kind of mountain rescue. Turns out he's married to the woman in the shop. She warned us about the weather.'

'He came in the middle of the night?'

She nodded. 'When the roof collapsed, Cameron remembered about the satellite you bought back in Aberdeen and called for help. Jim was the closest to us, so he was sent out to help and see if they needed to get the helicopters out when the weather cleared. We've been sheltering in his car. And it's not the middle of the night anymore.'

I looked up and finally, could see some thin pinkish light slipping through the grey clouds. The rain seemed to be easing a little. *Red sky in the morning; shepherds warning.* Suddenly, I wanted to gather up my family and get out of here. It was time to go.

Forty-Seven

Emily

We thanked Jim profusely and insisted that we didn't need an ambulance, but would all go to the local doctor when we got back to the village. I was worried about Tilly, but once she had a change of clothes, was wrapped in an old army blanket from Jim's car, and drank some warm tomato soup from Jim's thermos, she had stopped shivering and was warm to touch. Jim was going to drive back to the village the way he had come, along some old fire trails that he knew. He would alert the council and the laird about the storm and the damage, then come back for us around lunchtime.

The ceiling of the main room had a gaping hole in it, over a metre wide, but the bedroom roof was solid. Cameron and Tilly ate some tinned peaches and strawberries, and Jim left them a bag of sweets. We would have a big lunch, back in the village. I didn't dare bring up Tilly's vomiting; for now, she was eating, and she was safe.

While they got back into their sleeping bags and lay down for a rest, Paul and I went for a walk, inland, away from the swollen river. We couldn't talk near the bothy; words travelled miles in the clear air. We had needed this time to exist as one living, breathing family unit but now, we had to make a decision. I knew that our family circuit would never be repaired until we could either fix, or sever, the bond between Paul and me.

When we were about ten minutes' walk away from camp, up the hillside, we sat on a big boulder. From here, we could see

335

that the river had flooded the fields around us and was full of debris churning on its surface as it hurtled its way to the ocean. I shuddered at the thought that that could have been Tilly.

'I'm leaving, Paul,' I said, my voice strong even though inside I was quivering.

He nodded. 'I know.'

'Not just here. Scotland. I'm taking the children home.'

He nodded.

'So, what are you going to do?' I said sharply, turning to him. 'It's time to decide, Paul. I want things to go back to normal. The kids don't need any more uncertainty.'

'You're right. I want to come home, but... but I don't think I can live the same way.'

'It doesn't have to be the same. We can do anything. Quit your job, find something you love.'

'How can I?'

'Oh, for God's sake, Paul. You don't think we can survive on my income, the equity from the house and you having a normal job like everyone else? Mow lawns! Work in a supermarket! I don't care what you do! I love *you*, Paul, not all the trimming that comes along with it.'

'We'd have to sell the house, without my income. I don't think I could find another job that pays as well.'

'Then we'll sell the house!' I turned to him and clasped his hands. 'Paul. When will you understand that I have never needed a giant house and fancy cars? Think about where we grew up! But we do need power and we need water, and the kids need friends. They need an education. And all I need is stability, and my family.'

He nodded, his eyes hopeful. 'Would you really do that? Sell the house?'

I leaned forwards. 'Paul. I don't care about the house. We can have a fresh start. I've been thinking it was time to move anyway. Let's move away from Damian and Phoenix. Let's get back to the basics of what we need, as a family.'

His face crumpled and he pulled me towards him. 'Thank you,' he mumbled into my hair. 'I love you so much.'

I held him, then broke away, laughing. 'Are you sure about this?'

He grinned, and nodded. 'Definitely.'

'Let's do it! Come on, let's tell the kids!'

We stood up and hurried back down to our children.

Forty-Eight

Paul

Back at the bothy, I started to pack up everything quickly, to wipe away any evidence that we'd been here. There wasn't much we could do about the roof but I tried to sweep the debris to the side at least. Emily had taken Tilly and Cameron for a walk to get them out of the way.

I watched her walk, the children either side of her. Emily was pointing at the hillside, to the cairn visible at the top. I imagined the men and women who had made it, and what it had meant to them. I closed my eyes and felt dizzy. I let myself hear the sounds of their voices, the birdsong, the rushing of the river, the clack of pebbles under its pull. Everything here felt ancient and alive, but while everything around us had adapted to life here, we couldn't. And now, that was okay. I had to face the fact that despite everything I'd tried, I knew that our problems were not just in the world around us. I was part of a family and being part of a family made me a better person.

–

I was trying to stuff the sleeping bags into the tiny bags they had come in, when I heard voices laughing in the distance. I looked out of the window to the hillside and saw Emily and the kids busily scurrying around. I needed a break; I walked nearer to them and realised that they were staggering with rocks back to the pile I'd been making since I got here. I exhaled to compose myself as I kept walking towards them. Tilly saw me coming and waved. 'Dad!'

I waved back, wiped my eyes and hurried over to them.

'What are you all doing?' I said, smiling. 'Our last day and I finally get some helpers?'

'We thought we'd finish it, Dad, for when we come back on another holiday. Maybe the next visitors will think it was made by ancient people.'

'Hey, we're not ancient,' laughed Emily.

My chin trembled as I tried to keep my emotions in, but failed. Tilly whacked me playfully. 'Come on, it's not worth crying over! We need your help.'

I took a deep breath and smiled again. 'Right, let's get it finished.'

For the rest of the morning, the four of us searched along the shores of the river and up the hillside for the final stones, and when we had enough, we worked together to stack them, fitting the rocks together and keeping the structure stable. As the pile grew taller and narrower, it reached as high as Cameron.

'Here, the last one,' I said, handing it to him.

'Wait!' Emily said. 'Just before you do that, kids, can we all say thanks to Dad for taking us on this amazing adventure?'

'Thanks, Dad,' they chimed in unison. Cameron reached onto the top of the cairn and fitted the stone on top perfectly, and we all jumped up and down and cheered and hugged each other, and I could have wept again, but this time with sheer joy.

Forty-Nine

Emily

I hadn't let Tilly out of my sight since we left the bothy and she didn't protest when I followed her to the bathroom to make sure she'd stopped vomiting. As soon as we'd gotten back to Aberdeen I'd taken her to the GP for blood tests and to have her weighed. She was not great, but she was safe, and we could travel back to Sydney and get her the help she needed there.

Later that day, when the kids were watching a movie with Marjorie, I went to talk to Paul, who was lying on the bed with his laptop open.

'I've called Dr Davidson,' I said quietly. 'The psychiatrist. I've made an appointment for Tilly next week in Sydney. She'd like you to come too, if you can.'

He had looked up and after only a slight hesitation, nodded. 'Okay. I'll be there.'

'I haven't made one for Cameron yet. We'll see how he's going once we get back, he's been okay without the medication.'

'That sounds good.'

I smiled, relieved. 'Have you checked us in online?'

He nodded. 'Yes. I'm just emailing Damian.'

I paused, waiting.

'I'm just telling him that I'm giving him my notice that I'll be resigning.'

'That's brilliant,' I said.

He nodded, looked up at me briefly, smiled, then looked back at his computer.

'I'll leave you to it. We should take your mum out for dinner tonight, see if your sister wants to come, to say thanks.'

'Sounds great.'

He looked up again and I ran over and kissed him.

That night, we went out for dinner, chatted and laughed and said tearful goodbyes to Fiona with long hugs and then the next day, we got on the plane.

-

The flight home went so quickly and before we knew it, the four of us were trudging through customs then pushing our luggage trolley out into the balmy, heady air of Sydney. And then, with the kids squabbling in the taxi queue and our bodies heavy with fatigue, we were just another family returning from a long holiday, ready to get back to the hard work of real life.